Critical Acclaim for the Works of Veronica Sattler:

HIGHLAND FIRE:

"Spectacular!"

—*Romantic Times*

SABELLE:

"More than a bargain. It's warm and wonderful and gives you a story that makes you want more. Welcome back Veronica, you have been missed."

—*Affaire de Coeur*

"Sabelle and Sir Jonathan will charm you. Their rescue missions are very entertaining and their caring warms the book throughout."

—*Inside Romance*

A DANGEROUS LONGING:

"Eloquent . . . Beautifully written . . . A grand read."
—*Romantic Times*

PROMISE OF FIRE:

"Rich with colorful characters and compelling events . . . Vivid . . . Unforgettable."

—*Waldenbook Lovenotes*

Two shadowed figures prowled silently along the top of the cliff. Black kerseymere mantles covered each of them from neck to foot. On their heads they wore slouch hats with concealing brims pulled low over their faces.

It was a long way down to the rocks, but they withdrew from the cliff's edge and gazed down at something the growing light illuminated more clearly now: a deep green cloak, its velvet folds wet with spindrift and redolent of the sea.

"*There*," said the smaller figure. "Are you satisfied now?"

"Satisfied?" The other's tone was bitter. "How should *this* satisfy me? The chit was to have died *after* I had her! Besides, there's no body. What if—"

"She's dead, I tell you! Who could have survived a tumble from here? I'm only surprised she made it this far, in the storm."

"Perhaps," the other sneered. "But if she isn't . . ." He slid his companion a sly look. "She'd still be a virgin, you know. No matter what you thought to achieve with that nasty little business back there. The mere destruction of a maidenhead does not—"

"Enough!" the other snarled. "It doesn't signify. Not now. The chit is dead, and you, m'lord, will need to look elsewhere for your . . . satisfaction."

St. Martin's Paperbacks Titles
by Veronica Sattler

PROMISE OF FIRE
A DANGEROUS LONGING
SABELLE
HIGHLAND FIRE
HEAVEN TO TOUCH

HEAVEN TO TOUCH

VERONICA SATTLER

SMP

ST. MARTIN'S PAPERBACKS

HEAVEN TO TOUCH

Copyright © 1994 by Veronica Sattler.

ISBN: 0-312-95329-1

Printed in the United States of America

St. Martin's Paperbacks edition / October 1994

10 9 8 7 6 5 4 3 2 1

༄ One ༄

Rain . . . It seemed there would never be an end to it. It lashed the windswept moors with a relentless persistence. It beat on sedge, and bracken, and marram covered rock, as well as the slender figure that made its way across them with breathless, choking haste.

It was, thought the woman as she wrenched her sodden skirts free of yet another hidden blackthorn vine, as if the rain had a purpose of its own. As if it were a living thing that was bent on holding her back, on blocking escape, on—

Escape . . . The word rang in her mind like a warning bell, obliterating rational thought. *Escape . . . yes, must escape . . . mustn't let them . . . Dear God, please let me—*

A broken cry pierced the clammy darkness and was snatched away by the wind before she hit the ground. She lay sprawled, facedown, along a stony incline, her open mouth pressed into gritty mud.

She lay there for several seconds, vaguely conscious of the rain beating on her back, of sharp stones bruising her flesh through the ruined fabric of her spencer and the traveling gown beneath.

Slowly, she pushed herself to her knees, then made the arduous move to regain her feet. And stumbled on.

But it was a blind stumbling, the night and the wind-lashed rain making it impossible to see more than a few feet in front of her. Thunder rumbled overhead, attended by blue-white flashes of lightning that occasionally lit the barren moors.

Trying to get her bearings, trying to see with the aid of the flickering light during these moments, she used her fingers to rake away the sodden mass of hair that was plastered across her face. But it was futile. Wherever she chanced to look, it was all the same: acres of black moorland studded with tufts of gorse, an occasional wind twisted elm or clump of hawthorn, the ever-present marram covered rocks . . . and the rain.

On, she pressed, feeling at times akin to the rain, at one with it, flinging herself across the landscape with a will that was equally purposeful, equally driven. *Escape* . . . It tolled like a litany in her brain. . . . *Escape, if only you can.*

Twice more, she stumbled, each time finding it harder to rise than the last. She was rapidly reaching the limits of her endurance, and she knew it. Hers had not been the life of . . .

The life of . . . ?

She paused briefly, in the act of pulling herself to her feet for the third time, and froze as the blankness struck her. Surely, she should be able to remember. . . .

But at that moment a fierce crack of thunder split the night air, telling her that remembrance was of no import now, a luxury she couldn't afford. She had to find safety, or at least a way to go on. Sweet merciful heaven, she had to go on.

Her waterlogged half-boots squished through sand and mud as she made herself put one foot in front of the other. She could feel a gritty paste of mud and pebbles abrading the tender skin between her toes as she moved, but barely, for she was numb with the cold.

Somewhere in the world that teased at her memory, she knew springtime existed, but here, on England's Cornish coast, it may as well have been winter.

Her legs, under the soaked tangle of mud laden skirts, felt leaden, and still she forced herself to continue, her

mind consumed by the mechanics of her movements—
Right foot: lift . . . drag . . . step. . . . Left foot: lift
. . . drag . . . step. . . .

Dimly came an awareness that she was sobbing, but that
was all; it was an awareness devoid of articulate thought—
without analysis, without judgment. Just as her scraped and
bleeding knees formed such an awareness, or the raw,
throbbing pain between her thighs.

It seemed she'd been moving this way forever. How long,
exactly, she had no idea. Terror drove her, terror . . . and
the all-consuming need to escape.

Vaguely, she had a sense of being near the sea. Images
came and went, shifting, bringing more confusion. In one,
she saw herself looking down on jagged rocks and angry
waves that crashed against those rocks hundreds of feet
below a precipice on which she stood. And there was something . . . something about a cloak . . . a deep green
cloak that—

She slammed against the ground, the impact ripping the
image from her mind. Sharp pain shot from her elbows to
her shoulders.

She heard herself moan, the sound competing with the
wind before it was lost altogether in a roll of thunder. She
tried to raise her head from the tuft of flattened weeds that
scratched her cheeks . . . failed, then tried again.

Success this time . . . She could feel the rain beating
against her face, obliterating the heat of her tears. Was she
crying? *Silly girl* . . . *Crying won't help* . . . *no one to hear*
. . . *no one.* . . .

Despair engulfed her, and she collapsed under the force
of it, sobs racking her slender frame. And all the while the
rain beat down . . . driving . . . pitiless. . . .

How long she had lain there before the tears were ex-
hausted, she never knew. Nor did she know what caused
her to summon the will to try again. Something . . . the
thing called hope, perhaps, that beats against the darkest
places of the human mind . . . perhaps . . . she didn't
know.

She only knew that somehow she was on her knees again, ignoring the pain of scraped and lacerated skin. Then, bracing herself on one unsteady hand while she used the other to push the heavy, wet tangle of hair away from her eyes . . .

She blinked, then scrubbed at her disbelieving eyes with the back of her free hand, and blinked again.

There! Lights flickering in the distance . . .

Sobbing incoherently, she summoned the last of her strength and clawed her way toward them. And the thread of hope became a beating of wings in her breast.

Major Nicholas Sharpe slouched in a deep leather chair in the library of Caerdruth Hall, his family's ancestral home. That it was no longer his home, and hadn't been for a number of years, was only one of the things of which he was all too painfully aware as he sat gazing out at the storm.

A snifter of excellent contraband brandy nestled in the curled fingers of one hand, and a half-empty bottle of the warm brown liquid stood on the Axminster carpet near his feet.

He'd retired to the library immediately after a late supper he'd barely touched, intent on getting seriously foxed, but somehow the brandy wasn't working tonight. He felt little more than a mildly lethargic warmth stealing over him, and even that was more likely attributable to the fire on the hearth than the effects of his late brother's fine French brandy.

Thoughts of Aubrey called up more of the pain he'd been trying to quell, and a frown etched his perfectly chiseled features. Lord Aubrey Sharpe, sixth earl of Caerdruth, had been laid to rest in the family plot less than thirty-six hours before, and Nicholas was still trying to deal with the consequences of his half brother's death.

Bad enough a younger sibling—younger by six years— had predeceased him, but Nicholas knew that wasn't the deepest source of the pain. True, it had the effect of making him more aware of his own mortality, but as a military man just recently returned from the Peninsular campaign against Napoleon's armies, he'd long been inured to death.

Fact was, he'd always expected to die young. Had, in fact, been accused of courting death by those who knew him well—Aubrey among them.

God, Nick, you're the only man I know who seems to search out ways to look death in the eye, for the simple pleasure of spitting in its face! He could still hear Aubrey's words, spoken half in jest, half in awe, following one of the older brother's more-reckless-than-usual escapades, years earlier.

Nicholas could even recall the morning they'd been uttered. He'd just turned twenty, and Aubrey had been a gangling, hero-worshipping fourteen, following him around like an adoring puppy, despite the fact that Nicholas had been in disgrace that summer.

He'd been sent down from Oxford during the spring term, for conduct unbefitting a gentleman; and the bruises from the caning Nick had received from their father, the earl, were scarcely gone, when he'd decided to relieve the boredom of a summer's exile in Cornwall.

By throwing in with the local free traders and nearly getting shot by the customs men.

Nicholas smiled ruefully, recalling Aubrey's shining eyes when Nick had found it necessary to explain what had happened. There had been a bullet hole in a hat he hadn't been quick enough to hide when Aubrey had burst into his chamber, uninvited, the morning after the incident.

Ah, Christ, Aubrey! Why'd you have to die? You were only bloody twenty-eight years old!

He felt his next swallow of brandy settle, warming him further, but that was all. He was as sober as the proverbial judge, and likely to remain so.

Outside the floor-to-ceiling windows that were only partially obscured by burgundy velvet draperies, he could see the storm raging. The imported trees and ornamental shrubs his late stepmother had installed in the garden, to try to give Caerdruth some semblance of a civilized English manor house, were occasionally lit by sustained flickers of lightning. He could see them bend and twist, their branches glistening with rain as thunder rumbled in the distance.

An early spring squall. He recalled how he used to love them as a boy, frequently stealing out of the house and climbing the nearby cliffs to watch the sea churn and seethe with a primitive power that fascinated him.

He knew it could still draw and absorb him in exactly the same way, and he had a moment's inclination to ascend those cliffs again, now, while the storm was at its height.

But he let it pass. There were weighty matters to be considered, not the least of which was the brood of sleeping children in the west wing. Aubrey's children—all seven of them. And now they'd become his children, God help him.

And God help them all. That was, if there was a God, and of that, Nicholas was by no means certain.

He heard Aubrey's voice again, this time older and weak from the fever. The fever that had claimed his life only hours after Nicholas had arrived, having been summoned home on emergency leave, from his regiment on the Peninsula . . . *Promise me you'll look after them, Nick . . . my little ones. Promise you'll care for the children. There's no one else I'd entrust them with. Promise!*

And so he had, but with great misgivings. What did he, a military man all his adult life—and a bachelor, at that— know about raising a pack of children?

And then there was his career. He'd have to sell out, of course. But that comprised the least of his difficulties in accepting the burden Aubrey had laid upon him. All but one of the children looked like *her* . . . like Judith, Aubrey's wife, who had died two years before, giving birth to the younger set of twins.

Seizing the bottle that stood at his feet, Nicholas tipped it into the snifter, then took a hurried swallow.

Judith . . . whom Nicholas had loved with all the misspent fervor of youth—and who had cast him aside when his younger brother, the legitimate son who'd just inherited a title, had suddenly seemed a better prospect.

Nicholas's lips twisted in a bitter parody of a smile as he

contemplated the nasty twists of what fate had laid at his doorstep. He could still see Aubrey lying there, the painful regret of that singular betrayal residing deep in his fever-ridden eyes. Aubrey . . . dying, as he'd asked what others would have deemed the unthinkable, of the brother he'd betrayed.

Yet Nicholas had said yes. Yes, because in all the long years since, he'd never really blamed Aubrey. Never really stopped caring about him, he supposed . . . the baby brother whose care he'd taken upon himself when no one else had given a damn about him—not even Aubrey's mother—and certainly not their father.

He'd always known Aubrey to be the weaker of the two of them. The earl, their father, had known it too. Nick could remember him cursing the pair of them in one of his drunken rages—cursing Nick for his love of the land and the people when, as a bastard, he had no right to them, no legal ties or responsibilities; cursing Aubrey for being the legitimate heir to Caerdruth, while lacking the fortitude and intelligence to manage the earldom and earn Caerdruth its rightful due, its place in the new century which was just beginning.

"Soft, that's what you are!" he remembered the earl shouting at Aubrey. "A weakling, just like your mother, and no more fit to be an earl than an ass! Christ Almighty! I give you ten years before you run your entire inheritance into the ground!"

Taking a moment to run his eyes over the once rich, but now slightly shabby appointments of the library, Nicholas knew the old man—damn him to hell thrice over!—had been right. Caerdruth Hall had begun to show the effects of Aubrey's mismanagement of the estate.

And the Hall was most likely only the tip of the iceberg; on his return, while riding through Caerdruth lands to reach it, Nicholas had seen other evidence that the sixth earl had, indeed, impoverished the earldom.

Both tin mines, whose rich deposits had supported the estate handsomely for years, had been boarded up—both!

And from the looks of the village when he'd passed through it, the effects had been devastating to the locals, many of whom had been miners whose livelihoods had depended on those mines.

And a ripple effect would account for the number of shops he'd seen in disrepair, or closed down entirely, the faded and peeling letters on their signs advertising goods and services no longer available. Because miners who were out of work could no longer afford such goods and services, and so . . .

Heaving a disgusted sigh, Nicholas reached for the brandy again. Tomorrow he'd have a look at the books and call in Morgan, the estate manager, just to see how bad it was. Not that he relished the task. Caerdruth wasn't his, would never be his. Nor would Trevellan, the bordering estate attached by Aubrey's marriage to Judith—her dowry. *Ah, God! Trevellan.* How he'd planned and dreamed about it with her! It wasn't Caerdruth, but it would have been *his.* Only now Caerdruth and Trevellan both belonged to young Harry, the seventh earl—and all of thirteen years old.

Christ, Aubrey, didn't you ever think of your son? Your own heir? I know you didn't have a head for these things, but there are ways . . . hiring decent people to do it for you, or—

A sudden knocking at the library door jerked Nicholas out of his reverie.

Who in hell—

"Come in!" he growled, wondering who had the temerity to violate his orders that he was not to be disturbed.

The door creaked open on unoiled hinges, and Mrs. Hastings, the housekeeper, appeared, agitation apparent on her plain, no-nonsense face.

"Begging your pardon, sir," the woman gasped with uncharacteristic breathlessness, "but they sent me to fetch you."

"They? Who the devil are 'they'?"

"The butler and first footman, sir."

Nicholas nodded for her to continue, giving the old girl points for not being intimidated by his scowl.

"There's a stranger come to the door, out of the storm," Mrs. Hastings went on, her breathing somewhat less labored now. "A young lady, and she's hurt something awful. Will you come?"

∂ Two ∂

Nicholas reached the entry hall ahead of Mrs. Hastings, his eyes going to the figure slumped on the puddled floor. Several things registered at once. The stranger was in sorry shape. She was also a person of means, judging by the quality of her clothing, soaked and torn though it was. She was quite young, barely more than a girl.

And she was strikingly beautiful.

"Thank heaven you've come, sir," said the butler as he hovered over the young woman. The wide-eyed footman behind him nodded vigorously. "She's just lost conscious—"

"I can see that, man—now step aside." Nicholas knelt beside the supine figure, felt for a pulse at her neck. He noted at the same time, the pallor of her face, the scratches on it, the cold, clammy skin beneath his fingers. But her pulse, while a bit erratic, was strong enough. He doubted she'd die on them.

"Mrs. Hastings . . ." As Nicholas spoke, his hands moved expertly over the still form, checking for broken limbs.

"Yes, sir?"

"Have a guest chamber readied, but in the meantime, send someone up with hot water and towels. And blankets. We've got to warm her," he added as he scooped the dripping figure into his arms and headed for the stairs.

"Yes, sir . . . ah, up where, sir?"

"I'm taking her to my chamber for now," Nicholas tossed over his shoulder. He was already halfway up the staircase. "And, Parkins," he added, not stopping as he addressed the butler, "have someone build up the fire there, and send that gawking footman to the village for the doctor!"

All three servants scurried to do his bidding while Nicholas continued to his chamber. Outside, the storm raged on. It shook the rafters and pelted the windows with torrents. At its peak now, it rumbled over the roof of the Hall with scant regard for its ancient underpinnings.

Shifting the girl's weight to his shoulder so he could open the door, he had a moment to realize how light she was. A slender featherweight, despite the sodden clothing. But far from skinny. He'd felt soft, womanly curves when he checked her body for injuries. Young, nubile flesh of excellent proportions.

Badly bruised flesh, and bleeding in places. By the light of a lamp someone had left burning on the bed stand, he caught a nasty bruise on the underside of her chin. He saw another at the side of her neck as he drew near the bed. Its purple imprint bore the shape of a thumb. This was more than storm damage. Bloody hell, what could have happened to her?

Laying her carefully on the counterpane, he reached for the faded satin feather tick at the foot of the bed. He tucked it around her and began to massage her limbs through the thick covering, his movements brisk and efficient. Time enough to remove the wet clothing when the hot water and towels arrived.

Her lips were blue with cold, and he knew loss of body heat was a bigger danger to her now than what he'd been able to detect of bruises and lacerations. He was no physician, but he'd tended enough battlefield injuries to sort out that much.

A soft moan escaped her as he was reaching under the cover to pull off her muddy half-boots. Nicholas paused, his eyes going to her face. But there was no other sound, and her features remained unanimated.

He tossed the boots to the floor, then stripped away her muddy stockings. Her feet were icy, and he began to chafe them gently, but his gaze went back to her face.

It was heart-shaped, with a small, gently pointed chin. Exquisitely sculpted cheekbones and a straight, fine-boned nose were in perfect balance with the contours of her lips. These were wider and fuller than fashion dictated, and therefore more interesting to him.

But it was the shape of her eyes that intrigued him most. Even with her lids closed, he could see they were tip-tilted. Yes, a definite upward slant, and he found himself wondering what color they were. Further defining their unusual shape, their inky hue accentuating the pallor of her skin, were finely drawn brows that swept upward. Winglike, he thought. They matched the thick, dusky lashes sweeping her cheeks, and the jet black mass of hair soaking the pillow. A beauty, all right, or he was no judge at all.

But no one knew better than Nicholas, that he was.

Women, it was said in his regiment, were Sharpe the Bastard's foremost area of expertise. True, he might win at cards more than any man had a right to expect. And he was a picture of perfect grace on a horse—outstanding even in an army of expert horse officers. There was also no question he acquitted himself admirably in the field; and he could drink, swear, and box with the best of them.

Yet in each of these endeavors he'd been known to occasionally fall short of his mark. There was always the losing hand, the horse that stumbled, the opponent that landed a lucky blow.

But, it was widely proclaimed in the ranks, there wasn't a woman alive that Sharpe the Bastard couldn't have in his bed if he willed it. And more often than not, especially if she was beautiful, he did.

Nicholas stared, unseeing, at the small, bruised foot in his hands as these thoughts flashed through his mind, and his lips twisted in a bitter smile. If they only knew, those men who looked at him with envy from afar . . . if they only knew how empty it all was . . . how meaningless and—

Another moan drew his eyes back to the girl's face. The lovely features were contorted in a grimace, and a sharp cry sliced across a fading rumble of thunder. And then—

"*Don't!* I'm *begging* you! Oh, God, please don't—"

The scream that followed cut the air like a knife. She began to writhe and thrash on the bed, forcing Nicholas to throw his weight across her, pinning her down. She was sobbing now, tears streaming down the pale cheeks.

But he knew she still hadn't awakened. She had gone still against his chest, yet there was no discernible reaction to his nearness. No pulling away, no awareness at all. Her eyes remained tightly shut, their lashes spiky and glistening in the lamplight.

She was burning up. He could feel the heat of a fever right through the dampness of the bedclothes, her body trembling with chills.

She was moaning softly and tossing restlessly on the mattress. His mind groped for what to do next. He was beginning to feel helpless, and he didn't like it. Devil take it, where was that housekeeper with the things he'd summoned?

At that moment the door swung wide, and Mrs. Hastings appeared, a pair of housemaids in tow. They carried stacks of toweling and blankets, and a footman lugged a kettle of steaming water in their wake.

"How is she?" inquired the housekeeper, coming quickly forward.

"Burning with fever." Nicholas stepped away from the bed.

Hastings nodded and began issuing brisk orders to her staff. She sent a footman named Hawkins to the kitchens for cold water. She herself took charge of the patient, laying a hand on the girl's brow to check the fever, calling for a sheet of linen toweling to dry her hair.

Seeing she had the situation well in hand, Nicholas

headed for the door. He was preceded by the second footman, who'd been dismissed with the words, "Only female staff need remain, Bates."

Nicholas proceeded down the hallway toward the stairs. Sounds of the storm were no longer evident; it was likely headed out to sea by now. The tallcase clock at the top of the stairs read nearly midnight, and he supposed he ought to get some sleep.

Of course, the stranger occupied his bedchamber. Well, it hardly signified. It was a chamber he hadn't slept in for years—not until two nights ago, when he'd arrived just in time to watch Aubrey die.

Thoughts of his brother had him running his hand through his hair in vexation as he paused at the top of the stairs. The girl's arrival had actually made him forget for a while. Forget the seven children presently fast asleep in another wing of the Hall.

Not to mention Maud. The old girl's care would of course fall to him as well. And Maud was as mad as a March hare. *Christ, Aubrey, what a coil you've wrapped me in!*

Impatient with himself for the turn his thoughts were taking, he shook them off and headed downstairs. He'd never countenanced self-pity in others. In himself it was insupportable.

"How fares the young lady, sir?"

Parkins met him in the lower hallway. The old man had been in service at Caerdruth Hall since Nicholas and Aubrey were boys. Parkins was severe of countenance. Nevertheless, Nicholas knew he possessed a warm heart. It had been Parkins who'd gently tended the bruises and lacerations from the beatings the old earl had administered to Nicholas over the years.

"Well enough in some respects, Parkins, but she's taken a fever. When can we expect the doctor, do you think?"

"It's hard to say, sir. Bronson started for the village at once, but the storm would have made things difficult. I instructed the head groom to let him have the best horse in the stables—ah, barring your Lucifer, of course."

They shared a half-smile. Or at least what passed for such on the older man's part, given the habitual rigidity of his carved-in-stone face. They both knew Lucifer was a horse who acknowledged only one master. Both had been present the day the old earl had grudgingly deeded his most costly piece of horseflesh over to Nicholas.

Costly in more than one respect. Imported at great expense from the East, the young stallion was to have been the earl's prize addition to his stables. A superb stud whose Arabian bloodlines he'd studied and gauged the perfect outcross to supply the stamina and speed he desired in his breeding program.

But a combination of brutal injuries suffered in the long sea voyage and the earl's own stupidity had rendered the black unmanageable. Vicious. A maniacal killer who, by the time Nicholas arrived from Oxford and first laid eyes on him, had already trampled a groom to death, and broken the earl's leg in the bargain.

But it hadn't taken Nicholas long to learn his father had earned that broken leg. He'd been beating the animal unmercifully when it happened. And the dead groom had been following the earl's instructions to do the same.

"Untrainable, that's what he is!" his father had shouted when Nicholas questioned him about the animal. "Of no use whatsoever. Not even as a mount. And as for his stud potential, I'd be out of my mind to infuse my bloodlines with that temperament!"

"Then what do you intend to do with him?" Nicholas had questioned carefully. When he'd first seen the stallion, Lucifer had taken his breath away. A truly magnificent beast, the black was muscular and sleek—and large for an Arabian—with a deep chest and powerful hindquarters. Stamina and speed were written all over him. And the arched neck, the delicate triangular head with its fine, intelligent eyes spoke of sensitivity and courage.

He'd lusted for the animal. Lusted with as much passion as he'd ever known for a woman. Yet with that yearning had come pain. Pain, because he'd known at once the animal could never be his. His father would see to that. Just as he'd always seen to it that Nicholas didn't have the things he deeply craved. He was the earl's bastard, fit only for the scraps and leftovers.

"I intend to shoot him myself—just as soon as this bloody leg heals enough to get me to his paddock!" The earl's reply to his question had shaken Nicholas badly. But it had also given him an idea. A mad, impossible scheme he had no hope of achieving.

And yet he'd proposed it. Not at once, of course. The earl had been in a terrible temper over the whole business, and Nicholas waited for a more propitious time. Waited, and bided his own time.

He'd made excellent use of it by stealing down to the black's paddock at odd hours and patiently—patiently and gently—accustoming the abused animal to a humane touch. But eventually the right moment came, and he'd gone to the earl with his proposition: If Nicholas managed to tame Lucifer—to stay on his back for a specified, agreed-upon length of time—his father would deed the black to him.

He still remembered the dryness in his mouth when he'd dared the proposal. The sweating palms that came of wanting something so badly, he could taste it; and yet knowing —being absolutely certain—that if he gave himself away, if his father even suspected how much was at stake for him, he'd never agree.

"You damned fool!" He could still hear the earl bellow. "The bloody beast's a killer. And what if I do let you go down there and end your miserable life? If I should agree to this madness, what's in it for me, boy? Answer me that!"

Nicholas had affected a shrug. "If I'm thrown, or trampled to death . . . nothing, I suppose. But on the outside chance I tame him . . . why, you'll have a top-of-the-mark, manageable stud, of course."

And that had done it. The cupidity in the older man's eyes told Nicholas he'd won, even before the earl's sneering, calculated response. "Five minutes, by the clock. And you'll not only stay atop his back—you'll put him through his paces. At least two gaits—trot and canter—or I shoot him where he stands. After they've removed your body from the line of fire, of course."

He'd laughed then, wiping tears from his eyes as he ordered Nicholas out of the library. Nicholas had gone, doing his utmost to hide the triumph that hammered inside him like a drum. But not before summoning the temerity to request the agreement be put in writing, with Parkins and the estate manager as witnesses. And his father had been in such high humor by then, he'd agreed.

The rest was still a tale told about the grounds and stables of the Hall. Of how the Earl's Bastard, all of sixteen years old, had not only remained astride the fearsome devil, but put him through his paces just as nicely as you please, and then cleared the paddock fence with him.

Of course it had soon thereafter become apparent none but Nicholas could get near the stallion, let alone ride him. Learning of it, the earl had gone red-faced with anger. Roaring his fury, he'd yelled that it had all been "another damned gypsy trick," whatever that meant, one of the stable lads told Nicholas later.

Nicholas hadn't known what it meant, either. Not then. In the intervening years much had become clear on that score, however. *Christ, so many ghosts!*

Gazing wearily around the vast vestibule, Nicholas absently rubbed his fingers across the stubble on his chin. *So many damned ghosts and skeletons, and here I am, back in the midst of it!*

A slight movement from Parkins brought his attention back to the old man. "Did Hastings see to having that guest chamber readied?"

"The blue room, sir, nearest the stairs."

Nicholas nodded. "I'll take it for tonight. You'd best find your own bed, Parkins. Set someone to watch for the physician's arrival, and have me notified when he comes."

The old retainer bowed and turned to leave.

"And, Parkins?"

"Yes, sir?"

"My thanks for your ever calm efficiency this evening. But then you've always been the rock on which the running of this household rested. And bloody well more than the old man deserved. Good night."

The servant bowed again and retreated, leaving Nicholas alone in the empty entrance hall. Candles flickered and guttered in a pair of wall sconces near the stairs, but all the rest was dark and shadowed.

A fitting backdrop for the mood he suddenly found upon him?

Bloody hell, the ghosts would claim him again, if he let them! With an impatient shake of his head, Nicholas turned toward the stairs. *Not this time,* he told himself with a silent snarl. *Not bloody damned ever again!*

Two shadowed figures prowled silently along the top of the cliff. Black kerseymere mantles covered each of them from neck to foot. On their heads they wore slouch hats with concealing brims pulled low over their faces.

In the hour before dawn broke, the sky was clear, except for a few low-scudding clouds in the distance. Illuminating them was a heavy sprinkling of stars and the glow of a half-moon sinking into the far horizon.

Behind the pair and far below, on the flat tract of ground before the path leading to the cliffs, an unadorned carriage waited. Its wheels were wrapped about with rags to muffle sound when they moved. The black carriage horses' noses were buried in feed bags to keep them occupied—and silent.

"Look there!" said the taller figure in a rough whisper.

They both hurried toward a stunted bush that clung to the edge of the cliff. The smaller figure bent forward and reached gingerly for something that fluttered in the brisk sea breeze sweeping the cliffs; the object, whatever it was, hung from the bush's branches, and both were perilously near the edge.

As it was, a few stones became dislodged by the boot of

the one reaching for the object, and the figure withdrew hastily from the precipice. It was a long way down to the rocks, but they never heard the stones land; the crashing of waves below swallowed the sound, and that of the smaller figure's curse.

"Here, let me have at it," said the taller, and with a reach of his longer arm, he succeeded in capturing the fluttering object.

They withdrew from the cliff's edge and gazed down at the thing, which the growing light illuminated more clearly now: a deep green cloak, its velvet folds wet with spindrift and redolent of the sea.

"*There,*" said the smaller figure. "Are you satisfied now?"

"Satisfied?" The other's tone was bitter. "How should this satisfy me? The chit was to have died *after* I had her! Besides, there's no body. What if—"

"She's dead, I tell you! Who could have survived a tumble from here? I'm only surprised she made it this far, in the storm. We ourselves nearly had to abandon tracking her, and would have, if the storm hadn't let up when it did."

"Perhaps," the other sneered. "But if she isn't . . ." He slid his companion a sly look. "She'd still be a virgin, you know. No matter what you thought to achieve with that nasty little business back there. The mere destruction of a maidenhead does not—"

"Enough!" the other snarled. "It doesn't signify. Not now. The chit is dead, and you, m'lord, will need to look elsewhere for your . . . satisfaction."

The man holding the cloak hissed an obscenity that was carried away by the wind. Rolling the green velvet into a wad, he shoved it under his mantle and stalked back down the path.

His companion cast a last lingering look at the murderous rocks, at the salty spume sent crashing upward by the pounding waves. A smile formed beneath the concealing brim. Then this one too, turned and made for the carriage.

❧ Three ❧

"But who is she?"

Four-year-old Charlotte Sharpe tried mightily to make herself heard. The scene around the breakfast table was more chaotic than usual. This morning it seemed her older siblings would never acknowledge her at all.

Fortunately, someone finally did.

"No one knows, silly! That's why Nurse called her a stranger." Martin, the older of the twins, informed her of this with his customary impatience.

Charlotte considered this for a moment, spoon poised above her porridge. "Well, they should *ask* her! If *I* were to meet a stranger in the middle of the night, I should ask her straightaway, who she is!"

"They *can't* ask her, goose." Michael, the second twin, sounded only slightly less impatient than his brother. "She's uncon-uncon—"

"Unconscious," Harry supplied helpfully.

There was nothing of the lofty older sibling in Harry, Charlotte noticed. Harry was now the earl, and he normally no longer took his meals in the nursery. He'd remained with them these past two days, since Papa had gone to heaven, only because Charlotte had asked him.

"What's un-con-shuss?" Fanny, who was six, had a formidable voice and rarely encountered difficulty in being heard.

"It means that she's asleep and can't wake up," said Harry. Charlotte thought she heard a smile in his voice, although there was none on his face. None of them had smiled much since Papa couldn't wake up and went to heaven.

Fanny's eyes went wide. "Do you mean, not ever?"

"Is she going to go to heaven too?" Charlotte piped anxiously.

Harry did smile then. "We certainly hope not, Lottie." He ruffled Charlotte's flaxen curls. "That's why the physician's with her now."

"He'd best not be trying to wake her with those disgusting leeches!" Michael warned. "If they tried leeches on me, I'd *never* wish to awaken!"

"I'll bet Uncle Nicholas won't let him use the leeches," Martin added.

The twins had only seen their father's brother briefly—at the funeral—but Nicholas was already their idol. The tall, dashing figure he cut in his uniform had alone assured that. But last evening Harry had shared with them some clippings from the *Morning Post* which he'd stored away in his desk two years before. Containing reports of the "heroic bravery" of Major Nicholas Sharpe at Salamanca, they were the very stuff of hero-worship. As far as the twins were concerned, Uncle Nicholas could do no wrong.

"I'll wager *I* know why she can't awaken," Fanny declared suddenly. She had taken on that "squinty-eyed look," as the twins termed it, and both of them groaned.

Fanny, it was well known among the siblings, had a great imagination. They always knew when she was about to employ it by the way her eyes narrowed and stared into the distance at one and the same time.

"I think she must be a princess—just like the one in the fairy tale! A lost princess who was put to sleep by a wicked witch and held prisoner in a tower."

"But if she was asleep in a tower, how did she come to Caerdruth Hall?" Charlotte asked.

"She escaped, of course!" Fanny was rarely daunted by

annoying details in the scenarios she devised. "And naturally, being a princess, she must wait for a handsome prince to awaken her."

More groans from the twins.

Fanny was used to ignoring them. "With a kiss!" she ended dramatically.

"What drivel!" exclaimed Martin. He wasn't entirely sure what drivel was, but he'd heard Uncle Nicholas utter it during the eulogy the vicar gave for their father—the part about "a peerless peer of the realm"—and if Uncle Nicholas used it, that was good enough for Martin.

Michael reached for some marmalade to spoon on his toast. "I'd never kiss a girl, even if she was a princess," he said vehemently. "She could sleep until doomsday, before I'd do *that!*"

"I wonder where she came from . . ." Charlotte mused. Then, casting a glance at her older sister, "Before she was locked in the tower, I mean."

Harry was rising from the table.

"Oh, Harry, must you go?"

"Only for a short while, Lottie." The young earl checked the pocket watch that had belonged to their father until two days before he died, when he'd called Harry to his bedside and given it to him. "It's nearly half-past seven. I'll go down and see what I can learn of our sleeping princess, shall I?" He winked at Fanny.

"Oh, do, Harry! And come back directly and tell us!"

"Drat! I wish we could go," said Michael.

"Don't even think of it," Harry warned as he opened the door to the hallway. "Blodgett's bound to be done helping Nurse feed the twinnies shortly, and she'll skin you if you disappear."

Blodgett was their governess, and while Harry had graduated to a tutor the year before, he well recalled the woman's nasty temper. It was always worse after having to help Nurse with the younger set of twins, called "the twinnies" to distinguish them from the older pair. Judith and Nicky were real hellions, despite being only two years old.

Michael and Martin groaned in unison as the door shut behind him.

"Who wants to have lessons on the morning after a big storm?" groused Michael.

"And only two days after your father has gone to heaven," said Charlotte in a plaintive voice, but nobody heard her.

"By the time Old Sourpuss is done with us, all the village children will have picked the beach clean!" exclaimed Michael.

"Shh, she'll hear you!" cautioned Martin.

"Well, let her, then! She's only our sour-pussed old governess," Michael went on. "I mean, she's not our mummy, is she?"

Charlotte tried hard to remember Mummy whenever one of the older children brought her up. But she just couldn't recall anything. Mummy had gone to heaven too.

"No, but she's a lot meaner than Mummy, and Auntie Maud says we have to obey her," said Fanny.

"But why?" Charlotte asked.

" 'Cause that's the Way of Things." When she wasn't fantasizing, Fanny was given to quoting various grown-ups when no decipherable rationale could be found to explain the sometimes mysterious rules of Their World. "That's the Way of Things" was one of Auntie Maud's favorite expressions.

Charlotte eyed Fanny thoughtfully. "Auntie Maud says heaven's the place where the good people go. But what's it like, really?"

Fanny looked nonplussed for a moment. Then her eyes narrowed and she squinted into the distance. "Heaven," she pronounced, "is a place where it's always the day after a storm. It's ever so lovely . . . sunshiny, with no governesses whatsoever. Or lessons, of course. But there are miles and miles of beaches, with all sorts of astonishing things that have washed up on them."

"Are there cats in heaven too?" Charlotte asked.

"Yes, but only nice, pleasant cats. Never any fat, nasty ones like Old Sourpuss's Ernest."

"That cat will never go to heaven!" Martin declared.

"I should think not! Straight to The Bad Place, or nowhere at all!" his twin added.

"What's The Bad Place?" Charlotte looked worried.

"He ate my entire pudding when I wasn't looking," Michael complained. "Stole it right off the table!"

"What's The Bad Place?" Charlotte repeated, but no one was listening now. The subject of their governess's ill-mannered cat was always ripe for discussion, and this morning was no exception.

"That cat is so fat, he can hardly move," said Fanny.

"He can move for a pudding fast enough," Michael grumbled.

"The reason Ernest is fat is because he eats too much," his twin declared.

"And always has nasty bits of food clinging to his whiskers," added Charlotte, forgetting about The Bad Place for the moment.

"Why doesn't he clean himself ever so carefully, like the vicar's cat, I wonder . . ." mused Fanny.

"He's too fat and lazy, that's why!" Michael was growing incensed, which was nothing new where Ernest was concerned.

"He isn't too fat and lazy to scratch people," said Charlotte. "He scratched me awfully once, and I wasn't even *trying* to pet him!"

"Ugh! Who'd want to pet fat Ernest?" Fanny had taken her spoon and smeared porridge across her cheeks, which she now puffed out in imitation of their topic of conversation.

"Old Sourpuss, that's who!" said Martin.

"*Sst!*" Michael hissed. "Here she comes!"

At that moment an inner door swung ajar, admitting a ruddy-faced woman in black bombazine. A mousy looking woman wearing an aproned gray dress followed. Each held a struggling toddler by the hand.

"Mowtin!" exclaimed the towhead who could have been a female replica of the older twins at an earlier age.

"Oh, no you don't, you little monster!" Martin cried as little Judith lunged toward him. "I had enough of your strangleholds yesterday!"

"Martin." The large woman barely succeeded in corraling Judith as she escaped from her nurse. The toddler was shouting, "Picka-back! Picka-back!" but the governess made herself heard above the racket. "You will go to your room at once, and remain there until you can confine your speech to what is suitable for a young gentleman!"

"But—"

"At once!"

"Yes, Miss Blodgett."

Heaving a sigh, Martin trudged toward the other interior door. He wondered how much he'd risk if he informed Blodgett he'd overheard her use the term, *little monster,* herself, on a twinnie. But that of course had been said under her breath, and not meant for his ears; he thought better of the notion.

Around him, chaos still reigned. Both twinnies continued to struggle against Blodgett, who had a firmer grasp than the graying nurse. The governess restrained them successfully, though her face grew even ruddier with the effort. Nicky, the dark-haired moppet she'd come in with, had joined his sister in demanding a piggyback ride—this time from Michael, now that Martin had been banished.

Michael circled the room pretending to gather lesson books while trying frantically to catch his retreating twin's attention.

Fanny meanwhile had poured tea on her napkin, and was surreptitiously trying to remove porridge from her cheeks.

And Charlotte, who had ducked behind Michael, was eyeing a large orange tomcat which had followed Blodgett into the room.

"Hold still, you benighted imp!" Blodgett admonished Nicky.

"What's a 'nighted imp?" Charlotte asked her brother in a whisper. "Is it nicer than a little monster?"

Michael gave up trying to catch Martin's eye and half turned to her, cupping his mouth with his hand. "Only because *she* said it," he whispered back.

"Whispering secrets is rude," Blodgett announced as she handed Judith over to Nurse, whose real name was Mrs. Whitley though none of them called her that.

"Now, come along, Michael and—Fanny! Whatever have you done to your face? It's all-over splotches!"

"Perhaps the porridge has made her ill," Charlotte offered.

"Well, you see, Miss Blodgett," Fanny began while stuffing her soiled napkin into the teapot, on the table behind her back, "I awakened this morning with the most frightful of megrims. And I thought to myself, if only I could get some fresh sea air—"

"That will be quite enough, Fanny. Another of your fanciful tales is not to be borne after the morning I've—yes, Whitley, what is it?"

"Perhaps she's to be indulged somewhat," murmured the nurse as she distracted the wiggling Judith with a sweet from her pocket. "It being only two days after . . . well, two days since their—"

"Nonsense!" said Blodgett, eyeing the morsel with disdain. "Coddle them at such a time, and they'll never— Ernest! Come away from that cream this instant, you naughty cat!"

Ernest paid no attention to her as he lapped greedily at a spill of cream from the pitcher he'd knocked over.

Michael, on the pretext of being helpful, made a dive for the cat. He managed to grab its tail, which immediately sent the animal into a hissing and clawing frenzy.

"Look out, Michael!" Fanny yelled. "He's after your ear!"

"Stop this!" Blodgett yelled. "Stop it this instant!"

"Mikoo! Mikoo!" The twinnies laughed and cheered their big brother on, thinking it all great fun. Both had managed to tear loose of their captors now, and were racing madly around the table.

It was pandemonium at its wildest. Charlotte had bravely taken up a position on Michael's right, and was trying to distract the cat from biting her brother by swinging at it with a length of napkin. Fanny dodged to his other side, calling out advice on avoiding fang and claw. Meanwhile, Blodgett had advanced on all four, the ruler she used for hand whippings already withdrawn from the deep pocket of her gown.

"Measure alert!" shouted Martin from the door to the sleeping quarters. The noise and shouting had drawn him out of his exile; when he spied Blodgett with the ruler she used for striking their hands in punishments, he cried out the code words he and Michael had long ago devised to warn each other: *measure alert,* for "ruler warning."

Michael heard, and whipped about, releasing the cat. It was all Ernest needed. Claws bared, he lunged at the first object in his path.

Which happened to be Blodgett.

The governess went down on her rump in a flurry of petticoats and black bombazine. The cat, clinging to her bosom with the claws of all four feet, gave a final yowl, and sprang away. It raced for the open doorway where Martin was standing, openmouthed, while its mistress shrieked on the floor.

And this was how Nicholas found them when Harry led him up to the nursery.

"Bloody hell," Nicholas muttered disbelievingly.

Harry cleared his throat. "Um . . . yes, sir."

"What the devil's going on here?" Nicholas's eyes registered the bedlam before him, but he still couldn't credit what he saw; this was a nursery, not a war zone!

None of the room's occupants had noticed their arrival. All attention focused on the large woman who shrieked and flailed about on the floor.

True, the twinnies had ceased their mad dashes around the breakfast table; but now they were jumping up and

down in front of the toppled governess, cheering wildly and
clapping their hands.

Whitley had ceased chasing her charges and gone to
Blodgett's assistance, but her foot hit a smear of cream bearing a cat's footprint and sent her careening into the woman.
Serviceable gray cotton merged with black bombazine as
she landed on Blodgett's lap. Whitley's apron billowed like
a ship's sail and settled over both their heads, reducing the
shrieks to muffled bleatings.

Meanwhile there was a heated discussion underway between the twins and their younger sisters. Fanny was
urging the boys to Do Something, aided vaguely in her
endeavor by Charlotte. But the twins were having none of
it. Michael was yelling for Fanny to snatch the ruler, which
stuck out ominously from Blodgett's clenched fist as she
waved it about. Martin, however, had decided they ought
to make a beeline for the sleeping quarters, but he was
having a hard time of it because Michael had him by the
arm and wouldn't let go.

"It's . . . the nursery, sir," Harry answered in helpless
embarrassment. "The, um, schoolroom, to be specific."

He'd encountered his father's brother outside the guest
chamber on the second floor. The major had been instructing Parkins to send for the estate manager, saying he
wished to see him as soon as the physician left. At Harry's
query as to the welfare of their guest, Uncle Nicholas had
shrugged and indicated the closed door; behind it Mr. Cartwright, the physician, was apparently still in the process of
examining the young woman.

But Harry's query had prompted his uncle to ask about
the children. That's when Harry had suggested they look in
on the nursery wing, where he might see for himself. It had
seemed like a capital idea at the time . . . something to do
while they awaited the doctor's diagnosis. Only now Harry
was beginning to think it the most dashedly harebrained
notion he'd ever hatched.

"*Be still!—all* of you!" Nicholas's roar held the sound of
command, and the room went silent. The twinnies froze on

the spot, a mixture of awe and blatant curiosity on their faces. The seven-year-olds sprang to attention faster than a pair of new recruits. Charlotte's eyes went wide, and she clapped a hand over her mouth, while her sister eyed the newcomer assessingly.

As for the pair on the floor, there was no more flailing about because Whitley had a stranglehold on Blodgett that immobilized her; having managed to lower her apron, she held onto the governess for dear life while staring at Nicholas as if he had two heads.

"That's better," Nicholas pronounced. He turned to Harry. "The aproned one is yours, m'lord. I'll take the other."

Harry nodded, his chest swelling with pride at the manner in which his uncle addressed him.

In unison, they strode toward the pair of downed females and offered them their arms. In a moment they had both women on their feet. The governess appeared shaken until Harry looked at her eyes; they snapped with suppressed rage.

Whitley looked more embarrassed than shaken. She quickly curtsied to Harry and his uncle, then went to her two young charges and began to usher them into their quarters.

"Hold a moment!" Nicholas stayed her with his hand. "You are Mrs. . . . ?"

"Whitley, sir. Just Whitley," she mumbled, looking at the hem of her gown.

"Speak up, please!"

"I am Whitley, sir, the children's nurse."

"Very well, Whitley. And as I am Major Sharpe, the children's new guardian, I should like you to introduce me to your two youngest . . . charges before you *take* charge of them, if you please."

Whitley had some acquaintance with military men. Her long-deceased husband had been a corporal in General Burgoyne's regiment. She knew where her duty lay.

"This," she said, indicating the towhead who squirmed

under her right hand, "is Lady Judith. She just turned two. Mind your manners, Judith!"

Judith squirmed again, but made a passable stab at a curtsy.

"And this," said the nurse as she nudged little Nicky forward, "is her twin, Nicholas, although he only answers to Nicky at present. Nicky?"

Nicky's eyes never left his uncle's as he made a leg to ͸. That they were precisely the same shade of gray, and dark hair the exact same color as Nicholas's, had doubt- not escaped him. They were the only such in a nursery full of towheads.

Neither had the fact escaped Nicholas. A sardonic smile played about his lips as he mused on what mischief had been running through their mother's mind as she'd named the younger twins. For name them, she had. Aubrey had made a point of telling him so. On her deathbed, after having birthed them. Judith and Nicholas . . . for what might have been?

He didn't smile as he spoke to the two little terrors. "Well, Judith and Nicky . . . I am your uncle Nicholas, and the next time we meet, I shall expect something better in the way of comportment from the pair of you. You may be only two years old, but that does not mean you may jump about, acting like little savages. I expect you know how to mind your nurse when she tells you to do something. Is that correct?"

The pair nodded, wide-eyed.

"Mind Nurse," Judith mumbled around a thumb that had suddenly found its way into her mouth.

"Very well." Nicholas nodded at Whitley. "You are excused."

He turned to the governess, who stood stiffly before him, both hands bracing the ruler against her waist. "And you, madam, are—"

"I am Miss Blodgett, governess to the older children. That is, saving his lordship, who has a tutor now."

"Indeed. And may I assume, Miss Blodgett, that you were his lordship's governess before he progressed to a tutor?"

Blodgett's ample chest rose and fell as she seemed to consider where her answer might lead her. Sharp black eyes ran over the newcomer, taking his measure, and her grip on the ruler never wavered. "You may, sir."

"Then it is that which has saved you."

Her composure slipped for the first time since she'd been stranded on the floor like a beached whale, Nicholas noted, and he smiled inwardly. The woman was a bully of the sort with which he was all too familiar. He'd come across more than one of her male counterparts in his public school years. He'd probably end up sacking her, but not until he'd found a suitable replacement. For now, he'd enjoy making her squirm.

"Saved . . . *saved* me?"

"Saved your position, madam," Nicholas told her coolly. "The exemplary conduct of his lordship, here, indicates to me that you must have had some positive governing influence on the children of this household. Despite what the insurgent doings in this schoolroom revealed when I arrived. I shall therefore give you a chance to redeem yourself."

"Redeem my—" Blodgett's florid face deepened toward purple. "Well, I *never*—"

"You will tender me an explanation, of course. In writing. Have it on my desk in the library by tomorrow morning."

The knuckles on the hands gripping the ruler whitened, and Blodgett made a sputtering sound, but Nicholas had already focused his attention on her young charges.

"Michael and Martin, as I recall," he pronounced laconically. Nicholas speared the twins with silvery eyes that reminded them of Nicky's when he was being his most horrid. No, it was worse than that; these eyes belonged to the man they could well imagine decapitating one of Boney's frogs.

They wasted no time nodding—in unison.

"Speak up, gentlemen. You have voices, as I collect. Only

minutes ago, they were being heard clearly, I have no doubt —in the village square! Yes, I distinctly recall hearing your voices—even over the caterwauling of your siblings."

"I'm Martin, sir," said Martin, stepping forward with alacrity. He tried for as much military bearing as he could assume, given the fact that the only military personnel he'd ever laid eyes on rested solely in the person interrogating him now. He glanced nervously at his twin and indicated him with his thumb. "He's—"

"Michael Sharpe, at your service, sir," said Michael. He stepped forward to join his twin, and Fanny noticed how he made a splendid effort at snapping to attention. But the whole effect had been ruined, Fanny thought, by the way his voice squeaked on the *sir*.

Nicholas said nothing for a moment, looking them over with cool gray eyes. The twins were identical; he could envision all sorts of mischief brewing in future—given what he'd already seen of their fertile little minds—if he did not, on the spot, devise a means of telling them apart.

He finally spied what he sought: Each had a cowlick at the crown of his head, but Martin's spiraled in a clockwise direction, while Michael's went counterclockwise; they were truly mirror images of each other.

"Very well, gentlemen, it seems you know how to comport yourselves when you make the effort. Know, then, that I shall expect you to make that effort in future. Is that clear?"

"Yes, sir," they said in unison.

Nicholas nodded, turned to their sisters. The smaller girl had taken the time he'd used addressing the twins to inch behind her sister. She now peered out at him from behind the other's back, china blue eyes huge as saucers in the tiny face.

Yet it was the older girl's look that intrigued him. Sharp wits there, and no mistake. Good thing her face revealed everything that was running through that keen little brain, or he could find himself quickly in the suds.

He suspected he might anyway.

"And you are . . . ?" he said to Fanny.

"Lady Fanny, Uncle Nicholas. I was named after Mrs. Burney. I've never met her, of course. But she's a great friend of the Queen's—and a novelist!"

"I see . . ." Nicholas noted she'd been the only one to address him as Uncle. *Fearless, as well as bright . . . Damn it, Aubrey, what the deuce have you gotten me into?*

"Lottie's the one behind me," Fanny went on. "Her real name is Charlotte, but—"

A scratching on the outer door intruded, and as Nicholas called permission to enter, he found himself grateful for the interruption.

Parkins stepped into the room. "Begging your pardon, sir, but the physician has finished his examination and requests a word with you."

"Thank you, Parkins. Show him into the library, and tell him I shall join him presently."

"Very good, sir."

The butler left, and Nicholas eyed the group assembled before him. No one moved.

"No doubt, you are all aware that I am displeased with the state in which I found this chamber when I arrived. In future, you will each see to it that I have no reasons to feel such displeasure again. In short, you will conduct your-selves as ladies and gentlemen. Is that clear?"

There was a general murmur of assent. Giving them a final assessing glance, Nicholas nodded and turned to leave. Then he paused and turned back to the governess, who seemed not to have moved a muscle since he'd addressed her.

"Oh, Miss Blodgett . . . a lesson in lengths and mea-surements might be in order . . . particularly as you've that ruler already in hand. I cannot possibly construe any other valid use to which it might be put . . . can you?"

Meeting the outraged glare in the black eyes, Nicholas gave her a curt nod and quit the room.

* * *

Horace Cartwright was a country physician; not a gentle-manly surgeon, but he'd earned the approbation of the local people he'd been treating for years, and most showed him the respect of calling him Mr., as a true surgeon would be addressed. He was a short, balding man who wore his spectacles as he did his paunch—pushed somewhat ahead of where they ought to have rested. He readjusted the glasses that threatened to slide off the tip of his nose as Nicholas entered the library.

"Ah, Major Sharpe . . . good of you to come so promptly." Cartwright withdrew a watch from his waistcoat, glanced at it. "Due at the vicarage in half an hour," he added, returning the watch to its pocket. "Vicar's wife down with the megrims. No time to—"

"Get on with it, then, man! What the deuce happened to the girl? Is she awake? Did you speak with her?"

Cartwright had served the Caerdruth environs for most of his professional life. His wife had been born there. So he was not unacquainted with the background of the man who stood before him. Or his reputation.

The Earl's Bastard was what they'd called him, this almost indecently handsome illegitimate offspring of the late earl. But not only because he was born on the wrong side of the blanket.

Nicholas Sharpe had a reputation for being a hellion while he was still on leading strings, and it only grew worse after that. Wenching, gaming, brawling—the lord knew what else—these were the traits he was known by. They'd all breathed a sigh of relief when he managed to purchase a commission in the army and left.

Only now he was back—for good, by the looks of it. And Cartwright had no illusions of his being easy to deal with; his manner alone said that.

"Very well, sir. The young woman is resting quietly at the moment—but only because I dosed her with laudanum. She was tossing about restlessly in a half-wakeful state, and I feared she might further injure herself if—"

"Did she say anything? Anything coherent, that is."

"No. As I said, she was only half-awake and still feverish. Results of taking a chill in the storm, I'd say. As for the rest . . ."

The physician shook his head. "Major, I've never seen anything so brutal, and I've been a physician for thirty years."

"Rape is never anything less," said Nicholas grimly. He'd seen the evidence, of course . . . the blood on the camisole . . . the smears on her inner thighs. It wasn't his first encounter with this sort of thing. But the others had been victims of warfare . . . poor peasant women unfortunate enough to be in the way of marauding armies. *This* had happened right here in Cornwall. On Caerdruth lands, most likely.

"There is that, of course. But I was speaking also of the way she's been beaten. And the signs of rape have an odd look to 'em."

"Odd?"

Cartwright peered at him over the rims of his spectacles. "First, I'd lay odds the young woman was a virgin beforehand."

Nicholas swore softly to himself.

"I believe I was able to detect a newly ruptured membrane, although I cannot be certain," the physician went on. "You see, the tissue in the entire, ah, area has been so badly savaged, it makes an exact diagnosis impossible."

"Christ!"

"Moreover—and here is what is odd, young man—thorough as I was, I could detect no evidence of semen in—or on—her person." He paused to observe Nicholas scowling.

"But the rain last night—"

"Could have washed it away? Perhaps . . . but highly unlikely. She was fully clothed, and as I'm sure you—ah, discovered, female garments do a great deal of swathing of body parts—even in this day and age. Even the huge amounts of mud on the outer clothes I had the housekeeper show me hadn't reached her . . . more private places.

"As I said, sir," the physician went on, ". . . odd."

"What happens now?" Nicholas asked as his eyes met the physician's.

"We wait and see how she progresses. I've given Mrs. Hastings instructions for her immediate care, which includes keeping a careful eye on her and sponging her with cool water to keep the fever down.

"Beyond that," Cartwright continued as he picked up his medical bag and turned toward the door, "we can only hope she awakens soon, and is able to tell us something. Ordinarily, I'd want this sort of thing brought to the attention of the magistrate. It would appear there's someone vicious on the loose out there"—he turned and gestured at a view of the moors outside the library windows—"someone who could be a threat to our own wives and daughters.

"But," he added, standing by the door, "I believe we should wait on that score. The young woman is obviously of the Quality. Her garments alone attest to that and—oh, here . . ."

He began to fish in a waistcoat pocket, at length withdrawing something shiny, suspended from a delicate chain.

"We found this on her, tangled in her hair." He handed the object to Nicholas.

It was a gold locket . . . very finely wrought, and bearing the letter *H* engraved on its surface. Nicholas found the catch, and the piece sprang open; inside was a lock of blue-black hair.

"Of excellent workmanship, I'm certain you'll agree, Major. Surely something only persons of quality might afford. A nobleman's daughter, perhaps?"

Nicholas nodded. "Your reason for not wishing to alert the authorities, I take it."

"Not for the time being, at any rate. Wouldn't want to run afoul of an irate lord whose daughter's reputation we'd helped sully, would we? No, I'd say that for the moment, we keep this among ourselves . . . ah, by your leave, of course."

"Agreed. Although there is the staff to consider. Servants do gossip, and—"

"A rather closemouthed lot, this one. Known most of 'em all their lives."

Nicholas nodded, and thanked him. Cartwright turned again to the door. "Send word whenever she's regained consciousness, and I'll come straightaway. At any rate, I plan to look in on her again in the morning. Good day, sir."

The door closed behind him, leaving Nicholas to stare down at the locket in his hand. *A nobleman's daughter* . . . a rich man's at the very least. Bloody hell!

Muttering a curse, Nicholas opened the door and strode down the long hallway. He reached the landing at the central staircase and crossed it, proceeding purposefully down the opposite hallway, into the east wing. He spotted a footman on duty outside the chamber across from his own.

"The young woman . . . oh, it's you, Hawkins. They've removed her to this chamber, have they?"

"Aes, sir. Mr. Cartwright said 'twas all right t' move her across the hall."

Nicholas nodded, and rapped lightly on the door to the chamber. A tired-looking Mrs. Hastings opened it.

"Still the same, I gather," he said in a lowered voice, glancing at the still form on the bed.

"Yes, sir. I expect you've come from seeing Mr. Cartwright, then?"

"Yes. . . . You look done in, Hastings. Get some rest. Just tell me what to do, if anything, and I'll take over the watch for a while."

· The housekeeper nodded gratefully, and instructed him about keeping the patient comfortable, then turned to leave.

"Oh, Hastings?"

"Sir?"

"Has the old aunt been about . . . Aunt Maud, that is?"

"I haven't seen her, sir, but then I've been—"

"Of course. But if you can manage to spare the time, send someone to fetch her to me, will you? And one more thing: It's to be understood among the staff that this entire matter is of a highly confidential nature."

Hastings opened her mouth to speak, but Nicholas forestalled her. "I have no concern about some, like you and Parkins, for instance. But a firm word to the others might not be amiss, if you take my meaning."

"I'll see to it, sir," she told him, and took her leave.

Nicholas moved to stand beside the bed. And found himself unexpectantly mouthing an obscenity. The flawless face he vividly remembered was now marred in two places. On her chin and along one cheekbone were bruises which had deepened and purpled during the night.

Innocence violated at home. It disturbed him, though he didn't stop to piece out why.

Who could have done such a thing? True, there were vast tracts of the Cornish coast that were barren and inhospitable. A spawning ground for free traders and their rougher brethren, modern-day pirates and thieves. Was it brigands? Dressed as she'd been, she'd have been easily spotted as Quality, as the doctor had put it . . . high *ton*, if Nicholas knew anything at all. Had she been set upon and robbed before suffering violation and injury?

And if a lady of consequence, she'd hardly have been traveling alone, at night. Where was her escort, then? And the conveyance in which they'd been traveling?

The girl stirred restlessly on the bed, moaning softly. Nicholas wrung out the toweling that had been left in a basin of water beside the bed, pressed the cool cloth to her brow. She murmured something inaudible, twisted her head to the side, and quieted.

He felt his jaw tightening as the bruises on her neck and along the underside of her chin presented themselves again. *Savaged*, Cartwright had said.

Well, they'd have some answers eventually. And then maybe he'd help find the bastard.

Pulling up a chair, Nicholas settled down to wait.

The woman everyone called Aunt Maud made her way toward the east wing of Caerdruth Hall. Christened Maud Amelia Harriet Smythe, she'd been known "ages past," as she liked to put it, as Lady Throckmorton. And while she recalled having a married family name somewhere in that jumble, she frequently couldn't remember what it was. In any event, she was fond of saying, it didn't signify; sufficient to answer to *Aunt Maud,* for so she now was, to all and sundry.

Maud did her best to hurry, although she wasn't accustomed to it. Life held few surprises for Maud, and of things that mattered, fewer still.

Yet this morning something remarkable had happened. This morning Maud had been told she was needed.

She paused beside a hallway mirror, took in her seldom-examined reflection. Peering back at her was a small, wizened face that was certainly older than she recalled. Bright, birdlike eyes went to the purple turban wound about the top of her head; they ran the length of the dyed ostrich plumes bobbing above it, and here she frowned.

"Oh, dear . . ." she muttered. "That will never do, my gel. Not the way of things . . . not the way of things at all."

She whisked the plumes from her turban and thrust them behind a marble bust of Milton resting on the console table below the mirror. She glanced again at her image.

"There." She smiled approvingly at the face crowned by the purple headdress. "That's better!"

Without a glance at the pea green sarcenet opera gown she also wore, Maud hurried to the chamber where a footman had told her she was needed by the major.

Hearing a knock at the door, Nicholas opened it—and barely kept from gaping. The apparition in green and purple shouldn't have surprised him. Aunt Maud had been flitting about the house in outrageous modes of dress ever since he could remember. But perhaps he'd been lulled into forgetting.

"Aunt Maud . . ." He bowed courteously and gestured for her to enter.

"Good heavens, it's young Nick! Did the major send for you too?"

Nicholas's lips twitched, but didn't quite form a smile. *Same old Maud. Still with apartments to let upstairs.* "Uh, I am the major these days," he said as he led her into the chamber. "I thank you for coming, m'lady. Has anyone told you of our guest?" He indicated the still figure on the bed.

The birdlike eyes took in the sleeping stranger. "My goodness, but she's a prime article, isn't she? Awfully pale, though. Except for those bruises. Good heavens! Bruises! Has she had an accident?"

No, of course she hadn't been told anything. "That is precisely what we are trying to learn, madam. You see, the young lady . . ."

Maud listened carefully as Nicholas related the circumstances involving the stranger's appearance. She clucked sympathetically until Nicholas began to venture obliquely into the delicate matter of how the young woman might have come by her cuts and bruises.

"You needn't beat around the bush with me, Nick!" she cut in hastily. "What you're telling me is that the poor child was ravished!"

Nicholas breathed a sigh of relief. He'd feared it a devilish tricky business, getting such a message across to the old girl.

"I fear it is so, madam. And it is in this ticklish matter, I should like to request your help."

"My help . . . yes." Maud's eyes looked remarkably clear and sane to Nicholas as she said this.

"We really don't know what we may expect when the young lady awakens. But it stands to reason that, being female, she would benefit from the presence and support of one of her own sex when that occurs. I immediately thought of you in that capacity, m'lady. If you would be so kind—"

"Tut-tut, Nick . . . say what you mean. You immediately thought of me because there was no one else about to think of! No other female of her class, that is."

"How on earth did you know she was of your class?" he

questioned. The girl's finely made, if bedraggled, clothing which had given him a clue, had been taken away.

"Bah! A *tonnish* miss, if I ever clapped eyes on one—and I have, you know . . . in my time. Only look at her, Nick!"

Maud reached for one of the slim white hands resting on the coverlet and carefully held it up for his inspection. "See? Some scratches, but not a callus on 'em. Hardly the hands of a menial, m'lad!"

Nicholas nodded. He hadn't thought a jot about things like calluses. Beginning to suspect there was more to Aunt Maud than had ever met his eye, he listened attentively as she went on.

"But it's more than that, lad." Maud ran her eyes over the delicate features of the heart-shaped face. "The gel has a look about her . . . don't know how to explain it, but I know quality when I see it, Nick. And this one's a diamond of the first water!"

Nicholas met Maud's bright, birdlike eyes assessingly. He realized for the first time that they were not black, as he'd always supposed them to be, but a dark, penetrating gray. His own could take on that shade, he knew. One of his mistresses had told him it happened when he was especially vexed or distracted by something. Well, it stood to reason, didn't it? Maud *was* a relative of some sort.

He carefully ran over the details for the girl's care with the old woman, finishing with the rationale for discretion which he and the physician had agreed upon.

"You needn't instruct me on that score, Nick. A prime article who's been ruined is no longer a prime article! We must keep this whole nasty business under tight wraps, m'lad. Tight wraps, indeed!"

Breathing another sigh of relief, Nicholas thanked the old woman, planted a kiss on her papery cheek, and took his leave.

Hat in hand, John Morgan awaited Nicholas in the library. A small, bantam of a man, he was not without intelligence, judging by his sharp brown eyes. Nicholas had never met him directly, but he'd been Aubrey's estate manager for a dozen years. Nicholas had prepared to hate him on sight.

Morgan had more or less inherited the position from his father, who'd served the old earl in that capacity, and Aubrey as well for a year or two. That George Morgan had been an astute manager was evident. Not so, his son.

"I want you to tell me everything from the beginning," Nicholas said as soon as their greetings had been dispensed with. "How the estate had been operating when you came to it, what changes occurred, and when . . . how and when it all started to go bad—no, spare me any excuses or euphemisms! We both know Caerdruth's a shadow of what it once was, and I want to know how it happened."

They were still at it at nine o'clock that evening. Pausing only to eat some cold meats and cheeses he'd had sent up to them from the kitchens, Nicholas began to learn the full extent of what his sire and Aubrey between them had done to Caerdruth. His sire, Aubrey, and *Judith,* he amended, at one point.

Earlier, he'd ascribed the word *mortgaged* to what his brother had done to his inheritance, but only as a metaphor; now he realized it was all but fact. Heirlooms—jewelry and valuable paintings, silver—had been sold to pay off Judith's gambling debts. The income from Caerdruth's tenants had dwindled to nothing. And Trevellan's rents were nearly as bad, Morgan told him. He'd have to talk to Nettles, Trevellan's land steward, to learn the details.

Nettles, he confided, had recently mentioned his lordship wanted to mortgage Trevellan to keep Caerdruth afloat. Whether he'd acted on this before he died, Morgan couldn't say.

Nicholas met his grim gaze. They both knew Caerdruth, being entailed, couldn't be touched, which was likely the only thing that had saved it. Trevellan wasn't so favored.

God, not Trevellan! Nicholas agonized silently when they'd reached this point. If Trevellan was mortgaged—*Christ, Aubrey! If you weren't already dead, I swear I'd kill you myself!*

Just then a scratching at the door interrupted, and Nicholas called permission to enter.

It was the redheaded footman, Hawkins. "Beggin' yer pardon, sir," he said breathlessly. "The old mum sent me t' fetch ee. It be the young miss. She's awake!"

৯৯ Four ৯৪

Nicholas thanked Morgan and dismissed him, saying he'd see him again in the morning. Then he sent Hawkins to fetch the physician from the village. He'd no sooner left the library himself when a frightened-looking housemaid appeared. Stammering nervously, she asked what she was to do about a request from "the old mum" to fetch food to the guest chamber in the east wing.

"Find Mrs. Hastings and inform her of her ladyship's request. She'll know what to do," he told her, not waiting for the curtsy she bobbed in response. He made a mental note to see Hastings himself, adding the training of house servants to his growing list of what had been neglected at Caerdruth.

Maud met him at the door. "I think the fever's broken," she said in a low voice as he followed her inside. "She began to perspire fiercely, and all that dry heat went right out of her. Then she asked me for a drink of water, just as clear as you please!"

Nicholas approached the bed and pressed his palm to the girl's brow. It was cooler than his hand.

"Did she say anything else?" he asked as the old woman joined him near the bed.

"Oh, my, yes! After she'd taken the water, she asked who I was. I told her, of course. Except for that blasted name of Rodney's I keep forgetting. I told her about that too, and then the most extraordinary thing happened. A queer look came over the poor gel's face, and she said something even queerer."

"Go on."

"She said, 'A madhouse, then . . . a madhouse with a common affliction'!"

Frowning, Nicholas faced her. "You're certain?"

"As certain as I am of my na—oh, dear. Well, I'm certain, in any case. I assured her she was at Caerdruth Hall, and asked her then if she was hungry. But she never answered, poor dear. Just closed her eyes and drifted off to sleep."

"And that was when you sent for me?"

"Well, yes, but not before I waylaid that young woman with the freckles and asked her to fetch up some food."

"So you think our guest will be up to eating something." Nicholas said this almost absently, his eyes drawn to the heart-shaped face framed by jet black hair against the pillows.

"Our guest? Yes . . . well, perhaps," said Maud. "But *I* am sharp-set, my lad! Sharp-set, indeed!"

He wrenched his gaze away from the girl. "Devil take me for a lack-wit! Do you mean to say you've not eaten yourself? Since I set you here to watch, this morning?"

"Don't trouble yourself on my account, dear boy! I could have sent that ginger-pated fellow for some if I'd thought of it. But you see—oh, dear! We seem to have awakened her with all our rattling on."

Nicholas glanced down at the bed. The stranger was looking directly at him. He felt his breath catch. The eyes meeting his were tip-tilted as expected, yet their color was utterly unexpected: a startling shade of green.

"How are you feeling?" he asked for want of anything better to say. *Cat's eyes . . . feline . . .*

She wondered if she was still dreaming. The man who towered above the bed was the most beautiful creature she'd ever seen. But the beauty had a darkness to it. She felt it. Those eyes . . . perhaps she wasn't dreaming after all, but had died . . . perhaps this was some dark angel of death hovering over her. She wasn't certain she wanted to find out.

Her eyes shifted to the old woman beside him, and she felt a small jolt of recognition. "You . . . were here before."

"Indeed, I have been, my dear. All along. And I must say, you gave us all quite a turn with that fever. How clever of you to have disposed of it!"

The girl got that look in her eye that many did, who spoke to Aunt Maud at any length, Nicholas noted. "Do forgive my poor manners," he hastily put in. "I'm Major Nicholas Sharpe, and this is Lady Throckmorton, whom I take it you collect meeting earlier."

For some reason, he found himself wanting to touch the girl. Wanting to lend comfort. She looked so damned vulnerable lying there, and—

He nearly snorted. Sharpe the Bastard lending comfort? To an attractive woman? The only comfort he'd ever offered women was between their thighs!

The girl's eyes moved to his. "And now, perhaps," he began, "you'd care to tell us your own na—"

A sharp rap on the door intruded, and Cartwright rushed in. "That young footman says our patient has finally come round. If I might have a few moments alone with the young woman, Major . . ."

"Of course." Nicholas gestured for Aunt Maud, and they both withdrew.

"There's something queer about that gel," said Maud in a lowered voice after the door closed behind them. Farther down the hallway, Hawkins stood tiredly against the wall.

Nicholas was thinking the same thing. She'd had a kind of trapped look about her. He'd seen the same thing in the eyes of a fox brought to bay by hounds once. And more recently, in the looks of young soldiers about to go under fire for the first time.

Well, Maud was beginning to seem a good person to sound out, though he could hardly believe he was thinking it. "What do you make of it?" he asked her.

The old woman was silent for a moment. "My mind keeps going back," she said at length, "to that queer business about a madhouse. Nick . . . this ordeal she's been through . . . I daresay, I've known mature women who'd have stuck their spoons in the wall after suffering far less. Do you think it could have unhinged her?"

"Perhaps. We'll know more when Cartwright's finished examining her. In any event, m'lady, here comes the food you requested."

"Indeed. But the gel—"

"I suggest you have it taken to wherever you feel inclined to dine . . . your chambers, perhaps. I'll send down for more for the girl if it's wanted. Now, off with you, m'lady. She'll still be here, should you feel like returning later."

Maud nodded absently and led the tray-bearing servant away.

"Oh, Aunt Maud . . . ?"

She turned toward him, and Nicholas thought her eyes had that vague look he recalled, but hadn't seen all day.

"Thank you for all your help, m'lady. I couldn't have had better."

The vagueness vanished like a puff of smoke. "I'll wager you say that to all the dotty old ladies, Nick!" she quipped. And then, before she turned to leave, he actually saw her *wink* at him.

A good fifteen minutes passed before the doctor let himself out of the room.

"Well, Mr. Cartwright? How does our patient?" asked Nicholas, who'd been waiting impatiently outside the door.

The physician rubbed thoughtfully at his chin. "Ah, Major . . . perhaps we might withdraw—"

"Of course."

Cartwright commented that the girl seemed to be responding well to the excellent care she'd received, but was otherwise silent as both men walked toward the library.

"Very well, out with it," said Nicholas as soon as the door had closed behind them. "You've implied the girl's mending satisfactorily, I believe—or is she? What is it you *haven't* told me?"

The physician smiled. He liked direct men. He was one himself. "She has no recollection of who she is, Major."

So that was it. Nicholas was gratified to learn he and Maud hadn't been whistling in the wind at least. Small wonder she'd looked trapped!

"I'm not unfamiliar with such things, Cartwright," he said. "Saw a few such instances in combat. It's called amnesia, I collect."

The older man nodded. "We know very little about it, actually. But it frequently follows an inordinate assault to the nervous system. Sometimes a blow to the head causes it." He met Nicholas's eyes. "Or a severe fright or shock."

Nicholas nodded grimly. He remembered the terror in her voice last night as she'd cried out. *What kind of bastard would have—*

"What happens now?" he questioned abruptly.

"We wait."

"And . . . ? What's to be done for her?"

"Very little, I'm afraid. Aside from more of the rest and excellent care she's been given already."

"But surely—"

"As I said before, Major, we know very little about this affliction—or anything else that affects the mind, really. What we do know is that the patient frequently comes out of it himself. With proper rest and care, this one may do so."

"May . . . ?"

The doctor heaved a sigh and met his gaze squarely. "There are no guarantees. I've read about cases of amnesia that lingered for years, some indefinitely."

"Good Christ!" Nicholas ran a hand roughly through his hair. "Do you mean to say we might never learn who she is?"

"It's possible. From the young woman herself, that is. Of course, there are other ways of discerning a person's identity. If she doesn't come round in a few days, a discreet inquiry through your family solicitors might be in order. As we agreed while I was here this morning, the girl obviously belongs to the upper classes. For all we know, her family is searching frantically for her this very minute. It wouldn't be very difficult, I should imagine, for a solicitor to acquire knowledge of a member of the upper crust who's gone missing."

Nicholas smiled sardonically. "You'd be surprised at the lengths some of these titled lords and ladies would go to— or *not* go to—to prevent a breath of scandal from touching their noble names."

The physician looked taken aback.

"Tell me, Cartwright, what would you do if it was your daughter who'd disappeared mysteriously? Bandy it about? Call out the watch?"

Cartwright sighed heavily. "I take your point, sir." He reached for his physician's bag on the floor. "At any rate, I believe we may be premature in all this at the moment."

He turned toward the door. "The girl seems to be coming on well enough with regard to her physical injuries, and the fever's gone. She'll need bed rest for several more days, in any event, and in the meantime"—he turned back toward Nicholas—"oh, there was one more thing . . ."

Nicholas was frowning at a pile of ledgers on the desk. He looked up at the physician inquiringly.

"Regarding the injuries from the—well, I implied to the girl that she may have fallen inopportunely. She's such a mass of bruises and lacerations anyway, I'm not even certain she ascribed particular significance to those of a more . . . personal sort.

"So I took it upon myself," Cartwright went on, "not to inform her of the loss of her . . . membrane. No point to it, given what her state of mind is at the moment. As I said, she needs rest, and plenty of it . . . freedom from unnecessary worry, if you take my meaning."

Nicholas sighed tiredly and nodded. "She certainly won't hear anything on the matter from me. And I'll speak to Lady Throckmorton about it."

As he saw the doctor out, Nicholas began to feel the events of the past forty-eight hours taking their toll. He was weary to the bone, and none of it from physical exertion. *God in heaven, what else? First a pack of children I know nothing about. Now a ravished stranger who doesn't know who she is. Or even that she's been ravished! Oh, Aubrey, I hope you're laughing, wherever you are! Your bastard of a brother isn't, I can damned well tell you!*

The night was moonless and dark as a pair of figures in black emerged from their carriage. The taller one spoke a few words to the driver, who nodded and remained where he was. Pulling the brims of their slouch hats down to keep them from being snatched by the wind, the pair left the road and hurried down an embankment.

Moving as fast as they dared in the pitch-black, the two let their ears guide them, following the sound of waves in the near distance. The smell of the sea was strong as they made their way across the sand.

"They might not be here any longer," said the taller with considerable irritation. "We're late. All that time spent tracking down—"

"They'll be here," said his companion in a voice that smacked of smugness. "I told you, you worry needlessly, and—shh!"

Both paused to listen. Something was making a scraping noise that carried even over the murmur of the wind and the susurration of the waves.

"There! What did I tell you!"

Each cast a stealthy glance over the shoulder but could detect nothing untoward along the dark and lonely stretch of coast. Deciding it was safe, they hurried toward the shadowy outline of the longboat which had just scraped onto the sand. Although it was too dark to see, they knew the ship from which it had been launched had to be anchored only a short distance out, beyond the surf.

"You are late, *mes amis*," accused the man who sprang from the longboat.

"We had business which detained us," the smaller of the pair snapped. "It couldn't be helped."

The man from the ship grunted unsympathetically. "Another 'alf hour, and ze moon would 'ave risen, forcing our departure—*empty-'anded.*" He eyed the pair unpleasantly as the wind picked up and whipped their mantles about them and they shifted uncomfortably on the sand. "Our superiors do not pay us to return empty-'anded!"

The taller of the pair cursed under his breath and withdrew a packet from the folds of his mantle. "Well, you'll *not* be going back empty-handed, will you?" he sneered as he tossed the packet at him.

The latter caught the small bundle and flipped it to one of the sailors who waited beside the oars.

"And now, monsieur," said the smaller of the pair from the carriage, "I believe it is *your* turn. Kindly relieve *our* empty-handedness!" As if in demonstration, a gloved hand was thrust forward, palm up.

The man from the ship eyed the appendage disdainfully, and for a moment it appeared as if he'd do nothing. Then a furtive movement caught his eye, and in the next instant, he found himself looking down the barrel of a pistol. Held in the grip of the one who'd spoken, it was leveled directly at him.

"Our gold, monsieur," demanded the small figure in black. *"Now!"*

The Frenchman grinned mirthlessly at the pair, affecting a careless shrug. He turned toward the longboat and gestured for one of the sailors to bring forth the small chest resting at their feet. In less than a minute, the chest was transferred to the taller of the pair from the carriage, and his companion lowered the pistol.

"*Au revoir,*" said the man from the ship as he stepped into the surf. He turned briefly and gave the two a mocking salute before climbing into the longboat.

The boat cast off, and the pair turned to leave when the Frenchman called a final message. "Next time, *mes amis,* I would think carefully before making our rendezvous, eh?

Your services are, of course, much appreciated—but zey are not indispensable. I should 'ate to see our superiors decide to employ someone . . . weeth a less awkward sense of time, shall I say?"

The taller figure hissed an obscenity and spun on his heel, hastening to join his companion, who was already striding toward the carriage. "I told you there'd be difficulties if we—"

"And I told you, you worry too much!" the other snapped. "Besides, it was you who wanted to catch your precious little *virgin!*"

"Yes, and I'd have had her if you hadn't—"

"Enough! She's a dead virgin now, m'lord, and I suggest you begin looking elsewhere for your . . . pleasures!"

The tall man grated an obscenity and followed his companion to the carriage.

ᗜᕚ Five ᕛᗝ

The woman who'd worn the locket with an *H* on it gazed absently out the window of her bedchamber. She was trying desperately to make some sense out of what had happened to her. *Amnesia,* the physician had called it. A simple word, really. Three brief syllables, yet in their import they encompassed a world of confusion, self-doubt . . . and pain.

Dear God, who was she? She had no idea. Yet surely she was someone. Someone with a past that gave meaning to who she was. How she lived. Someone with a name . . . with a family, surely . . . with hopes and dreams and— yes, even fears would be welcome now, if they could tell her something about herself.

God in heaven, why couldn't she remember? What had happened to her to cause all this . . . blankness? This sense of floating in an endless void, with no way out.

The physician had mentioned something about shock. Shock sometimes caused it, he said. She gazed down at the purple bruises encircling her wrists. She was gripping the arms of the chair so tightly, her knuckles shone white beneath the skin. Making a conscious effort to relax, she released them as she thought about bruises.

Bruises said she'd been hurt. She nearly laughed. She hardly needed to look at them to know *that.* Her entire body was a mass of aches, some dull and throbbing, others more acute. Had the injuries she'd suffered been even worse than what she felt now? Had they been so severe, her mind needed to blot them out of memory, as the physician's words suggested? A terrible accident of some sort?

She pushed back the sleeves of the fine rose wool wrapper they'd found for her. Turning her wrists slowly, she examined the bruises. These were the result of no accident. Something, or someone, had gripped those wrists—gripped them hard. Hard enough to hold her still, perhaps, while she struggled to—

Oh, God! *Why couldn't she remember?*

A movement down below drew her eye, and she bent forward to get a better look. The man who'd introduced himself as Major Nicholas Sharpe strode onto the circular drive fronting the house. With him was a slighter man dressed in the plain clothes of a tradesman or man of business. She watched Sharpe exchange a few words with the man, who then mounted a horse a groom led forth.

More specifically, she just watched Sharpe.

He was tall and beautifully built. The body of an athlete . . . a true Corinthian, as the *ton* put it. The *ton* . . . now how did she know that? Apparently there were some things lodged in her memory which hadn't been erased. She knew how to speak the English language, for example. She knew how to walk, and eat with the proper utensils, and—

Her breath caught as Sharpe turned from seeing the man off, and looked up at the window. She knew he saw her, yet he didn't move, made no sign of recognition. He simply stood there, gazing up at her.

She let her breath out slowly, not moving a muscle herself. Again, as when she'd first set eyes on him, his dark perfection penetrated her awareness like a blade. He no longer seemed an angel of death, as she'd feared in those first waking moments, yet a dark angel nonetheless. Hair as black as her own being swept by the wind . . . high, angular cheekbones framing a long, straight nose, and a mouth—dear God, it was so perfectly chiseled, she itched to touch it!

She felt her breathing go shallow with the thought, made her gaze move on, but not far. It was his eyes that held her now. Darkness again . . . a deep, gunmetal gray that watched and brooded beneath fierce slashes of brow. No light here. A keen intelligence, cynicism, bitterness . . . and smoldering anger—these she sensed at once, but no light. No light at all.

A shiver coursed through her, and she pulled back into the chair. Into herself. It seemed to break the thread that held him, and he turned abruptly and strode out of sight, hidden by the eaves. She began to breathe normally again.

Nicholas reentered the house and made straight for the library. But not to spend time with the books. He and Morgan had finally completed that task, and the grim picture he'd feared was now firmly established in his mind.

What to do about it was another matter, but he would sort that out later. It wanted time, and a careful scrutiny of the estate . . . exchanges with the tenants, certainly . . . and, of course, some discourse with his brother's bankers. Not that he was sanguine about what the latter might afford.

But for now there was something he could act upon, and it was high time he took care of it. The girl. Cartwright had mentioned sending an inquiry to the family solicitors as a means of ascertaining her identity. He should have thought of it himself—would have if he hadn't been so damned preoccupied with that trapped, vulnerable look about her . . . a look he couldn't get out of his mind.

Even now, seeing her again in that window, he'd been struck by it, even more than by her beauty. It threatened to wrap itself around him and make him feel things he had no business feeling, didn't want to feel. Never again, by God— *never*. Women had exactly one use he could trust, feel comfortable dealing with, and the green-eyed mystery upstairs had no part to play in that.

But she has a body that was born to satisfy a man, a silent voice taunted. *Made to lie beneath a man in his bed and*

*accommodate the hardness of his own with lush, ripe curves.
She'd fit around you like a—*

Christ! The sooner he got her off his hands, the better!

He wrote the letter quickly, establishing the details with
as few strokes as possible, underscoring the need for discretion above all.

Deciding to kill two birds with one stone, he also apprised the solicitors of his intention of journeying to London in the near future. He needed to discuss with them
details pertaining to his half brother's estate. He had only
Aubrey's word about the guardianship of the children, for
one thing. And nothing at all had been said about Caerdruth, although one would suppose warding Harry included wardship of the entailed estate.

And then there was Trevellan, which wasn't entailed, but
had likely been willed to Harry as well. On the other hand,
perhaps it went to the next male in line. Lesser estates,
especially those arriving through the mother's dowry, occasionally went to younger sons. The next in line would be
the elder of the twins—Christ, wouldn't that prove a sticky
wicket! Yes, a look at the will was definitely in order.

He sanded and sealed the letter, then sent a footman to
carry it to the village. The mail coach was due around noon.
With luck, his missive would reach the offices of Witherspoon and Clark by late tomorrow.

This accomplished, Nicholas went to collect his riding
coat from his chamber; if he set out now, he'd have time to
visit the three nearest tenants before dark. He arrived at his
door when he spied a housemaid approaching. She carried
a tray laden with food.

"Is that for our guest?" A sudden impulse had seized him,
and as he dipped his head in the direction of the door
opposite, it solidified into decision.

"Y-yes, sir."

He grasped the tray before the startled woman could respond. "Just knock for me, if you will."

Nicholas shouldered the door ajar and entered. The girl
—Holly, he amended, recalling the name his little vixen of

a niece Fanny had invented for her—was no longer by the window. In bed now, she glanced up from a book she was reading. He saw her flush.

The blush of a young woman at his appearance was nothing new to Nicholas, but this disconcerted him. *God, are there still women that young and innocent in the world? After Salamanca? After Spain?*

"Good afternoon, Miss Holly." He made a stab at a smile. "I took the liberty of waylaying your nuncheon tray. It appears the staff is taking quite seriously the physician's orders to see you on the road to recovery."

"Good—good afternoon," she managed. She'd gone nearly speechless at his sudden appearance. Feeling herself flush, she quickly lowered her eyes to the book in her lap.

Following that disturbing sight of him from the window, she'd withdrawn to the bed and tried to blot the man from her mind. The irony of this, in view of her present circumstances, was not lost on her, and she'd stifled the urge to giggle wildly with it. Yet immersing herself in the copy of *Sense and Sensibility* Aunt Maud had left had seemed a good means of distraction; now she realized she'd been reading the same sentence over and over, and still didn't know what it said. She snapped the volume shut.

"Not to your taste?" Nicholas asked as he set the tray on a table which had been drawn up to the bed. He picked up the book from her lap, glanced at its spine, then at her. "Miss Austen's novel, I mean. The food here's quite tasty, I assure you. My brother kept an excellent larder, if nothing else."

Holly felt more heat invade her cheeks. The brush of his fingers along the blanket covering her lap as he'd taken the book . . . she'd felt it clear through to the skin of her thighs.

"Your brother?" She willed the blush away, made herself look at him. "This is your brother's home, then?"

"Has no one told you anything?" Nicholas was frowning. He'd followed the impulse to drop in on her because of the item in his pocket. But also as a means of assuring himself that he'd been needlessly concerned with the creature. With that unspoken vulnerability, that look about her that drew him, despite himself. A few moments with the chit, he'd told himself, and he'd see she was as ordinary as rice pudding.

Now he was more concerned than ever. What the deuce had Hastings and the others been about? Bad enough the girl had no memory of her past; letting her languish for hours without apprising her at least of her present circumstances was tantamount to neglect. Small wonder she looked so lost. She had to be totally at sea!

"Told me? Told me what, Major Sharpe?"

"About Caerdruth Hall"—he gestured with a sweep of his arm—"where we are. About who we are. Haven't they said?"

She paused in thought, catching her lower lip between her teeth. A full, sensual lower lip, he noticed not for the first time. One that in other circumstances he'd have immediately marked for kissing.

Christ! Are you that depraved? Been too long without a woman, old boy. It's affecting your judgment. Best arrange that trip to London soon!

"Well," she said, "I do know about Caerdruth, that it's a country estate in Cornwall. And that you have several children, Major. Although, how many—is something wrong, sir?"

Nicholas followed his snort with an uncomfortable smile. "They're not mine, exactly."

"I beg your pardon?"

"Here," he said, placing the tray on her lap. "Have some of this food before it grows cold, and I'll explain it all to you . . ."

A bowl of chicken broth and two slices of mutton later, Holly was in full possession of the Hall's immediate history. She looked a deal more comfortable than when he first came in, Nicholas decided, though whether from the nourishment or his briefing, he couldn't say.

He eyed the tray's remains as she blotted her lips with a serviette. "Not one for sweets, are you?"

Her glance fell on a small bowl that remained untouched, and she smiled apologetically. "I'm afraid I don't fancy the pudding." She drew in a sudden breath. The green eyes went wide with it, and Nicholas felt stunned by their emerald clarity.

"Oh, how very odd!" she exclaimed. "That I would know I'm not a rice pudding person without even tasting—is that amusing, Major?"

Nicholas wiped a sardonic grin from his face. "Not at all, Miss Holly. I was merely agreeing. Indeed, I find not a single rice pudding thing about you." *In fact, only an ass could have thought it.*

He ignored the puzzled look she gave him, and reached into his pocket. "I have something which belongs to you. I'd meant to return it earlier, but—at any rate, here you are."

Before she could decipher what he meant, Nicholas lifted her hand from the blanket, turned it palm up, and dropped the locket bearing the *H* into it. "I believe they told you about this?"

Slowly, Holly nodded, her eyes on the object in her palm. Her hand tingled, but not from the locket with its fine engraving and delicate gold chain. The sensation had begun the instant Major Nicholas Sharpe grasped the hand. The object in it created no awareness in her. Except for the warmth it imparted. She felt herself blushing again, too aware the gold retained the body heat of the man who'd carried it in his pocket.

She forced her attention back to the locket. With her forefinger she lightly traced the ornate *H* on its surface. They found this on her the night she'd sought refuge here from a terrible storm. That much, she knew—but only because she'd been told about it by the housekeeper.

But if it was hers, why could she summon no recognition? Surely the initial signified a name. Her own? *Why can't I remember?*

Sensing the expectancy of the man waiting silently beside the bed, she knew she ought to say something. She cleared her throat, made herself speak. "It—it's quite lovely, isn't it?"

Nicholas nodded slowly as she met his gaze. Her eyes shone bright with unshed tears. *She looks more hopeless than ever . . . like a lost child who can't find her way home in the dark. . . .*

"But you don't recognize it, do you?"

Blinking back the tears, she shook her head and looked away.

"There's no faint stirring of memory? No familiar—"

"There's nothing, I tell you! *Nothing!*"

She'd rounded on him like some cornered wild creature, and Nicholas felt two things at once: remorse, for having pressed her—and a surge of admiration. Both surprised him. Remorse was alien to him; he'd never troubled himself with such a useless emotion. As for the admiration, he'd previously regarded her as vulnerable . . . weak as a kitten, and therefore deserving of his—what? Solicitude? Pity? He'd never concerned himself with those either.

But now it seemed the kitten had claws. Good. She'd need them, he suspected, in the days and weeks to come.

"I—I beg your pardon, Major," she said. "I don't know what came over me. I never meant to raise my—"

"A flea bite," he said with a shrug.

Holly felt mesmerized by the breadth of shoulder that made the gesture. Nicholas Sharpe affected her in ways she somehow knew in her bones she'd never felt before. Before the flush could deepen, she quickly cast about for something to say.

"Your housekeeper was the one who told me about the locket." She managed this calmly. "She also mentioned one of the children . . . the one who conjured a name for me from it." He'd briefly summarized his brother's children as "four boys and three girls," had mentioned their ages, but no names. "Fanny . . ." she went on. "Which one is she?"

"Um . . . the six-year-old, I believe."

"She sounds an unusual child."

"She is."

Why the wry smile? "I should like to meet her . . . meet all the children, actually. Might that be possible?"

"It might be arranged, yes."

More than wry . . . positively sardonic . . . He's not comfortable with children . . . but then, being a bachelor, how could he be? "I find it remarkable that a six-year-old would take it upon herself to name an utter stranger. In particular, one in my . . . unusual circumstances."

Nicholas was thinking "remarkable" too mild a term for that lot in the nursery. "Lady Fanny, I would say, has at least two immediately discernible traits: She is quite bright, and, uh, extremely imaginative."

She nodded thoughtfully. "Why *Holly,* I wonder."

"She first decided to call you *Princess* Holly, actually. According to her eldest brother, the child was born on Christmas Day. And she'd always rather fancied the name for herself, had she been allowed to choose it. Consider it a testament to Fanny's fascination with your appearance here at Caerdruth, that she bestowed the name on you. And to her more-than-vivid imagination, that she added 'Princess' as a title."

Holly smiled. "Indeed, I shall consider it an honor, and so inform her when we've met. Ah, might that be soon?"

The grin was decidedly cynical this time. "Sooner than you'd have wished, I suspect, once it's happened."

"I beg your pardon?"

His laugh was cynical too. "I might find myself begging yours, once I've introduced you," he said, rising to take the tray.

She realized he was leaving, and tried not to let the surge of disappointment she felt show on her face.

"My brother's children," Nicholas said matter-of-factly, "are a pack of holy terrors. All seven—count them!—*seven* of them! Have I shocked you? Very well, then I've shocked you."

Holding the tray as he faced her, ignoring her incredulous look, he went on. "Their education may have been perfunctorily seen to, but only that. They are ill-mannered, cheeky, and up to every rig they can think of. But if you're still inclined to meet them . . ."

He let his words trail off, made for the doorway, then threw a parting shot over his shoulder. "But never say I didn't warn you!"

Leaving Holly to stare openmouthed at the door he shut firmly in his wake.

ৡ৯ Six ৡৡ

Nicholas awoke with a start. The chamber was dark, but moonlight limned the draperied windows. Combat-honed senses told him it was a long time till dawn, yet . . . *What the devil—*

Then he heard it. A high-pitched scream, somewhat muffled but reverberating through the oak panels of the door. It was coming from across the hall.

The girl—*Holly!*

He was out of bed as the realization hit. Bounding for the door, he checked his movement, returned for the breeches he'd discarded when he retired. The screaming became a high, keening wail as he hastily drew them on.

By the time he reached the hallway, others were approaching, drawn by the terrified sounds. Parkins, his dignified posture at odds with the nightshirt he wore, came from the stairs bearing a chamber stick. Its flickering light revealed the nightgowned figure of Hastings behind him.

Nicholas motioned them forward as he crossed to Holly's door. When he opened it, moonlight flooded the chamber. It spilled across the high tester bed where a slender figure huddled against the headboard. Screaming.

"Holly—what is it?" Reaching the bed, Nicholas realized she hadn't heard him. Her eyes were closed, and she'd begun to twist and struggle fitfully, much as when she'd lain unconscious. The screams had dwindled to deep, broken sobs.

"Holly, wake up!" Nicholas went to shake her awake, thought better of it, and climbed carefully onto the bed. There he placed both hands on her shoulders and began to speak in soothing tones.

"Holly . . . it's all right. You're having a nightmare, that's all. Wake up now, and you'll be fine . . . Miss Holly . . ."

As he spoke, he drew her rigid body against him. He could feel her shudder with each convulsive sob. *Christ! Whatever she's seeing—must be hellish.*

"Holly, shh," he murmured, running a hand along her back as he held her, cupping her head and smoothing the tangle of tear-dampened hair.

He'd heard sounds like this before . . . in tents pitched on blood-soaked ground . . . in field hospitals, amidst the maimed and dying . . . but this was England . . . this was civilized, goddamned Cornwall, for Christ's sake!

He heard her gasp, and knew she was awake. Parkins drew near, and placed his chamber stick on the stand beside the bed. Out in the hallway footsteps sounded, and a murmuring of voices.

"It's all right, Miss Holly," Nicholas said, and loosened his hold on her. "You've had a nightmare, but you're awake now. All's well . . . there, now . . ."

He heard her exhale—a long rush of air, then suck in more, expel it. Dazedly, still cradled in the crook of his arm, she raised her head. Eyes not green, but shimmering quicksilver in the moonlight, gazed up at him through lashes spiked with tears. And despite the terror in them— ebbing now, but by no means gone—despite the moon-blanched pallor of her face, Nicholas felt his breath catch: She was exquisite.

He knew he'd never seen anything lovelier in his life. Knew with a certainty that after this, the beauty of other women would pale in comparison. Knew too, he must wipe the thought from his mind.

He was poison to someone like her . . . an innocent, despite what the *ton* would make of what she'd been through. He only hoped he had some semblance of decency left; enough at least to give that innocence a wide berth.

"Better now?" he questioned evenly.

She was still breathing hard, but gave him a hesitant nod. He immediately set her away from him, propping her against the pillows.

Holly felt the loss of body heat at once. It had begun to penetrate the stark terror of the dream . . . the dream that —what had it been? She groped for fading images that teased her recall, but they were gone.

Instead, she remembered a deep, calming voice . . . strong arms . . . a warm, hard-muscled—*Dear God! He's half-naked!*

"I—I had a bad dream," she managed, and tore her eyes from Nicholas's chest. "It . . . was frightening." She dropped her gaze to her lap, began rubbing her temples with her fingers.

"Oh my, aes, miss!" exclaimed the freckled girl they'd assigned her as an abigail that morning. "Ee gave us all a turnin', that ee did, what wi' yer screamin'! Bain't never been so scared in all me—"

"That's quite enough, Mary." The housekeeper planted herself between the tableau at bedside and the crowd gathered at the door. "Return to your rooms at once," she told the gaping servants. "The sun will rise soon enough, and I hope I make myself understood when I say there had best be no sluggards about their morning duties!"

The crowd dispersed with alacrity, some of them darting furtive glances at the major, who also made his way toward the hallway. Hastings had administered a warning lecture about slipshod service recently, and none had any doubts as to its primary source.

Nicholas turned at the doorway, and nodded at the senior servants who remained. "Thank you both." He glanced at Holly, offered a perfunctory bow, then turned back to Parkins and Hastings.

"I'll leave things in your capable hands now," he told them. Without another word, avoiding the bewildered eyes of the girl on the bed, he crossed the hall and shut his own door behind him.

Holly politely declined the housekeeper's offer of a cup of tea. She did, however, accept the butler's suggestion that he light her lamp before they left. Assuring them she'd be fine, she watched the door close behind them, then settled back against the pillows.

So much was happening that she couldn't understand, had no frame of reference to deal with. Bad enough to awaken in a strange place, surrounded by strangers. But she was a stranger too . . . alien to herself. And these dreams . . . she felt certain they were trying to tell her something, but what? Who she was, most likely, but—

No, there was something more . . . something, she suddenly realized, she didn't want to—what? *What? What? What? Dear God, I shall go mad if I don't stop this!*

She turned toward the bedside table where she'd left the volume of *Sense and Sensibility,* then saw that someone had placed it on the mattress near at hand. Nicholas?

She felt herself flush, knowing she shouldn't be referring to him by his Christian name, even in her mind. They were barely more than strangers—that word again.

And of all that was strange in this place, Nicholas Sharpe was the strangest. Such a somber, brooding man! Hardly the stuff of a young girl's fancies, yet she couldn't get him out of her thoughts.

She chuckled ruefully to herself. Little surprise in that. Regardless of his temperament, with those looks of his, she wasn't likely to be the only woman who reacted that way. He probably had them lining up in cues whenever he went out socially, just on the chance he'd speak to them!

Did he go out and about, though? He seemed such a solitary man. Yet even Lord Byron, with his dark, brooding underlook, went out in society, so—*Lord Byron?*

Now, how did she know that? Know *him?* But she must

have! How else would Nicholas Sharpe have reminded her of him? Yet when she tried to summon an instance of meeting the famous poet, nothing came.

Or, rather, Nicholas Sharpe came to mind instead. Devastatingly handsome Nicholas Sharpe, with his women in the dozens. Slim chance he'd notice her, a girl with bruises on her face, without even a name to call her own.

Still . . . there was something about the way he'd looked at her a little while ago . . .

Smiling to herself, Holly clasped the book to her chest and drifted off to sleep.

It was several days later, and the physician had just seen Holly that morning. He'd pronounced her recovered sufficiently from her physical injuries that she need no longer be confined to bed. And a good thing too, she told herself. Kind as the staff and certain members of this household had been, she'd begun to grow frightfully bored. She meant to take full advantage of her new freedom!

The first order of business had been to summon the little abigail. With the housekeeper's assistance, she'd managed a bath for Holly, and the washing of her yard-long hair.

"Ooh, miss!" Mary now exclaimed as she brushed the shining tresses before a dressing table. "Bain't never seen hair this thick an' loverly in all me life!" Mary's own hair was ginger-colored, and on the fine side.

Dressed once again in the rose wool wrapper, Holly nodded absently, her gaze on the image in the looking glass. Her face, at least, was familiar. Although whether from the daily perusals she'd given it in a hand mirror Maud had provided, or from a far longer acquaintance, she couldn't say.

But the face in the glass did give her the impression of being thinner . . . than it had once been? Perhaps she was remembering. In any event, it was not an unattractive face, especially now that the scratches were gone, the bruises fading.

She wondered if Nicholas would think her pretty, then

forced the thought aside. She'd not seen that dark angel—
for so she'd begun to think of him—who'd soothed away
her nightmares since that night, and she made a resolution
only this morning, not to let it concern her. The fact that
Aunt Maud came to visit each day didn't mean everyone
ought to do so, did it?

It was merely, she told herself, that he'd agreed to let her
meet the children, and now that she could dress and go
about, she was more than ready to have him arrange it.
Dress and go about . . .

Her eyes strayed to the jonquil yellow sprigged muslin
gown Mrs. Hastings had found in the sewing room. Holly
had resisted wearing it at first—the household was in
mourning, after all—but in the end it was decided she
might be forgiven the lapse, given her circumstances.

The late Lady Sharpe's clothing had been donated to the
parish after she died, but this gown, relegated to a mending
basket because of a loose hem, had escaped notice. She'd
already tried it on, and it would more than do. Lady Sharpe
had apparently been a shorter woman, but hemlines had
come up since she'd had the dress made; Aunt Maud had
assured Holly that in reaching only to her ankles, the gown
would appear "all the crack."

Holly fought a giggle. Aunt Maud? Informing her of what
was all the go in fashion? She was terribly fond of the old
dear, but if she didn't begin to enjoy the company of others,
she feared she'd begin to think like that queerly bedizened
soul!

Mary braided her hair into a high coronet, then softened
its severity by arranging a few wisps and tendrils about the
hairline. After Holly had donned her own stockings and
shift—washed and mended now—she allowed the abigail
to help her into the sprigged muslin. A pair of yellow kid
dancing sandals—donated by Aunt Maud, and only a bit
too large—completed the ensemble.

Or so she thought, until she stood before the pier glass in
the dressing room. The gown, with its high waist and

square neckline, looked lovely on her, but it also drew the eye to the remnant of bruises at her throat.

"Mary," she said, "I'm all for matching up colors, but yellowing bruises are not exactly what *Le Beau Monde*'s fashion pages would dictate for a *jonquille* gown!"

"Aes, miss." The girl heaved a sigh. "Bain't knowin' what t' do 'bout it, neither."

"But I do," said a familiar voice from the doorway. "Just the thing, in fact!"

"Aunt Maud!" Holly turned toward the old woman. "I was hoping you'd come, but was afraid you might be napping."

"What, and miss your coming out? Not exactly a Coming Out with capital letters, I realize, but an event in any case!

"I do hope you'll excuse my not knocking, my dear," the old woman added as she joined them in front of the glass, "but the door was ajar, and—"

"Of course," said Holly, "but what was it you were saying about 'just the thing'?"

"Indeed," said Maud as she began to fish about her person. Or, in particular, to rummage through numerous huge pockets of different colors which had been sewn onto a black court mourning gown complete with hoops. (Maud had already explained to Holly that she wore mourning when she could remember to do so, but that her fondness for color sometimes made that difficult.) "Let me see . . . I know I had it here somewhere."

As she rummaged, she pulled out various bits and pieces of paraphernalia which had been stuffed into these pockets. The maid's eyes widened, and Holly stifled a giggle as there appeared all sorts of oddities . . . a boy's slingshot . . . a quizzing glass . . . even a ball of yarn complete with knitting needles stuck through it!

"Drat!" Maud muttered. "Stitched these pockets on, myself, you know . . . never could remember where I'd put my reticule when they came into vogue . . . didn't grow up using one, y'see . . . but sometimes having all these pockets—Ah! Here we are!"

From a pocket of amaranthus-colored velvet, she extracted what looked like a handful of Brabant lace. "It's one of those elegant little ruffs emulating the Elizabethan mode," Maud explained as she motioned for Holly to bend down to her level. "Came into fashion not too long ago, I collect, and—there we are! Just the thing!"

And it was, they saw at once. Completely hiding the bruises, it set off the high coiffure beautifully and was accommodated by Holly's long, slender neck. All it wanted was for her to remove the chain with the locket, but here she hesitated.

The locket was all she had to remind her of who she was —or might be. Her only real link to her forgotten past . . .

She was feeling less at sea now than she had felt in those first awful hours and days. But the dreams still terrorized her nightly, although she'd managed to awaken without screaming since that one time. And no matter how much of a "normal" face she tried to put on it, her life was little less than a shambles . . . or should she say a sham?

With a decisive nod, Holly tucked the locket into the square bodice, and went for a tour of the Hall with Maud.

"Not a proper conservatory any longer," the old woman murmured a short while later. They had entered a vast, windowed enclosure at the southeast corner of the house. "The countess, Aubrey's mother that is, hailed from Somerset, and missed the tamer landscape of her native soil."

Maud chuckled softly as she led Holly to one of several stone benches dotting the aisles. "Don't know how she did it, but she somehow convinced that scapegrace earl of hers to have this conservatory built. Got the old skinflint to engage Nash for it too. Then went to work importing not only Somerset roses and whatnot, but all manner of exotica as well. Even tackled a garden out of doors."

She sighed, gazing around at the few pitiful specimens of trees and shrubs that stood among more numerous pots and plots of bare earth. "But Aubrey's countess was a different sort entirely. Took no interest in the thing. It's been years now, since Caerdruth's retained a gardener."

Holly looked around her and nodded, privately thinking this was more articulate discourse than she'd heard from Maud since she'd met the woman. Despite her shimble-shamble ways, Maud could be a fountain of information if she chose. Holly made a mental note to pay close attention to what the old woman said in future, and perhaps to encourage her along certain lines.

"Well then, Aunt Maud, do you suppose the major has any interest in reviving any of this, now that he's—"

"The major? Oh, but my dear, my husband stuck his spoon in the wall years ago! And he received a promotion to lieutenant colonel, as I recollect, before he met his Maker."

Holly blinked bemusedly, then hid a smile. "Ah, I was referring to Major Sharpe, actually . . . Major *Nicholas* Sharpe?"

"Major Nicholas . . . do you mean *Nicky?*"

Holly did smile this time. In fact, she almost burst out laughing at the thought of that dark angel with such a sobriquet. "Yes," she answered. "Nicky."

"Oh, good heavens, no, my dear! I can no more imagine Nicky standing about waiting for things to grow, than I can picture the devil praying! Too restless, y'see . . . always haring about, getting into scrapes! No, never Nicky!"

"Never Nicky, what?" said a deep male voice.

Both women turned toward the arched doorway, and Holly felt her heartbeat quicken. Nicholas Sharpe's big frame nearly filled the space. He stepped inside, followed by a tall, slender youth.

They were dressed similarly, in loose-fitting black shirts —they were in mourning too—with flowing sleeves caught tight at the wrists, thigh-hugging black breeches, and Wellingtons. Each held a fencing rapier at his side.

But there the similarity ended. The boy was neatly handsome in a youthful sort of way; but Nicholas's dark male beauty seemed to burn the air around him. Beside it the youth's slim blondness faded to an echo of the man whose mode of dress he shared.

"Come now, Aunt Maud," Nicholas insisted as he advanced toward the bench. "What *about* Nicky?"

"I was telling the gel you'd never be promoted to lieutenant colonel if you insist on rapiers, Nick. It's all barking irons these days, m'boy. Rapiers are not the way of things any longer, and high time a rum young buck like you knew it!"

Nicholas flashed a grin that told the old woman he was onto her flummery, and Holly's heart skipped a beat. He was handsome enough in any case, but with that roguish grin . . .

"Ah, but then how should I show Harry proper fencing techniques, m'lady?"

"Better, I expect, than you've shown him manners, you young scamp!" Maud gestured archly at the earl, then at Holly.

"How remiss of me," Nicholas replied, not sounding the least bit chastened. "Miss Holly, allow me to introduce my nephew, the earl of Caerdruth. Lord Harry . . . our charming guest, Miss Holly."

He watched Holly execute a curtsy worthy of a candidate for presentation at Court. And suddenly felt certain she'd been through that very procedure. *No green country miss, this . . . I'd wager the home farm on it . . . that is, if I had a home farm!*

His mouth curled in a self-mocking smile as he watched the rightful heir to Caerdruth bow awkwardly over Holly's hand and murmur a politeness.

"We've been looking forward to meeting you, Miss Holly," said Harry. "And we do hope you're feeling . . . er, better."

Holly chuckled wryly. "Thank you, m'lord. While I cannot say I am feeling, ah, quite myself yet, Mr. Cartwright assures me I am on the mend in some respects, at least."

"Indeed, Miss Holly," said Harry, "you are looking . . . um, remarkably well."

Nicholas watched Harry's ears redden, and stifled a snort. *The young pup's smitten already! Devil take it! The entire household's agog over the chit—and I've an estate to run!*

"M'lord Harry," Nicholas said with asperity, "if you're through exchanging pleasantries, I believe we had a fencing lesson to accomplish before your tutor arrives." He glanced at the women. "Ladies, if you will excuse—"

"But, Nick," the old woman protested, "the Hall has no fencing parlor!"

"Indeed, which is why I've brought m'lord to this"—he gestured about them—"wasteland, to practice his *demi-volte.* Now, if you will kindly—"

"Would it be possible for us to watch?" Holly wanted to bite her tongue the instant the words were out.

Too late. Nicholas looked at her as if she'd sprouted two heads. Fencing was a totally male endeavor, and no lady of the first stare would think of entering the premises of Angelo's Haymarket fencing rooms, or—*Angelo's . . . I've recalled something else!*

"Tell me, Miss Holly," said Nicholas crisply, "do you feel a fancy coming on, to watch gamecocks as well? Perhaps we should arrange a journey to the Royal Cockpit, or—"

"Uncle Nicholas!" Harry's ears flamed redder than before as he heard himself speak to his guardian in such tones; but the fact was, he was embarrassed that his uncle had spoken so rudely to a guest. A guest who was a lady—and a beautiful one at that!

"Er . . . I apologize, sir," he went on, "but—well, frankly, I shouldn't mind at all if the ladies cared to watch. Might even help improve my feints and parries, and . . ." The words trailed off in the face of Nicholas's unrelenting glare, and Harry wound up staring miserably at his feet.

"Very well, m'lord," Nicholas replied tightly, and held out a staying hand to Holly, who was gesturing at Maud to take their leave. "You have said it, and you are the ultimate master of these premises, after all. The ladies will remain.

"As for your lordship," he added as he rounded on the

youngster and raised his rapier in a swift, graceful movement. *"En garde!"*

Harry barely raised his foil in time to meet the salute, let alone parry the thrust that followed. He stumbled backward under the force of several lightning-quick executions from his mentor, and Holly winced as she urged Maud out of the way.

Apparently Nicholas had allowed Harry's acceptance of her audacious request with the aim of teaching him a lesson. And not a lesson in swordplay. It was clear from the way he was engaging the boy—mercilessly, using all of his vastly superior skill to embarrass the youngster. He'd make him regret the day he dared overset his guardian's wishes . . . *from his vantage point of privilege?*

Holly blinked as this last realization hit. She didn't know any such thing about Nicholas's motives, did she? Yet, somehow she sensed it was true. Nicholas was angry with the boy, not merely for countering his wishes, but for having the superiority of birth to dare it, despite his youth!

But, why? Why be so intolerant of a green boy? Surely, as a man of the world, he'd run across titles throwing their weight around before—and Lord Harry hadn't even done that! He'd actually been acting the gentleman, defending her!

Oh, God, what have I gotten us into? She stared helplessly at the merciless spectacle of the professional soldier trouncing a thirteen-year-old boy, and wanted to scream. Thrust, parry, thrust again . . . Nicholas was relentless.

Harry was dripping perspiration, yet his uncle hadn't broken a sweat. He lunged, parried the boy's half-formed ripostes, lunged anew . . . always gaining ground, moving across the stone floor like a great, angry cat on the prowl: a panther out for prey.

Maud was clutching Holly's arm as if the weight of the world depended on it. Holly had no doubt the old woman knew what was going on as well as she did, and they were both helpless to stop it. As the boy's guardian, it was Nicholas's right to do this thing, but it branded him heartless as far as Holly was concerned. *Bully!* she wanted to cry. *Monster!*

Then finally it was over. Harry stood backed against a potted fig tree as his foil clattered to the floor. Head drooping, thin chest heaving, he listened as Nicholas said a few words to him which Holly couldn't hear.

The boy nodded wearily, then bent to pick up the rapier. But he managed to keep his head high as he approached the women. "Aunt Maud . . . Miss Holly," he said around labored breathing, "I'm sorry if the display wasn't as good as I'd hoped. I fear I wasn't really up to—"

"Nonsense, lad!" said Maud, taking his free arm. "You showed excellent mettle, and that is what counts in this world—isn't it, Miss Holly?"

The young lord couldn't seem to look at her, but Holly offered him a smile just the same. "Indeed it is, m'lord." She saw Nicholas approach out of the corner of her eye, and raised her voice slightly, "I daresay, battles have been won on just that sort of courage."

"Or lost, for just that sort of foolishness," Nicholas put in behind them.

They were nearing the doorway, the two women on either side of the young earl. At his uncle's remark, Holly saw the boy wince, but he didn't turn around.

She did.

"Oh, bravo, Major," she told the man who seemed more devil than angel to her then. "Bravo, indeed!"

She turned, and saw Harry had broken free of Maud's arm and was dashing down the hallway. She started after him, but a firm hand on her shoulder stayed her.

"Let him go," said Nicholas. "I won't have the boy mollycoddled. He'll need to lick his wounds in private if he's to become a man."

Holly gaped at him, feeling she almost hated Nicholas Sharpe at that moment. "Fine words, Major. Especially for a child who's just lost his sole remaining parent! Is that how they do it in the regiment? Find an orphan, trounce him soundly while he's still in mourning, and call it making a man of him?"

With a look that said exactly what she thought of him, she showed Nicholas Sharpe her back and accompanied Maud from the room.

❧ Seven ☙

After their encounter in the conservatory, Holly saw nothing of Nicholas for two days. She told herself she was glad of it; she couldn't like him after his odious treatment of Harry. Yet he was rarely out of mind.

His image would break into her thoughts with the least provocation. As when she'd embarked upon Miss Austen's *Pride and Prejudice,* and met the character of Mr. Darcy, with his highhanded ways. Or when Mary had been brushing her hair, and its blue-black color recalled his midnight locks.

He was also with her on nightly arousals from nightmare. She would awaken with a silent scream clogging her throat, heart thudding, perspiration soaking her gown. Then a recollection of Nicholas Sharpe's soothing voice and hands became the thing she used to dispel fear. He would become her dark angel again, and never the devil she'd tried to paint him.

But the real Nicholas was keeping his distance. She spent hours about the Hall with Maud, and never caught a glimpse of him. So it was with some surprise she read the note a footman brought three mornings after The Incident —as she'd begun to think of it—its boldly scrawled signature unmistakable:

Miss Holly,

Reminded of your desire to meet my wards, I invite
you to sup with all of us at table this evening. The
younger children normally take their meals in the
nursery, but we have made an exception in this instance, and hope you will join us in the drawing
room across from the dining salon at seven.

                              Maj. Nicholas Sharpe

The note was so much like him, Holly had to smile. No
salutation beyond her name . . . no courteous address
. . . no closing beyond his signature—with military rank,
of course.

She quickly jotted off a reply, saying she'd be happy to
join them, and sent it back with the same footman. Then
came the dilemma of planning her toilette for the occasion.
What to wear. The gown and spencer she'd arrived in were
in sorry shape, and unsuitable for dining *en maison*, in any
case.

That left the *jonquille* muslin. Holly sighed. She had a
faint sense of never having such a difficulty before. Had she
led a privileged life, then? Never having to worry about
dress because whatever she wanted had been available?

Feeling herself succumb again to frustrating longings for
the memory she'd lost, she quickly set aside this train of
thought. She'd concentrate on something within her control. Smiling to herself, she rang for Mary, and asked Aunt
Maud to join her in her chamber.

"There you are, my gel," said Maud. "A diamond of the first
water, if ever I've laid eyes on one!"

It was a quarter to seven, and she and Holly were standing before the pier glass in the dressing room. Mary was
kneeling on the floor behind Holly, adjusting a trim of fine
lace on a sort of garment she'd never laid eyes on, although
she'd been required to stitch it together.

"Er . . . what'd ee say the name of them be, mum?"

"Well," said Maud, "that fashion journal where I

glimpsed them years ago spoke of pantalettes, but I collect Lady Montague pronounced them *drawers*. Invented by the frogs, y'know . . . but then, wasn't everything that's becoming all the kick this side of the Channel?"

"Do you really think they're being taken up here?" Holly questioned. She felt oddly certain she'd never worn such a garment in her life.

"Oh," said Maud, "I daresay they will be, if they haven't quite gone the mile yet. We English simply cannot resist Continental fashions. Just see what's happening with that outrageous dance, the waltz! We may be shocked by it, but the vicar's wife assures me it's invading the land. Her husband's preached three sermons against it already!

"Now, let's have a final look at you, gel," she went on. "Hmmm . . . definitely the first water, though I do wish you'd borrow my demi-turban. I was an absolute toast in it at the old King's birthday ball."

Holly smiled, recalling the outrageous wad of bishop's-blue muslin. They'd done what they could to transform the sprigged *jonquille,* but a bright, purplish blue turban would have been the outside of enough!

The dining salon was perhaps the least shabby room in the Hall, Nicholas thought as he surveyed its length shortly before seven. The solid oak furniture of an earlier age had proven impervious to years of wear, and he didn't give a damn that it was no longer in vogue. Prinny and his set could keep their Chinese-pagoda whatnots, or Egyptian tables with sphinxes for feet. He'd had a bellyful of foreign climes and their appurtenances . . . in the mud and blood of Salamanca . . . in the heat and cannon fire of Vitoria. Give him a good, solid Tudor piece any time, and devil take the exotic!

Parkins entered with two small feather ticks tucked under his arms.

"What the deuce are those for?" Nicholas asked.

"Seating aids for the twinnies, sir."

"Seating aids?"

"Ah . . . yes, sir," replied the servant as he proceeded to place the ticks on a pair of dining chairs. "The little ones are hardly tall enough to reach the table. These should elevate them to the proper height."

Nicholas managed not to groan as he recalled the little terrors. What the deuce had possessed him to include them in this dinner?

But even as he asked himself, he knew. That green-eyed chit in the guest room, that's what! Miss Holly, the Question Mark, and her tender little heart.

He allowed a small smile, glimpsed the sardonic shape of it in the Chippendale mirror over the sideboard. She wished to meet the children, did she? Excellent. By the time the evening was half done, she'd have her craw full of the little monsters!

The tramping of feet alerted him, and he came through the salon's double doors just as his inherited brood was approaching from the stairs. At the front of the assemblage was Blodgett, who of course he'd had to include in this charade. She held Judith and little Nicky by their hands, and for once the twinnies didn't appear too restless. Wide-eyed at this seldom-glimpsed part of the Hall, their heads swiveled in each direction as they took in the furnishings about them.

All the children, Nicholas noticed, had been washed and polished to a fare-thee-well. Since they were dressed in mourning, however, they resembled nothing so much as a pack of land-bound starlings.

"It's Uncle Nicholas!" Martin exclaimed to Michael and Harry, who were bringing up the rear.

"Silence!" said Blodgett. "You may speak when addressed, and not a moment sooner!"

Fanny mouthed the syllables of "Good evening, Uncle," as they filed into the drawing room. Nicholas eyed her archly. Trust that one to find a way through the loopholes!

He was just nodding a greeting to the older boys when a flash of yellow on the stairs caught his eye. He turned, and there was Holly. She'd paused halfway down to assist Maud with the hem of the old woman's gown, which had caught on a ragged piece of stairway runner.

Because she was focused elsewhere, he took the moment to look his fill. She was breathtaking.

He'd seen her in the yellow gown before, of course. But too much had been going on in that meeting for him to really take her in. Slender as a reed, yet showing ripe curves at breast and hip as she bent to attend the old woman, she was something to be savored at one's leisure, like a fine wine.

The hair gathered at the crown of her head shone in a wealth of glossy curls, while the finely etched profile beneath . . .

She walks in beauty like the night . . . The words of Byron's sonnet ran in his mind, and he gave his head a sudden shake. *Quoting poetry? Like a besotted schoolboy? Idiot!*

He greeted the two women politely when they made their way down, then showed them into the drawing room. With the exception of Harry, the children were lined up in front of the fireplace beside Blodgett. Harry stood just inside the door, greeting Aunt Maud with a courteous bow, and then Holly.

"I am ever so pleased to see you again, Miss Holly," said the young lord.

"Thank you, m'lord. I am pleased to be here."

Nicholas glanced at the line of squirming children. "The time grows late, even with country hours. Perhaps you'd care to introduce our guest, m'lord."

Harry looked surprised, then offered his uncle a delighted smile. "Happy to, sir."

From what Holly could tell, there was no evidence of any bad feelings, no indication Harry resented his guardian for what had passed between them two days before. In fact, the young lord seemed totally at ease with the man.

A remarkable child, Holly found herself thinking . . . *or is it,* a small voice niggled, *the* man *who's remarkable, for instilling such respect and acceptance in the boy?*

Harry led her forth, and began by introducing the gov-

erness, as was only proper. Miss Blodgett was formally polite, but Holly found herself taking an instant dislike to the
woman. There was nothing she could put her finger on, but
the governess was stiff and Friday-faced in her black bombazine. Holly couldn't help thinking she'd be the last sort
she'd entrust with a lively brood of children.

For lively, they were. And adorable, with their mops of
blond hair (excepting the smallest boy) and winning smiles.
The smaller twins giggled when she addressed them, but
managed a bow and a curtsy nonetheless.

"Princess!" chirped the towheaded Judith.

"Pretty lady!" added little Nicky.

Nicky? It was all Holly could do, not to glance at the
major behind her and grin.

"And how old are you, Charlotte?" she asked the middle
girl.

Charlotte stared at her slippers and held up four fingers,
then got past her shyness. "How old are you, Princess
Holly?"

"Lottie!" Harry chided. "It's not polite to ask!"

"But she asked me!"

"Indeed I did," said Holly with a laugh. "Serves me right
too, asking a question I'm not prepared to answer in kind."

She bent down until she was on the four-year-old's level.
"Shall we share a secret?" she asked in a whisper.

Charlotte gave the governess a furtive glance, then nodded eagerly.

"I'm in a bit of a muddle right now, and can't recall how
old I am. But when I do—you, Lottie, will be the first
person I shall tell. Will that do?"

Wide-eyed, Charlotte gave her a grave nod.

Fanny was next in line. "So this is the young lady who is
responsible for giving me such a lovely name," said Holly.
"How very thoughtful of you, Fanny. Thank you."

" 'Twas nothing, Your Highness. It came to me in a blaze
of ins-inspir"—Holly hid a smile as the child struggled with
the word—"in a blaze of light!" Fanny finished grandly.

"I see." Holly was still fighting the smile. "And are you frequently given to these . . . blazes?"

"Oh, ever so!" exclaimed the child. "They come upon me on a moment's notice."

"They come upon her with the squints!" one of the twins put in.

"*Michael* . . ." said the governess in dire warning.

"I'm not Michael—I'm Martin!"

"You're also not long for this gathering if you continue in that vein," said Nicholas, coming forward. "You will apologize for your impertinent address, Martin."

"I beg your pardon, Miss Blodgett," said the boy in a subdued voice.

As introductions were completed and they advanced into the dining salon, Holly wondered about a governess who couldn't tell her charges apart. Even if they were twins. She, a total newcomer, already knew a major difference between Martin and Michael; Martin was the one with a rational bent—it showed in his eyes as they followed a conversation —while his brother favored action. And of course they were mirror images, not exact duplicates of each other. Didn't that dour black crow see any of this?

The meal proceeded without mishap through the first course. The children seemed absorbed with the food, a tasty mulligatawny, along with platters of salmon and turbot. They managed to display acceptable table manners, Holly noted, neither slurping their soup nor wolfing anything down.

Then it happened.

The footmen were just beginning to clear for the second course when an odd, yowling sound emanated from beneath the table. Holly saw the twins stiffen. They cast knowing looks at each other.

"It's Ernest!" said Charlotte around a mouthful of bread and butter. Just as Holly saw the damask tablecloth twitch, a little to the left of Blodgett's plate.

Too busy remonstrating, the governess didn't notice.

"Charlotte, how many times must I remind you not to talk with your mouth full? You know—"

She got no further as a large ball of orange fur leapt onto the table in front of her. Blodgett's florid face went purple, but all she could emit was a strangled gibbering sound as the fattest cat Holly had ever seen proceeded to help himself to the remains of her turbot.

"What the devil!" shouted Nicholas.

"Get him!" yelled Michael to his twin.

"He's too big for me!" Martin stood on his chair and glared at the feline. "Let's do it together!"

"Who the deuce let that animal in here?" Nicholas thundered.

The cat evaded a dual lunge by the twins, and made a flying leap for the salmon. A pair of footmen came toward it, but backed away when it arched its back and hissed at them.

"Oh, you needn't be afraid of Ernest!" Fanny assured them. "He may be large, but it's all fat!"

"We'll get him!" shouted Michael, motioning Martin around the table.

"He's planted his feet in our salmon!" cried Charlotte.

"Parkins!" Nicholas yelled, but the twinnies had raised such a din cheering their brothers on, Holly doubted he'd been heard.

The room was in total chaos now, with the twins stalking the cat, and footmen running to and fro as Ernest leapt from plate to platter. Fanny managed to grab the cat's tail at one point, and this brought on a yowling loud enough to raise the dead. Only Blodgett remained silent. Her eyes bulged—a pair of currants stuck in meringue. Her face had gone the color of ripe gooseberries.

Meanwhile, Harry was leaning toward Nicholas, trying to hear what his uncle was yelling at him over the racket. And as Fanny called instructions to the twins, the twinnies stood upon their seats and jumped about on the feather ticks, screeching at the tops of their lungs.

Through most of this, Holly and Maud sat slack-jawed. But then their glances met, and they burst out laughing.

"That does it!" roared Nicholas.

With a decisive gesture, he lurched forward and grabbed the cat by the scruff of its neck. Ernest was standing four-square on the platter of salmon, gorging himself. When he felt the major's hand on him, his nasty hiss sent bits of salmon flying. Nicholas closed an eye as several of these missiles struck him head-on.

Nicholas dislodged the fishy debris with a violent shake of his head, then fixed the animal with a malevolent glare. And hissed back.

Ernest froze, and a great cheer went up from the younger children.

The cat looked utterly startled. Its eyes fixed unblink-ingly on the large man who'd dared to lay a hand on it. Who now proceeded to grab the salmon platter and lift it, cat and all, clear of the table.

"Parkins!" barked Nicholas. The butler finally appeared, drawn by the racket. "Take this . . . *creature,* and dispose of it! Then fetch the next course—but under no circum-stances allow it to be served until the diners about this table have composed themselves!"

The words had an instantaneous effect on the children. The twins hastened back to their seats, Charlotte quit gig-gling, and Fanny carefully replaced the bread she'd been prepared to hurl at the cat. Even the twinnies complied, scrambling quickly down onto their feather ticks until they were seated again, their eyes trained on their uncle.

Silence reigned, except for the quiet movements of the footmen who began to set the table to rights. But the odd thing was, Fanny noticed, Uncle Nicholas hadn't been ob-serving the children when he'd issued those instructions to Parkins. Nor was he observing them now. He was looking straight at Princess Holly.

Their guest was bent nearly double with silent laughter. Her lovely shoulders shook, and she pressed a fist to her lips, which twitched with her effort to contain her mirth. As the silence lengthened, Fanny noticed that Aunt Maud's lips also twitched. She was looking at Princess Holly too.

But Uncle Nicholas wasn't laughing. He wasn't even smiling. He was glaring at their royal guest!

Nicholas had reached the limits. Not only had that wretched cat caused more disorder than he'd imagined possible—even amongst this brood; it had done so while failing to give Holly any sort of negative impression. Instead of having her craw full of this pack of miniature hellions, she was laughing. Laughing!

How the devil was he to maintain the discipline these children required? He was no ogre, but by God, they needed a firm hand!. How was he to employ one if she undermined him this way?

He raised a staying hand to Parkins, who'd come forward with the intention of ushering in the second course. "Miss Holly . . ." he intoned in a too-quiet voice that had had seasoned soldiers quaking in their boots. "If you are quite through, perhaps we may recommence dining . . . ?"

Holly went still and raised her head. The green eyes grew wide with astonishment as she took in what was happening. Blushing to the roots of her hair, she managed a quick nod, then busied herself with arranging her serviette on her lap.

Nicholas gave the butler a nod, and the meal continued. Except for the occasional clink of silver against porcelain, the major noted, it was so quiet one might have heard the proverbial pin drop. Too quiet. In truth, it was downright deadly. *Bloody hell!*

The meal proceeded without incident. The quiet, Nicholas told himself, was nothing more than a civilized peace. There was no rule said they had to rattle on—like magpies on a garden wall!

At last the evening drew to an end, and the company parted—as quiet as mice. Only then did Nicholas wonder at the satisfaction he should have felt—but didn't.

* * *

Later the same night Holly found herself in bed, but unable to sleep. Or rather, to return to sleep. She'd drifted off quite easily earlier, the events of the day and a full stomach no doubt contributing to her drowsiness.

But she'd awakened a short while ago, to a heavy rain pelting the windows, the sounds of distant thunder and wind whistling through chinks in the sash. An April storm . . .

Like the one that brought me here? The words hadn't finished forming in her mind when she shivered—and not because she was cold. She could recall nothing of the storm that had brought her to Caerdruth; she knew of it only from what she'd been told. But whenever she tried to reach for some detail of it in her mind, the way was blocked. Not merely by the blankness. By fear.

She was afraid to learn about that night, she realized. But it was a nameless fear, its cause, something she couldn't even guess at. Yet it had the power to freeze her blood, make her want to scurry off in search of someplace safe and warm.

Without thinking, Holly found herself climbing from beneath the covers. She was tying the sash of the rose woolen wrapper about her and easing her chamber door ajar before she even realized she'd left her bed. A few minutes later, she glanced down, absently aware she carried her chamber stick, when her footsteps brought her to the library door.

The books in the library had been a godsend in the aftermath of her arrival at Caerdruth. Of the frightening discovery that she didn't know who she was. Between their pages she'd discovered worlds of sense and order, which she used to help dispel the chaos that threatened in the real world. Refuge for the mind.

But as she opened the door, Holly realized there'd been something else associated with this room, which drew her when she needed calming . . . or someone. She'd seen the masculine stamp he'd left on it each time she'd come here . . . a pair of military cuff links lying on the desk . . . an empty brandy glass . . . a riding jacket thrown casually over a chair . . .

Nicholas! she heard her mind exclaim as she took in the lean length of the man who stood gazing into the fire.

"What the devil are you doing here?" he demanded as his head swung in her direction.

"I . . . I couldn't sleep and . . . and came looking for something to read." Holly hated the apologetic sound in her voice, but the accusing tone of his, indeed, the surprise of finding him here was so off-putting, she nearly turned and ran.

And yet, she found herself rooted to the floor. He looked so formidably male standing there, in shirtsleeves, with his cravat removed, the long, muscular length of his legs outlined by firelight. Yes, male . . . and darkly, dangerously beautiful.

Words formed in her mind . . . "Cloth'd with transcendent brightness didst out-shine/ Myriads though bright . . ." and even as she heard them, she knew they were Milton's, from *Paradise Lost* . . . describing the fallen angel, Lucifer.

In the silence that fell between them, Nicholas's eyes raked her from head to toe. The inky hair spilling over her shoulders accentuated the flawless whiteness of her skin; the green eyes were enormous in the heart-shaped face as she eyed him with apprehension. She stood perfectly motionless, a willowy, slender sylph in the dim light. A creature out of faerie, too evanescently lovely to be real. Yet he knew she was, and from the look in her eyes as she began to take him in, he knew he could have her. Then and there, if he wished it.

And he was mad to even think it.

"Find yourself something to read then, and be quick about it," he growled.

He watched her as she hesitated, then made her way hurriedly to the bookshelves far to the left of the fireplace. He'd come here directly after the supper, needing to be alone. Reading had always been one of his pleasures, even when he was a boy. When his father had learned about it, he'd sneered at him, calling it bookish and unmanly; worse, he'd taken great pleasure in forbidding him the use of the library thereafter. Not that that had stopped Nicholas. He'd sneaked into the earl's inner sanctum to pilfer books whenever he could, often earning canings when he was discovered. The books, *and* thwarting his sire, had been worth it!

But tonight he hadn't come here to read. He'd come to mull over all that had happened since his return and try to put it in some perspective; his own plans for the future were in shambles, and he'd wanted to lay out the options that were left to him . . . plan anew.

Only, that hadn't happened. Instead, he'd found himself going over more recent events in his mind . . . that business with Harry in the conservatory . . . tonight's debacle of a supper . . . the children . . . and, yes, the lovely Miss Holly.

His gaze shifted to the slender figure who'd wandered along the shelves and was now no more than a few feet away. Lightning flickered at the windows, highlighting the details of her face and form. She held her chamber stick aloft and pored over the titles on the shelves nearest the fireplace; he could discern the outline of her breasts beneath the wrapper.

Again, the lightning flashed, and he couldn't take his eyes off her. He was suddenly acutely aware of her deshabille . . . the way her hair tumbled down her back . . . the fact that she had nothing beyond the thin barrier of some nightclothes to shield her young and nubile body from his eyes.

Christ! Didn't she realize she oughtn't be alone with him like this? Didn't she—

A loud clap of thunder boomed overhead. It was followed by another, even louder, and he saw her shrink into herself, lowering the chamber stick so fast, the candle was snuffed out. The only remaining light came from the fire, but in its glow, he could see her trembling.

Nicholas cursed under his breath and was beside her in

an instant. "Here," he said taking the chamber stick that seemed to dangle from nerveless fingers and setting it on the mantel.

Holly barely heard him. The sudden proximity of the storm had come upon her unawares, and she was seized by the nameless terror she'd come to associate with that other storm . . . the one she couldn't recall. Ghostly images threatened and chased themselves in her mind . . . the handwritten pages of a tattered book . . . rain, lashing her face . . . the squish of her half-boots on boggy ground . . . the need to flee—*oh, God!*

"Holly, stop!" Nicholas's voice echoed in the room. "Whatever you're thinking about—don't! Think of something else!"

She felt his arms close about her, felt the steady beat of his heart beneath the soft linen of his shirt as he gathered her against his chest. "Something else," she murmured, "yes . . ." *Safety . . . Nicholas.*

Nicholas felt the tension drain out of her, yet he didn't release her immediately. He remained as he was, with his arms folded about her, her head tucked under his chin, where he could feel the silk of her hair against his skin. The elusive scent of something floral drifted up to him as well, and he closed his eyes against a sudden shudder of need that threatened. Christ, he was growing hard!

Grinding his teeth and silently cursing the mindless lust he knew to be part of his nature, Nicholas disengaged and set her sharply away from him. "I think it's time you returned to your chamber," he growled.

"I . . . yes, of course." Wide, bewildered eyes stared up at him for a fleeting moment, then lowered as she groped for the chamber stick.

Nicholas turned away and grabbed a spill from the mantel, then quickly set about relighting the candle from the fireplace. "Here you are," he said gruffly, then turned his back to her, gazing into the fire as he had when she'd first come upon him.

Confused totally by his sudden shift of mood, Holly

stared dumbly at him for several long seconds. What had she done to earn this latest disapprobation?

"Good night, Miss Holly," he said pointedly when she still hadn't moved after several seconds.

"G-good night," she answered, and hoped it hadn't sounded as forlorn as she felt while she moved toward the door. But she did feel forlorn. It had felt so wonderful, so comforting to be held like that by him! And then, for whatever reason—

Holly sighed as she closed the library door behind her. She was halfway to her chamber before she realized she'd come away with nothing to read.

❧ Eight ❧

It was a mild day, especially for April on the Cornish coast, where buffeting winds from the sea still held spring in winter's icy fist.

Thank goodness Mrs. Hastings had come across the old riding habit in an attic trunk, Holly thought to herself as she followed the path to the stable block. Without this ensemble she'd have had to make do with the gown and spencer she'd arrived in, and although cleaned and mended, they truly looked like something fit for the dustbin. Although years out of date, this was a near perfect fit, and the leaf green fabric accentuated the color of her eyes.

The sun felt warm on her back as Holly reached the stable yard where a groom held the blood-bay hunter Harry had selected for her. She was almost as sorry as the young earl, that his lessons were keeping him from joining her. She would have enjoyed his company on the ride.

Still, it was a glorious day, and for once, she'd slept the night through, untroubled by nightmares. She smiled at the groom, a young man of about twenty whose black hair and eyes were typical of the Cornish she'd met.

There was a magnificent black saddled and waiting near the stable entrance, and she was admiring it when Nicholas appeared from the shadowy interior of the stable.

Her insides succumbed to one of those queer little lurches that the sight of him always seemed to call up.

Dressed in a full-sleeved white cambric shirt and dove gray riding breeches that hugged his thighs like a second skin, he was coatless and bareheaded, his only nod to fashion the mirrorlike shine on his tallboots.

He took the black by the bridle and came toward her, just as the groom finished helping her mount. Dismissing the servant with a nod, Nicholas assumed the task of adjusting her stirrup himself. He hadn't said a word, and he was scowling.

"And good morning to you too, Nicholas," she said tartly, disliking the way he could pique her mood.

He finished with the stirrup, gave a quick check to the girth, and, stepping back a pace, ran his eyes over her.

"Who gave you that riding habit to wear?"

"This? Why, it's something that belonged to your late sister-in-l—"

"I know very well whose it was. I asked who gave it to you."

He'd have known that green outfit anywhere. It was from her youth, before she'd wed Aubrey and borne children, which was why it fit Holly so well. Not that she had ever grown stout. Oh, no, not Judith. But on the few occasions when seeing her had been unavoidable, he'd noted the added pounds and fuller, riper curves. Curves that had been implicit in the sweet lushness of a younger, girl's body on the day he'd taken her riding and she'd worn the green habit. On the day he'd carefully stripped it from her body and—

"Never mind," he growled as Holly was about to answer his question. "I'll be escorting you on your ride today. Lucifer needs the exercise, and he doesn't tolerate anyone but me on his back."

Holly watched him swing up into the saddle with the same effortless grace he displayed whenever he moved. She eyed the stallion that stood quivering with excitement as its master settled his weight onto its back. *Lucifer* . . . Somehow the name seemed apt. A devil of a mount for a man who seemed beset by devils. Were they of his own making?

Or had fate dealt him one savage blow too many, so that he'd come up snarling and stayed that way?

They eased their mounts into a trot, and then a canter. The bay was behaving beautifully, responding to the lightest pressure of knee, or hands on the reins. Lucifer was another matter. He fought for his head several times, clearly impatient with the sedate pace Nicholas had set. She heard Nicholas swear several times under his breath before getting the stallion settled.

They rode this way in silence for some time. Overhead, curlews called their shrill cries, and the air bore the sharp tang of the sea.

Then, as they approached a flat, grassy lea leading to the cliffside trail Harry had told her about, Nicholas slowed and drew to a halt, forcing her to do the same.

"I'll be running Lucifer flat out, now," he said. "He needs it. But I want you to remain here."

When Holly opened her mouth to protest, he seemed to be expecting it. "I can tell you're a capable equestrienne. Your seat is excellent, and you have soft hands. But there's still the matter of your injuries. They cannot have healed completely, and there's no sense in tempting fate. I'll be giving Lucifer his head, and—"

"I *am* recovered!" she cried. "Mr. Cartwright said so!" She felt heat rise to her cheeks and knew it had more to do with the realization that he'd been studying her than with her annoyance at being left behind.

But the latter grated too. From the moment she'd eased her weight onto the sidesaddle, she'd known, somehow, that she'd ridden all her life and, what's more, enjoyed it above all things. It was as if a tiny window had appeared for a moment in her mind, and she'd been allowed a glimpse of the person she was, or had been, before the darkness. She'd seen—no, it was more that she *felt*—herself putting a blooded filly through its paces, and the filly's name was—

"Nightwing!"

Nicholas looked at her sharply.

" 'Twas the name of my horse!" she supplied with a giddy

sense of accomplishment. "A filly, as black as the ace of—as
—as your Lucifer." She was grinning now. "Oh, Nicholas!
I've recalled something solid and concrete for the first time!
Something important to me."

Nicholas watched her face come alive in a way he'd not
seen before. Watched the green of her eyes take on an emerald shimmer and sparkle, dominating that heart-shaped
face that was all eyes anyway.

Helpless to stop himself, he grinned back at her, sharing
her triumph. "Cartwright said you might begin to remember things at any time. Perhaps this is the beginning. Do
you recall—" A shadow crossed his mind as he remembered
what had happened to her, and how damaging the full
recovery of her memory would likely be. "Is there anything
else?" he asked carefully.

Holly closed her eyes for a moment, then opened them
and shook her head. "Not really. Or certainly not anything
quite so concrete." She shook her head again, as if trying to
dislodge something. "But the sense of . . . of my command of horsemanship is very strong, and," she added with
another grin, "I do believe I've taken up the ribbons on a
few occasions and tooled along quite handsomely, I daresay."

"Have you, now?" He was grinning again too, and he
couldn't take his eyes off her. Several strands of midnight
black hair had come loose of the ribbon she'd used to secure it at the nape of her neck, and he felt his loins tighten
as he imagined what it would be like to run his hands
through it and free it entirely—on a pillow. *Christ, what in
hell am I thinking of?*

With a scowl, Nicholas abruptly returned his attention to
the meadow. "Expert horsewoman or no, I'll not have you
risking your neck on *my* watch. You may follow, but keep
the gelding to a canter." He gestured toward the far end of
the grassy straightaway. "I'll wait for you where those rocks
mark the start of the cliff trail. Then, if you're a good girl,
I'll show you a view from the top that will take your breath
away."

He took off like a shot, the stallion's hooves churning up chunks of turf as it lunged into a full gallop.

Bewildered by his sudden change of mood, Holly frowned at the departing pair.

" 'If you're a good girl . . .' " she mimicked, and she found herself scowling as blackly as Nicholas had a moment before. Order her about, would he? She'd show him a thing of what she could do on his watch!

Bending low over the bay's withers, she urged it forward and into an all-out gallop.

Nicholas let out all the stops, giving Lucifer his head, feeling of a piece with the stallion as its powerful strides ate up the ground. The black couldn't run too fast to suit him. It was as if, by putting a distance between himself and the green-eyed enigma that was Holly, he could outdistance his lust. Lust that had no decent place in exchanges between them.

He grinned to himself, thinking how the men of his regiment—not to mention the *ton*—would be shocked by this sudden display of conscience. Hell, he was bloody well shocked, himself! Imagine! Sharpe the Bastard, actually considering the consequences before helping himself to whatever he wanted beneath a woman's skirts!

The grin disappeared after some sixth sense told him to look behind him, and he spotted Holly riding straight toward him, hell-bent-for-Hades, coming head-on, and maybe too close to stop safely without colliding with the black. He reined the stallion in and urged it to the side. A few seconds too late.

Holly saw what was happening, but failed to slow the bay in time. When she did rein in, it was far more sharply than good sense dictated; and that, combined with the fact that she was riding sidesaddle, sent her careening over the gelding's side and onto the ground.

The next few seconds were a blur of movement and sound as Holly sensed several things happening at once. There was the flash of powerful hooves all too near her head as she struggled to get her breath, and because the old-fashioned riding habit had necessitated wearing stays, she was having a difficult time of it.

One of the horses neighed shrilly as she heard Nicholas shout, "You little fool! What in hell possessed you to disobey me?"

Then he was bending over her, gray eyes fiercely intent on her face. "Are you hurt? Can you move?"

"Can't . . . can't breathe."

A string of oaths threatened to turn the air blue while she felt him tearing at the fastenings of her bodice, and then the lacings of the stays beneath.

Air! Sucking in huge gulps of it, unmindful of anything beyond the blessed relief she found, she could imagine no sweeter sensation in the world.

"Better?" she heard Nicholas ask, and she could only nod, grateful for every breath that precluded speech.

"Damned, foolish contraptions!" he growled, and she felt him yank at the offending stays again. "Are you hurt anywhere else?"

Closing her eyes, she cautiously moved each of her limbs, considering. "No . . . I don't believe so."

"Good," he pronounced—and ripped the stiff garment out from under her, freeing it from the gaping bodice and hurling it away with a grunt of disgust.

Holly's eyes flew open, and she gasped, intently aware of her deshabille. Of the coolness of the air on her exposed breasts, freed not only of bodice and stays, but of the shift he'd torn in his efforts to release her.

And of Nicholas's eyes on her.

She uttered a small cry, and her hands shot to the parted flaps of the bodice to draw them together. But then Nicholas lifted his eyes, and their gazes locked.

Holly felt her breathing go shallow as, suddenly, she was acutely aware of her body. She tried to swallow, but a thickness had claimed her tongue and throat, making it impossible.

And all the while Nicholas's eyes burned into hers.

Again, she tried to swallow, and ran her tongue along her lips.

Nicholas's gaze dropped to her mouth, catching the movement, and she heard him groan before his own mouth captured hers in a kiss that devoured.

A need as fierce as anything she could imagine exploded deep inside her body when she felt his mouth claim her, and she parted her lips as if to cry out. But this only gave him access for his tongue, which slipped between to graze her teeth and then explore the moist recesses beyond.

She shivered at the intimacy of this, and without thinking, slid her hands upward and about his neck. Closer . . . she had to have him closer.

She was vaguely aware of his grunt of satisfaction, even as he gathered her against him with one arm while, with the opposite hand, he tore the ribbon from the nape of her neck. And then he was threading his fingers through her hair, sending ripples of pleasure along her spine while his mouth slid to the sensitive skin below her earlobe.

"Ah, God, Holly . . ."

Something wild and dangerous snapped inside her when she felt his hand close over her breast, but before she could piece it out, his thumb grazed her nipple, and she found herself arching against him. A sweet, piercing shaft of pleasure had shot from where his thumb teased the aching bud, to the very core of her, high between her thighs. She heard a moan, and it took a moment to realize it had come from her own throat, before it broke into a sob that was his name.

Nicholas was lost, drowning in the sweet, heady pleasure of her flesh beneath his hands. And the heat in her! He'd known passion in women before, but never from someone so untried, so obviously inexperienced at—

"Christ!" He tore himself away from her and threw himself onto his back, on the grass. The sounds of his own breathing came to him, ragged and harsh, as he flung an arm across his eyes. *Untried?* an inner voice mocked. *You stupid sonofabitch! Untried?*

"N-Nicholas?" Holly's voice, bewildered and uncertain, penetrated the fog of self-recrimination.

He felt her shift beside him, and somehow found the strength to tear his arm away and make himself look at her.

She was heartstoppingly lovely, despite the bewildered frown. Inky hair tumbled over her shoulders and down to her waist in a wealth of shiny curls. Her lips were cherry red and swollen from his kiss; her eyes, thick-lashed, and green as old emeralds in lamplight, were huge in her face.

He saw she was clutching the panels of her bodice together with awkward fingers, even as she continued to look at him with eyes which were still dilated with passion. It was enough of a reminder to make him wince.

"Put yourself together," he growled, and saw her recoil as if she'd been struck. Well, there was no help for it now. She might suffer some hurt briefly, but it was the only way he knew, to reduce the damage he'd done.

"Nicholas, please, I—"

"Do it!" he snapped, and jackknifed to his feet.

He made himself look away from her while she complied, keeping his attention on the horses, which had wandered less than a dozen yards away and were contentedly grazing on the new spring grass.

Holly fumbled with the fastenings of the bodice, hating the heat she felt burning her cheeks. She was having some difficulty securing the garment, owing to the absence of the stays, and her recollection of what had happened to them made her face grow even hotter.

But even as she made herself concentrate on the task at hand, her mind was a jumble of conflicting emotions. The pleasure! Dear God, she hadn't known such pleasure could exist!

She succeeded in fastening the frog that secured the habit's high collar and dared a look at him. He was standing a few feet away, with his back to her, his posture rigid and military in its bearing.

She swallowed, determined to try to come to terms with what had happened.

"Nicholas . . ."

Holly's voice sounded quavery and uncertain, and despite something that twisted in his gut, Nicholas forced himself to turn around and meet her eyes.

"Nicholas, please talk to me," she continued. "I need to understand . . . about what happened—about what's happening now—between us. I don't—"

"Don't you?" he inquired in a clipped voice. "Well, then I suppose I had better tell you."

He strode a pace closer to her, and she noted his eyes had gone flat and expressionless, a dull, gunmetal gray.

"What has happened," he went on, "is that you barely escaped being seduced and ravished by a man regarded, far and wide, as a past master at such doings.

"Don't look away, and don't shake your head. I want you to see me as I am, Holly. As the man known all about these parts, during the years he grew up here, as the Earl's Bastard. Not to mention later, in the military, as Sharpe the Bastard.

"And lest you think those designations merely literal descriptions of the circumstances of my birth," he went on, "let me assure you they are not. They were figurative sobriquets I earned by every deed you may imagine—and some, I'm certain, you may not be able to. Ask! Did I take any female I fancied, heedlessly? The answer is yes. Young, or not so young; virgin, or married; peasant, or highborn lady —it didn't matter. The niceties were lost on me—as was all sense of scruples. What mattered was my lust, and the heady knowledge that while I may have been born without a right to land or title, I'd also been favored with a face and body that drew women to me like flies to a honey pot.

"Indeed, you may wince," he went on ruthlessly. "Others did too, and a lot I cared! Ask again: Did I kill? No, I am not referring to the war, but even before that—while I was still busy carving out a reputation to suit 'the Earl's Bastard.' Let me see . . . there were at least two duels with irate husbands—"

"Nicholas, stop it!" Holly was white-faced and shaking,

but somehow determined to end his torrent of self-abuse. "I'll not listen to——"

"Ah, but you will," he insisted, drawing a step closer and grasping her chin with his fingers when she tried to turn away. "Look at me, Holly! See me for what I truly am, dammit!"

"Why?" she cried. "Why tell me these things? So that I'll hate you?"

"Yes, if that's what it takes!"

"I . . . I don't understand."

"And I don't give a bloody damn if you do! I only care that you keep yourself out of my path. Stay away from me, Holly."

He released her then, and whirled toward the horses, gathering both sets of reins in silence. When he led them toward her, his face was a mask of indifference.

Nicholas made himself look through her as he assisted her in mounting. It was a technique he'd perfected in the war, to enable him to function amid the carnage. And the tears shimmering in her eyes were nothing, compared to that.

Taking the lead, he turned the stallion's head toward the manor.

It was done, he told himself, denying the regret that nagged from an unbattened corner of his mind. *Done.*

✣ Nine ✣

Sitting on a bench in the walled garden, Holly pretended absorption in the embroidery she was helping Charlotte stitch. But the sound of male voices drew her. Out of the corner of her eye she watched the open gateway. A moment later Nicholas passed, talking to a man wearing crude country clothes. Nicholas was informally dressed as well, much as he'd been three days ago, when—

Go on, say it—if only to yourself. When he touched you in a way he'd no right to. When he said those awful things to you. When he left you unable to get him out of your mind, day or night!

Dear God, even your nightmares have been replaced by dreams of him. Of the way he made you feel.

She was being stupid. No sane woman would continue to concern herself with a man like that. Nicholas Sharpe was every inch the rake he'd painted himself, and it was time to put him out of mind.

After that devastating scene near the cliffs, she'd holed up in her chamber for hours. Bewildered . . . hurt by those things he'd said, she'd tried to make herself believe otherwise. Those vicious self-deprecating words had been at such odds with the Nicholas she'd glimpsed before.

But at length, unable to stand the doubts and confusion any longer, she'd gone to Maud. And the old woman had told her: It was true; Nicholas Sharpe was all the things he'd said—perhaps worse. Not that Maud had gone into any great detail; a lady simply wouldn't. Although Holly had sensed that Maud knew a deal more than she was telling. She'd had the feeling the older woman was conducting some kind of inner debate with herself as to how much she might reveal.

"Well, my dear," Maud had said, "it's no secret, the circumstances of his birth . . . born 'on the wrong side of the blanket,' as they say. Didn't you know? It's the reason Aubrey inherited, even though Nick was the firstborn."

But she hadn't known. Hadn't thought about it. Not with all the other things which took precedence . . . like trying to cope with a mind gone blank. . . .

"I daresay," Maud had continued, "it played its part in making him bitter. Nick was always the one who loved the land, y'see . . . loved Caerdruth . . . but as a . . . um, merry-begotten son, he couldn't inherit . . . had to stand by helplessly while it all came to Aubrey, who didn't much care. Oh, he cared about the income Caerdruth gave him. But about Caerdruth itself? Never . . . not in the way Nick did."

"But there must be thousands of younger sons in similar straights," Holly had reasoned. "Many of them in the military, unless all I've been reading in books like Miss Austen's has misled me. Never say they've all given themselves over to . . . to . . ."

"Being rakehells?" Maud had supplied with a sad smile. "No, but then none of them had Nick's father to contend with, growing up."

She'd asked Maud what she meant by that enigmatic statement, but the older woman proceeded to change the subject, wandering off into a barely intelligible murmuring —about gypsies, of all things! It was odd, but just at those moments she was convinced the old dear was as sane as a bishop, she'd overturn it by lapsing into these queer bits of prittle-prattle.

Holly murmured absently as Lottie showed her a stitch she called a love knot. A moment later the child's words registered, and Holly's lips twisted in a wry smile. *Love knot,* indeed! Love *not,* you mean. As in love *not a man whom no decent woman would be seen with!*

Love? Now, where did that come from?

Love had nothing to do with it. She wasn't entirely certain she knew what love was, but she suspected she'd never felt it. Not toward . . . a man. Not in the sense that the poets spoke of it . . . Byron, with his "full but soft emotion/Like the swell of Summer's ocean" . . . Shelley's "One passion in twin-hearts," or Wordsworth's "joy of my desire" . . .

She helped Charlotte with the stitch, then found her gaze wandering toward the wall, where a low murmuring could be heard coming from the other side. Glancing down, she saw the child was deeply engrossed in finishing a large cluster of the knots; they'd hold her interest for a deal of time.

Holly rose from the bench, and began walking slowly about the garden, as if bent on examining its flora. There was actually little to examine. What hadn't been lost through years of neglect had obviously suffered serious winter damage. Perhaps by storms like the one which had brought her here.

Still moving slowly, she appeared to be wandering aimlessly, but before long Holly had brought herself to a place where the voices were audible enough to make out the words. Feigning interest in a climbing rose that looked more dead than alive, she ignored an inner voice that said it was positively *de trop* to eavesdrop, and listened.

". . . lost *my* brother to natural causes," Nicholas was saying. "You lost two—in an accident that never should have happened. Dammit, man, I knew Robbie and Colin as *well* as brothers! We shared many a pint together in the old days. They were younger than both of us—too damned young to die in such a senseless—"

" 'Twas their time, sir, as I look at it. Beside all, they knew the risks . . . we all knew 'em, what worked in the mines."

There was a silence, heavy with unspoken things.

After a while Nicholas broke it, his tone suddenly businesslike and unemotional. "What about the sense in what I'm trying to do, Tim? Are you sure there are enough placer deposits to warrant—"

"I tell ee, sir, there be ore aplenty down there. 'Tis the shaft's collapsed, not the tinstone."

Holly pictured the rough-clad local, a square, sturdy man of middle years from what she'd been able to see of him. He sounded more respectful than deferential, despite the difference in their stations. And confident in the way of a rustic who is certain of his craft, though how she knew this Holly couldn't have said.

"I'm not doubting you, Tim," said Nicholas. "It's a matter of making sure there's something to mine before I—well, let's just say a man doesn't go courting if he's learned all the daughters of the house are long married."

Tim chuckled. "Nay, sir—lest he be courtin' trouble!"

They shared a laugh over this, and Holly saw a different side of Nicholas. This wasn't the difficult, brooding man of military bearing. Or the harsh, rejecting creature of three days ago, either. Nicholas Sharpe was able to share easy banter with one many in his position would have regarded as mean . . . well beneath them, and do it without losing a jot of respect.

She pictured him among the men of his regiment, sharing a joke here, a quiet word there. But never giving up the respect a commanding officer required from the men under him.

At length she heard the man called Tim take his leave. She glanced at Charlotte, who was still busy with her stitches. About to return to the child, she was stayed by the sound of Harry's voice calling Nicholas's name. He sounded different . . . out of sorts somehow.

"What is it, Harry?" Nicholas sensed it too. "What's wrong?"

"Uncle Nicholas . . . I . . ."

"Devil take it, lad—out with it! It's not like you to beat

about the bush with me. Here, have a seat on this bench—
talk to me."

There was a moment's pause, and then a low moan from
the boy. "Oh, God, sir, it-it's about Miss Holly!"

"Holly?" The owner of that name went rigid—as shocked
as Nicholas sounded.

Harry seemed near tears. "I-I've just come from the stables. Some of the men . . . the undergroom and one of
the stable lads, I think . . . they were talking, and they
didn't know I was there—on the other side of the stall, that
is—and . . ."

"Go on."

Holly stood perfectly still, every nerve attuned to the
young lord's words. Hands clenched at her sides, she wasn't
aware her nails were carving moon-shaped gouges into her
palms.

"They said"—Harry choked on the words, had to begin
again—"they said she was r-ruined . . . *Raped!* Miss
Holly! Before she—on the night—the night she came here!
Oh, God, Uncle. Is it true? Did someone—Who'd *do* such a
thing? *Who?"*

The gouges began to bleed, and still Holly stood there
. . . frozen, unable to move . . . or breathe.

Nicholas swore viciously under his breath, and put an
arm around the boy's shoulders. They were shaking. "Who
told them this?" he managed in a voice tight with rage. He'd
left explicit instructions about the need for discretion. If he
found out who, he'd kill the bastard! "Did anyone say?"

The boy was sobbing now, great choking sounds that all
but cut off speech. "One . . . one of them said . . . said
it was c-common gossip . . . be-belowstairs . . . said he
had it from a n-new laundrymaid who was given Miss
Holly's linens to . . . to . . ."

"It's all right, Harry . . . you needn't say any more on
that account. I don't—"

"But is it *true?*" demanded the boy through his tears.
"Uncle Nicholas . . . ?"

Nicholas heaved a sigh, trying to gauge how much the

boy could be told. Could understand. *Damn the bloody gossips! Damn them to hell thrice over!*

"The doctor thinks it's possible, yes," he replied finally.

Harry looked at him. A mix of confusion and anguish filled his eyes, but he was silent. Overhead, a curlew cried. At the same instant Nicholas thought he heard another behind them in the garden, but that was ridiculous; curlews didn't frequent the garden.

"I said possible, Harry," Nicholas went on, "but not definite." Seeing the confusion build, he sighed again, forcing damning thoughts of his dead brother from his mind. "You see, Harry, these things are not always as clear-cut as they seem. They—"

"I know what rape is, Uncle."

Nicholas assessed the taut lines in the boy's face, the hard, angry look in his eyes, and nodded. *One hurdle down. Now for the tricky part* . . .

Choosing his words with care—no small task for a man accustomed to military directness—Nicholas laid out the essentials of what he and Cartwright had discussed. He made certain the boy understood each fact as it arose, knowing the lad was gaining an education in matters no tutor would include in his lessons. But when he'd finished, he was also confident the young earl was far better prepared for an aspect of life he and most other men had had to acquire only through raw experience. And not always without a high price.

The most difficult part, however, had nothing to do with female anatomy, or the physical aspects of rape. It had to do with the nature of being "ruined," as their society saw it. Harry's tutor had done an adequate job of developing the boy's sense of reason—but there was nothing rational in the *ton's* assessment of what upheld a woman's reputation.

"But, sir—it doesn't seem logical," Harry said as they broached this aspect of what had happened. "Or fair!"

"No one said it was fair," Nicholas replied with only the hint of a sardonic edge. *No one said life was fair, but I suspect you'll have to learn that lesson for yourself.*

"But according to what you've told me, a lady can lose her reputation—can be cut off from all decent society—not on what has *really* occurred, but on what the Polite World *thinks* has occurred!"

"And there you have it," said Nicholas. "With the *haut ton*, appearance is all."

Harry looked astonished. "But what a devilish queer lot of claptrap and nonsense! If that's true, Uncle, it means that we'll need to—"

A child's high-pitched voice intruded. "Princess! Your Highness, wherever have you gotten to?"

"That's Lottie!" said her brother. "I didn't know she was—"

"Oh, Harry—Uncle Nicholas!" Charlotte exclaimed as she came through the gate and saw them. "I've lost Princess Holly. Have you seen her?"

Nicholas felt a smile forming as he looked at the moppet he'd begun to regard as the least troublesome of the nursery crowd. She came toward them clutching a piece of wrinkled linen and a sewing basket that seemed larger than she was.

"No, Lottie;" said Harry. "Was she with you . . . in the nursery?"

"She was helping me with my stitches," said Charlotte as she held up the linen proudly. "But not in the nursery—in the garden, silly!" She gestured behind her. "We were sitting right over there, in the garden."

Harry and Nicholas exchanged a glance.

"Do . . . do you mean just now?" her brother asked.

Charlotte nodded. "But while I was working my love knots, she wandered off this way, and next I looked up—she was gone. Are you certain you haven't seen her?"

Nicholas hissed something under his breath. Bending his head, he pinched the bridge of his nose with his fingers, while Harry started to ask her something else. But at that moment a couple of sharp yells drew their attention, and they saw the twins racing toward them.

"Harry!"

"Uncle!"

"It's the princess—Miss Holly!"

"You've got to stop her!"

"It's dangerous!"

"She's taken—"

"Whoa!" said Nicholas, rising and holding out his palm to stop the fusillade. "One at a time, and clearly. Martin, you begin . . . what about Miss Holly—and what's dangerous?"

The boy pointed in agitation toward a path that led to the stables. "Miss Holly—she came down to the stables at a fearsome run—didn't say a word to any of us, even though we called out to her! She looked in quite a twitter, sir, and then—"

"Uncle!" Michael cut in. "We saw her ride out—on Lucifer!"

Harry's groan only partially obscured the oath his uncle swore as Nicholas bolted down the path.

The little fool! I don't care what *she overheard—if she's on that stallion—*Nicholas cut off the thought he didn't want to contemplate, and doubled his speed.

Holly dug her fingers into the stallion's mane, and hung on. With scalding tears blurring her vision, she had no idea where she was going. And didn't care. Since the big black's stall was the first she'd spotted as she fled to the stables, she'd jumped on the horse bareback; Lucifer had likely allowed her on him only out of surprise, and now she had no control over the dangerous animal beneath her. She didn't care about that either.

She cared about very little right now—except dulling the pain. Ruined! She was ruined . . . unfit to live with decent people . . . people like . . . like the Sharpes . . . like those innocent children!

The stallion stretched its neck, pushing its nose into the wind. It was clearly exulting in the freedom of being given its head, and meant to make the most of it. Clods of turf flew in its wake like missiles flung from a catapult.

A small stream bisected the meadow. It had been a dry

gulley before the recent rains, but now it presented an obstacle in their path. Too late, Holly saw they were almost on top of it.

Lucifer had seen, though. The big horse collected itself—and soared into the air. Holly slid sideways on the stallion's back as it cleared the stream. They landed with room to spare. She'd come perilously close to falling off, but managed to hang on.

Not that it mattered. She felt so dirty . . . soiled . . . Ah, God! No wonder he'd warned her off him! He'd merely tried to spare her feelings! It wasn't Nicholas who was beyond the pale—it was *she!*

They were thundering up an incline now, and Holly clung to the horse's withers, her mind a chaotic jumble. Behind them, she thought she heard a shout. The wind was whistling in her ears; she'd likely imagined it.

But she knew she wasn't imagining the smell of the sea. The smell of salt was strong, even through her tears. She concentrated on it. On the steady beat of the stallion's hooves. On anything that would blot out thought.

The wind dried her tears as fast as they fell now. When she perceived the horse had stopped climbing, curiosity got the best of her; she raised her head to look around . . .

And screamed.

❧ Ten ❧

Nicholas heard the scream before he saw her. He'd seen where Lucifer was headed, known the direction long before they reached the trail to the cliffs. But Aubrey's gelding, fine as it was, hadn't been able to catch the black.

Now his pulse thrummed in his ears as a second scream carried on the wind. Was he too late? Lucifer knew the trail well enough to keep to it, but Holly had to be in a panic. What if she'd startled the stallion, made it stumble, or—

He clenched his jaw and urged the gelding on.

Her eyes riveted on the waves churning against rocks far below, Holly pulled futilely at Lucifer's mane. The stallion had slowed, but wouldn't stop. It seemed to know the narrow trail, but—Dear God, so close to the edge!

Suddenly aware of her foolishness, aware she didn't want to die, Holly pressed her face into the horse's mane and began to plead. "Please, Lucifer . . . please slow dow—"

A sharp whistle sliced the air, and she felt the stallion's head come up as it slowed to a halt. Before she had time to ponder the miracle, hoofbeats sounded behind them, and then Nicholas's voice.

"Don't move, Holly. You've had a fright, but you're all right. Just remain where you are, and I'll help you, understand?"

She tried to answer, but the sound died in a throat gone

dry with fear. Wordlessly, she nodded, her gaze still fixed on the rocks below. She was shaking with terror, but with a strange sense it came from something other than this narrow escape. There was something ominous about those rocks, something that went beyond their immediate proximity . . . something she didn't want to—

"Here, I have you."

Nicholas's arm caught her about the waist, and she sank into the strength of it. Into the wall of hard muscle that was his chest as he pulled her off Lucifer's back.

She was trembling violently as Nicholas pulled her into his arms. *Christ! She could have died down there!*

He'd seen a lot of death in recent years . . . slaughter on a grand scale. He wondered he wasn't inured to it . . . had thought at times during the roar of cannon fire, that perhaps he was . . .

But suddenly he knew he wasn't. Especially where this woman was concerned. This utter stranger had become . . . important to him somehow. In ways he didn't understand . . . didn't want to understand if he were honest about it.

He led her to a flat space curled into an indentation in the cliff wall. A sense of *deja vu* struck him as he murmured assurances into Holly's hair, held her close. How many times would he be cast into the role of her protector? He, Sharpe the Bastard—protector of women? He wanted to roar with laughter.

Instead, seeing her begin to quiet, he urged Holly down onto the plane of marram covered rock. The rock was warm. Heated by the sun and protected from the wind's bite by the brief stretch of cliff that rose above them, it formed an ideal shelter. He'd stood on this spot countless times before . . . by himself . . . with Judith . . . but he wouldn't think of Judith now.

As for the woman in his arms—

He found himself suddenly furious with her. "You little fool!" He seized Holly's shoulders and gave her a shake. "You could have broken your neck! I told you about Lucifer, so don't pretend you didn't know! What the deuce possessed you to do something that stupid?"

Her head came up, and a warning flashed in the green eyes. Something . . . anger, visceral and raw, Nicholas thought, and then it was gone. Perhaps he'd imagined it; what he saw now had more to do with pain. A look so vulnerable, his heart caught in a sharp twist.

"Ah, Christ, Holly . . . I didn't mean—"

"Don't!" He'd begun to pull her back into his arms when the single word crackled between them. Nicholas froze.

"Don't . . . ? Holly, I know I was angry with you just now, but—" He reached out to her, a gesture meant to reassure.

She recoiled as if struck. "Don't . . . don't *touch* me, Nicholas!"

"Dammit, I will! You're still in shock, and—"

"No . . . not in shock—unclean! Unf-fit . . ." She began to sob. Wrapping her arms about herself, hanging her head. All he could see was a tumble of inky curls.

A brief dawning, then a stab of guilt. For the first time since the wild chase up to the cliffs, Nicholas recalled what had sent her running. Hell!

"Holly . . ." he began carefully, "I know what you think you overheard—"

"Think!" She raised her head. Her eyes blazed at him behind the shimmer of tears. "*Think?* Stop saying what you don't mean, Nicholas! I couldn't bear it if you said one more dishonest word!"

He met the blaze of green head-on, and his eyes narrowed. "What the deuce are you talking about? When have I ever been dishonest with you? When?"

She straightened, raking the tumble of hair out of her eyes with her fingers. "Are you pretending you didn't tell Harry I was"—she nearly choked on the word, forced herself to say it—"*raped?* Are you?"

Nicholas looked out to sea and swore softly, plowing a hand through his own hair. When he swung his gaze back to her, her eyes had taken on a hollow look . . . unflawed emeralds, devoid of emotion.

"Holly, listen to me. I told Harry the doctor concluded there was the *possibility* of . . . of—"

"You see? You can't even *say* it! You're s-so repulsed by it —by *me!*—you cannot—"

"By *you!* You? Holly, is that what you think? Because—"

"It's what I *know,* damn you! It's the real reason you said all those things to me the other day! You couldn't stand being near me . . . touching me—and who could blame you? I'm a woman defiled, and the *t-ton* wouldn't even deign to speak to me—m-much less touch me!"

"The *ton!*" The gray eyes went wintry. Holly shivered, reminded of the cold sea that churned below.

"Who the bloody hell gives a damn about the *ton!*" He spewed the final word at her as if it had made him sick. We're talking about *me,* goddammit! And you cannot *begin* to know what I am. But the last thing I have anything to do with is the bloody *ton!*"

Before she could react, he grabbed her arm and pulled her toward him. His face was inches from hers. "Whatever may or may not have happened to you out there"—he gestured wildly with his free hand in the direction of the moors—"has no bearing on what I think of you. I do not— repeat, do not—think you defiled. Disabuse yourself of that, here and now!"

She closed her eyes and moaned, reminding him of an animal in pain. An emotion totally alien sluiced through him, wrenching at his gut. He knew he'd painted himself a bastard—but not that sort of bastard!

"Holly . . . look at me." The words were soft, spoken so quietly she almost didn't hear them. But the sound of her name on his lips was a siren's call, soothing her battered mind. It was the sound she'd heard in dreams . . . dreams that kept the nightmares at bay, and she could no more ignore it than ignore herself.

Her eyes opened. She met the full impact of his gaze, and

it struck her to the core. There was truth there, naked and bold. How could she ever have thought him capable of less?

But beyond the truth of how he felt about her, beyond the honesty of his eyes, she now glimpsed something having more to do with Nicholas than herself. He wasn't simply telling her he thought her pain unfounded, and wouldn't put up with it . . . wouldn't let her put up with it. He was feeling it himself.

Maud's words came back to her with sudden clarity. *I daresay it made him bitter . . .* Nicholas *knew*. Knew what it was to be an outcast . . . to be made a social pariah through no fault of his own. And he had to have been a mere child when it began . . . *Ah, Nicholas, I've begun to know you better than you think.*

Nicholas saw comprehension in her eyes, and nodded slowly, his gaze never leaving her face. "You're an innocent, sweetheart. And I don't mean simply because you've no memory of what happened to you that night. There are a dozen things about you—more, if I chose to count them— that proclaim you untouched."

He saw her tilt her head slightly. Her eyes searched his. Not expressing doubt, but as if waiting for him to explain this thing so she might understand it.

"Untouched here"—he tapped his fingers lightly against her chest—"inside, where it matters."

He smiled wryly. "And trust me, sweetheart," he told her. "I'm no mean expert where matters of innocence and experience are at work. I know about such things." The smile changed, became open . . . genuine. "Can you do that?"

It was the first true smile Holly had seen from him. Nicholas. She was astounded at how it transformed him. He seemed years younger. And his eyes, crinkled at the corners, were the color of a misty sky shot with sunlight. A bubble of pure joy seemed to burst inside her, and she suddenly felt weightless . . . lighter than air.

She was smiling back at him. "Yes," was all she said.

"Good girl!" he answered on a laugh. A laugh! And then he was hugging her. Hugging so hard, he lifted her off the ground and swung her around in an arc, and she was laughing too.

When Nicholas lowered her to her feet, they were left standing toe to toe. They looked at each other. The laughter drifted away, leaving only the sounds of the sea, the cry of gulls in the distance. Still, they looked, each acutely aware something had changed between them.

Holly wanted to speak, say something. God, the world was suddenly filled with him! She wanted to tell him, but a dryness had settled in her mouth. She swallowed, wet her lips with her tongue. Still, the words wouldn't come.

Nicholas's eyes followed the tiny movement, settling on her mouth. He felt the tightening in his loins, knew what was happening, even if she didn't. Knew he should break away before anything began. He was the one with the experience. He'd just told her that.

But her mouth . . . no fashionably prim Cupid's-bow, this. Wide, full lips that proclaimed a vital, flesh-and-blood woman. Christ! He could still recall the taste of them, the way they'd moved under his . . . mobile . . . sweetly blossoming . . . opening to him at the merest—

He tore his eyes away, focusing on a point somewhere above her head. A full erection strained his breeches, and he was desperately counting on that innocence he'd cited to keep her from noticing. A few seconds . . . that's all he required, and he'd be able to move . . . get himself safely out of range . . .

An inarticulate murmur from Holly had him glancing down at her again without thinking. Without a conscious will, he let his gaze feast on her face . . . on her eyes this time—ah, Christ, her eyes! *Don't look at me that way, sweetheart! I'm only a man, and—*

"Nicholas . . . ?"

He gritted his teeth against the unexpected sound of her voice. It sounded throaty . . . rusty . . . as if she hadn't used it in a long, long time. Christ, he was hard as a rock!

"Nicholas . . ." she repeated, "I know you told me to keep away, but . . . but I *can't*. There's something perverse in me that—well, it's just that the more I try *not* to think of you, the more I . . . Nicholas, if it's so wrong, why can't I get you out of my—"

With a groan, he caught her hard against him. His mouth plunged like a bird of prey, stopping more than her words, stopping thought itself. Only feelings existed for Holly now. She flung her arms about his neck and welcomed his kiss as a starving beggar welcomes food.

Warm . . . his lips were warm, and the tongue that slid along the seam where hers were joined bore greater heat. When she opened for him, a jolt of immense energy seemed to surge through him, and he made a hoarse, inarticulate sound deep in this throat.

She felt him widen his stance. One hand slid to her buttocks, pinning her against him while the other moved up her back. Higher, until his fingers tunneled through the curls at the nape of her neck. She felt them spread, cup the back of her head as he angled in for a closer joining.

Now his tongue was exploring the moist recesses of her mouth with open access. She couldn't deny him. Rather deny herself. But what might have felt like an invasion was not. For all the fierceness of the embrace, he used his tongue lightly . . . teasing her own with its tip . . . grazing her teeth . . . tangling with hers in a gentle onslaught that made her giddy.

Everything about her was sensation, and at the center of it all was Nicholas . . . Nicholas with his hard planes of muscle and delicious heat . . . with his hungry mouth and fierce, possessive hands . . . *Ah, Nicholas, Nicholas!*

Somehow, he'd lowered her to the ground . . . without once breaking their kiss . . . or rather it was kiss upon kiss, with a new one beginning before the other ended. Now he was harsh and demanding, now soft and coaxing, but always his mouth covered hers in an endless exchange of taste, and touch, and throbbing, burning heat.

"Christ, Holly . . ." she heard him whisper hoarsely as she suddenly became aware of the sun warmed rock beneath her. His mouth had left hers at last, sliding to her ear.

Warm breath feathered tendrils of her hair and made her shiver.

His hands braced on the rock to either side of her head, he suddenly pulled away. The loss of his body heat jarred her, and she opened her eyes. The harsh rasp of his breathing played counterpoint to the thudding of her heart. Both filled her ears, but it was his eyes that consumed her . . . dark with passion . . . the night sky silvered with moonlight . . .

"Holly," he rasped. "You're the loveliest creature on God's green earth, and I can't stay away from you either . . . but I should . . . God help me, I sh—"

Her fingers stilled the words. "I need you now, Nicholas. Don't pull away again. Don't—don't leave me . . . please . . ."

He knew what she meant. He'd just told her there was nothing in her to repulse him . . . nothing he saw in her to drive him away. In her . . . but what about him? What about things in him that were unclean . . . unfit for such as her?

Yet how could he pull away without falsely signalling it was she who stood between them . . . between them and this fire their bodies screamed for?

"Ah, hell," he murmured hoarsely, and pulled her back into his arms.

The kiss was sweeter this time, Holly thought through the soaring joy that sang inside her. As if Nicholas had made up his mind to proceed with greater care. But for all its gentleness, she felt a candent fire begin to build, and build . . .

His hands were moving over her with soft persuasion, yet wherever they touched, she burned. The interlude in the meadow came back with sudden clarity when he cupped her breasts and grazed their tips with his thumbs. When the deft teasing sent the same lance of pleasure darting to the secret place between her thighs. When she recalled the pleasure, felt it as before . . . *Dear God, the pleasure!*

Nicholas heard her moan, and the sound nearly pushed

him over the brink. Desperately, he sought for control. He'd made up his mind to do this for Holly, not himself. In the light of what she'd overheard, of her doubts about herself, he'd elected to continue. But with care and restraint. Only to the point where he could be sure he'd overcome those insidious misconceptions.

He'd known frozen women in his time. Women who couldn't respond because of feelings of degradation . . . of no self-worth. One had been a miner's wife, newly widowed. And though he'd been little more than a lad at the time, he'd known enough to realize her stiff responses and tense limbs were related to the bruises her abusive husband had left on her flesh, and not to him. Bruises he'd discovered in time to end their bedding before it began.

And of course in later years there'd been whores and courtesans who'd been unable to feel, though they pretended passion. But he could always tell. A woman's body might not react as blatantly as a man's, but it did react.

Like the way Holly's was now. Pebbled nipples that puckered into even harder buds when he teased them further. The tiny pulse that hammered at the base of her neck . . . especially when he pressed his lips to it . . . like this . . . *Ah, God, Holly* . . .

She'd begun to thrash restively beneath him now, but that was something that could be feigned. So could the sharp cries of delight that issued from that delicious mouth when he took one of her nipples in his, suckled it right through the muslin of her gown . . . but he didn't believe they were. She was too innocent to feign . . . innocent, but with a natural passion that left him burning, burning . . .

Again, he fought for control, succeeded, but felt like a man hovering on a razor's edge. She moaned again, and he shuddered with need. Christ, what had he gotten himself into?

Still, he made himself go on. Kissing her . . . learning her body with all its lush curves and delicious hollows.

At length he reminded himself there was the ultimate

spot on a woman's body that never lied to a man . . . he would just test it . . .

Murmuring words of praise into her ear, he nuzzled the spot just below it, nibbled at the lobe as his hand swept the length of her thigh. "Holly . . . so sweet . . . so responsive . . . God, sweetheart, you were made for this. . . ."

He found the hem of her gown, delved beneath it, and began to caress, slowly making his way upward. . . .

Holly felt the newest touch as a sailor feels a gust of wind in a full-blown storm. Her body quaked with sensation, and the caress of Nicholas's hand on the bare skin of her inner thigh, though dimly perceived, seemed only to stoke a fire that already blazed. Blazed with each murmur of Nicholas's voice in her ear, with each renewed longing for something she couldn't put a name to, but which thrummed through her body like the notes of a horn.

She'd tell him . . . he would know what it was she wanted . . . wanted . . . longed for . . .

"Nicholas . . ." she breathed, "I—Oh, God—*No!*"

Nicholas went absolutely still, his fingers wet with the slippery heat of her. Moisture and heat that had just proved her anything but frozen. He looked down at the white-faced woman beneath him.

Her eyes held pure, undiluted terror.

"Get away from me! Oh, God, *don't*—please don't!" She was shouting now, and twisting violently under him. He knew he'd heard similar words before . . . on the night she'd come to Caerdruth . . . on the night she'd been violated.

He released her at once, rolling away and onto his side. Holly barely noticed. She was staring straight ahead, terrorized by ghosts he couldn't see.

She was breathing hard, chest heaving, sucking in huge gulps of air, but the shouting had stopped. The hands that had reached for him in passion were now clenched into fists.

"Holly . . . ? Can you hear me?"

No answer. Just a violent trembling that shook every inch of her.

"Holly," he repeated. "It's all right now. You're safe. It's Nicholas, Holly."

She shuddered, released a final rush of air. The image of a green velvet cloak receded, and with it, the nameless terror. "Nicholas . . . yes."

He saw her turn to him, and knew she really saw him. "Nicholas? Oh, God, Nicholas, what . . . ? What have I done?"

Stumbled across a part of you that's frozen after all. Ignoring the unsatisfied clamorings of his body, he held out his arms to her. "Nothing so terrible, sweetheart." He forced a chuckle. "In fact, probably something very wise."

She looked at him oddly, didn't answer.

"Holly . . . ?"

With a smothered cry, she threw herself into his arms. They closed around her, cradled her against his chest as she began to sob brokenly.

He felt that sense of *deja vu* again, stronger than before . . . and mocking . . .

"Shh, love, it's all right," he murmured, wondering if anything ever would be for her. Wondering, given what she was, what he was, why in God's name he cared.

❧ Eleven ☙

Agnes Blodgett stood before the four Sharpe children who were her personal charges, viewing them with supreme dislike. The twins were the arch troublemakers, to be sure. But the girls aided them in no small way. Spoiled, that's what they were, the lot of them!

Agnes had never been fond of children. But a curate's daughter with nothing to recommend her beyond the modicum of education drilled into her by a strict religious upbringing had had little choice in the matter. She'd been on the shelf for years when her aging parents had died within a year of each other, leaving her in need of a means of supporting herself. So when the vicar of Saint Albans in Caerdruth sent inquiries throughout the diocese regarding a governess for the earl's children, she'd secured a reference from her own vicar, and been taken on.

Now, as she ran her eyes over the four she'd lined up before the nursery windows, Blodgett found herself wishing for the first time in her life that she were a man.

A man would have other employment options. A man wouldn't have to suffer the indignities visited on her by this odious pack of brats. Not without being able to resort to a fine disciplinary tool like her ruler. If a male tutor were threatened by someone like that major—Blodgett shivered with disgust—he could pick up and go elsewhere. To a household that knew the merits of "Spare the rod, and spoil the child."

But there were other methods of correcting wayward charges, and she would use them. She eyed the flaxen-haired foursome in front of her with distaste. How dare they look so angelic when their nasty little minds were so demonic!

"Very well," she told the four, "I shall give you one more chance to confess. If I do not learn who the culprit is within the next sixty seconds, I shall assume you are all guilty, and all will be punished. Punished . . . until I learn the truth!"

The governess's eyes narrowed, beady pupils spearing each of the silent youngsters in turn. "Who fed that noxious concoction to my Ernest? Who?"

Not a child moved. Blodgett consulted the watch pinned to her bosom. But as the seconds ticked by, a soft popping sound broke the stillness of the schoolroom, and four pairs of china blue eyes darted to the pile of cushions behind the governess. Specifically, to the bloated creature sleeping on those cushions. Ernest.

The governess had heard it too. Her eyes narrowed further as the source of her displeasure reminded her of the sedition perpetrated against them both. A moment later there was a perceptible quivering of Blodgett's nostrils. Those sensitive portals were being assaulted yet again! As they had been all night long, while poor Ernest lay atop her coverlet, miserable as she from that infamy!

The twins watched Blodgett's nostrils assume a pinched look, and each privately decided that whatever the punishment was, it would be worth it. And of course they'd all be punished. Because they were all innocent.

No one had fed Ernest that lot of beans. He'd fed them to himself. Stolen them, was Martin's guess; they'd found out Cook was preparing beans and bacon for the staff's supper last night, just around the time Ernest had gone missing.

It wasn't their fault Ernest had kept Blodgett up all night by breaking wind in her chamber. But would Old Sourpuss listen? Oh, no! She'd made up her mind one of them had done it, and here they were, lined up like pigeons for the plucking.

Fanny almost grinned as she watched the governess sidle away from the noxious fumes. Wouldn't it have been famous to see Old Sourpuss's nose twitching all night while that lardy cat made wind in her face? Not that Ernest seemed the least bit discomfited by what was going on with his innards. But Blodgett, now . . . *Old Sourpuss and her odorous puss! Oh, Lord, I mustn't laugh!*

Of the four, only Charlotte was upset. They were going to be punished, and they hadn't *done* anything! Sometimes, it seemed to Charlotte, Blodgett did nothing but punish. She certainly punished more than she taught. She'd been ever so fond of using that ruler.

Of course, she'd not used it since Uncle Nicholas had come to stay. Fanny said it was because their uncle had warned her off it, and if that was so, Charlotte was glad. The ruler stung her small hands awfully, and sometimes she hadn't even been certain why the governess was using it on her. Blodgett didn't believe in Explaining the Obvious, as she said—whatever that meant.

But Charlotte didn't like the way Old Sourpuss's eyes were narrowed on them this morning. It was worse than those times she'd reached for her ruler, and it worried the child. Punishments were difficult enough when you'd done something bad, but when you hadn't done anything, they were much more frightening. Then they made Charlotte feel the way she had when she'd learned Papa was going to heaven, and there was nothing she could do to make him stay.

"Your time is up!"

The crack of Blodgett's voice jarred Ernest from his nap. The obese feline rolled over, producing a prodigious explosion of sound. Startled, Ernest raised his head and glanced curiously in the direction of his tail. Then he curled into the cushions again, oblivious to whatever had caused the momentary distraction.

The indelicate interruption fed Blodgett's ire. "You will all," she pronounced with tight-lipped satisfaction, "remain exactly as you are for the duration of the morning. Hands at your sides, eyes forward. There will be no fidgeting, no moving about, and absolutely no sitting."

She was tempted to add "no talking," but surmised that would be impossible to police. Also, they might just talk the guilty one into giving himself up. "Is that clear?" she added with a snap of her black eyes.

"Yes, Miss Blodgett," they replied in unison.

"When it is time for your dinner," the governess went on, "I shall return to inquire if you've learned your lesson, and are ready to divulge the abuser of animals in our midst. If not . . ." She let the words trail away ominously.

Bending to pick up Ernest, she gave a grunt, hefted the somnolent feline to her bosom, and headed for the door to the hallway. Reaching it, she turned and eyed them all before issuing a final threat. "Do not think you can disobey me in the interim. I shall be returning to check on you during the four hours, and if I find one toe misplaced"— she glanced at the children's feet in dire warning—"there will be consequences!"

Fixing them with a parting glare, the governess suddenly glanced at the ponderous ball of fur in her arms. The children managed to remain silent as they watched her wrinkle her nose in vile disagreement with what had obviously just emanated from it. Quaking with indignity, Blodgett turned and slammed the door behind her.

"Good thing she took Ernest with her!" Fanny clamped her nose with her fingers. "If he'd remained, I shouldn't want any dinner."

"We may not be having it in any case," said Martin on a sigh. "When she returns and gets the same answer, it would be just like her to leave us standing here without it."

"For the rest of the day, do you mean?" asked Fanny.

"I wouldn't put it past her," said Michael. Martin nodded agreement.

"But I shall become unbearably hungry without my dinner!" cried Charlotte. "And we didn't do anything!"

"Don't cry, midgin," said Martin, feeling inordinately solicitous of the four-year-old. "We're all in this together, you know."

"Yes, and we shall starve together too," said Fanny, "unless we figure a way out of it."

"I don't *want* to starve!" Charlotte began to cry more loudly.

"Shh, Lottie," said Michael. "If she comes back and hears you, it'll just make her glad. And we don't want Old Sourpuss glad to see us so unhappy. We want her—"

"Sorry!" exclaimed Fanny with that faraway-squint they all recognized. Yet instead of moaning at her as they usually did when she got the squints, the twins turned toward Fanny and waited. Their sister could be devilishly clever when she wanted to be, and they were in need of some quick thinking right now. Forget about missing dinner; standing still for four hours wasn't exactly a pleasant prospect.

"We'll make her sorry she's punished us so horribly," Fanny added.

"Well, it hasn't gotten horrible quite yet," Martin put in reasonably.

"No, but it will! It will, I just know it!" wailed Charlotte.

"What we've got to do," Fanny went on, "is to remain as we are for at least a little while . . . before it grows too tiresome, I mean."

"I'm tired some already!" sniffed Charlotte.

"Yes, Lottie, I know," said Fanny. "But you must try to be very brave—for a little while, at least. Until Sourpuss has had a look-in once or twice. We must first convince her we've been suffering a deal of time. Then . . ."

"Go on," said Martin. He ignored the squint entirely now, utterly focused on his sister's words.

"Then, after a bit of time has passed," said Fanny, "and she's convinced we're in here Suffering Horribly . . ."

"Dash it all, Fanny!" exclaimed Michael. "Don't keep us hanging!"

"The next time she comes for one of her look-ins, we let her find us passed out on the floor!"

"On the floor!" Charlotte's tears had dried, and she eyed her sister as if she'd suddenly sprouted horns.

"We'll pretend to have fainted dead away," said Fanny. "From cruel and wicked punishment!"

"And from hunger!" added Charlotte, tuned in to her sister now.

"Capital idea!" said Michael.

"It might work!" said his twin.

"Of course, it'll work," said Fanny. "It merely wants the proper moment. Are you all with me, then?"

"Yes!" the three exclaimed.

Catching one another's excitement, they settled down to wait.

Maud sat up in bed, no longer trying to sleep. She'd lain awake since dawn. Something was terribly amiss with Holly. First, according to the twins, she'd gone haring off on that wild horse of Nick's a couple of days ago, with no care for her safety. And after that, she'd grown blue-deviled as a mourner. She kept entirely to her chambers, refusing all Maud's efforts to draw her out.

Maud had grown quite fond of their guest since she arrived in their midst. She'd begun to worry about the child's welfare in a way she couldn't recall worrying in years. Not since—

Well, no sense in going into all that. What was done was done. It belonged to the past, and no amount of rehashing would put it straight.

But Holly was another matter. Holly had been given into Maud's care. Had needed her. And she'd been coming along rather nicely, thought Maud as she slid out of bed, despite not knowing yet who she was. But the physician had given them all cause to hope that with proper rest and care, the dear girl's memory would return.

Only now something had happened to disturb the child. Something was interfering with the rest she required, and Maud had no idea what it was. But she intended to find out.

Reaching into her wardrobe for the first thing at hand, the old woman hurriedly donned a carmine sarcenet gown. She must hurry to Holly as quickly as possible. The child *needed* her.

Maud made her way to the east wing as fast as her ancient bones would allow. As she hurried, she sifted through her mind for something to draw the girl out. She must get her to cast aside whatever was making such a brown study of her. Getting Holly involved, that's what was wanted!

By the time Maud reached Holly's door, she'd come upon just the thing. Holly was extremely fond of the children. She had a natural bent for mothering, Maud guessed—else she was a Christmas goose! The child might put off an old woman's entreaties to leave her rooms, but what about an urgent summons to aid the children? Let her resist that if she could!

Less than ten minutes later, Holly was accompanying Maud to the nursery. She wasn't at all sure why they were rushing there at such a frantic pace, but Maud had given her a definite impression it was necessary. Although, she did wonder why Maud had summoned her. Why not the children's guardian?

Nicholas . . . She felt herself shrink, as from a blow. The mere thought of him was enough to make her want to scurry for cover in her mind. To forget, just as she'd forgotten her past and her essential self, what had happened between them two days ago.

Her lips twisted in an ironic smile. Where was her amnesia when she needed it? Why couldn't she misplace her doubt in her mind as conveniently as her mind had misplaced her?

For it was doubt she felt, of her innocence, despite Nicholas's urgings to the contrary. He had to find her repugnant after all. Why else was he keeping his distance again?

She'd learned from Mary that he left the house each morning at dawn, and didn't return until nearly midnight. He was keeping away from her all right, just as she was avoiding him.

Even if she couldn't avoid him in her mind. Couldn't avoid recalling her delight in his touch. Or reconcile it with the sudden panic she'd felt, which was triggered by something Nicholas had done—or was it? She'd felt overwhelmed by a sudden darkness that was akin to the cloud hiding her memory, yet not entirely. This had been far worse. Terrifying. There'd been something about those rocks, something that had nothing to do with Nicholas.

"Oh, look—it's Nick!"

Maud's words sucked her back into the moment, and Holly stopped dead in her tracks. *Speak of the devil* . . .

Nicholas swore softly as Maud called a greeting. He shouldn't have gone back for the damned ledgers. Nettles had said they could get along well enough without them this morning. But he'd stubbornly done so, and now he'd pay for that stupidity. There was Holly, when he'd sworn off contact with the chit. For good.

Damn it, Holly, stay away from me! But even as his mind formed the words, Nicholas found himself walking toward her . . . absorbing the sight of her. Innocence in a yellow gown. Abused innocence, yet innocence, still . . . but with pitch-black, yawning edges that threatened to suck her into an abyss. An abyss he'd touched two days ago, and wanted to drive from his mind . . .

Christ, Holly, I can't help you! I'm the last person on earth who can help! I've abysses of my own!

"Good morning, Aunt . . . Miss Holly," he made himself say. "A bit early for the pair of you to be about, isn't it?"

While Maud made some pleasantry, Holly scrambled for something to say. Anything to establish the distance she needed between Nicholas and herself. He was too near. Dear God, much too near, with that black lock of hair curling over his forehead just as it had when——*Oh, God, don't think about it!*

"Major Sharpe, it's about the children," she hastily put in. "There's something amiss in the nursery, and we're off to investigate."

Nicholas grated something inaudible under his breath, and took off like a shot for the nursery. The women hurried after him.

Blodgett felt a measure of satisfaction. Her charges were responding properly to the punishment. One of the twins (she could never be sure which) began to sway on his feet when she'd looked in on them. And that crybaby, Charlotte, had obviously been weeping; Blodgett was quite familiar with those puffy eyes, the way she'd sniffled from a reddened nose. Excellent. Perhaps they'd be ready to confess at the next look-in.

Savoring the luxury of an entire morning without the little monsters, the governess turned away from the nursery. She'd gone halfway down the hallway toward her own chamber when the sound of rapid footsteps drew her up short. She turned and saw that wretched Major Sharpe striding toward her, the sound of his tallboots echoing loudly on the tiled floor.

"The children, Blodgett——where are they?" she heard him demand, just as she spied the dotty aunt and that odd female guest hurrying in his wake.

"The . . . the children?" Blodgett could think of but one reason he'd demand the whereabouts of her charges in this fashion, and she blanched. Had the devious little beasts gotten word out somehow——but that was impossible. Furthermore, she had nothing to fear. After all, she hadn't used her ruler.

"Devil take it——of course, the children!" snapped Nicholas. "We've had word——oh, never mind!" He strode to the nursery door and flung it wide.

"Christ!" The word died on his tongue as the shock of four children slumped on the floor nailed him in place.

Behind him came a gasp from Maud and a smothered cry from Holly. Jarred into action, Nicholas sprang toward the still forms near the windows.

"God in heaven, what's happened to them?" Holly cried as she came up behind him. Nicholas was bending over Fanny, who'd begun to moan.

"Oh dear, oh dear," Maud muttered as she drew near.

Fanny seemed to rouse as Nicholas chafed her wrists, and the twins had begun moaning just like Fanny. Only Charlotte remained still, and Holly dropped to the floor beside her.

"Charlotte! Charlotte, dear, can you hear me?" Holly heaved an audible sigh of relief when the four-year-old's eyes opened. "Oh, sweetheart, you've given us such a fright! Are you all right? Whatever happened?"

China blue eyes blinked back at her. "We've fainted . . . from Horrible Punishment," said Charlotte. Her small mouth began to tremble. "And we didn't *do* anything!"

"Punishment?" Nicholas's head whipped around, and he eyed the child sharply. Seeing she was near tears, he turned toward the twins, who'd joined Fanny in sitting positions by now. "What's she talking about, lads? Martin . . . ?"

Martin darted a look at his twin. Michael nodded encouragement. Martin swallowed, and glanced at Fanny. His sister gave him the thumbs-up sign. Still, Martin hesitated.

It had seemed devilish good luck to be found this way. By someone beyond Old Sourpuss. That would show her! But now Martin wasn't so sure. It was one thing to pull the wool over Blodgett's eyes; she deserved it. But telling a clanker to Uncle Nicholas . . . and Miss Holly . . . somehow it didn't feel right.

"Poor Martin's still in shock," said Fanny just in time, "but I can tell it, Uncle."

"He looks quite capable to me," said Nicholas, eyeing his nephew suspiciously. The boy had begun to squirm, and if there was one thing Nicholas recalled from his own childhood, it was that squirming boys and the truth seldom went together. "Now, Martin, I want you to—"

"Oh, do let Fanny tell it!" Holly broke in, then wanted to cut off her tongue. The look Nicholas shot her was so reminiscent of that time in the conservatory, she could hear the clash of rapiers in her mind. "I—I merely meant that Fanny . . . well, Fanny's so willing, you see . . ."

Nicholas continued to spear her with that unnerving gaze she recalled only too well. Seconds passed, and Holly had all she could do to continue meeting his eyes, but she dared not look away. Something more than whose wishes would prevail with the children was at stake here; she sensed it, even if she couldn't put what it was into words. Something she wanted to call *trust* nibbled at the edge of her awareness. She held her ground.

"Very well," Nicholas said at length, and Holly let out a silent sigh of relief. So did Martin.

"Well," said Fanny, not squinting the least bit as she eyed each adult in turn, "it all began when that fat cat . . ."

It was a full five minutes later when she'd finished, and Holly was torn between laughter and tears. The picture of a bilious feline imposing its digestive distress on the Friday-faced governess, was priceless! She'd wanted to burst out in giggles. But the sight of Charlotte's tear-stained face was more than enough to quell Holly's amusement. The poor children!

Maud seemed to share these mixed emotions, but Nicholas demonstrated no such ambivalence. His face was a study in barely controlled fury as he rose and made for the door.

"Nick, what are you about?" queried Maud.

"Finding that miserable governess!" he said between clenched teeth.

"Oh, dear," said Maud, just a shade guilty that the Banbury tale she'd concocted to stimulate Holly had begun to have too many unforeseen consequences. "And when you do?"

"I'm going to sack her!" came the taut reply.

"But, Nick," Maud protested, halting him in his tracks at the door, "we've no one to replace her!"

"Oh, yes we have." His eyes drilled into Holly. "Our *guest* seems to have no end of notions on the rearing of children. I shall therefore let her put those notions to use. Besides," he added with a nasty smile, "it's about time she earned her keep!"

Ignoring the gasps of both women, he spun on his heel and left.

❧ Twelve ❧

Nicholas scanned the letter a second time, as if this might let him read between the lines. But the terse summons was vague even for Whitehall: "The Minister requests your presence," it read. "Return to London at once."

His request to sell out had likely hit some snag, though why that would require a meeting with the War Minister was beyond him. Nicholas crumpled the heavy vellum with its official seal, tossed it into the fireplace.

He turned to the footman who'd brought it. "Tell Parkins I wish to see him. And inform the stables I'll want my horse saddled and ready by the front door in half an hour."

The servant left, and Nicholas glanced at the ledgers lying on the library desk. The meeting with Nettles would have to wait now, but it hardly mattered. He'd seen enough of Trevellan's accounts to learn the basic facts. He grimaced: not as disastrous as Caerdruth maybe, but bad nonetheless.

The grimace faded, and he almost smiled. The prospect of leaving struck him suddenly as just what he needed. A break from the enormous pressures weighing him down since Aubrey's death. London, great whore of a city that she was, beckoned with uncommon brightness. He could already savor her crowded thoroughfares with their teeming masses . . . yes, and her filth, and fog, and even the stench of her gutters. Christ, he couldn't wait!

Declining Parkins's offer of a footman the butler had begun to train as a valet for Harry, Nicholas changed clothes and packed his own scant belongings. While he did this, he gave the old retainer instructions for what was to be done in his absence.

"I think that covers everything," Nicholas told him as he snapped his bag shut some twenty minutes later. "You sacked that laundrymaid as I ordered?"

"Indeed, sir." Parkins had seen to it personally. He'd pulled rank on Hastings for the honor after learning of the wench's indiscretions with regard to their houseguest. Most of the staff had begun to grow inordinately fond of Miss Holly. They'd felt sacking too good for the loose-tongued jade. "And, ahem, Miss Blodgett left on the mail coach yesterday afternoon."

Sensing the old man's wish to add more—Blodgett's departure was common knowledge about the Hall, after all—Nicholas set the bag on the floor, and eyed him archly. "And . . . ?"

"And . . . well, sir, I was wondering if there were any particular instructions for—ahem, with regard to the children?"

They both knew he was obliquely referring to Blodgett's replacement. Nicholas had no doubt the Hall was abuzz over the events which had transpired in the nursery the morning before. This was the first anyone had alluded to them in his presence, however, and a good thing too.

He'd left the schoolroom in a rare fury. He'd always dealt easily with women. In taproom, drawing room, or bedroom, he'd made his way about their skirts as deftly as a good cat caught mice. Whether charming, intimidating, or seducing them, he had no trouble getting women to do his bidding. And in these exchanges he was always in control. Only once had he ever allowed a woman to determine the course of his life, and the results had been painful, but instructive.

He was not about to let it happen again. Ever.

"Has there been word from . . . the nursery? Problems?" he asked the butler.

"Not at all, sir. Hastings and I have each taken the liberty of looking in on the schoolroom since, ahem, the change in staff, and it appears things are progressing well."

"I am gratified to hear it," said Nicholas, reclaiming his bag and heading for the door. It was the truth. His wards had been subjected to enough turmoil in their lives of late. He wanted a return to normalcy for them.

As for their new governess, he bloody well didn't want to think of her at all. She'd been the first female to make him lose that control he'd mastered since Judith's—*Bloody hell! The baggage has me dredging up a past I counted long buried!*

A pointed clearing of the old man's throat had him turning at the door. "Oh, very well, you old sly boots," he said testily. "Out with it—quickly. You know Lucifer doesn't idle well, once saddled."

"It's about something Miss Holly said when I last saw her, sir. Ah, not that she indicated she wished me to speak to you about it, but—"

"Just tell it, man."

"Yes, sir. She said she feared the schoolroom held too many unpleasant memories for the children, and wondered if she might not arrange, for a while, to hold their lessons in different surroundings."

"Which surroundings?"

Parkins was impervious to the impatience in Nicholas's voice. "Ah, she mentioned taking them to the library, sir, and perhaps out of doors when the weather—"

"The library is out." Nicholas could bloody well imagine the little terrors laying waste to what was still a decent collection of books, despite what Aubrey had sold off. He shuddered to think of the havoc they could wreak.

"As for the grounds," he threw over his shoulder as he stalked from the room, "she's welcome to the whole bloody acreage for all I care!

"And, Parkins—one thing more . . ." He turned at the head of the stairs, faced the butler, who'd trailed him from his room. "You will tell her this: I expect to see evidence upon my return, that her charges have not run roughshod over her. Convey that personally, Parkins—from me!"

Told that the groom she wished to see had business up at the entrance to the Hall, Holly walked the blood-bay toward it from the stables. She'd noticed a lameness in the gelding's foreleg while returning from her morning ride, and wished to speak to the groom in charge of the horse.

But she had to hurry. Whitley had agreed to feed the children breakfast so Holly might steal an early ride; she'd needed it to relieve the tension building since yesterday's incident in the nursery. But the horse's limp had forced her to return at a walk, and now she was running late.

With her eyes on the gelding's foreleg, she didn't notice the groom—or more importantly whose stallion he was holding—until a familiar voice drew her attention.

"Why the devil aren't you with the children?"

Holly's head shot up, and she saw Nicholas striding down the steps. He wore the dress uniform of his regiment, and despite the frown he directed her way, her heart took a mad, involuntary leap.

He was impeccably turned out. From the perfect cut of the red military coat to the gleam of his boots, the man seemed a hero out of myth, and masculine as thunder. It didn't help her state of mind that he was also the last person on earth she wanted to see this morning.

"Don't worry," she snapped, "I'm just now on my way to the schoolroom—*to earn my keep!*"

Reminded of his rudeness, a more sensitive man might have winced. A well-mannered one would have apologized. Nicholas did neither. He laughed.

"I fail to see the humor in that!" Holly raised her voice over the rumble of laughter. "And you, Major, certainly didn't find it amusing yesterday!"

Nicholas mounted the stallion and looked down at her. Laughter still lurked in his eyes. "Ah, but that was yesterday, Miss Holly!" he told her with a mocking grin. He affected a careless shrug. "For now, I find my mood remarkably altered."

It was actually the truth, he realized. Irritated as he'd been with her, the moment she opened her mouth with that set-down, he'd lightened. She'd looked so damned adorable with her eyes flashing, like a green-eyed kitten spitting fire. Hell, a man would have to be a saint to resist the chit when she looked like that!

Her chin set at a stubborn angle, Holly refused to respond. Would that the rest of him were altered as well, she thought. He was too handsome, too worldly, too magnetic, and too close at hand. She felt herself irresistibly drawn to this devil on a black horse, and she couldn't afford to be. She didn't even know who she was, for God's sake! No, she couldn't risk it, and he didn't want it. He'd made that clear, if nothing else.

"If you'll excuse me, Major Sharpe," she said crisply, "I need to discuss something with the groom." Holly turned to the servant who'd stepped a few yards away, dutifully pretending to have heard none of the exchange between his betters.

"Discuss all you wish," Nicholas replied with a shrug. He urged Lucifer forward, turning in his saddle as he passed her. "But I'd pay attention to a particular message that's been left with Parkins if I were you. I won't be in London forever!"

London? He was off to London? Just like that? Without so much as a by-your-leave? A word of explanation?

The groom asked if he could be of assistance, and Holly tore her eyes from the uniformed figure on horseback. She quickly described the gelding's limp. Nodding absently when the servant offered to take the bay, she returned her gaze to the rider disappearing down the drive.

And despite her admonitions of moments before, Holly felt suddenly bereft.

It was the day after Nicholas had left for London, and the air in the garden smelled of sun-warmed earth and growing things. Spring was finally settling in on the Cornish coast, thought Holly as she saw a footman approach with the item she'd requested.

"Ah," she said, nodding her thanks to the servant, "the last part of our lesson has arrived!"

Smiling, she faced her four charges, who were speechless for once as they gaped at the item in her hands.

"How shall we divide this into quarters?" Holly bent over the table lately removed from the schoolroom. Still smiling, she set the item in front of her pupils.

Four pairs of identical blue eyes fastened on the object in question, hardly able to credit its use as an arithmetical device. An iced currant cake, fresh from the kitchens!

Fanny voiced what the other three were only thinking. "Um . . . does the one who answers first get to have some, Princess Holly?"

"No," said Holly.

Four frowns.

"*Everyone* may have some"—she smiled at the astonishment on their faces—"but only after it's been properly divided! In quarters, if you please. Our lesson was about halves and quarters."

She gestured at the figures she'd scratched out for them in the dirt to teach the lesson. "Take your time," she added, "and you may refer to these, if you like."

Silence ensued as the children pondered the scratchings. At length, Martin broke it. "Um . . . begging your pardon, Miss Holly," he said, "but I should like to—that is, may I ask a question?"

Again Holly smiled. Martin being Martin, she'd been expecting it. "You may."

"Well," said the boy, "if we're all to have a piece in the end—"

"*If* there's a correct answer," Holly reminded.

"Yes, Miss Holly. But if it's possible for all of us to have some . . . that is, mightn't there be a *special* reward for the one who knew the correct answer?"

"Hmm," Holly murmured, knitting her brow, pretending

to consider the problem. She secretly enjoyed the ever-rational bent of the seven-year-old. In truth, she was finding this group of quick-witted youngsters a constant source of delight. And a challenge, of course, but that only kept things interesting.

Nicholas Sharpe may have thought he was setting her a punishing task when he made her their governess, but hers was the last laugh: She couldn't imagine anything more satisfying—and fun!

"Very well," she said. "The one who answers correctly may select first. And to prevent any wild guessing, each wrong answer puts you at the end of the cue."

There was a chorus of groans. It died when Holly lifted a brow at them. Fanny had already labeled this her "I'll-tolerate-no-rudeness eyebrow."

Again there was silence at the table, but Holly noticed Charlotte frowning. It wasn't a frown of concentration . . . more of consternation, she thought.

"You seem in a pucker, Lottie," she ventured. "Would you like to tell us about it?"

Charlotte gaped at her. Had she actually *asked* if one of them would like to say something? This was such a far cry from Blodgett's "Speak up!" (which daren't be disobeyed) she could hardly believe it. Imagine! *Asking!*

Charlotte swallowed, then took the plunge. "It was always Michael who got first pick before," she said plaintively. She saw Michael glare at her and hastily amended, "Well, sometimes it was Martin—but it was never Fanny or I because the boys can run faster! They were always getting to the sweets first, and they always selected the largest piece!"

Holly held up her hand to silence the protests forming on the twins' mouths. "But, Lottie" she reminded, "that was then, and this is now. We shan't have the race going to the swiftest, so to speak, because there is no race. Not in the running way, at any rate. And the quarters will be all the same size, won't they?"

"Not if the one who answers cuts the cake!" cried Charlotte. "He'll cut his piece larger! It's the most unfairingest thing in the world!"

The twins grumbled. Their sisters ruminated. It was Fanny who suddenly brightened. "I know! Will *you* cut it, Princess?"

Holly eyed them thoughtfully, wondering if this was all merely a rattling on to stall for time. But no, Charlotte looked truly troubled, and perhaps she should be. In the adult world, Holly suspected, such an exchange would be labeled a Discourse on Justice.

Smiling at all of them, she withdrew the dull knife Cook had given her from her pocket and laid it on the table. "I shall do better than that," she said. "The losers will cut the cake—and then the winner will select!"

All four puzzled over this for a moment. Then a rash of grins broke out. "Oh, Miss Holly," Charlotte exclaimed, "you are the most fairingest grown-up in the whole world!"

Nicholas frowned as he faced England's Minister of War. "Let me see if I comprehend what you've told me thus far," he told the corpulent man sitting behind the desk. "My request to sell out has been denied, yet I am not being sent back to my regiment. Is that right, sir?"

"It is, Major Sharpe, so far as it goes. As to the rest . . . the, ah, reasons for the denial, I'm afraid I'm not at liberty to tell you."

"Not at lib—" Nicholas took a step forward, then froze as the Minister held up a silencing hand.

"As you were, Major. And calm yourself." The older man eyed the officer who'd come so highly recommended by Wellesley. Was he the right man for the job? Sharpe was utterly in control of himself now, his face an impassive mask. Still, that momentary outburst . . .

Of course, the man had just lost his only brother . . . and not long before, had been in the thick of it on the Peninsula . . . bound to affect a man, that.

Yet they'd been told he'd served courageously in the field,

displaying nerves of steel and incisive thinking. Furthermore, he was the only one in a good position to—

The Minister sighed. It wasn't his problem, after all. Napoleon was on his way to Elba, and the Foreign Office was running things now. Let them deal with it.

"Major Sharpe," he said abruptly. "I told you I am not at liberty to discuss the ramifications of this, but I didn't say no one else would. Fact is, we're waiting on the arrival of—"

There was a knock at the door, and a young lieutenant appeared. "Sir," he said, "the Foreign Secretary will see Major Sharpe now."

Nicholas darted a glance at the War Minister. *Castlereagh? Here in London? But he's supposed to be—*

"I know what you're wondering, Major," said the War Minister as he rose and ushered him to the door. "But the Secretary will explain it all to you shortly. Suffice it to say he's here in England only briefly. And secretly, I must add. He will be returning to Paris as soon as his business with you is completed. Does that say it plainly enough?"

Nicholas nodded, his mind spinning as he thanked the man and took his leave. Following the lieutenant down the corridor, he was still trying to take in the implications of what he'd heard. Lord Castlereagh, England's Foreign Secretary, and currently her representative to the peace negotiations—here in secret, to see him? What the devil was going on?

Robert Stewart, better known as Viscount Castlereagh, had never been overly popular with the public. But he was well regarded within the inner circles of government, and most saw him as the chief architect of the Grand Alliance that had just defeated Napoleon.

People might not like Castlereagh, but they respected him. This, notwithstanding the duel in which he'd wounded George Canning, the former Foreign Secretary who'd opposed him politically a few years back. An austere man, he didn't smile as he greeted Nicholas, but it was done with courtesy.

"Please sit down, Major. I'm neither your commanding officer, nor here in any official capacity. That is to say, only a select few are aware of my return to London, and what we discuss here will remain private. Am I clear?"

"You are, m'lord." Nicholas took a seat in an armchair he indicated. His eyes swept what was obviously a little-used office which had doubtless been commandeered for the purpose of this secret meeting.

Castlereagh took a position behind a desk devoid of any objects. Not even an inkstand graced its mahogany surface.

"No doubt you are wondering what this is all about," said the Secretary. "Or, more specifically, what it has to do with you."

"Those things did cross my mind, m'lord."

There was a hint of a smile on the stern mouth, but it quickly faded. "I shall come straight to the point, Major. We want you to do a little intelligence work for His Majesty's government."

Nicholas stared at him. "Spying?" he finally managed. "Why the devil do you want *me?*"

"I shall come to that in a moment." The Secretary propped his elbows on the desktop, steepled his fingers in front of his chin, paused in thought.

"Despite the defeat of Bonaparte's army," he began at length, "the allies are by no means convinced we are out of danger. Not all of us, at any rate. Even among Napoleon's enemies, there are men who admire him, including some with whom I've just met abroad.

"Moreover," he went on, "in the waning days of the campaign, the War Office became convinced there were leaks of vital secrets . . . battle plans, that sort of thing. And more to the point, we've now reason to believe there's someone here at home, the same someone as before, who's sabotaging the peace negotiations. In short, Major, we've a traitor in our midst."

Nicholas swore under his breath. Coming home for Aubrey's summons had been less difficult than it might have been. In early April it had been apparent it was just a matter of time until victory was at hand; he hadn't felt as vital to the campaign. He'd thought—they'd all thought, the officers in his regiment—Boney was finally finished. Now, from what Castlereagh was saying . . .

"Save your oaths for later, Major," said the Secretary. "If you take this assignment, I've no doubt you'll be wearing them thin."

"*If* I take—do I have a choice?"

A thin smile appeared on the solemn face. "You're not under military orders to do this, Major. The decision to decline your request to sell out was more a matter of allowing you a decent cover under which to function, should you accept. Of course, should you decide not to accept . . ." Castlereagh shrugged.

"Back to basics, m'lord." Nicholas leaned forward in his chair, his gaze intent on the patrician face. "Why me?"

The Secretary nodded. "It may not surprise you to learn we've been working on this leak for some time. And from the intelligence gleaned thus far, we've narrowed down our suspects to three people. Difficult as it is for me to tell it, all three"—his eyes held Nicholas's as his voice shook with disgust—"are highly placed members of the peerage."

Nicholas let out a long, low whistle.

"Precisely. Which is where you come in. Wellesley vouches for you, for one thing. You're loyal, intelligent, and reputed to have a cool head under fire. But beyond that, we require someone who can move among the highest levels of society without causing suspicion. You, sir, while not a peer, have certainly had access to the *haut ton* all your life, if only on the fringes."

Nicholas smiled sardonically. "We bastards have a way of being betwixt and between, m'lord."

Castlereagh allowed another smile. "What makes you perfect, however, is a couple of things. First, the recent change in your personal life. That you are now in charge of your late half brother's estate will account for your suddenly appearing among the *ton* in situations where you previously hadn't."

"And the second thing . . . ?"

The Secretary looked grim. "The three suspects, Major. Two were intimate acquaintances of your late brother and his wife. The third, I'm afraid, is an old friend of *yours*."

৪১ Thirteen ৭৬

James Witherspoon smiled apologetically at the flint-eyed man across from him. He'd not met the illegitimate son before, but he could see at once Nicholas Sharpe was different from his brother. Different from the old earl too. And not just because his extreme male beauty hovered on the edge of impropriety. This was another kettle of fish entirely.

No, none of the excesses and weaknesses of the other two here. The father had been a difficult, selfish man with cruel eyes. He'd seen to his estate, but self-indulgently, at a great cost to others. And Lord Aubrey Sharpe had never been up to snuff. It had shown in his eyes. The solicitor had noted his weakness long before the heir began the blatant mismanagement of his inheritance.

But the bastard looked awake upon every suit. The gray eyes held no cruelty, he was relieved to see, but neither were they soft. He'd need to step lively in his dealings with this one.

"It is indeed unfortunate, Major," said the solicitor, "that you made the journey to London before receiving my letter. It explained about the fire in our offices, you see."

"Fire?" Nicholas had noted the solicitor's apologetic manner from the outset. *What the devil's gone wrong now?*

"Yes, sir. Six weeks ago, Tuesday. Um, nothing major, mind you, but extensive enough to destroy some of our files before it was put out. Unfortunately, as my letter was to inform you, one of the items destroyed was the office copy of your late brother's will."

"Bloody hell!"

"Indeed, sir, but do not overset yourself. As I said, it was the office copy which was destroyed. Fortunately, it was not the only copy. There were three altogether, sir." Witherspoon smiled, obviously pleased with his firm's efficiency in such matters.

"I see," said Nicholas. "Then where the deuce are the others?"

"Well, Major, I was hoping you'd come across one of them yourself . . . the one in your brother's possession."

Nicholas knew he'd gone through Aubrey's papers thoroughly. He'd seen nothing resembling a will. Of course, Aubrey hadn't been the most organized man in the world . . .

"If it's at Caerdruth, I haven't the faintest idea where," he told the solicitor. "What about the third?"

"Ah," said Witherspoon. "As my letter also explained, my associate, Mr. Clark, has it, as he has copies of all our legal papers. It's a system we devised in the event of a catastrophe . . . ah, such as a fire."

"Well, man—have him fetch the damned thing up!"

Again, Witherspoon offered an apologetic smile. "Unfortunately, Major, Mr. Clark is out of the country at the moment. Went to Paris in the interests of some of our clients, now that the peace—"

"So what you're telling me is that I'll have to wait for his return to learn the contents of my brother's will."

"Unless you can locate Lord Sharpe's copy, sir, I'm afraid so."

Nicholas heaved a sigh and gave the man a level look. "I don't suppose it'll hurt to wait—as long as you can tell me I'm not in deep water in the meantime."

"Ah, with regard to what, sir?"

"As I said in my letter, my brother asked me before he died, if I would be the children's guardian . . ."

Witherspoon listened as Nicholas outlined the state of

things as he'd found them in Cornwall. He nodded agreement with his preliminary assessments of both Caerdruth and Trevellan—of the dire financial straits they were in. It was only when Nicholas broached his intention of finding a means of restoring Harry's patrimony that the solicitor interrupted.

"My dear sir, allow me to say I am gratified to hear of your intent in this. But I would caution you on two accounts: First, I must urge you to do nothing until we've perused the will. I confess, it was Mr. Clark who drew it up, and my memory of its details is limited. Secondly, the rebuilding you've outlined—reopening the mines, especially —will require a deal of the ready. Where do you intend to come by it?"

Nicholas smiled grimly. He'd already been to see Aubrey's bankers. "I was hoping you might tell me."

The solicitor shook his head sadly. "Although you must understand, sir, that I'm not at liberty to discuss the circumstances of your nephew's inheritance until the contents of the will indicate I may, I can unofficially tell you this: If there were anything amounting to liquid assets lurking about, I seriously doubt your brother would have taken to selling off the items you say you noted in the accounts. Does that say it plainly enough?"

Nicholas sighed, running a hand through his hair. "If I could borrow—".

"Forgive me, Major, but against what collateral? The entailment forbids—"

"Yes, yes—I know! But there's Trevellan, and—" Nicholas clamped his jaws shut when the solicitor held up a hand.

"Again, you must forgive me, Major, but you know such a possibility isn't likely. From what you've told me of Trevellan's books . . . well, let me just say I doubt even the cent-per-cents would touch it. Even usurers demand—"

"Bloody Christ, man! Do you think you're telling me anything I haven't told myself? But I can't let it alone—don't you see? Caerdruth was once a thriving estate! And Trevellan! I won't just sit by and let them fall into dust!"

Privately, the solicitor was thinking that if at first he'd only guessed this man was different from the other two, now he was dead certain of it. He'd never seen this kind of fervor in a man's eyes, not even when they belonged to a legitimate heir on the verge of losing everything.

But what motivated him? Was he inordinately attached to his young nephew? Somehow, he suspected Nicholas Sharpe's interest was far from anything so simple.

From the way he spoke, it was clear Sharpe had no private fortune at his disposal. A landless, penniless bastard, then. Yet, as he looked at the perfectly chiseled features, the solicitor reminded himself there were fortunes to be had in things other than land and bank balances.

Toying with the quill from his inkstand, Witherspoon cleared his throat. "Ah, there is one way you might try to regroup . . ."

The gray eyes were instantly alert. "Go on."

"It isn't unheard of, Major, for bankrupted heirs to *marry* their way into financial solvency, and—"

A derisive snort cut him off. "My nephew the earl, may I remind you, is thirteen years old!"

The apologetic smile was beginning to irritate Nicholas. "Forgive me, Major. I wasn't making myself clear. You see, it was you I meant. For a, um, plump-in-the-pockets bride, that is. In that event, with the proper arrangements, you could extend funds to your nephew's estates with the understanding that they would eventually be repaid . . ." The words trailed off as Witherspoon noted his visitor's eyes. Frost had a chance of being warmer.

"Let us move on to the other matter I mentioned in my letter," Nicholas said abruptly. He had the satisfaction of seeing the deucedly all-too-clever solicitor flush. *By Judas's balls!* he swore silently. *I've used whores in my time, but I'm thrice-damned if I'll be a whore! Sell myself on the marriage-mart? That'll be the bloody day!*

"Um, yes," said Witherspoon, managing to take the cue. "Your amnesia victim. No change in the poor young woman's condition, I take it?"

"Not as of the time I left Cornwall. Have you learned anything with the details I gave in my letter?"

"No, sir, I am sorry to say. We've made numerous discreet inquiries, but thus far it would appear no female remotely resembling the young woman has gone missing."

"Or been *reported* missing," Nicholas injected.

"I take your point, Major." Witherspoon withdrew a paper from a desk drawer, scanned it briefly. "Of course, all we had to go on was that she is, ah, comely . . . green eyes, black hair, and likely belongs to the Polite World . . . ah, yes, and that a locket found on her person bears an *H*."

Nicholas shrugged. "It isn't much, but the *ton* is a small, closed world where everyone knows almost everyone else. I have the feeling, if we only approached the right parties, this information would elicit something."

"Mm . . . possibly, Major—unless there's been a concerted effort to keep it under wraps, as you've already suggested. But there are always weak spots in the walls erected around these secrets. The servants' grapevine comes to mind . . ."

Witherspoon withdrew a sheet of foolscap from the drawer, dipped his quill in ink. "Perhaps, if you were to give me a more detailed description of the young lady . . . ?"

A few minutes later, as he finished recording additional details about the young woman they called Holly, the solicitor lowered his quill and studied his client's face. It was impassive, giving away nothing. Yet Witherspoon wondered if Sharpe knew how much he'd revealed in spite of this. *Eyes that tilt upward at the corners, especially when she laughs . . . small, perfect nose . . . flawless complexion, with a tiny mole—good heavens! The man sounds besotted!*

Masking his surprise, the solicitor suggested hiring some Bow Street runners to aid in the search, and Nicholas agreed. Nicholas thanked him, and they walked toward the outer office when he added one more suggestion.

"It might also be helpful, Major, if you were to bring the

young woman to London. With the Season getting under way, the entire *haut ton* will be in evidence. Excellent chance someone might recognize her, you know."

Nicholas frowned. "I don't need to reiterate the delicacy involved in this matter, Witherspoon. Bad enough she has no recall who she is, but the other . . ."

"I understand, sir. Unfortunate . . . most unfortunate."

"Criminal" says it better, Nicholas thought as he pictured the terror in Holly's eyes, heard her nightmare screams in his mind.

"I'm not certain I have the right even to suggest it to her," he told the solicitor. "But I'll ask—only because she can't very well go on with things as they are. I'll ask, and we'll let *her* decide."

Telling Witherspoon he could be reached at the family town house, and that he'd be in touch, Nicholas left. One small bit of good news he'd had from Aubrey's bankers was that his brother had proposed mortgaging Sharpe House in Queen Street shortly before his death but hadn't gotten any further. The town house wasn't all that grand, though. He doubted whether even its outright sale would have made a dent in the dun territory Aubrey had put himself in.

Nicholas had that morning collected some back pay he had coming, but it hardly amounted to what he'd need to do the undercover work for the Foreign Office. Castlereagh, however, had assured him that His Majesty's government would subsidize the venture. "If you're to move among the *haut ton*," he'd said, "you must appear flush in the pockets. Send the bills to Whitehall."

On his agenda, therefore, were several establishments that dealt in fashionable attire for gentlemen; dressing like the *ton* meant a deal more than wearing the two uniforms currently comprising his formal wardrobe.

After a stop at his former tailor in Saint James's, he went to Hoby's about boots, and finally Lock's for a top hat. In Queen Street he checked with the small staff at the town house to see how they were getting on, instructing Finch, the majordomo, to "find me a bloody valet." Then it was on to White's.

Brooks's was the club he favored, what with its Whiggish bent. But Castlereagh had made it clear he was also to frequent White's and Boodle's and Watier's too, if he was to glean the information they sought. He didn't even enjoy membership in the latter two, but the Secretary had told him it was being arranged. All sorts of doors were being opened for him with his assignment, and he only hoped it would pay off.

No one had a stomach for traitors, but the thought of betrayal from the highest echelons of society made Nicholas's blood boil. How many of the men he'd seen die might still be alive without the information passed to the enemy by this piece of human garbage? The upper echelons—it went against reason! They'd had the most to lose if Boney took Europe!

He saw no other uniforms at White's, but it didn't surprise him. Most officers confined themselves to the Guards' across the street, though likely not out of preference. Prinny and Wellesley himself had formed the Guards' Club a few years back; they'd learned many officers returning from the Peninsular Wars were being denied entry to the loftier establishments, and needed a place to meet.

He smiled cynically to himself as Raggett, White's proprietor, greeted him courteously. A bastard without title or blunt, he was welcome at the haughtiest establishment this side of Almack's, when dozens of legitimate younger sons were turned aside.

But the *ton* had an affinity for those who bested them at their own game, and in this Nicholas knew he was a master. He'd been welcomed into White's and Brooks's but a fortnight after his initial arrival in London. He'd barely reached his majority, but a winning round or two in Jackson's Rooms, a successful duel, and the appearance on his arm of the Town's most fashionable Cyprians had had sponsors running to recommend him.

Nicholas returned the greetings of several who recognized him, making his way toward the card rooms. But a quiet word from a footman diverted his course, and he headed for the bow window overlooking Saint James's.

"Sharpe," said the impeccably garbed man at the table. "Heard you were back in town." He ran his eyes over Nicholas's immaculate uniform. "Still wearing your colors, I see. Would've thought you'd sold out by now."

"As I've only arrived this morning," said Nicholas, "I ought to say I'm surprised word's already out. But it's comforting, I suppose, to learn some things never change. An *on-dit* in London still travels faster than the pox through a whorehouse."

Beau Brummell's eyes signalled amusement, while the other two at the table laughed aloud. "It don't appear you've changed either, Sharpe—eh, Skeffington?" Brummell nudged the man next to him, a dandy with rouged cheeks.

"Oh, Sharpe's sharp, all right!" Sir Lumley Skeffington laughed at his own wit.

Lord Alvanley, the third man, raised his quizzing glass. "I say, Sharpe," he remarked, "Boney's tricks don't seem to have done you any damage. 'Pon my word—not a mark on that pretty face of yours!"

"Oh, the frogs wouldn't have dared," said Brummell. "Half the muslins in England would have scratched their eyes out!"

"Half?" quipped Nicholas. "I must be slipping!"

There was a chorus of guffaws, and after another minute of such badinage, Nicholas took his leave. As he made his way toward the whist tables, his eyes took in the throng clustered around White's betting book. He registered a few familiar faces, but something else was apparent. There was a good number—all young bucks—he failed to recognize. Far more, in fact, than those he knew. The discrepancy hit him like a punch in the gut.

He was no longer one of them, those scapegrace young bucks that made up the pink of the *ton*. The war had put a distance between him and that sort of life, and he could never return to it. Other, younger faces crowded Gentleman

Jackson's Rooms now . . . got foxed at topping houses
. . . raced their cattle to Salt Hill.

He'd been regarded as a buck of the first head before he
left for the Peninsula, an out-and-outer, despite his mean
heritage. Now he wondered where he fit in.

Furious betting at the book usually indicated a common
interest. He asked a passing waiter what the wager of the
moment was.

The man looked at him with surprise. "Why, they're betting on *you,* sir!"

"On *me?*"

"Yes, sir. On how long it takes you to, er, visit the rooms
of the Misses Wilson."

Harriet Wilson and her three sisters were the most elegant of the courtesans who serviced the men of the *ton.*
Nicholas had long been a favorite patron of these popular
Cyprians who could afford to pick and choose among their
fashionable clientele. He even counted Amy, the intelligent
sister, among his friends.

"Longest odds on ten this evening, or before," the waiter
added. "Much shorter ones on the hours after midnight, of
course."

Nicholas thanked him, smiling sardonically as he strode
past the cluster of youngbloods. He no longer made up one
of them, but they apparently hadn't noticed.

He found a seat at a whist table, settling down to play
while he kept his ears open. He needed first of all simply to
reacquaint himself with the current scene if he was to move
amidst it with ease.

Beyond that, he listened for almost anything. As Castlereagh had pointed out, the most arcane bit of gossip sometimes contained a key to valuable information.

The play went in his favor, tricks almost falling into his
lap. The *on-dits* were less interesting. He learned that the
Duchess of Oldenburg, the Tsar's sister, had arrived in town
last month in advance of a state visit by her brother. And
that she and Prinny had detested each other on sight.

He'd already heard about the falling out between Prinny

and Brummell, but gossip still hovered in its wake. Two men behind him were remarking on the surprisingly large number who still befriended Brummell; their conclusion was that Prinny was aging, and didn't have the cachet of his youth.

Bored after a couple of hours of play, Nicholas gathered his markers and rose to go. He deemed the afternoon a waste in terms of his spy mission, but he'd won more than two thousand guineas. Enough to purchase a pair of high-steppers at Tattersall's. He'd let Whitehall spring for the rig they were meant to pull.

As he was cashing in the markers, a deep voice claimed his attention. "Nick! Nick Sharpe, as I live and breathe!"

He turned, and saw a tall, good looking blond man striding toward him. *Good God, it's*—"Rex! How are you, man?"

Lord Rex Wickham was the closest thing to a boyhood friend he'd had. Eldest son of the earl of Braithwaite, whose estate neighbored Caerdruth, Wickham was the same age as Nicholas. He'd joined in many of the young bastard's infamous boyhood escapades—despite the disapproval of Rex's family. The Earl's Bastard hadn't been deemed suitable company for the Braithwaite heir.

"I'm well—no, *better* than that!" Wickham replied. "Congratulate me, Nick! I'm newly married—and happily so in the bargain!"

"My felicitations, of course! A love match, was it? I wonder his lordship sat still for it."

They both knew it had been Rex's father who'd barred the way to a closer friendship between them. Lady Wickham had been easy, charmed by Nick's good looks, and a way with women that had already begun to emerge when he was a boy. But the earl of Braithwaite was a high stickler, especially where his heir was concerned. By the time the boys reached their late teens, he'd forbidden Rex the Bastard's company.

· Wickham's grin faded. "My father passed on a year ago, Nick. You didn't hear?"

Nicholas offered belated condolences, although he privately wished old Braithwaite an eternity in hell. Tales carried by the son of a bitch to Nick's sire had resulted in a number of brutal canings "for leading Rex astray"; Nicholas bore the scars on his back and buttocks to this day.

Nicholas explained his recent arrival from the Peninsula, as well as its cause, quietly accepting Wickham's condolences on Aubrey's death. "It appears, m'lord earl, we've a deal to catch up on," he told Rex as they made their way out of White's. "I don't even know who your countess is, for one thing, and when did you sell out?"

He'd been surprised to learn Wickham's father had allowed him to buy a commission a few years back. Although as he recalled, Rex was largely indulged as a boy, despite the earl's strictures in some respects. Rex, he'd been shocked to learn when they were both about eleven, had never been caned in his life.

Braithwaite laughed. "Here's the best part of all, old boy —because you'll hardly believe it! I've married Diana Travers!"

"Good God, man—never say so!" Lady Diana Travers was Rex's distant cousin. She and her family had come to visit the Wickhams the summer she was eight, and the two boys, ten. She was a pretty little hoyden, and had trailed after Rex and Nick like an eager puppy.

But the significant thing that had transpired that visit was a semi-innocent exploration among the three. A comparison of male and female body parts in a hayloft. Nicholas recalled it perfectly; it had produced his first non-nocturnal erection.

"I do say so." Braithwaite chuckled. "And if you've any pretense at being a gentleman, Nick, you won't say another word!"

"My lips are sealed!"

"Devilish hard when you're sporting an ear-to-ear grin!" Wickham replied, but he was grinning too.

"By the by," said Nicholas, "I recollect seeing the lady here during the Season some years back. Didn't she wind

up spoken for—engaged to Lord Kemball's heir—before it
was over?"

"She did," said Rex, "and became a young widow scarce
two years later. Bad luck for young Kemball, who broke his
neck in a hunting accident—but good luck for me! I'd have
offered for her as soon as she was out of black gloves, but
my father wouldn't hear of it. Proposed to her—discreetly,
mind you—the day after Father's funeral. And when my
own mourning was up, got happily leg-shackled!"

So Wickham's father hadn't been so tractable after all.
Nicholas wondered how many young lives were thwarted
by the absolute power parents had over their children. God
knew, his own might have taken a widely different course if
he'd had a father who gave a damn about him, a mother
who hadn't abandoned—*Enough! They're all ghosts now, anyway—and good riddance!*

With an eye to renewing their acquaintance, Nicholas
suggested Rex accompany him to Tattersall's in the morning, and then perhaps the pair could have a go at the town.

Braithwaite shook his head regretfully. "Wish I could, old
boy, but the deuce of the thing is, I'm off to Cornwall in the
morning. Promised Diana I'd return straightaway to collect
her for the Season, and I'm a day overdue now. Had some
business in town that, uh, couldn't be postponed. But she'll
be in high dudgeon if I delay any longer."

Nicholas nodded, pensively silent for a moment, then
told him he was planning to return to Cornwall himself.
Why didn't they ride home together?

Rex agreed at once, and they parted after arranging to
meet at the Wickham town house in the morning.

Watching his old friend leave, Nicholas's face was grim.
The purchase of cattle at Tatt's could wait, as could the
business of eavesdropping at clubs. He only wished he
could put aside the thing he'd arranged with Rex as well.
Indefinitely, if he had any choice. But he didn't.

Rex Wickham, fourth earl of Braithwaite, was one of the
three suspects on Castlereagh's list.

৯৯ Fourteen ৯৯

Mrs. Hastings muttered to herself as she made her way to the garden. A footman had informed her Parkins was to be found there, and find him, she would. She needed to speak to him about supplies which were running low in the larder. But this was not the first time in the past few days she'd had to chase the butler down, and she was growing impatient with it.

Parkins had always been the perfect upper servant as far as she was concerned. The two of them had enjoyed a well-oiled partnership in running the Hall. She could rely on him. She always knew where to find him. Until lately.

Since Major Sharpe left for London, Parkins had taken to vanishing at the most inopportune moments. Yesterday, when she'd needed his cost estimate of the week's menus, he'd been helping Miss Holly select a book from the library —to teach the children about the stars and planets! And just last night, when she'd required his assistance with a recalcitrant footman, she'd found him carrying Lady Charlotte to her bed—the child had fallen asleep in Miss Holly's bed when the governess had sung her a lullabye.

Indeed, whenever she tracked Parkins down, it was to find him doing the most extraordinary things. *Unbutlerlike* things. It really was the outside of enough!

Bursting through the garden gate, the housekeeper came to a dead halt. Good heavens! There was movement everywhere, and Hastings had an impression of bees swarming over a hive. A hive of . . . gardeners?

All of the children were there—even young Lord Sharpe. The thirteen-year-old was standing in the middle of a plot of ground with his shirtsleeves rolled up, and he was— *raking!*

Nearby, and covered with mud from the knees down, the twins were intent on digging a pair of holes in the ground. Armed with shovel and spade, they too were in shirtsleeves. Excitement animated their faces as they rapidly exchanged words.

Lady Fanny carried a bucket of water toward the far corner, where an assortment of uprooted plants and seedling trees lay on the ground. There, Whitley supervised the twinnies, who—joyously, it was quite clear—were using their hands to heap dirt into a jumble of clay pots. All three were singing!

The housekeeper's astonishment grew as she at last spied Parkins. The butler was also in shirtsleeves. *Parkins—in shirtsleeves!* He stood in the middle of the walled enclosure holding a basket. Focused on the upper branches of the only live tree in the garden, an old pear, Parkins was grinning!

Barely recovering from the shock of it—she'd never seen the old man smile, let alone grin, not in all the years she'd been here—she followed the upward direction of his gaze. And gaped.

Had the world gone mad? There, sitting in the pear tree, was Miss Holly—with little Charlotte! The houseguest-*cum*-governess was dressed in what looked like Lord Harry's old breeches and a shirt Hastings had thought relegated to the dustbin. There was a smudge of dirt on her chin, another on her nose. She was swinging her legs and laughing at something the young earl said, though Hastings missed what it was (she wasn't certain she comprehended her own name, let alone the King's English at this point).

Lady Charlotte swung her short little legs in an exact imitation of her governess. She was similarly attired as well, in something one of the twins had outgrown. She laughed with Miss Holly, who was busily pruning away at the dead branches. The governess handed the cuttings to the child who, grinning back at Parkins, pitched them into the basket.

Suddenly Holly looked up and saw the housekeeper. "Why, Mrs. Hastings! Have you come to join us?"

"Join . . . join you?"

"It's a botany lesson, Mrs. Hastings!" Harry exclaimed.

"And wonderful physical exercise!" Fanny called from her corner.

"And ever so much fun!" piped Charlotte from the tree.

"Fun!" shouted little Nicky, waving his muddy hands. "Make gawden gwow again!"

"But first, we took a nature walk . . ." said one of the twins, indicating the fields beyond the wall with his spade.

"Learning the names of all the plants we gathered," his brother finished with a nod.

"In Watin!" cried little Judith.

"Harry supplied the Latin," Fanny added as she sloshed water over a seedling—and her slippers. "But Princess Holly suddenly found she could remember things! Like their English names! Isn't that famous?"

"Famous . . ." Hastings muttered, still in a daze. She'd seen the nursery lot in disarray before. All of them had, the staff who'd been here from the days their parents had begun haring off to London at every opportunity. Leaving them in the dubious care of that dour governess who, for all her strictness, hadn't seemed able to do much with them.

Yet they'd never seemed this wild. They looked like ragamuffins! She'd seen beggars in Saint Giles's look tidier. But as she got her bearings and took in the scene more closely, as she let their words sink in, she realized there was a certain order to this madness.

The children might be dirty and ragged, but they were all working together toward a common purpose. A purpose with merit, as she understood the nature of what governesses were supposed to teach.

That had never happened before. The gossip belowstairs had often included descriptions of chaos in the schoolroom, but always with the sense of things gone out of control. Of quarrels, and children at odds with one another, as well as with the hatchet-faced governess.

But there was something else as well. As the realization dawned, Hastings began to understand the grin that cracked Parkins's face. Indeed, she felt like grinning herself. The children—all seven of them, and for the first time, ever —were unquestionably *happy!*

Nicholas and Rex Wickham parted at a crossroads a mile south of the village. The weather had at last turned spring-like, and they'd made good time from London. Nicholas had suggested Rex stop at the Hall for tea, or perhaps something more bracing, but Wickham was in a hurry to reach his bride. He declined the invitation, but promised to bring Diana for a visit before they returned to London.

Turning Lucifer's head toward Caerdruth, Nicholas pondered what he'd learned of his old friend's activities since they'd last seen each other, years before. It was certainly nothing to write Whitehall about.

Wickham had convinced his father to let him buy a commission, but just barely. The war had been going badly for the allies, and a fervor of patriotism was prompting all sorts of men, highborn and low, to do their bit for king and country. Rex was among them.

Wickham was an excellent sailor, as Nicholas knew from their youth; they'd enjoyed many a wild time in the young lord's skiff, and Rex had been in on some of his freebooting exploits. His friend had wanted to join the Royal Navy, but the countess, his mother, was fearful of his being lost at sea, leaving them without even a body to bury; the earl would hear none of it.

Rex had retaliated by haring off to London and leading the profligate life of a young buck on the town. When word of his gambling debts reached Cornwall, they'd compromised on an army commission. But Rex had had to promise to sell out at the first word he was needed at home. He told Nicholas he doubted he'd even have gained that, were it not that he had two younger brothers to carry on if he died in battle.

They'd touched on the war, but only that. No exchange of war stories in the way of old soldiers. The Peninsula had left Nicholas empty of delusions about honor and glory. War was a brutal, inhuman business, and there was no way he could bask in reminiscences in its aftermath. Rex Wickham's eyes had said he felt the same.

So when it came to assigning a possible motive to this particular suspect, Nicholas could honestly say he hadn't found any. There was no evidence of a disgruntled officer who might sell out his country to even some score, that sort of thing. Not yet, at any rate. That could change, but Nicholas truly hoped it wouldn't.

He liked Rex Wickham, and not just because in his youth Rex had stood against the opinion of the majority, that the Earl's Bastard was not fit company. Although that had mattered more than Nicholas liked to recall, to a young man trying to find passage into manhood in the face of being made a pariah.

But Wickham shared a history with him, as he'd allowed no one to do since. Nicholas was by now comfortable in the niche he'd carved for himself—though initially he'd been thrust into it. He was a loner, and there was a certain comfort in that. He could do largely as he pleased, and owed no man an explanation.

The army, of course, had required explanations, not to mention adherence to rules, but he'd chosen that way of life; he'd known he could leave it if he wished. At least he'd had no family hovering over him, demanding he put familial duty first. His sire couldn't stand the sight of him and had jumped at the chance to advance him the money for the commission, just to have him off his hands.

Nicholas smiled bitterly, recalling the day he'd left. His father had taken great pleasure in reminding him the advance was not a gift, telling him he was obligated to pay it back . . . "if some frog doesn't put a hole in your useless hide first."

The smile deepened, underscored by its bitter edge. He recalled the day he'd ridden back to Caerdruth with the winnings from a high-stakes card game in his pockets. The day he'd flung his repayment in the son of a bitch's face. No, he'd wanted no obligations, especially those of his so-called family.

Suddenly the smile changed, became self-mocking. Fine words from a man who'd just taken on seven children! "Ah, Aubrey, I won't know myself before your ghost is done with me!" Nicholas laughed then, and the laughter was mocking too.

Lucifer's ears flattened at the sound. The black didn't like it, and perhaps, thought Nicholas, he didn't either. He shifted his weight in the saddle, and with a slight pressure from his knees, the stallion picked up his pace. Soon they were racing neck or nothing for Caerdruth. And as the black's hooves tore up the turf and flung it in their wake, Nicholas wondered if he was running from himself.

Holly brushed remnants of tree bark from her hands and clothing, humming to herself. Beside her, Charlotte was doing the same. It was some wordless tune, but she knew she had to have learned it somewhere. *Somewhere in my past life . . .*

"Lottie," she asked, "do you know what it is we're humming? The name of the song?"

She hadn't known the name of a lullabye the child had shyly asked for last night, either. But when Charlotte had begun humming a few bars of something she'd heard Nurse singing the twinnies, Holly had picked up the melody at once.

"We know that one!" exclaimed Martin, and his brother nodded. "It's 'The World Turned Upside Down.' Soldiers sing it when they march on parade."

Lullabyes and army songs. What did that tell her about who she was? Had her mother or a nurse sung the one to her . . . a father or brother, the other, as he went off to war? A lover, perhaps?

She felt heat rising to her cheeks with the word. *Lover . . . Been reading too many novels, my girl.*

But even with the admonition, an image of Nicholas flooded her mind, and she blushed harder. Where was he now? Riding in Hyde Park with some lucky miss he'd favored among the dozens who flocked around him? Arranging to attend the theater with some high-flyer on his arm?

God above, why is he so much in my mind? My dreams? Even when he's nowhere near, he has me acting the lovesick schoolgirl! And I don't have a life! I'm not free to fall in lo—

Dear God, had she really begun to consider such a thing? That she might actually be falling in love with a man like Nicholas Sharpe? A man with, by his own admission, a wicked past? With more dark shadows hovering about him than Byron's Childe Harold?

One of the twinnies called to her, startling Holly out of the troubling reverie. Burying the ache she finally had to admit to, the ache of missing Nicholas with a telling yearning, Holly ran to see what Judith wanted.

Nicholas left Lucifer at the stables, deciding to walk up the side path past the garden instead of entering the Hall by the front door. He somehow wasn't ready to meet head-on, whatever awaited him inside.

Not that he anticipated a welcome-home. He'd never in his life been shown a welcome at Caerdruth, and he wasn't about to look for one now. Quite the opposite, in fact. He craved solitude before facing all those newly acquired obligations. His mission for Whitehall had preempted his plans to cut loose in London, and now he needed some space about him, time to regroup.

A bath . . . and perhaps a glass of brandy sounded a good idea, and if he slipped in unnoticed through the side entrance . . .

A trill of feminine laughter from beyond the garden wall had him stopping in his tracks. Holly.

He hadn't thought of her at all since leaving the solicitor's office, and he wondered why. She'd been part of the reason he'd gone to London, and a better part of his reason for returning so soon. But he'd resolved to dismiss her from his life as fast as possible, hadn't he?

Why, then, was he standing here with the sound of her laughter wrapping around him like a song, feeling suddenly glad to be back? Why were notions of a brandy in solitude no longer appealing, replaced by an urge to follow that sound? To run his gaze over that impossibly lovely face, and smile into tip-tilted eyes as green as leaves in the shade?

The garden gate creaked on its hinges, and Nicholas looked up to find his imaginings become flesh. *Holly . . . Christ, what was she wearing?* Breeches? And those smudges on her face—she looked like a waif from the streets . . . a lovely . . . adorable . . .

He saw her lips form his name in a soundless whisper, yet she didn't move.

Their eyes met, held. The sound of children's voices beyond the wall faded from ken. It was as if they were the only two people in the world.

A smile tugged the corners of his mouth upward, and without a thought to what he was doing, Nicholas held out his arms.

It was enough for Holly. More than enough. With a small cry, she closed the distance between them, and flung herself into his arms. They wrapped around her like a warm benediction, and then he was kissing her with a fierceness that matched the thrumming of her pulse. *Nicholas . . . oh, God—Nicholas!*

Nicholas's mind refused to analyze what he was doing. It was enough to let the reality that was Holly fill him. He savored her sweet, welcoming warmth. His senses reeled with the scent and feel of her. Awareness centered on the soft, pliant lips that opened beneath his, the well-remembered taste of her going to his head like a fine wine. It was madness, and he didn't care. Holly . . . sweet, vibrant, and willing in his arms. Ah, he could hold her, kiss her like this forev—

"I'm sure she was right out here, Lottie. She—*oh!*" Fanny's eyes widened. The adults jumped apart as if they'd been scorched. And perhaps they had. Princess Holly's cheeks burned with two bright flags of scarlet, and Uncle's gaze radiated a heat she'd never seen in them before.

Nicholas was the first to recover. Watching six more children troop out of the garden, each shouting his name, he started to laugh. At first it was merely a rumble, deep in his chest, but it soon had him clutching Holly's shoulder and shaking with mirth.

"Sweet God Almighty," he gasped when he could finally manage speech, "so this is what a welcome feels like!"

What Fanny had witnessed outside the garden was known throughout the Hall, and Holly knew it. Although no one said a word to her, of course. But her charges eyed her with a naked, telltale curiosity, and Harry had blushed furiously the one time they'd spoken.

She wondered if they regarded Nicholas in the same way, but she hadn't seen him since they'd parted at the garden gate yesterday afternoon. Perhaps he was deliberately keeping out of sight, and if she had any sense, she'd have done the same.

Little chance of that though, what with her duties toward the children. Besides, she loved working with them, and had begun to feel she was having a positive influence on them. Lottie in particular had begun to blossom, and she wouldn't disappoint the child for anything.

Not that it was easy. The servants too—at least the lower staff—threw smiling, speculative glances her way when they thought she wasn't looking. And her abigail! The silly chit had taken to singing folk songs about "my own true love," and the like while she dressed her hair! Holly wanted to sink into the ground.

So it came as no surprise when Maud had run her eyes over Holly assessingly at breakfast this morning. Or when she'd invited her to her chambers for afternoon tea. Holly knew the household gossip was behind it. She'd never been asked to Maud's private chambers before, and tea wasn't called "scandal broth" for nothing! She feared an embarrassing lecture from the old woman.

Teatime arrived, and Holly dragged herself to Maud's quarters. Mary had given her directions, and a good thing; the rooms were tucked away to the rear of the west wing, and she'd never have found them by herself.

Despite her unease, Holly smiled when Maud led her inside. All the furnishings of the Hall belonged to an earlier time, but Maud's were from the more recent past, with graceful, curving lines and a delicate balance to everything.

"Why, Aunt Maud," she said, "how lovely!"

"Like it, do you? Knew you would. Queen Anne's period . . . seems to suit you. Brought it all with me from my old home. It suited me too when I was a young thing like you."

They were in a small sitting room where graceful furniture with cabriole legs and padded feet stood on an Aubusson rug done in soft pastels. Yellow velvet draperies lined the windows, faded perhaps, but not impossibly so. And the walls were covered in a blue and cream fabric that showed no wear whatsoever.

Maud led her to a small settee upholstered in yellow and blue striped satin. Before it stood a tea table of the period, laden with a silver service. And delicate porcelain with blue and yellow flowers. The name, Sevres, popped into Holly's head.

They made small talk, remarking on the fine weather while the old woman poured. After they'd taken their first sips, Maud eyed Holly silently for a moment, then set down her cup.

"I'm going to tell you a story, my dear, and before I'm half into it, you'll no doubt know why. Although I suspect you've an inkling of some of the reason already."

Holly wanted to grimace, but a kindly twinkle in the old woman's eyes stopped her. There was nothing censorious in Maud's manner. She gave a small, grateful smile.

"This is a bit of ancient history," said Maud, "family history. I thought I'd put it behind me forever, so bear with me if I seem to have misplaced parts of it.

"At any rate," she went on, "it concerns someone we both care about, and I've begun to think there are things about him you should know."

"Nicholas," Holly said barely above a whisper.

"Yes . . . Nicholas. But before I come to him directly, I need to tell you about his . . . parents.

"The old earl, Nick's father," she continued, "was a hard, embittered man. He hadn't always been that way, although I collect sensing a selfish streak in him from the beginning. Perhaps it would have shaped him into the cruel, uncaring person he became, no matter what. But that is only speculation, and of no account.

"What is of account, however, is what happened to him around the time Nick was born. The worst of it sprang from that, and that was bad enough."

Maud took another sip of tea, and Holly had to force herself to wait. Nicholas's story, from the beginning. She was half frightened of learning it, yet knew she had to hear every word.

"Well," said Maud, "I'd best begin even before that—with Nick's mother. Her name was Catherine, and Nick resembles her. She was more beautiful than my poor words can describe. Perhaps if you put a feminine aspect and form to Nick's, you'd have an idea. A beauty, yes—but wild."

The old woman smiled ruefully. "I suppose Nick takes after her there too, but in his case there are reasons. With Catherine . . ." She shrugged. "Who knows where it came from? She certainly didn't suffer any of Nick's abuses growing up. Why, her parents doted on her! I collect—well, never mind. Where was I?"

"You were speaking of . . . the woman's wildness." Holly longed to ask about the abuses, but she didn't. Maud was being inordinately lucid—for Maud—and she wanted to keep her on track. *But abuses . . . to a child! Dear God! Can I bear to hear it? Can I bear not to?*

"Ah, yes. The gel was wild, all right. Nothing could hold her. She had everything . . . lovely home . . . clothes, jewels . . . a Season with all the trimmings—but it meant nothing to her. Didn't give a fig about it.

"She loved to ride, though nothing so tame as a sedate mare with a sidesaddle. Oh, no. It was bareback, on the wildest horse in her father's stables. She'd race it over the moors, y'know, and along the water's edge. 'Twas where she met Branwell Sharpe . . . Nick's father."

Holly realized the old woman knew them all by name, not just their titles. She wondered how Maud knew them, what her own relationship to these people had been. But she didn't ask. She felt it might be too forward—these were personal reminiscences, after all. If Maud wanted her to know, she'd tell her.

"Bran was already earl, and more than a dozen years older than Catherine, who was only seventeen at the time. He fell madly in love on the spot, and knew there'd never be another woman for him"—she looked up from her tea, meeting Holly's eyes—"a potentially dangerous trait which tends to run in this family, my dear.

"Suffice it to say he offered for her at once, but Catherine refused. Wanted her freedom, she said. But she didn't refuse his bed. And less than a year later, Nick was born.

"When he learned she was breeding, the earl was at first overjoyed, thinking she'd have to wed him now. But as the months passed, he began to realize Catherine was a free spirit who wouldn't be bound by society's rules, and he was right. Less than a week after Nick's birth, she ran off with a band of passing gypsies—"

"Never say—"

"And was never heard from again."

"Dear God!"

"Indeed, you may invoke God's name. We all did, but to no avail. Catherine was gone for good, leaving behind, not only the man who loved her more than she deserved, but the bastard son she'd borne him.

"The earl never forgave her. Neither did he forgive the

son who reminded him of her . . . nor the woman he never loved, but whom he later married instead. No, nor even her son—Aubrey, his legitimate heir."

Holly could only shake her head. To leave one's child, newly birthed, and needing his mother . . . it was unthinkable!

But Maud was far from finished. "Then came the terrible years. Branwell began to drink heavily, but that was a symptom, not a cause. As I said, I suspected a selfishness in him, and it certainly came to the fore. He was a brutal man . . . cruel, especially to his wife and sons.

"But he seemed to have a special affinity for taking his bitterness out on Nick. Canings became a routine part of the child's existence, I'm afraid, and none of us could stop it. We did what we could, but—oh, dear! I see I've made you cry, and I'd no wish to do that! Oh, Holly, my dear . . ."

Fussing about for something to dry Holly's eyes, Maud finally seized a damask serviette from the tea tray, handed it to her.

"Th-thank you, m'lady," Holly murmured. "I—I didn't mean to react so emotionally. You must think me the worst sort of—"

"Nonsense, gel! If anything, I think all the better of you for it. Should have realized anyone with a heart would weep buckets to hear it. Collect I wept buckets myself in those years."

Nodding sadly, Holly handed back the serviette.

"Well, I have rattled on," said Maud, "and there was more, but perhaps I shouldn't trouble you with it just—"

"Oh, please do! I—I mean I'm quite up to hearing the rest, really I am!" It was her first true insight into what had made Nicholas what he was, and if there was more, she had to hear it. *Had* to!

Maud nodded, poured them some more tea. And finally she told Holly about Nick and Aubrey. And Judith.

ಲಿ Fifteen ಲಿ

Holly stopped and peered into a hallway mirror for one last inspection before moving on to the library. Nicholas had sent word he wished to speak with her, and she couldn't help wanting to look her best . . .

For him, she added, silently addressing her image in the glass. *Own up, my girl. You're hopelessly drawn to the man, for all your levelheaded admonishments! You make not a move without considering him. Without wondering if he'll find you interesting . . . or clever . . . or pretty . . .*

Would he find her pretty this morning? she questioned, vexed with herself even as she did it. Mrs. Hastings had engaged a seamstress in the village to make up a couple of frocks for her; this one, an apple green morning gown, accentuated her eyes, which she decided were her best feature. The matching ribbon Mary had threaded through the pile of curls at the crown of her head wasn't unattractive either.

At least, she thought as she pinched her cheeks to give them some color, she hadn't had to trot out the yellow muslin again. She suspected Nicholas had a low tolerance for a deal of things, boredom first among them, and she was bored to tears with the yellow herself.

Aware she was delaying their meeting out of nervousness —it would be their first since that scene by the garden—

Holly told herself Nicholas likely had no tolerance for being kept waiting as well. She hurried on.

Reaching the library door, she realized her palms were sweating, and resisted the urge to dry them on her frock before she knocked.

Nicholas opened the door himself, and for a long moment simply stood there, looking at her. The seconds passed, and Holly felt absolutely tongue-tied. His sheer male beauty was almost too much to take in. And why didn't he say something? Was the apple green wrong for her after all? Was she too thin for the gown? Perhaps her hair wasn't—

"No matter how well I think I remember," he said abruptly, solemn gray eyes still moving over her face, "each time I see you, it is to find myself overwhelmed by how utterly beautiful you are . . . come in, Holly."

She hoped he couldn't hear the thudding of her heart as she followed him into the room. *Beautiful*. He'd said she was beautiful! And not while in the throes of passion, which could be misleading according to the romantic novels she'd been reading. He'd said it in the ordinary light of day, right here in the library!

Ignoring a tiny voice that called her a fool for attaching such importance to it, Holly fairly floated to the chair he indicated by the fireplace. Yet the voice nagged again as she sat, reminding her of his vast experience with women, of how that would have schooled him in meaningless flattery.

But then Nicholas smiled at her as he took the chair opposite, and the voice was lost in the singing of blood in her veins.

"Both Parkins and Hastings have told me what you've been doing with the children," said Nicholas. "And Harry and the twins made a point of showing me the results of the, ah, botany lesson themselves. My congratulations. It seems you've a natural talent for dealing with children."

He didn't add that he'd expected her to fall flat on her face. That he'd set her up to fail, and she'd turned the tables on him. He didn't have to. The glint of amusement in his eyes proclaimed a self-mockery she was beginning to recognize.

And understand. Maud's recounting of his history had opened her eyes to much that had puzzled her about Nicholas. She could see how a child who'd been shunned by his own parents might develop a sardonic edge to arm himself against the pitfalls life held.

"I . . . am gratified to learn you think so," Holly said. "But perhaps all it wanted was someone who *cared* about the children. That, and taking the time to ask, 'What would I wish for, if I were in their place?' Simple things, really."

"Indeed. So simple that most individuals who call themselves teachers—or parents—fail to recognize them. Or choose not to."

The sardonic edge was back, and Holly could well surmise its cause. *His* parents had certainly chosen not to!

Nicholas leaned casually back in his chair, stretching out his long legs and crossing them at the ankles. He grinned, the amusement in his eyes suddenly glinting with devilry. "Have the little beggars been tweaking your sensibilities over Fanny's discovery by the garden?"

She felt her cheeks catch fire. The man was a master at throwing her off balance! Quickly dropping her gaze, she brushed an imaginary piece of lint off her skirt, and heard him chuckle.

"I can see they have. Well, no matter. I've no doubt they're fond enough of you, not to think ill of you in any event. And now they've seen you and I are less than strangers, perhaps some of that affection they bear you will rub off on me."

Less than strangers. Was that what they were? Holly felt a stab of disappointment at the vague characterization, then grew annoyed with herself for it. *What did you expect him to say? That we're two people with a* tendre *for each other? Lovers? Don't be a goose!*

"I-I'm certain they're already quite fond of you," she replied, still not looking at him.

"Are you? I can't imagine why. I'm certainly not in the habit of causing people to like me."

Because you were raised with the expectation that they wouldn't? That even those who should have loved you couldn't bring themselves to do so? Feeling suddenly uncomfortable with the knowledge Maud had given her, certain he would be furious if he knew, Holly tried to put it out of her mind.

"Speaking of the children," she said, glancing at him as she started to rise, "they'll be expecting me in—"

"Stay a moment," said Nicholas, placing a hand on her forearm. "I still need to talk with you."

Her gown was short-sleeved, the touch of his fingers on her bare skin, warm . . . inviting, she thought as a frisson of helpless longing ran through her. "About"—she had to clear her throat—"about what?"

His hand returned to the arm of his chair, and Holly felt the loss of warmth like a flower suddenly denied the sun. *Better get ahold of yourself, my girl. He's had this effect on countless women!*

"About a meeting I had with my solicitor in London," he replied. "A discreet meeting in which I engaged him to do what he can to help us determine who you are. Don't look so surprised. I recollect asking Cartwright to inform you I was writing the solicitors to that effect weeks ago. He did tell you?"

"Oh, yes . . . yes, of course. It's just that you never mentioned, when you were leaving—"

"Nothing to mention. Hadn't heard from them at the time. It was one of the reasons I wanted to speak with them direct—"

"Have they learned anything? Has someone like me gone —gone missing?" She felt suddenly anxious; a film of perspiration had broken out on her brow, and she had to make a conscious effort to unclench her fists.

"Nothing whatsoever." Nicholas noted the tension, saw it drain out of her with his reply. He had an instant's recollection of the nightmare, of Holly screaming in terror, and wondered if he wasn't making a mistake in pursuing this for her. Well, as he'd told the solicitor, he'd let her decide.

He went on to tell her what he and Witherspoon had discussed, finishing with the question he hoped wouldn't distress her all over again. "How would you feel about coming to London with me? I've outlined the arguments for it, but I wouldn't blame you if you said no. It's entirely up to you, Holly."

She sat very still for a moment, giving him no clue as to what was in her mind. She didn't look tense, exactly, just . . . thoughtful.

"What about my duties here?" she said after a moment. "The children."

"Does that mean you're thinking you might go?"

"I'm considering it," she said, sounding more at ease than she felt. *London . . . where someone might know me . . . be able to give me a name . . . a past . . . perhaps tell me who it could have been that held me by the wrists and—No! Don't think about that! Think about London itself . . . about being there—with Nicholas.*

She seemed to be demonstrating a kind of quiet courage that Nicholas couldn't help admiring. He tried to imagine what it must feel like to be asked to face a blank wall that was your past. The possibility of unknown terrors lurking behind it. The knowledge that you'd been violated, and not knowing how, by whom—but that that someone might be lurking there too.

He couldn't. The nearest he could come to it was the war . . . Salamanca, and there, at least, he'd been able to see the enemy, fight him.

Yet when he'd put the question to her, Holly's first concern had been for the children. Hell! She was beginning to shape up altogether admirable. Too damned admirable by far!

"If the children are all that's holding you back," he said irritably, "disabuse yourself of that concern. You're not their actual governess, you know."

"Yes, but they've begun to—"

"Bloody hell! We'll take them with us, if you like! They wouldn't be the first to gain an education by what London has to offer." Had he said that? Had he really said that? He must be going soft in the head!

Holly was grinning at him. "Why, Nicholas! That's a splendid—"

"But not the twinnies!" he growled. "I'll take the older lot, and Maud should come of course, but those little imps from hell stay right here!"

Her grin was ear to ear. "Of course," she told him. "Whatever you say. When shall I start the packing?"

She was going. Nicholas felt a mixture of relief and something less familiar—regret—although he had no idea why. This was what he'd wanted, wasn't it? A positive step toward having her off his hands?

"Not for a day or two," he told her. "There's estate business I must see to, and—oh, by the by—we're having visitors this afternoon for tea."

"Visitors?" She'd had the sense that no one ever visited Caerdruth Hall.

He told her about Lord Wickham and his new wife. "Do you think you're up for it? Might be a good test, you know. To see if you're able to handle a social occasion such as you're likely to encounter in town."

"That sounds a good idea," she said, wondering if it was at all. But it might be interesting to meet someone Nicholas said was an old friend; she hadn't pictured him having any. He seemed too solitary, too much the loner.

As for herself, she was apprehensive, yes, but she had to take the plunge sometime. "I'll be ready," she told him. "This way we'll know straightaway, and if I'm not up to scratch, you can leave me behind when you return to London."

She flashed him a pert smile. "Um, with the children, of course!"

Nicholas laughed. "Just make sure that includes the twinnies!"

*   *   *

Holly tucked a coverlet around Charlotte, who'd again fallen asleep on Holly's bed as she'd read her a story. She smiled down at the child, tenderly brushing a stray curl off her forehead. She'd call on Parkins to carry her to the nursery, but not yet. For now, just watching the child sleep gave her the most peaceful feeling she could imagine, and she wanted to savor it. The prospect of meeting strangers for tea would destroy it soon enough.

Of all the children, Lottie seemed to need her the most. She pulled at her heartstrings with the little things she revealed by her innocent questions: Were Mama and Papa truly in heaven? Would Lottie see them there some day? Would Mama know her, even if she couldn't remember what Mama looked like?

But this afternoon the child had asked the most wrenching question of all: Would Holly please be able to stay with her, and not go off to heaven too? Dear God! Barely out of leading strings, and viewing as practically inevitable the loss of adults she counted on!

Holly knew something about loss. If nothing else, the amnesia had taught her that. She knew what it felt like not to be able to recall one's own mother. Bad enough for an adult, but Lottie was a four-year-old!

Assuring the child she had no intention of haring off to heaven, she'd told Lottie of the trip to London. "I made Uncle Nicholas promise"—it was bending the truth a little, but she wanted Lottie to feel secure—"to let you older children come along," she'd said. "So you see, there's no chance I'll go popping off without you."

And, oh, the dazzling smile that had produced! But best of all—and this had prompted tears in Holly's eyes—best of all, was Lottie's response. "Oh, Princess!" she'd exclaimed. "I love you!"

Holly rang for Mary to help her change into a new afternoon gown of bottle green sarcenet. There was another matching ribbon for her hair, and the abigail declared she must wear green whenever she could, as it made her look "jest lovely."

Sending the maid to fetch Parkins, Holly had a final look-in on Lottie, took a deep breath, and headed downstairs. Because their guests could encounter one of the children, and given that children talk, she and Nicholas had agreed to apprise Lord and Lady Wickham of the bare essentials of how Holly came to be at the Hall.

They would learn of her arrival in the storm, that she had amnesia, but that was all, Nicholas had said. He hadn't had to add there was no need for them to know of the assault to her person. He hadn't had to; it was there between them, as it was here with her now: Would they see? Be able to tell she was impure? Ruined?

These fears and worse running through her mind, she approached the drawing room, its double doors partially ajar. She almost turned back. But the sound of men's laughter and a woman's upper-class accent reminded her that she'd given Nicholas her word; she couldn't embarrass him by taking French leave before she'd even arrived!

But she needed to calm down. They were only guests for tea! *But a titled lord and lady,* said that nasty little voice she was beginning to hate. *Ninnyhammer!* she answered. *That doesn't mean they bite!*

But perhaps if she just stood here outside the doors, and grew accustomed to their voices for a moment . . .

Nicholas glanced at the mantel clock, noting it was ten past four. It wasn't like Holly to be late, but he shouldn't blame her if she—

"Nicholas, don't you agree?" Diana Wickham's voice bubbled with laughter. "With Boney being bundled off to this Elba, why shouldn't we all hare off to Paris, and meet him before he goes? I hear he's been throwing the most lavish parties for all sorts of Englishmen at the Tuileries!"

"Ha!" exclaimed her bridegroom. "This from the same woman who, just a few short months ago, was ranting on about 'that impious monster, Bonaparte!' "

Diana affected a pout, but her expressive brown eyes glinted with humor as she turned to her husband. "Nonsense," she sniffed. "I *never* rant."

"Liar," Rex replied, tapping her playfully on the nose. "I suppose you never pout, either."

"Never," said his wife with a chuckle, "unless I've been served pilchards. I detest pilchards!"

"Devil take it!" exclaimed Nicholas, snapping his fingers as if he'd just recalled something. "I'd best ring for Parkins at once. He's bound to trot out some of the smelly little things on the tea tray."

"Never say so!" Diana's eyes widened as she gazed up into Nicholas's face. She'd been flirting with him since the moment they'd arrived, but her husband's composure said it was harmless.

"Ah, but I do," said Nicholas, flirting back. A past-master at the game, he did it with just the right amount of insouciance; it let Rex know it was harmless on his part too.

Not that Diana Wickham wasn't a fetching baggage. She had the same outrageous red hair he recalled from her childhood; and a generous sprinkling of freckles across her nose called attention to a pretty gamine face. But she was Wickham's, and he had no taste for cuckolding a man he liked and respected.

"Pilchards and tea at Caerdruth," he went on in the same teasing banter, "are as inseparable in the imagination as Brummell and his valet. Indeed, as Prinny and Brighton!"

"Or Prinny and his corset!" added Rex with an irreverent laugh.

"Which he's taken to lacing even tighter since Brummell's insult!" Diana said with a giggle.

The final break between the Prince-Regent and his old friend had come after an argument, when Prinny had given Brummell the Cut-direct; in retaliation, Brummell had remarked loud enough for Prinny to hear, "Alvanley, who's your fat friend?"

"Time was, it was women who stuffed themselves into whalebone and lacings." Wickham, who was as muscular and fit as Nicholas, grimaced with distaste. "Now, God help us, it's the men! Nick, old boy, has the world gone mad, d'ye think?"

But Nicholas wasn't listening. A flicker of movement beyond the doors had caught his eye. "Ah," he said, striding toward them, "I believe our Miss Holly has arrived for tea."

Well, there was no help for it now, thought Holly as she pasted a smile on her face and allowed Nicholas to all but pull her inside.

"Courage, lass," Nicholas murmured only loud enough for her to hear as he led her forth on his arm. "Lady Wickham . . . m'lord," he announced as the earl and his bride turned toward them, "I should like to introduce our guest. This is—"

"Good God!" Diana exclaimed. "It's Helene Tamarand! We'd heard you were drowned at sea!"

৯ Sixteen ৩

Holly's head throbbed. Speechless, she stared at Lady Wickham. A buzzing began in her ears, compounded by three voices speaking all at once:

"*Tamarand* . . ." Nicholas repeated.

"My God, Diana, are you certain?" asked Rex.

"We attended a memorial service for you not a fortnight ago!" the countess exclaimed, looking at Holly as if she'd seen a ghost.

"Here, Holly . . ." Nicholas began—her name refused to translate into the alien Helene—"perhaps you'd better sit down." He took her hand, began to lead her toward one of the settees flanking the fireplace. The hand was ice-cold.

Parkins appeared at the doorway with the tea tray, and Nicholas glanced at him. "Some vinaigrette, man—and hartshorn, if you have it!"

"I-I'll be all right," Holly murmured, but she didn't believe it herself; her head felt squeezed in an anvil.

"Rot." Nicholas ran his eyes over her face. "You're white as a ghost!"

Diana murmured something else about ghosts while Parkins disappeared down the hallway. Holly's hands flew up and pressed her temples as Nicholas started to seat her.

"Hang it!" he exclaimed, and swept her up in his arms. He turned toward the doorway, ignoring her protests. On his way across the room, he darted a look over his shoulder at the Wickhams. "Stay there, you two. I'm taking her up-stairs, but once she's settled—by God, we have to talk!"

Nicholas carried Holly up the stairs, remembering an-other time he'd done this. The night of the storm came back to him with wrenching clarity, and he stared down at her. Her eyes were squeezed shut, and he could feel the tension in her body. Diana's words had obviously shocked her. They'd all been unnerved by the revelation. Something else had jolted him as well, but he couldn't dwell on it now.

His immediate concern was Holly. He suspected some-thing more than simple shock. He was no physician, but he'd warrant this wasn't an ordinary headache. The way it had come on—the instant Diana's words were out—sug-gested its cause lay in the secrets buried in her mind.

It was as if a battle were being waged there. A battle between her body's natural inclination to heal itself—in this case, to restore her memory—and a force just as powerful: the instinct for self-preservation.

Entering her chamber, he laid her gently on the high tester bed. She was trembling, and he pulled the counter-pane up around her. He remembered doing that before too.

Holly opened her eyes, and he could see the pain in them as she started to say something. He placed his thumb gently against her lips. "Shh, sweetheart . . . don't try to talk. It'll likely make the pain worse. I've sent for—"

The inner door opened, and her abigail rushed into the room. Nicholas put his finger to his lips, then motioned her forward.

"Miss Holly has the headache," he told the girl in a soft voice. "Stay with her, and make her as comfortable as you can. I'll see what's keeping—ah, Parkins."

The butler entered, followed by Hastings with a tray of vials and powders, a pot of tea. Nicholas instructed them to tend to Holly, adding that perhaps a footman ought to be sent for the physician.

The butler nodded, and after giving Holly's hand a squeeze, Nicholas headed back to the drawing room. As he strode downstairs, he allowed himself to think about the second shock he'd received with Diana's news: a Lord Tamarand was another suspect on Castlereagh's list!

The Wickhams rose from the settee as he entered, their faces a study in concern. "How is she?" both asked at once.

Nicholas told them, bidding them to be reseated. Glancing at the untouched tea tray, he suggested they all take something stronger; they concurred, and he poured Diana a sherry, brandy for Rex and himself.

"Now," he said as he settled on the settee across from them, "tell me about Helene Tamarand."

Rex said he'd only seen the girl at a distance, had never been introduced to her, although he'd attended the memorial service with his wife. It was left to Diana to fill Nicholas in.

"Well, to begin," she said, "it's *Lady* Helene Tamarand. She's the only child—and the very high-water heiress, I might add—of Lord Basil Tamarand, the marquis of Lansdowne."

Nicholas's brow knotted at this, yet he didn't interrupt. Diana continued with as much as she knew.

Lansdowne lost his wife three years before, just as Helene had begun her initial Season at the age of seventeen. At the time many among the *ton* thought it an especial pity, since Helene Tamarand had already become a toast: the most celebrated debutante in years. Her mother's death, and the period of mourning that followed, ended her brief reign as *the* belle of the Season.

Then, only a year later, Lord Tamarand remarried. The *ton* was rife with gossip over it; his bride, Lady Angela Phipps, was the same age as his daughter; indeed, she'd come out the same time as Helene. It was widely supposed the marquis hoped Angela would provide him with the male heir his first wife hadn't been able to give him; but so far, the couple remained childless.

Lady Helene, however, had remained immune to gossip. The high-sticklers approved of her circumspect behavior: she stayed in black gloves for two years; she was never heard to say an unkind word about her father's remarrying; and she treated her young stepmother as a dear friend.

Nicholas nodded from time to time through all of this; but at Diana's next piece of information, he seemed to freeze, then reached for his brandy: After her period of mourning was over, Helene became engaged to wed an Ango-Irish peer—Lord Trevor Regis.

They'd all heard, Diana went on, that Helene was on her way to the North of Ireland, to meet his family; that a storm overtook her ship on the Irish Sea, and Helene was swept overboard. Devastated, her fiancé and stepmother, who'd accompanied her on this voyage, had ordered the ship back to England.

". . . was when the marquis arranged for the memorial service we attended in Saint Paul's a week later." Diana finished the account, shifting her gaze to the double doors through which Holly had disappeared. "My God—Helene Tamarand . . ."

Nicholas's eyes swept from his empty brandy glass to the decanter. He looked as if he'd like to down the whole thing. *Lost at sea . . .* How did that explain—

"What do you intend to do now?" Rex's voice pulled him back to the moment.

"Now? Nothing beyond waiting to see how this news has affected her. I've sent for the physician, but for all I know, by the time he arrives, she may have recalled everything." *Everything? Christ! What if—*

"Well, I should think that would put it all to rights," said Diana. "She'd be able to get on with her life, not to mention clear up the mystery of how she came to be here in Cornwall . . . everything!"

That word again, thought Nicholas. And what if everything were to be more than she could bear?

Rex was skeptical. "She didn't look on the verge of remembering to me, poor girl. I should think she'd have shown some recognition of you if she were, Diana. I collect your saying the two of you were rather friendly."

Reminding himself he had a mission to accomplish,

Nicholas sifted this information in his mind. Did Diana's friendship with the daughter admit a link between her husband and Tamarand? Was it possible their traitor wasn't *one* of the three suspects, but a combination of two of them? Or even—

"Well, what if she doesn't remember?" Diana asked. "What then, Nick?"

Nicholas sighed, plowing a hand through his hair. "It will be up to her, of course—and to the doctor after he examines her—but I should think her family must be informed." *And if her father's the man we're after? He'd be potentially dangerous. Do you want her thrust in the midst of—Christ! What if she's already mixed up in this somehow? What if—*

He reached abruptly for the brandy decanter, pouring himself another drink. Diana and Rex still hadn't finished theirs.

After taking a hefty swallow, he explained to them the plans that were in place before their arrival. Omitting any reference to Holly's assault, he emphasized the need for discretion should she still decide to go to London. There was enough in her dilemma to start tongues wagging even without that information. The Wickhams would have to see that.

"But of course we'll be discreet," said Diana. "In fact, until you say otherwise, we shan't mention her at all. Isn't that right, darling?"

"That's my girl," said Rex, giving her hand a squeeze. "You can trust us," he told Nicholas, and after a barely perceptible hesitation, Nicholas nodded.

They finished their drinks, the earl and countess promising whatever help was wanted in addition to their discretion. Diana enjoyed a certain popularity amid the *ton,* and thought she might be of use in easing Helene back into society, should she require it.

Nicholas thanked them, and was seeing them out when Parkins came down the stairs. The butler informed him Miss Holly was resting, although the headache remained.

But Cartwright's gig had been spotted from an upstairs window; he'd arrive in a few minutes.

As the Braithwaite carriage was brought round, Nicholas knew he had to ask one more question. "What of this Regis . . . Holl—the lady's fiancé? How's he been taking her death—and how do you expect he'll take the news of—"

"Regis?" Diana looked amused. "Oh, not grieving all that much, I assure you! The latest *on-dit* has it, he's been having a dalliance with a married woman. The gossipmongers hadn't ferreted out her name, though, last I heard."

She chuckled. "Yet I daresay he'll be glad enough to learn Helene's still among the living. Heiresses that plump in the pocket are not all so easy to come by! And Regis, they say, is in need of a fortune."

Their carriage pulled up at that moment, and Nicholas promised to be in touch as they took off down the drive. Only after they'd gone did he ponder the odd little twinge he'd experienced at Diana's words. It felt curiously like pain.

Cartwright came, and left a scarce half hour later. His patient was still unable to recall anything; but he'd administered a powder mixed in some willow bark tea his wife had sent along; the headache, he told Nicholas, was on the wane.

As Nicholas saw him to his tilbury, the doctor also told him she might begin remembering again at any time; but an effort was to be made to keep her from the kind of shock she'd had that afternoon.

"And how the devil am I to do that?" Nicholas shot back. "I'd no idea what Lady Wickham was about to impart! Neither had she or her husband. We were all bloody well shocked together! Besides," he added, "didn't you say Holl —the lady's still talking of going to London?"

"Dead set on it, I'd say," replied the physician. "Seemed especially determined the children should accompany her for some reason."

Nicholas snorted. He might have guessed! "Didn't you

point out to her that London wouldn't do her or the children any good if she spent it in sickbed—or worse?"

The doctor sighed. The Bastard was a deal more worked up about his patient these days. Far more than he'd been when Cartwright had first seen her. He didn't know whether that was good or bad. But Mrs. Cartwright was waiting a good roast mutton dinner for him, and it had been a long day.

"Major Sharpe," he said as patiently as he could, "it has been my experience that if a patient craves something, unless he is an addict—let him have it. In that way I've learned a great thirst usually means dehydration; great hunger, a need for nourishment. Occasionally it's tossed up in a basin, but not often.

"To that end," he concluded, "I shall say this: Miss—that is, her ladyship—wishes you to take her to London. In a word, Major—*go!*"

By the time Nicholas went upstairs to check, Holly was asleep. The abigail sat in a chair by the window, and when she started to rise, he motioned for her to remain. He walked to the bed, gazed down at the slender figure who struck him as small and vulnerable against the vast expanse of sheets.

His next impression was how young and innocent she looked. The new green dress he'd barely had time to appreciate on her had been exchanged for a lacy white sleeping gown; what he could see of it was buttoned nearly to the chin. Someone had taken down her hair, perhaps brushed it, and it lay spread out on the pillow like a young girl's.

Well, she was only twenty, according to Diana. Young enough, although many women were married and had borne children at that age. As for innocence . . .

He smiled wryly to himself. He knew her for the innocent she was. She had an innocence of heart and mind, despite what their culture would make of what had been done to her body.

And in that moment Nicholas knew he would move

heaven and earth—yes, and hell too, if it came to it—to protect that innocence.

Glancing up, he caught the abigail staring hungrily at the leavings on the tea tray. It was past the supper hour, and the wench had likely missed hers. He dismissed her, saying he'd keep an ear open from across the hall. She was to inform Hastings m'lady was in good hands; as an afterthought he added she was to tell the housekeeper he'd see to his own supper as well.

He watched the girl leave, and was about to follow her out when a soft moan from the bed stopped him. Holly was no longer sleeping peacefully. Her face was strained, and she moved her head restlessly from side to side.

Nicholas went to the door, shut it, then made for the chair the maid had vacated. Angling it to afford him the best view of the bed, he made himself comfortable. He'd no idea what idiocy had driven him to it, but he'd told himself he meant to protect her, and that watch began now.

It was dark in the room when Nicholas awoke from one of several catnaps he'd allowed himself. He identified the sobs coming from the bed at once, and jackknifed out of the chair. He was beside the bed in an instant.

"Holly . . . Holly, wake up." He kept his voice low. He'd no wish to frighten her more than she already sounded: The sobs had given way to terrified little whimpers.

He was about to join her on the bed as he'd done that other time, then decided some light might help when she awoke. Moving quickly, he located the tinderbox he'd seen on the mantel. Holly's whimpers were growing louder, frantic. He lit a lamp he'd spied which still contained some oil, carried it quickly to the bed stand.

"Holly,"—he doubted he'd ever call her Helene—"it's Nicholas." He climbed on the bed as the whimpers dissolved into a moan of agony. "You're having another nightmare, and you—oh, God, sweetheart—don't!"

The moan had given way to wracking sobs, and Nicholas

pulled her into his arms, careful to avoid any jarring movement. "Holly . . . ah, Holly, you *must* wake up." In a soothing voice, he murmured this against her hair, her face, both wet with tears. "It's Nicholas, Holly, and I promise—"

There was a gasp of recognition, and Nicholas felt her arms tighten abruptly around his waist. *Awake, thank God.*

"Nicholas . . . ?" Holly's voice was still thick with tears, his name almost lost as she pressed her face into his shirt.

"Unless you know someone else insane enough to climb into your bed while you're under this roof," Nicholas said dryly.

He tried to keep his voice light, but it wasn't easy. The old fury at whoever had done this to her welled up inside him like lava, and he wanted to smash something—someone.

Holly chuckled. It was watery, but he was relieved to hear the mirth in it. "You're not really *in* my bed, Major Sharpe. More . . . *on* it, I should say."

Nicholas eased her away from him until he could see her face. *Beautiful . . . so damned lovely, it staggers me every time I look at her.* "Oh, so we're going to quibble over the niceties, are we?"

She would quibble over the color of the sky if it would keep him grinning at her like that. The deep grooves bracketing his mouth—an utterly male version of dimples—turned her bones to water.

"I don't know about niceties," she said, sighing and snuggling in closer, "but you, Major Sharpe, feel very *nice* right now."

Without warning, Nicholas felt himself grow hard. He'd been concentrating so completely on keeping things relaxed, he wasn't prepared for the change in her: the melting softness that said her body was aware of him as a man, even if her mind wasn't trained to it.

Gritting his teeth, he tried to focus his mind elsewhere. "Don't think I'm not awake upon every suit with you, m'girl," he bantered. "You mean to use my cravat to mop up those waterworks, and you think I won't notice!"

"Oh! I truly didn't mean—" She tried to pull away, but Nicholas held her fast. "But your cravat! It's—"

"Hang the cravat!" he growled, angry with himself for giving her even a second's upset. She'd been through enough. And if he couldn't hold onto his lust any better, *he* ought to be hanged!

Holly's heart was hammering against her rib cage. His utter maleness nearly overwhelmed her. The scent of him, the rock-hard muscle of his chest, his arms . . . awareness of them seeped into every pore.

"Nicholas . . . ?" she queried tentatively. "Are you angry over—over anything Lady Wickham revealed? Because if you are, I must tell you I can't remember—"

"Hang Lady Wickham too!" He lowered her to the mattress in a trice, his face intent as he bent over her, meeting her eyes. "Holly, I'm not the least angry with *you*. As for what Diana said, there was nothing . . . untoward about it. And I know you've not regained your—Good God! You know nothing about it yet—beyond your name! Shall I—"

Her hand came up, stilling him. The feel of his lips against her fingertips sent a shiver of longing through her. "No," she said. "I don't want to hear about it . . . yet."

Half-formed images shifted in her mind . . . the shocked face of Lady Wickham . . . the interior of a carriage . . . a leather-bound notebook that—She shivered again, not from passion.

"What is it?" Nicholas demanded. "You're white as a—You've seen something, haven't you? Remembered something."

Slowly, Holly nodded, licking lips suddenly gone dry. "Some—some things . . . I think they're f-from the nightmare. I—I'm—"

"Don't," he told her. "Don't try to remember if it's too—"

"But I think I must! Nicholas, I can't go on hiding from it forever, don't you see? Sooner or later, I'll have to face it. It's part of my life—part of *me!*"

He stared intently at her, doubtful. She looked drawn, the green eyes doubly huge against the pallor of her face.

"Try, then," he said, doubt still evident in his voice. "But don't push yourself. Proceed slowly, and if there's any—" He sighed, touching his knuckles lightly to her cheek. "Just don't push yourself," he repeated.

She nodded, her eyes sliding away from his as she concentrated on summoning the images. "There's a carriage— the inside of it, really—and it's moving very fast. It—it's dark outside, I think, and—and there's a storm!"

"Are you certain?" he asked, caught up in it now.

"Yes . . . a storm . . . lightning. And—and there's a book . . . a notebook of some kind. It has a brown leather binding, and—*That's my riding crop! What are you doing with*—"

A look of unholy terror seized her. Nicholas saw it, knew at once she'd gone far enough. Without another thought, he pulled her against him, cutting her off with a hard, demanding kiss.

The image flew from Holly's mind as Nicholas filled it. His hands came up and held her head as his mouth moved over hers, branding her with a heat that seared. Ah, God— his mouth! Possessive, hungry, it took what it wanted—no more than she wanted to give, but where it plundered, it drove out thought.

Very soon, though, the kiss gentled. The pressure eased, lips clinging lightly as his tongue sought entry, found it. Now Holly's world became a center of pleasure where tongue met tongue, gliding, teasing, sending shivers of delight along her spine.

Again and again, pleasure rippled through her, then again, as he nibbled, and tasted, and savored. Minutes passed . . . eons, while the joining of their mouths became the only reality, a law unto itself. There was only one truth, and its name was Nicholas . . . Nicholas, and the sweet, honeyed madness of his mouth on hers.

Nicholas! His name was a song in her soul. *Nicholas!* it chimed, flooding her with an aching sweetness that left her giddy. His hands were tangled in her hair, his big body pressing against hers. Ah, the weight of him—the very feel of him! She wanted to drown in it!

She was weak with need when it ended, Nicholas easing her down against the bedclothes while a shudder claimed him.

"Nicholas . . . ?" The throaty timbre of her voice sounded alien in the hush that fell between them. He loomed above her in the lamplight, eyes shut, the rigidity of his jaw proclaiming an inner struggle. "Nicholas, what's wrong?"

There was an explosion of air that might have begun as a laugh. Nicholas dropped to his back beside her, throwing an arm across his eyes. "What's wrong?" He did laugh then, but it held no mirth. "Think, Holly! Doesn't this all seem too familiar?"

She had a sudden recollection of that time she'd been thrown from her horse. Yes, she remembered . . . only too well. He'd warned her off, told her to forget about him, about . . .

She raised herself on an elbow to look at him. "That was different!"

"Was it?" The irony in his tone was unmistakable.

"Yes, it was. We—we were nearly strangers then, Nicholas! But we are hardly so now."

"Holly . . ." His voice held a warning as he levered himself above her, spearing her with his eyes.

Unflinching, she returned his gaze, though it felt as if he would pin her to the bed with it. "Nicholas . . ." Her heart was pounding so hard, she thought he must hear it. "Would . . . would you please kiss me again?"

The ticking of the mantel clock was the only sound in the room as Nicholas looked at her. The seconds flew by, and Holly's heartbeat increased as she watched his eyes roam over her face.

"You know what you're asking, don't you?" he said at last, his voice low and husky. "We *are* in your bed, and with the way I'm feeling right now, a kiss won't be enough."

He saw the doubt in her eyes, knew she was questioning

herself again . . . wondering still, if he wasn't put off by her loss of virginity.

"Give me your hand," he told her, and when he had it, he guided it to the front of his breeches. She let him do this, passively curious, but when she felt the hard bulge beneath the cloth, her eyes flew to his face.

Slowly, Nicholas nodded. "I want you, Holly—more than I can remember wanting any woman. That's why it won't stop with a kiss. It was all I could do to stop a moment ago."

Holly felt herself flush, but she kept her eyes on his face. "I only know," she told him solemnly, "that I feel as if I'll die if you don't hold me again . . . kiss me . . . yes, and all that implies! I want you too, Ni—"

A groan tore from his throat as he pulled her into his arms.

This time his mouth was everywhere. He used it to explore with a thoroughness that left her reeling. She had no time to think, could do nothing but feel as it traced a scorching path across sensitive flesh. He ran his lips over eyelids . . . temples . . . ears. Pressed kisses to the tiny indentations at the corners of her mouth, and when his tongue darted in to touch them, he caught her gasp of delight with the full of his mouth on hers.

Nor did the modest confines of her gown deter his exploration. Dragging his mouth from hers, he met her eyes as his hands found her breasts through the cotton, cupped them. Holding her gaze, he used his thumbs to graze their tips, and at her sudden intake of breath, he smiled.

"Like that, do you, sweetheart?" His voice was husky, gently teasing.

Again, his thumbs worked their magic, turning the peaks into upthrust buds; and when Holly uttered a sharp little cry, that beautifully sculpted mouth curved even wider.

"I love the sounds you make when I pleasure you," he murmured before capturing her lips with a kiss that promised more than fulfilled. Her hands came up to try to hold him for a more thorough kiss, and he laughed, low in his throat, then gave it to her.

She was still reeling when his mouth left hers and he lowered it to her breasts. These, he fondled with his hands, and the thin batiste of her gown again proved no barrier as the heat of his mouth closed over one taut peak. Holly cried out again, then louder as a thumb played havoc with the other.

Nicholas was on fire, yet he schooled himself to move slowly. She was a virgin in every way but one, and he meant to make it good for her. Too, at the back of his mind lay the question of whether she'd freeze on him again. It was possible. But if there was any way of getting past the fears lodged inside her mind, he would find it. She was sensually responsive. Her body's reactions proved it. He only had to take his time with her, get her to trust him completely . . .

Ah, but it was so damned hard! The erection straining his breeches was becoming painful, and he hadn't even relieved her of that silly sleeping gown!

Seized with an idea, he kissed her quickly on the mouth, then grinned at her. "I want you to do as I ask," he told her. "Will you?"

Holly smiled through the haze of passion claiming her senses. She'd have flown to the moon with him, if he'd asked. The widening of his grin when she nodded made her insides feel like jelly.

Quickly, he propped himself against the headboard, the pillow behind him. Then he picked her up as if she weighed nothing at all, and sat her in front of him. Her back rested against his chest, and her hips were nestled between his thighs.

"Comfortable?" he murmured, bending over her ear while his arms slid about her waist from behind.

His warm breath feathered tendrils of hair at her ear, sending a shiver of desire through her. She was barely able to nod, and then his hands came up to her breasts, and she heard herself moan, but as if from a distance. Nicholas was doing devastating things to her ear with his mouth, and her breasts, as he cupped them, felt languorous, heavy.

"I remember how beautiful these were when I looked at them before," he whispered between nuzzlings and nibblings of the sensitive skin at her ear. He lifted each breast slightly, as if testing its weight, but did nothing more.

"And I want to see them again, sweetheart—but you'll have to help me." He lowered his hands from her breasts— she almost moaned at the loss—and found her own hands, bringing them to the tiny button at the top of the long row that marched down the front of her gown.

"Here," he said, and his voice seemed thicker now. "Unfasten it, darling."

Holly's fingers were unsteady, but she managed to push the tiny button through its loop, and then she gasped. The instant the button was undone, Nicholas followed with something he did to her nipples, something so wickedly teasing, she felt a rush of liquid heat at her core.

Then, suddenly, he stopped, and she tried to turn and look at him, wondering what he was about, but he held her as she was.

"Well . . . ?" she heard him ask lazily, again at her ear. "You aren't stopping now, are you?" He planted a kiss at the small expanse of skin afforded him by the slightly loosened neckline, but did nothing else.

Holly shuddered with an intensified longing, somehow made her fingers go to the second button. And when it was undone, he rewarded her again. It was exactly like before: a deft movement of his fingers, and her nipples jutted into hard, aching points, while the shaft of pleasure to the place between her thighs was so intense, it made her squirm.

"Mmm," Nicholas murmured, nuzzling the exposed column of skin along her neck. But those magical fingers had stopped. Again.

Holly called him a devil, which only made him laugh, but she was already at work on the third button. The pattern repeated itself, and then again, as she made her way down the row, but in the end, Nicholas had to help; her fingers grew clumsy, her movements uncertain and stumbling as the game he played sent her into a delirious frenzy of pure, undiluted passion.

"Shh, love," he whispered as the last three closures proved too much for her, and she tore at them with reckless, trembling fingers. He made quick work of them; then, before she knew it, had the gown completely off and was turning her toward him, and kissing her senseless as his hands returned to her breasts—and this time they didn't stop.

He began to make love to every inch of her then, but slowly, knowing exactly how to make her moan and beg for more. But soon Holly became a wild thing in his arms. She arched and twisted beneath him, pulling at his clothes in a desperate attempt to remove the last barriers of cloth between them.

Nicholas was caught in the rising tide, wanting her with a desperate passion that was new to him. He was nearing the edge of his control, and Holly didn't make it any easier. Yet he made himself resist, remembering what was at stake. If he rushed her to the finish now, she might never finish at all.

She didn't seem to notice when his hand trailed its way across her belly and found the silken triangle above her thighs, although Nicholas held his breath. He held it again when his fingers slipped lower and found the liquid heat of her, but she only moaned, digging her nails into his shoulders.

But when his thumb grazed the tiny bud below the inky curls, a sob welled up from her throat, and Nicholas knew a moment of panic. Then it melted away as he recognized a second sound as his name—cried in passion.

"Oh, God, yes!" he breathed, feeling her climax against his hand. His own need was shuddering through him like a drum, but he paid it no heed. She was whole—he was sure of it—and relief washed over him in waves.

She was crying softly when he pulled her into his arms, but he knew this was something different from the panic he'd feared; the release of pent-up passions, a healthy thing. He smiled as he held her, stroking her back, pressing light kisses to her brow, her hair.

And he made up his mind to something then, which astounded him even as he did it. He would go no further tonight. No, not even with the need he felt, raging for release. He could plant a seed in her belly this night, and then where would she be? With a bastard growing inside of her —a bastard such as he himself had been . . . was.

And she was engaged to another man as well, goddamn it! Nicholas tried to wipe the thought from his mind as quickly as it came, but it lingered. The bastard was after a fortune, was he? And what effect would it have on Holly, on her feelings about her self-worth, if he should also be the type to regard her, with his discovery on the wedding night, as damaged goods?

Beside him, tucked into the comfort of his embrace, he felt Holly drift into an untroubled sleep. But Nicholas didn't join her. He lay awake long after her even breathing told him she was deep in slumber. Awake, and pondering something that had been pushed to the back of his mind by a riptide of chaotic events: Lord Trevor Regis—her betrothed —was the third name on his list.

❧ Seventeen ❧

Seated beside Maud as the Caerdruth coach lumbered along the post road, Holly gazed pensively out the window. She was vaguely aware of the chatter of the four children sitting opposite, but none of it penetrated. Even the reality of going to London had retreated from her thoughts. They were focused on the man astride the black stallion up ahead, just beyond her view.

Nicholas. How had she ever thought she might understand him? She'd awakened only yesterday in the bed where he'd learned the most intimate secrets of her body; yet today he was more of an enigma than ever.

She'd awakened alone in that bed. She could still feel her sharp stab of disappointment on rousing. When she'd reached for him, replete with dreams so sweet, they made her ache—and found him gone.

Yet that had been the least of it. After all, she'd told herself, it only made sense that he should leave her chamber before someone discovered him; servants, as she'd already learned, could be the worst of gossips.

But the real puzzle came of what had happened since. Nicholas hadn't so much as spoken a word to her! A message had come, through Parkins, that she was to have the older children ready for travel this morning if she was still set on London. That was all.

He was clearly avoiding her, and she didn't know why.

Although she had her suspicions. He'd left it to Aunt Maud to inform her of what they'd learned of her past. The old dear had come to her room yesterday morning, and cheerily imparted the facts as she'd had them . . . from Nicholas. Nicholas, who couldn't bring himself to face her after—

Dear God, was I such a disappointment to him? Perhaps I shouldn't be surprised, what with the countless women he's bedded. Well, I'm not, of course—truly I'm not, only . . . only . . . Dear God, but it hurts!

Another suspicion of what lay behind his actions nibbled at the edges of her mind like a stealthy predator, but she beat it back. He'd told her the thing didn't matter, hadn't he? She had to cling to that reassurance, *had* to, or the pain would—No . . . she wouldn't think about it, not even for a second.

But she very much feared she was falling in love with Nicholas Sharpe. Feared it with good reason. Clearly, he returned not a whit of what she felt. It was all one-sided, and she'd been a fool to allow herself to succumb to him. He'd warned her off him, hadn't he? She had only herself to blame. Not that knowing so made it any easier to bear.

Suddenly vexed that he should consume so much of her thoughts, she forced them to other things. She was on her way to London, where pieces of the puzzle that was her past awaited her. More than enough food for thought, and—

"But I like 'Princess Holly' ever so much better!" The high-pitched insistence of Charlotte's voice cut across her musings. "Must we call you Lady Helene now?" the child asked, placing a small hand on Holly's arm to claim her attention.

Holly smiled at her. "Perhaps not all of the time, Lottie. Do you remember what I told you about things that happen in private? About how they're special?"

Solemnly, the child nodded, as did Fanny and the twins, who'd suddenly grown quiet on the seat beside her.

"Well, suppose I were to say you may continue to call me Miss Holly—"

"Even *Princess* Holly?" Fanny broke in.

"Even 'Princess Holly,'" she echoed with another smile. "But only in private, I should think. Otherwise, we might confuse the people in London who already know me as Lady Helene."

This seemed to satisfy all four of them. They quickly returned to what had apparently been an earlier discussion: whether they'd catch sight of Princess Charlotte and the Prince-Regent in London. Across from them, Aunt Maud snored gently, her turbaned head lolling against the squabs.

Helene . . . Lady Helene Tamarand . . . Staring at her lap, Holly tried the syllables out in her mind. Just as she'd done several times since Maud had uttered them yesterday morning. She felt nothing. No sudden jolt of recognition, no memories bursting, full-blown, into her mind.

But why? She'd been desperate for clues for ever so long, and now she had something even better: solid facts. An identity . . . the names of loved ones . . . Dear God, even a fiancé! What was so terrible in all that, that her mind refused to link with it?

But a flash of the shifting images of her latest nightmare suggested a reason, and she quickly shut her eyes, concentrated on Nicholas again. Nicholas, who, for all her uncertainties about him, represented safety.

A chorus of male laughter drew her attention back to the window. Nicholas was in view now, and Harry, who rode beside him on a chestnut gelding. John Coachman was relating something to them from the box, and Harry laughed again. But Holly's eyes never left the man on the stallion.

His dark curls caught glints of sunlight as the wind blew them. In uniform again, he was so impossibly beautiful, so utterly male astride the big black, Holly had to look away. She clenched her fists against a great tide of longing that swept through her. Nicholas . . . who represented safety . . . Nicholas . . . who didn't want her . . .

* * *

Maud eyed the smaller drawing room of the house in Queen Street with raised eyebrows, but said nothing as Nicholas rose from a chair by the fire.

"Not to your liking either, is it?" Nicholas waved a careless hand at the *ton*'s idea of the last word in furnishings. Egyptian motifs and X chairs abounded, and the "Turkey rug" beneath their feet pulled the eye with its bright, jewel-toned colors.

"Garish frippery!" he muttered as he led the old woman to a lion-footed chair by the fire. "And I daresay it cost Aubrey a bundle he could ill afford. What the deuce happened to the old stuff? Adam, wasn't it?"

"Queen Anne. Judith wanted to auction if off, but I reminded Aubrey it wasn't theirs to dispose of, as they did those lovely Turner landscapes your stepmother loved. But the furniture was mine. Still is, thank heaven, even if it is under covers in the attic."

The adamant glint in Maud's gray eyes reminded him of someone, but Nicholas couldn't place who it was at the moment. He shrugged. "At least these rooms aren't shabby, like most at the Hall. I expect we've that to be thankful for, now we've a marquis's daughter on our hands."

"Indeed," said Maud. "And I expect you've asked me down to discuss what to do about her."

Nicholas smiled. Maud was as quick on the uptake as anyone he knew these days. She still wore outlandish dress —the current parrot green with silver lace furbelows, a case in point—but he realized it had been weeks since he'd noticed any windmills in her head.

"Speaking of which, where is m'lady at the moment?" he asked her as Finch brought in a tea tray.

Maud thought it best not to mention she'd left Holly directing a game of leapfrog while her charges recited irregular French verbs back to her. "Ahem, conducting a French lesson in the garden, I collect."

Nicholas shook his head. "The chit truly takes this governess business seriously. I'd have thought—what the devil's so amusing?"

"Nothing . . . nothing at all." Maud busied herself pouring tea, then met his eyes as she handed him a cup. "Have you attempted to contact Lansdowne yet?"

"No, but I've made inquiries as to his town address, and whether he's in residence. Seems he and his young marchioness arrived a fortnight ago from their estate in Kent."

Maud nodded, taking a sip of tea. "I suppose you're obliged to inform him of the gel's presence—of her remarkable return from the dead, I should sa—"

"Of course I'm obliged, but—devil take it! I don't even know her feelings in the matter, and—"

"You might ask her, Nick," Maud cut in quietly.

Ask her . . . two simple words, but they were caught in a coil of "What ifs" that made his gut clench: What if she saw in his eyes his memory of that night? Of how hard it had been to leave her bed? What if the lovely light in her own eyes had him promising things he'd no right to, no hope of fulfilling?

He hadn't been able to get her out of his mind since he'd left her—aching in his loins and craving her like a drowning man craves land. *Ask her! Brave words for a man who's feeling like a coward for the first time in his life!*

"I was hoping I could persuade you to do that," was all he said to Maud.

The old woman eyed him thoughtfully over the rim of her cup, then set it down, leveling her gaze at him. "You realize none of us may have any choice in this, don't you, Nick? The man is her father. He has every legal right to do with her as he wishes, with or without her consent."

Nicholas studied his untouched tea. *And what if she doesn't consent? What if she's terrified, or recalls something suddenly on seeing him, something her mind's tried to shut out forever?* "He'd need to know she's alive first," he said pointedly.

Maud snorted. "And just how long d'you think you can keep that a secret, now she's here? This is London, Nick! And if the marquis finds out later that the gel's been here under wraps? He's a powerful lord, I seem to collect from something I heard somewhere. Men like him can crush the likes of us, m'boy."

Or crush armies when they turn traitor. But there it was, the real reason he had no choice when it came to contacting Lansdowne. The tie to Holly was a perfect entrée, and he had a duty to perform. Shirk it, and *he'd* be the traitor.

He gave Maud a curt nod. "Rather than ask, you can perhaps . . . gently apprise the lady of what I intend, if you will. I'll waste no time contacting her father in any case."

Maud nodded approvingly. "There's bound to be scandal broth at teatime in any event. Heiresses don't simply turn up alive after their memorial services without causing a sensation—not to mention all sorts of vile speculation. The gel will need all the support she can get, and that begins with her family."

She eyed Nicholas appraisingly. "Of course, a deal will depend on us as well. Are you still set on implying it was a rescue from drowning?"

"I think it's the wisest course, providing the marquis agrees. No need, that way, to explain anything that might have happened . . . on the moors. The clever trick will be to explain how she got anywhere near the Cornish coast."

"Ships are blown off course, I dare—"

"Not that far off course. The devil of the thing is, the fiancé and stepmother already put it out, she was lost on the Irish Sea."

He heaved a sigh. "I suppose the best thing is to remain vague about the details. The scandalmongers will be inventing enough of their own, in any event."

"Indeed . . . and what about the gel with regard to that? Is she strong enough to withstand it, do you think? Has she the courage?"

Images came and went. Holly defying him over a fencing lesson. Holly taking Lucifer—Lucifer!—out at a dead gallop. Holly deciding to come to London—no matter what awaited her here—because she'd promised some children who weren't even hers.

"She has the courage," he said.

Following the talk with Maud, Nicholas went to the small room his father had always used as an office while in town. It had recently been swept and dusted, but there was still evidence of long disuse. He doubted Aubrey had ever occupied it. But then, he and Judith had come to town to play—not work.

He dashed off a letter to Whitehall, employing the special code Castlereagh had given him. In it he apprised the Secretary's man of what he'd learned so far. He included Holly's story—with a plea for exceptional discretion in the matter. The letter finished with a query as to the possibility of a link between any two, or among all three, of their suspects.

He wrote a second letter to Witherspoon, bringing him up to date on Holly's case, inquiring as to the status of Mr. Clark and his copy of the will.

A third letter was brief and bare of details. Written on parchment bearing the Caerdruth coat of arms, it requested an interview with the marquis of Lansdowne. He told Lord Tamarand only that he had information to impart which was of great consequence to him and his family.

He dispatched these last two by way of a footman; the one to Whitehall, he would see to himself—there was a "fishmonger" in the East End who'd see the letter into the right hands.

This done, he made the acquaintance of Rigby, the valet Finch had procured—with great difficulty, as it turned out. Rigby was a cousin to none other than Robinson, Brummell's celebrated valet, and had been trained by the man.

Finch proudly informed Nicholas that he was almost as much in demand as his cousin. Indeed, the only thing which had pried him away from his former employer—a high-flying nabob—had been Brummell's personal assurance that Major Sharpe was a man of superior taste.

"Bloody hell," Nicholas muttered when he heard this.

The creature would likely demand a fortune for his services, and he only hoped Whitehall would stand for the cost.

Still, the man had his uses. Rigby set out at once assembling his new wardrobe, freeing Nicholas for more important business. This included making the rounds of the clubs, where he meant to glean as much as he could about Regis and Lansdowne.

But first a visit to the Braithwaite town house was in order. He'd sent a note to the Wickhams before leaving Cornwall, updating them on Holly's condition, telling them they were off to London. A reply had repeated the couple's offer of help, and also invited Nicholas to call on them in town.

Little did he guess his visit would gain him a piece of news more interesting than any he'd hear at the clubs.

Diana was fetchingly turned out in a gauzy blue concoction, and he told her so as she met him in the tastefully appointed drawing room.

"Flummery!" she accused with a twinkle, "but I adore you for it nonetheless. Sherry—or something stronger?" she added, leading him to a chair by the fire.

"Sherry's fine, thanks. Is Rex—ah, speak of the devil!"

Rex reminded him which of them had been called a devil in their youth, and Diana laughed as her husband joined them.

"Ah," quipped Nicholas, "but that was only when ladies were present, and 'bastard' might have offended them!"

"Really?" Rex rejoined. "I collect it was the ladies most often called you that themselves!"

"Among other things," Nicholas added wickedly as the three settled by the fireplace while the butler served the sherry.

"Well, Nick," said Diana after he'd caught them up on things at Sharpe House, "I take it you've not had time to hear the latest *on-dit,* so—"

"Oh, more than an *on-dit,* darling," said Rex. "I had it directly from Alvanley, who was asked to stand by and serve as Lansdowne's second when the time comes."

"Lansdowne?" Nicholas tried to keep from sounding too eager.

Rex grinned at his wife. "You tell it, darling. Didn't mean to usurp—"

"Fudge!" Diana laughed, wagging her finger at him. "But I'll make you pay later, Braithwaite! See if I don't!"

Rex actually flushed, producing a grin from Nicholas before he urged Diana to finish her tidbit.

"Nick, it's all over town," she said. "Lansdowne caught Angela—his child bride, if you'll collect—being indiscreet with a younger man! No name given, last we heard—or Alvanley wouldn't tell—but it's said the marquis is out for blood!"

Lord Basil Tamarand was an attractive man somewhere in his mid-fifties, Nicholas guessed as the marquis joined him at White's. And every inch, the proud aristocrat. Average in height, he retained the slim musculature of someone much younger, and the way he carried himself said he took more than a little pride in it.

A resemblance to his daughter wasn't immediately apparent. But then Nicholas noted the iron gray hair that might have been black in his youth, and that his hazel eyes tilted upward at the corners.

"Hope this won't take long, Sharpe," Lansdowne told him brusquely after a waiter had closed the door to the private room behind him. "Dashedly busy today." He slipped a pocket watch from his waistcoat, glancing at it as if to make his point.

Busy arranging pistols at dawn, no doubt. "What I have to relate won't take long, m'lord," Nicholas told him. "What you'll do upon hearing it, however, is another matter."

"Must tell you, Sharpe, had you not mentioned my family, I shouldn't even have come. Get on with it, sir."

The imperious tone didn't sit well with Nicholas. *Demanding, are you? Very well, m'lord, you want directness—then you shall have it!* "Lord Tamarand, your daughter, Helene, is alive. She is at this moment residing with my family at our London town house."

All the color drained from Tamarand's face. "If . . . if this is some kind of a vile joke, Major—"

"I assure you it is not. Lady Helene is alive and well, and currently living at Sharpe House in Queen Street. She has black hair and green eyes that tilt at the corners just like your own."

Lansdowne stared numbly at him, as if trying to take it all in. "What—that is, how—" he began. After a long pause, "*Alive . . .*" was all he seemed able to add.

Seeing him so obviously in shock, Nicholas went to a decanter of wine and a pair of glasses the waiter had left on a sideboard. When he returned to the table with the glasses filled, he saw tears on Lansdowne's face.

"I—I must tell you, Major," said Tamarand as he grate-fully accepted the wine, "though I am not a young man, I would gladly have given half the years of my life for what you've just told me. Please, sir—can—when may I see her?"

"As soon as we can arrange it, m'lord." Nicholas watched him closely. Though shaken, the man seemed genuinely overjoyed to learn the news. "Though I think you should hear some of the details of her story first."

"Yes . . . yes, of course. She—she's well, you say?"

"Physically, she's been pronounced fit by our family phy-sician. But there's something else I think you should know before I proceed . . ."

Nicholas went on to tell him everything: Holly's appear-ance in the storm, the amnesia, all of it. It was a full quarter hour before he'd finished, and when he was done, the mar-quis appeared to have aged ten years.

"My poor child . . ." he murmured brokenly as Nicho-las hastened to pour him some more wine. "Who could have done such a—"

"Exactly the question we've all been asking, m'lord," Nicholas replied grimly. "I suggest you have another glass of wine. Then, perhaps, we can discuss how to go about finding the bastard!"

ঌ Eighteen ঌ

After all that had happened in recent days, Nicholas told himself nothing should surprise him. Yet the sight of Lady Tamarand on her husband's arm did exactly that. The *ton* was simmering with gossip over her indiscretion; nonetheless here she was, smiling sweetly at the marquis as he performed introductions in the Sharpe drawing room.

Perhaps the surprise showed on Nicholas's face. He hadn't finished bowing over her outstretched hand before she rushed to explain.

"Do forgive my coming along uninvited, Major Sharpe. But surely you'll understand, won't you, when I tell you Lady Helene has been far more than a stepdaughter to me? She's my dearest friend! Why, after we came out together, we were inseparable!"

"Not at all, m'lady," Nicholas said smoothly as he ushered the couple toward the chairs by the fireplace. "It is I who was remiss in not including you. May I ask to be forgiven?"

"You are too kind, Major." She smiled at her husband again as he seated her. "La, but when I think upon all that has happened . . ."

She went on to explain how grief-stricken she'd been, how filled with remorse that she'd not been able to protect Helene from being washed overboard. As she spoke, dabbing at her eyes with a black-bordered handkerchief her husband provided, Nicholas studied the woman.

Angela Tamarand was a beauty by most of the conventional standards of the day. Blond and blue-eyed, she had that porcelain-fair complexion that marked Englishwomen's skin as a paradigm of perfection throughout the Western world. A nose that was slightly aquiline in her oval face was balanced by fashion's perfect rosebud mouth and a sweetly rounded chin.

The singular exception to her conventional beauty was her size. She was tall for a woman, topping her husband by at least two inches; and while she was in no way given toward fat, the width of her shoulders, and hands that were on the large side, suggested a deal of physical strength.

She was still in black gloves; but given the circumstances of her stepdaughter's reemergence among the living, he felt it only circumspect: Lady Helene was still dead as far as the *ton* was concerned.

Angela used a black silk fan with practiced grace as Nicholas outlined the domestic arrangements of the household. When he explained Lady Helene's involvement with the children, she tapped her husband lightly on the arm with it.

"There! You see, m'lord? I *knew* she was ready for marriage! She fairly longs for children."

"I own, you may be right, m'dear." The marquis beamed at her, and given their current marital coil, Nicholas could only conclude the man was head-over-heels for her.

Wrapping up his sketch of the household with a brief explanation of Maud's place in it, Nicholas caught sight of Finch at the doorway.

"Well, I shan't keep you waiting any longer, m'lord . . . m'lady." He rose from his chair with a slight inclination of his head in the majordomo's direction.

"Lady Throckmorton and Lady Helene Tamarand," Finch announced.

A rustle of fabric behind him told Nicholas his guests had risen too, but his gaze remained fixed on the doorway. Maud entered first, and he was vaguely conscious of her unexpectedly modest dress: a black bombazine gown that looked suspiciously like those worn by the former governess.

But it was the slender figure following quietly in her wake that riveted his attention. Holly . . . looking lovelier than he'd ever seen her, despite the uncertainty in those incredible green eyes. Dressed simply in a white muslin afternoon gown with a deep green satin sash at the high waistline, she moved across the carpet with an elegance that took his breath away.

As the two women approached the group by the fire, Maud stepped astutely aside, and the marquis rushed forward. "Dear God, it *is* you!" he cried, throwing his arms about his daughter. "Oh, my dear child—I hardly dared believe . . . !"

Again, Lansdowne's display of emotion impressed Nicholas. The marquis would have needed to be a better actor than Kean to appear so genuinely moved if he didn't feel it. He was holding Holly as if he'd never let her go.

When he finally did, it was the stepmother's turn, and Angela embraced her fiercely. "My dearest Helene!" she exclaimed. "We were desolate . . . *desolate!* And now—oh, you cannot know the joy we feel, to have you again!"

But the stepmother's words barely reached Nicholas as he pondered Holly's reaction. She appeared almost wooden in the midst of these greetings. Neither returning nor shying away from the embraces of either of the Lansdownes, she seemed merely to . . . endure them, he thought.

Stepping quickly to her side after Angela released her, Nicholas gently took hold of Holly's arm. "Steady, lass," he murmured as he seated her on a settee by the fire.

He watched her carefully, even while introducing Aunt Maud to the marquis and his wife. *She doesn't know them . . . doesn't remember them at all.*

Holly's thoughts echoed his. *The man's my father, but I don't know him. I don't know either of them!* She shivered, suddenly grateful for Aunt Maud's presence when the old woman joined her on the settee.

Fighting back panic, she stared at the lordly man across the tea table from her. It was no good. Both he and the tall woman who rattled on about getting out of black gloves were utter strangers.

Helpless to prevent it, she found her gaze drawn to the man who watched with that brooding silence that had always unnerved her. Nicholas's eyes met hers, but gave away nothing. *Oh, Nicholas, help me! I need to feel safe again!*

Nicholas signalled Finch to enter with the tea tray he held ready in the doorway, then went back to observing Holly. He was particularly alert for signs of stress, but while she still wore almost no expression, she seemed to be functioning well enough.

Then, as Maud poured the tea, Lansdowne said something that finally brought a reaction. Alarm flooded Holly's face as her father spoke of taking her back home with him immediately.

"Ah, forgive me, m'lord," Nicholas cut in, "but is it wise to move so quickly?" *Doesn't the man realize she doesn't recall anything? Doesn't know him?*

"Wise?" Lansdowne looked utterly bemused. "Sir, she is my daughter! Why shouldn't she return home with us?"

"Because the gel still remembers nothing," Maud cut in quietly. "Isn't that right, my dear?" she added, patting Holly's arm.

Holly offered the old woman a faint smile, then faced the marquis. "I fear it's so, m'lord. I . . . I still suffer from the amnesia. I'm sorry," she added lamely.

"Well, of course you don't remember us, poor dear!" Angela's tone relayed deep sympathy, but when she turned toward Nicholas, her eyes held an odd light he couldn't decipher. "All the more reason she must come home with us at once, Major."

"Exactly so, m'dear," said her husband. He too turned toward Nicholas. "I've no intention of debating this with you, Major. But in light of the kindness you've shown my daughter, I'll add a word to elucidate Lady Tamarand's point: Since Lady Helene doesn't remember us, there is no better means of jogging her memory than her immediate return home. It is where she will see her family, all that was once familiar to her, on a daily basis."

Nicholas said nothing, and there was a pregnant silence. He scrutinized Holly for a clue as to her feelings. No help there. She wouldn't look at him. At any of them. She sat immobile, staring at the fire.

He very much feared Lansdowne would have his way in this. Not that he hadn't been prepared for the man to be taking her home. But not this soon. The marquis was under a cloud of suspicion, damn it, and time was needed to contact Whitehall! *Bloody hell, why isn't she resisting, asking for a little more time? I need time! I need to arrange protection for her!*

It was Aunt Maud who broke the silence. "You must all forgive an old woman for putting in her oar, but I daresay, shouldn't we be consulting the gel on the matter?"

Holly seemed to come out of a trance as Maud placed a hand on her arm. A harrowing image of a bloody riding crop faded from her mind, and she blinked, turned to the old woman. "I"—she took a deep breath—"I'm sorry, Aunt Maud . . . what was it you said?"

Maud repeated it, and they all looked at Holly expectantly.

What do I want? Holly's gaze travelled over the faces of the marquis and his wife. The marchioness's appeared hopeful, while her father . . . his eyes seemed to plead with her for recognition—or was she just being fanciful?

But they were her parents, weren't they? Amnesia or no, wasn't her place beside them?

Her gaze moved on. Nicholas . . . who still wore that shuttered look that gave away nothing. She somehow sensed, however, that he wasn't happy with her father's idea of taking her home straightaway.

But why should she remain? There was really nothing between them. He'd made her no promises . . . had indeed shown no inclination toward doing so. No, not he. Never Nicholas . . . who didn't want her!

"If you'll give me a chance to gather some things, m'lord," she said to the marquis, "I shall be ready to leave with you shortly."

Word of Helene Tamarand's miraculous reappearance was carefully put out to the *ton*. Nicholas had no contact with her after she left. But he had word through Maud, who enjoyed a regular correspondence with Holly—they all still called her that—that the lady had begun to appear at small, select social functions. These were always in the private homes of close family friends, where she was escorted by her parents.

But Nicholas had another means of keeping track of her. The moment she departed Sharpe House, he'd hurriedly contacted Whitehall; a pair of His Majesty's loyal government agents were currently masquerading as new additions to Lansdowne's household staff.

There was a third means of hearing what Holly was up to, but it was hardly reliable; *on-dits* blazed through the *ton* like wildfire: The heiress had tried for a runaway match at Gretna Green, but been hauled back by her father before the deed was done; she'd been rescued at sea by an Irish fisherman, and hovered near death for weeks before recovering enough to contact her family; she'd been washed ashore and buried alive before making a miraculous recovery, and digging her way out!

Because the majority of these were so ludicrous, those who knew the true story began to relax. The wilder the tales, the greater the smokescreen. Beyond her father's insulating power and prestige, it was her best insurance against being ruined.

All this was on Nicholas's mind on a balmy May evening when he had his first sight of Holly since she left Sharpe House. The occasion was a small "at home" hosted by William, duke of Clarence, younger brother to the Prince-Regent.

Nicholas told himself the only reason he was here had to do with one fact: It was the first time he might observe all three of his suspects together. Lord Regis had been in Ireland when Holly came to London, and this was to be his first appearance with his fiancée; Rex Wickham had been invited to Clarence House as well——he and the bluff, jovial duke were old friends who shared an interest in sailing.

But if spying on the suspect trio was the reason for him to have dragged himself to this stuffy affair tonight, a quiet observation by Wickham suggested it might not be his only one.

"You'd better not let m'lady Harlowe see you staring at the chit like that," Rex murmured to Nicholas as they watched the Lansdowne party enter Clarence House's grand salon.

"What the deuce are you talking about? Lydia's nowhere in sight." Nicholas had all but forgotten the wealthy widow he'd escorted to the gathering.

Rex chuckled wickedly. "Damned good thing too! She'd scratch your eyes out before she let them feast on another woman that way——especially when it's the one woman in the room who can put Lydia in the shade!"

"*The one wom*——" Nicholas dragged his gaze away from the green-eyed sylph performing a graceful curtsy before their host. "Devil take it, Braithwaite, say what you mean!"

"I mean, my dear Nick, the Tamarand chit. You haven't been able to take your eyes off her since she arrived!"

Nicholas's scowl deepened, then vanished with a laugh. "You hardly need to announce it as if it were news! When have you ever known me to give a beautiful woman the go-by?" He shrugged. "The chit's a prime article, and I've still got eyes."

"If you say so." Wickham's tone said otherwise. He was accustomed to his old friend's lazy perusals of beautiful women——usually as preludes to conquest. He ran his eyes over them in the same way most men would assess prime horseflesh at Tatt's. But this was different. Nick drank in the sight of Helene Tamarand as if she were the last source of water on a desert island.

"I do say so—and what the devil was that nonsense about Lydia?"

Rex gave him an insouciant lift of his brows. "According to the latest *on-dit,* the beauteous widow's out to leg-shackle you, old boy. Care to put that one to rest?"

Nicholas gave him a lazy grin. "What she's out for, and what I'm out for may be two entirely different things." In truth, Nicholas knew it went further than that. Lydia Harlowe had been left enormously wealthy by her husband's demise. In real property alone, her assets amounted to a fortune—the sort of wealth Nicholas needed if he were to restore Caerdruth and Trevellan.

An inner voice reminded him this was exactly the notion he'd disdained in Witherspoon's office that day. Nicholas smiled sardonically to himself. Lydia was as inventive in bed as some of the highest-priced courtesans; if he were to *play* the whore to a woman who could *act* the whore, why, it was a fitting exchange, wasn't it?

A ripple of musical laughter drifted over to him, and he glanced across the room. Holly was delighting in something being whispered to her by the tall, dark-eyed man at her side. The fiancé.

Biting back a sharp twinge he was beginning to recognize, Nicholas turned abruptly away, telling Wickham he was off in search of Lydia. There was no room for regret in his life.

Holly sighed as she let Prudence, her old abigail, remove her mother's emeralds from her neck. *My emeralds now,* she corrected silently as she removed the matching ear bobs herself and handed them to the maid.

"Just put them in the case, and that will be all, Prudence. It's been a long night, and I can manage the rest myself."

"Yes, m'lady . . . and thank you, m'lady." The girl had waited up for her mistress's return from the "at home," and was obviously grateful to be allowed to seek her bed.

Holly smiled as the girl bobbed a curtsy and withdrew, but the moment the door closed, the smile faded. Her mouth ached from the smile she'd pasted on it all evening. Just one more, she felt certain, and it would crack.

The wide green eyes staring back at her from the dressing table mirror studied her reflection. Was she anywhere near as beautiful as Regis had told her she was? Repeatedly, all evening?

She owned she couldn't find fault with the elegant coiffure Prudence had styled, its Grecian curls still artfully arranged. And she supposed the emeralds *had* brought out her eyes. This too was something her fiancé had mentioned several times during the evening, although she'd gotten the distinct impression *his* eyes had been more on the emeralds than on her.

She heaved a sigh, vexed with herself. She could hardly complain. As Angela said, she must be grateful Lord Trevor still meant to have her; he could easily have cried off. Many men would have, in the face of the gossip that dogged her steps like a relentless shadow.

She thought about her fiancé for a moment, trying to assess her feelings toward him. But the problem was, there *were* no feelings. True, he was suavely handsome . . . a pleasant surprise when she'd been reintroduced to him tonight. And he did have impeccable manners, from the way he wielded a snuff box to knowing just the right thing to say.

He'd even made her laugh . . . a witty remark about Mrs. Jordan, Clarence's *chere amie,* and their ever-increasing brood of little Fitzclarences. And, of course, he'd been the soul of devoted attention, never leaving her side all evening.

While another never came *near* her all evening.

Was it only decent of him, as Angela had pointed out when she'd caught Holly's eyes straying in Nicholas's direction once too often? "If Major Sharpe were to pay any court to you," her stepmother had pointed out, "your reputation would be in shreds, Helene. Bad enough, he enjoys a rakish one of his own. But being seen in his company might be all it wanted, to link you to those rumors that you were with him in Cornwall."

"But I *was* with him in Cornwall!" Holly had cried.

"All the more reason to put the lie to it!" had been Angela's rejoinder.

So. He was being decent. Doing the right thing. She ought to be grateful, Holly told herself as she quietly watched tears slide down the face of her mirror image. Grateful . . .

ও Nineteen ৬

After the night at Clarence House, Holly saw Nicholas frequently, but it was always the same; he would somehow materialize at any gathering she attended, but keep himself at a distance. She'd look up suddenly, and there he was. Sometimes she was certain she could feel his eyes on her, but he never acknowledged her, not even with a nod. And he always had a woman on his arm.

Lately, it had been a particular woman: a stunning creature with chestnut hair. Holly had learned from Angela her name was Lady Lydia Harlowe, and that she was a wealthy widow. She flirted outrageously with Nicholas, and clung to his arm with a possessive air that was apparent even from across a room.

At first Holly tried to tell herself it didn't matter: Nicholas was out of her life now, and she'd be spared those colossal ups and downs of trying to keep her balance with him. But after a while, as she saw him returning the widow's looks with unconcealed interest, she could no longer pretend. The pain ran deep.

It ran deep because she knew now for a certainty, she loved him. And she feared nothing she could do would change it. Not that she didn't try. Trevor was always near, and she tried desperately to summon whatever it might have been that had once interested her in the man.

But it was no good. Trevor Regis was handsome, urbane,

charming—all the things most young women would adore in a husband. Yet when he'd kissed her once, she'd had all she could do to suppress a shudder of revulsion. And when she thought of spending a lifetime with him, she invariably found herself putting Nicholas in his place.

It was Nicholas she wanted to grow old with, Nicholas whose children she envisioned having . . .

The thought of children inevitably brought another pain. She missed the Sharpe children unbearably. More than that, she knew she'd brought them to London because it was a means of reassuring Lottie, all of them, really, that she'd not disappear from their lives.

And now she had.

She'd for all intents and purposes broken her promise. And it simply wouldn't answer that she kept in touch with them through her correspondence with Maud. The old woman assured her the youngsters were getting on famously; but whenever Holly saw the childish scrawl of Charlotte's name added to a sheet of foolscap that arrived from Maud, she wanted to weep.

All of these things were running through her brain one day in early June, when Trevor took her riding. As they skirted Rotten Row, she was glad Nightwing was feisty from lack of exercise; controlling the filly gave her an excuse for not engaging in repartée. Her fiancé had given up trying a quarter-mile back, and now rode silently at her side.

She turned to check on Prudence, who followed some distance behind, in the barouche with Angela. Holly knew Prudence didn't like Lady Tamarand very much, though she never said so of course. It was just the stiff manner she had whenever the mistress of the house was near.

Holly shrugged. Angela was a bit high-handed, she supposed, but she and her stepmother got on well enough. Of course, there were those few instances in which she'd caught Angela eyeing her rather strangely . . .

It was almost as if she were trying to gauge what Holly was thinking. She frequently asked about the amnesia too,

so perhaps she was trying to understand what it must feel
like, to have no memory of things.

Prudence was looking particularly uncomfortable with
something Angela was saying to her. Perhaps it would be a
good idea to smooth the waters. Prudence was a decent
sort, though a bit given to the blue devils when repri-
manded.

She was about to tell Regis she wished to ride back when
she spied something that made her freeze. Nicholas . . .
with Lady Harlowe. Unthinkingly, her hands tightened on
Nightwing's reins as she watched the pair canter toward
her. They were laughing together, oblivious to her presence, and the thought flashed in her mind, that she had to
get away, get out of sight before—

She must have communicated the message to the filly.
Before she could act, Nightwing leapt forward, and broke
into an all-out gallop that nearly cost Holly her seat. Years
of experience in the saddle saved her; but as the horse took
off at breakneck speed, Holly realized to her horror, this
hadn't been enough. She'd foolishly allowed the filly to
seize the bit between her teeth. She couldn't control her!

They were tearing down the path, Regis's shouts in her
ears, when the final horror hit: The sidesaddle was slipping.
It had broken free of its girth!

A mocking sense of *deja vu* loomed in her mind as she
leaned over the filly's withers and threw her arms about the
sleek neck: another mount's neck . . . thicker, more muscular, but just as black . . . gulls crying . . . the smell of
the sea . . .

She fancied her brain playing tricks as the image clung,
grew in her mind until she could hear the same thunder of
hooves behind, the same—

Nicholas! She knew it was his arm closing about her, his
strength she felt, even before she heard his voice.

"Let go!" he shouted as Lucifer's head appeared beside
the racing filly's. "I've got you now, dammit! Let go of her!"

Trust him! The voice screamed in her brain. But she
couldn't relinquish her hold! It was a death-grip, all that

stood between her and the ground flashing beneath the filly's hooves. *Trust him*, it cried again.

She let go.

The choking dread eased as Nicholas felt the weight of her in his arms. One more second, and she'd have—

He reined the stallion in, watched with a sickening in his gut when Lucifer's hooves narrowly missed the sidesaddle on the path. His grip on Holly tightened as he circled and brought the stallion back to the spot.

"Helene!" Regis approached at a canter. "I say—is she all right?"

Nicholas ignored him, his eyes going from the saddle on the ground to Holly's face as she freed it from the folds of his cravat and looked up at him.

"Are you?" he asked quietly. More calmly than he felt. He was all too aware of the thudding of her heart—or was it his?—as she pressed against him, her hands fisted in the cloth of his coat.

Regis was addressing her directly now, demanding to know if she was injured, but Holly didn't seem to hear. She continued to meet Nicholas's eyes, and he saw her lips tremble as she forced a smile.

"I . . . seem to give you no end of trouble when I'm on horseback, Major. S-seems I've made an annoying habit of—"

"Nicholas!" Lydia's tone was insistent. "I've been talking to you! Release that woman at once, as her escort says! People are staring!"

Nicholas ignored her too. "Indeed, you have, m'lady," he told Holly as if there'd been no interruption, no crowd of curious onlookers gathering. "Fact is, I'm beginning to feel like a bloody hero. Best watch it . . . bad for my image, y'know."

Holly saw the familiar grin, felt at once, the giddy warmth curling through her. "Yes," she said, grinning back at him, aware of the mad acceleration of her pulse. "We can't have Sharpe the Bastard rescuing damsels in distress, can we?"

Suddenly Nicholas frowned, casting another glance at the saddle on the ground. Around them, voices resonated . . . Regis, insisting Lady Helene be surrendered to her carriage . . . Angela, urging something along the same lines . . . Lydia, demanding his attention in a strident voice . . .

Nodding as if he'd suddenly made up his mind to something, Nicholas turned Lucifer's head and nosed his way through the crowd. It took only a moment, and then suddenly, he was cantering away.

Holly gaped at him. "Nicholas, where are—?"

"Nicholas!" Lydia's shriek rose above Regis's startled shout.

"See here, Sharpe!" The fiancé's voice carried over Lucifer's pounding hooves.

Nicholas glanced over his shoulder at both of them as he urged the stallion on. "See Lady Harlowe home, will you, Regis? There's a good fellow!"

Holly's grin had long since faded. She issued her own query, though not as demandingly as the outraged widow in the distance. "Where are we going? Nicholas, I insist you take me back—at once!"

"In reply to your question," he told her as Lucifer picked up his pace, "to Sharpe House." There was a grim look on his face as he went on. "As to the other, m'lady—not a chance!"

Holly started to put up a struggle, muttering angrily about the scandal of an abduction in broad daylight, but he quelled her with a look.

He'd been a fool to let her out of his sight—of his personal protection. He could still feel the freezing of his blood as he'd taken in the sidesaddle on the path. There had been no need to dismount: Even from where he sat, he'd seen the severed edges.

The girth had been cut.

"Aunt Maud! Aunt Maud!" Fanny rapped urgently on the bedchamber door. When the old woman opened it, the girl seized her by the hand. "She's back, Aunt Maud! But you must come at once! Oh, please hurry! They're—"

"Dear me, child! Whatever are you rattling on abou—"

"It's Princess Holly, Auntie! Uncle's brought her back, only now they're having a terrible row, and—oh, please won't you come?"

Maud agreed at once. Muttering that she was not as young as she used to be, but hurrying nonetheless. Doors along the hallway opened as they headed for the stairs. Charlotte appeared, sleepy-eyed from her nap; the twins, from the room opposite; then Harry, from the chamber nearest the stairs.

"What's happened?" the young earl asked. He noticed Lottie straggling at the end of the family parade and scooped the four-year-old up in his arms. They followed the others down the stairs while Fanny hastily explained.

"I was coming downstairs to ask Mr. Finch if he'd seen my lesson book," she said, pausing to allow Maud to catch up. "I'd gotten to about here"—she indicated the step on which she'd stopped—"when the front door opened, and Uncle Nicholas came in. He was carrying Princess Holly in his arms!"

There was a chorus of exclamations, and Maud urged them on down. They could hear angry voices coming through the closed doors of the drawing room as they descended.

"They were shouting at each other and didn't see me," Fanny told them. "Not even when I called their names! They were ever so angry! Then Uncle carried her in there, though the princess warned him not to."

She looked at Maud as they all drew up before the drawing room, which had suddenly grown silent. "That was when I came to fetch you, Aunt Maud—straightaway."

"Did the right thing, child," Maud assured her. Yet she couldn't imagine what she was to do, now she was here. Still, the shouting had stopped . . .

Hoping she wasn't setting a bad example for the children, Maud squared her shoulders. Then she adjusted her turban with both hands, took a deep breath, and thrust open the doors. *"Oh!"*

Nicholas and Holly stood in the middle of the room. She was on tiptoe, her arms entwined about his neck. He appeared to be kissing her senseless.

"Bloody hell!" Nicholas muttered as he tore his lips from Holly's. The drawing room echoed with the sound of doors slamming.

"Wh-what was that?" Holly asked in a daze. She hadn't had a coherent thought since Nicholas had stopped her protests with his mouth.

"That," he said, not releasing her, entirely aware of her pliant curves pressed against him, "was most of the Sharpe family, if I'm not mistaken."

He grinned at her as she groaned. "Seems they're making a habit of this sort of thing, doesn't it?"

"H-habit?" Holly was still trying to gather her senses, not a likely proposition with him so close. She could feel the muscled length of his thighs through the material of her riding skirt, smell the familiar scent of him . . . redolent of leather and wool, and an elusive something she knew to be utterly male.

Nicholas laughed, kissing her lightly on the lips. He began to set her away from him, then appeared to think better of it. Widening his stance, he pulled her back into his arms.

Holly managed to collect her wits. "No, you don't—you devil!" She forestalled the kiss with a hand she freed just in time, clapping it over his mouth. "We have things to settle!"

Nicholas sighed, released her with a reproving look. "Not at the tops of our lungs this time, I hope." He gave the doors a disparaging glance. "Though I've no doubt we've an audience waiting to hear what's happened."

"Then they're the only ones in London who don't already know!" she snapped.

"Dammit, Holly, you were in danger!"

"The danger was past!"

"Like hell, it was! It was closer than—"

Holly eyed him sharply when he snapped his mouth shut.

"What . . . ? It was closer than *what,* Nicholas? What aren't you telling me?"

Bloody hell! Nicholas shoved a hand through his hair. He hadn't meant to tell her anything. Not now, at least. Maybe not at all, if he could figure out a way to protect her without alarming her.

But the way she was looking at him told him it was no good. Devil take it, then. It appeared he had to tell her if he was to convince her to remain. She had to be where he could watch her!

He described the severed girth strap. He did it calmly, choosing his words with care, yet Holly's eyes widened as the truth sank in.

"It's followed me to London, hasn't it?" she asked in a toneless whisper. "Whatever . . . whoever it was who—"

"Here—sit down," he ordered when she began to tremble. He led her toward a settee, joined her on it.

"Now, listen to me, Holly . . ." he told her, taking both her hands in his. He went on to state his case for keeping her at Sharpe House. Mentioning nothing about his clandestine mission—because he couldn't—he nonetheless intimated there were people he could call on, connections he had in the military; they would help him guard her, he said. But his final argument was the most persuasive.

"I won't let anyone harm you, Holly," he told her, his eyes grave with concern. "I swear it."

It was the first moment since learning about the girth that Holly felt an easing of the tension coiled tightly inside her. "I'll stay," she told him.

❧ Twenty ❧

"She'll not stay!" Basil Tamarand railed at Nicholas in the drawing room. "Have you lost your mind, sir? Kidnapping my daughter in plain view of half the *ton?* Expecting me to stand idly by while you detain her here? I could call you out for half of it!"

"Yes, but you won't." Nicholas leaned casually against the fireplace mantel, looking for all the world like a relaxed country squire. But his voice was steel.

"You won't because you know there is a household in Cornwall full of servants who know the truth of your daughter's reappearance, and that I am all that stands between their potential for indiscretion and the *ton.* The lady remains here."

"Major, that—that is *blackmail!* It won't answer, sir. I won't have it!"

"Ah, but you will, m'lord. That is, if you value your daughter's safety."

"Safety! *Safety,* sir? She is already in jeopardy as a result of your indiscretion this afternoon! Carrying her off bodily —*bodily!* I cannot—"

"I was not speaking of the danger to her reputation, m'lord. I was addressing the danger to her person—her life!"

"Eh?" Tamarand looked confused. Nicholas watched

carefully for anything that might suggest knowledge of the sabotaged saddle, but he saw only bemusement.

"Lady Helene's saddle girth had been tampered with, Lord Tamarand. Someone tried to kill her. And not for the first time, I believe."

"I . . . I . . ." Tamarand looked stunned. Nicholas continued to watch him carefully as he led him to a chair; this reaction too, appeared genuine. He quickly poured him a brandy.

While the marquis downed it, Nicholas described the incident in detail. Next, he described Holly's exact condition upon arriving at Caerdruth.

Tamarand knew of her violation of course; they'd had to tell him. But he'd been spared the uglier details of her injuries. It was time to raise what Nicholas had long suspected: that the loss of her virginity had been incidental to a greater assault—on her life.

Tamarand's face was drained of color as Nicholas finished. He asked for another brandy and managed to respond only after he'd taken a hefty swallow. "Appears I owe you an apology, sir. You've saved Helene's life, not once, but twice. But who could have—the girth strap! My groom tells me it's—"

"Disappeared?"

"Yes, but how did you—"

"I sent my own man back for the saddle, and when he saw it was gone, he had the foresight to go to your stablemen and ask if they'd secured it. They had, and complained angrily about someone in the crowd having pinched the girth strap in the confusion."

"A wide-awake thief, my head groom said." Tamarand took another hefty swallow. "Called him brazen, to be chalking marks in Rotten Row!"

"Brazen, I've no doubt. But not a thief. *Would-be murderer's* the accurate phrase."

The marquis nodded grimly. "Didn't want evidence of what he'd done lying about."

"It would have been enough to warrant contacting the magistrate. As it stands—"

"We have only your word to go on. Not that I doubt it for a second, Major. But where do we go from here?"

Nicholas outlined his plan for keeping Holly under his roof, citing the fact that they already had evidence she wasn't safe at the Lansdowne town house.

"But what makes you think she'll be any safer here?" the marquis asked. "And there's the added difficulty of it linking her name with yours. After that abduc—er, rescue, sir, I fear we've enough wagging tongues to deal with."

"She'll be safer here because I have time on my hands to watch over her personally. I've a leave of absence from the military, owing to my brother's death. Can you deny your own duties in the Lords keep you too occupied to watch over your daughter night and day—for however long it takes?"

"No, I don't deny it. I even concede, if there's anyone who can protect her, you're the man. I've checked on you, Major—your war record among other things. Your ability in such matters is unquestionable. But there's still—"

"The scandal—yes, I know. But I believe I've a solution. We'll give it out, I'm the one who rescued her at sea. Say I was sailing to Ireland with my aunt to attend to matters involving my brother's estate . . . whatever. I'm reasonably certain no one will check. They'll all be too busy savoring the romance of it, and Aunt Maud's presence will provide the proper—"

"That still doesn't explain—"

"I'm coming to that, m'lord. We'll say today's incident began as nothing more than a rescue from a runaway horse. There are people who saw that much, in any event, and it will compound the glamor of the previous rescue.

"The, ah, abduction," Nicholas went on, "we'll explain this way: One of my brother's children—all of whom m'lady had grown quite fond of while recuperating with my family—was ill and asking for her. In fact, I'd been riding toward her to inform her of that very request. She insisted on being taken to the child at once, and here we are."

Tamarand looked skeptical. "Word has it, Lydia Harlowe's in a taking over being abandoned by you this afternoon, Sharpe. She'll put the lie to your reasons for riding in the Park, if no one else does."

Nicholas laughed. "Half the town knows she's hardly the first to fly into a jealous tantrum over my antics, m'lord. Seems I've a bit of a reputation as—"

"A rake. I'm well aware of it, Major, which is all the more reason not to—"

"Rakes have been known to reform, m'lord, which is exactly what you are about to witness. Rely on it! By the time we're through pushing this tale through the pipelines"—Nicholas smiled sardonically—"my own mother wouldn't recognize me!"

The marquis shook his head doubtfully. "I don't know, Sharpe . . . seems all too much a Banbury tale, to my thinking."

"No more than the nonsense already going about. All this wants is the official stamp of your word on it. You've a sterling name in this town, m'lord." *And I can only hope you haven't sold it for thirty pieces of French silver,* he thought. "Surely you can employ it to save your daughter."

Tamarand was silent for a moment, staring into his brandy. At length he sighed, meeting Nicholas's eyes. "I'm not keen on it, but I suppose we'll need the thing to explain away the abduction, no matter where she resides. The child who's supposedly ill—you have one in mind? One who can be relied on, to go along for a time?"

Nicholas grinned, picturing a certain towheaded hoyden with an imagination to rival Sir Walter Scott's. "Trust me, m'lord. I've just the one!"

Nicholas met with Holly and Maud immediately, informing them of what he and the marquis had devised. The women had no trouble dealing with the concocted sea rescue; it was closer to the truth than anything put out thus far, and would free Holly from many of the evasions she'd had to manage recently. But the business of involving the children was another matter.

"How can you put the children in such an untenable position?" Holly questioned hotly. "Asking them to lie! It simply won't answer, Nicholas!"

Nicholas heaved a sigh. He might have known she'd be more of a stickler about the children than her own welfare! "Now, see here," he told her without bothering to hide his annoyance, "there are some things in this world—"

"No, you see here, Nicholas Sharpe! I won't be a party to teaching those children deceit! Why, it's . . . it's—"

"If I may interrupt, my dears?" Maud tried not to smile as she rose from the chair where she'd been listening.

They looked like a pair of belligerent children themselves —squared off, nose-to-nose, in the center of the room. But while they continued to glare at each other, they appeared to be waiting for what she had to say, at least.

"An outright clanker may not be necessary—may not be what it will amount to, that is." She had their attention now.

"The children *have* been asking for you, gel, far more than I let on in my letters. Little Lottie, in particular, although all their appetites have been off, Cook tells me. Even the twins have been moping about. And Fanny! Why, the child hasn't been given to squints in days!"

"Oh, Aunt Maud!" Holly chided. "Why didn't you—"

"And serve you up a case of the megrims as well? Give me credit for some sense, gel! But back to my point: Who's to say their megrims aren't an illness? *I* certainly shan't!"

Nicholas wanted to hug the old woman. "Will that answer, you little hair-splitter?" he asked Holly.

"Hair-splitter! Why, you glib-tongued—"

A noisy clearing of throat interposed, and when Holly saw the vexed look on Maud's face, she burst out laughing. "Very well, you wretched man!" she said to Nicholas. "It seems it will have to."

* * *

But there was one more person Nicholas had to satisfy with his arrangement, and their encounter wasn't a pleasant one. He'd hardly sent the women off to talk to the children when Finch announced Lord Regis's presence without.

"Bloody hell!" Nicholas muttered. But he sent the major-domo to admit the man to the drawing room. He'd asked Lansdowne to inform Regis of matters, but the fiancé apparently had his own arguments to marshal.

Outraged arguments, as it turned out.

"I wish to speak to my intended, Sharpe—at once!"

The man's mood was ugly, arousing Nicholas's ire. With the exception of his commanders in the military, no one ordered him about so peremptorily—no one!

"Impossible, Regis," he said tightly.

"Impossible! What's impossible is your flagrant kidnapping of my fiancée this afternoon! I don't care what concocted drivel you fobbed off on Lord Tamarand, Sharpe! Lady Helene belongs at home with her parents. I intend to take her there—at once!"

"Oh . . . ?" Nicholas's voice was ominously soft. "And to what end, may I ask?"

Regis sputtered with indignation. "Why . . . why, to save her good name, of course!"

"Hmm . . . and if I may be so indelicate, m'lord, just how do you think that will save it? What with all the rumors already flying about, that is. Surely you're aware it was already in jeopardy before this afternoon's . . . incident?"

It was a subject he'd long dreamed of pursuing with Regis. He hadn't stopped worrying over Holly with regard to her violation. Over how her fiancé would take it. Over how it would affect her, if the man devalued her for it.

How much had Regis been told? Even without being given particulars, was he man enough to overlook what many already considered a given? Or did he secretly resent his betrothal to a woman who was "damaged goods," by *tonnish* standards?

"I realize there's been . . . speculation, if that's what

you mean," said Regis. "Fact is, who *wouldn't* speculate, what with this devilish amnesia and whatnot!"

Nicholas suppressed a creeping sense of loathing as he noted Regis couldn't look him in the eye. "Yourself included of course," he prompted.

"Yes—well, dash it all, Major! You're a man of the world! How would you take it if—"

Suddenly Regis did look at him. "But of course! You were there. I wonder if you might settle something in my mind, Sharpe. When Helene turned up . . . that is, when she was found, how did she, ah, appear? Was she . . . ?"

The loathing grew, became disgust as Nicholas had his answer. The son of a bitch was fishing for verification! He wasn't quite certain Holly's virtue had been compromised, and he actually believed Nicholas would tell him!

Never more aware of his vow to protect her, Nicholas knew he couldn't allow Holly to fall prey to this jackal. *Christ! I was just getting her to believe in herself as a woman again!*

"M'lord Regis," he said with barely suppressed rage, "I take your point. But consider: You needn't keep to this betrothal. Given her lack of any memory of you, I'm certain Holl—the lady will understand, and release you from such a commitment. I'd even be willing to speak to her for you."

It was both a discreet affirmation of Regis's worst fears, and a bolt-hole for his escape. Nicholas eyed him archly, prepared to see him jump at this chance.

What he wasn't prepared for was the raw pain that engulfed him with Regis's response: "Hardly that, old boy. You see, Sharpe, it's her virtue that's in tatters—not her fortune!"

Nicholas reluctantly allowed Regis to meet with Holly. The fiancé insisted on being "reassured, through her own words," that she was in accordance with the plan. During the interview he begrudingly agreed to step to the sidelines; he'd allow Nicholas and Maud to be her escorts about town while she took time "to adjust," as Holly put it.

There was one final note to all these arrangements. That evening word arrived from Lord Tamarand, that Helene's stepmother wished some reassurances as well. But this was an easy request to satisfy; Angela wanted "mainly to meet with those marvelous children who seem to have captured Lady Helene's interest."

The meeting took place the next day. All five children stood beside Holly and Maud in the drawing room as Nicholas introduced the marquis and his wife.

"She doesn't *look* like a wicked stepmother!" Michael whispered to his twin while the marchioness cooed over their "angelic" sister Lottie.

Martin was about to tell him that not all stepmothers were wicked when Fanny cut in under her breath: "They don't need to be ugly to be wicked, you ninny!"

"Come, children," said Aunt Maud, "no rattling on in whispers! Lady Tamarand was addressing you, Fanny."

"Yes, m'lady." Fanny curtsied to the marchioness, and even Blodgett would have approved of her form. What happened next, however, would have earned the remonstration, "Young ladies do not gaze forthrightly into the eyes of their betters!"

But Fanny was curious about this woman who looked no older than her stepdaughter. She fixed china blue eyes on Angela; bad enough. But her question would have had Blodgett reaching for her ruler: "Do you take snuff, m'lady?"

Angela gasped, then quickly recovered. She was already smiling sweetly at her as Uncle Nicholas told Fanny not to be impertinent.

"But Nurse used to tell us she took snuff to keep the ague out of her bones!" Fanny protested. "I was only wondering what kept m'lady looking so young!"

Nicholas scowled at her, but Angela seemed delighted. "What a cunning child! So young and fresh! So innocent!" She tapped the marquis's arm with her fan. "Don't you think, so, m'lord?"

Lord Tamarand responded with a noncommittal grunt, but his wife's attention was back on the girl. "Tell me, Lady

Fanny," she said, stroking the child's cheek with the tip of her fan, "did you really miss Lady Helene's company so terribly?"

Fanny had been duly coached by Aunt Maud as to the "game" they were playing to keep Holly at Sharpe House. "Oh, it was awful, m'lady!" she exclaimed with one of her best squints. "I languished for days without her! There I was, all splotches and megrims with it. Ghastly, it was! Simply ghastly!"

"Sarah Siddons herself couldn't improve on it!" Nicholas muttered to Holly in an aside as Angela called Fanny her "poor darling."

Holly grinned at him. "Why, I should think you'd feel she's doing you proud, Sir Stage Manager!"

Nicholas muttered something about Fanny not being the only impertinent chit in evidence; but Holly was already focused on her stepmother's overtures toward the twins.

And overtures, they were. She'd not suspected Angela might be so interested in children. From all this, she'd have surmised her stepmother longed for her own—perhaps the heir she hadn't yet produced; but Angela's recent comments about a *ton dame* who was *enceinte* dissuaded her: "Fat as a sow, and proud of it! *Can* you imagine?"

But the fact was, there was little about Angela that Holly could connect with herself. She truly wondered what had wrought the closeness they'd enjoyed before the amnesia. But it was the same with Trevor, and her father hardly called up filial feelings in her.

Was that how the illness worked, then? A severing of the self from all previous emotions, human connections? And if that was true, would she wake one morning with her memory restored, only to find the old in place—and the more recent attachments gone?

But that would mean a severance from the children! And of course from Nicholas. It would be the perfect solution to her hopeless longing for him, yet Holly felt panic rising with these thoughts. *No!* her mind cried out. *Not the children! I can't give them up!*

And Nicholas? the inner voice mocked, and she called herself a fool as her heart answered: *Memory be damned! Not while I have breath!*

"Holly, are you all right?" Nicholas whispered as Angela exchanged small talk with Harry. "You look as if—are you in pain?"

Holly felt Fanny had nothing on Siddons as she pasted a bright smile on her face. "Not at all! Really, Nicholas, the way you fuss, you could give mother hens lessons!"

Finch arrived with the tea tray, and Angela urged Charlotte to sit beside her, but the child wouldn't go. Lottie had been unusually silent throughout the interview, and Holly surmised it was because she'd missed her nap. She asked Angela to understand as the four-year-old sucked her thumb and retreated behind Harry.

Angela shrugged, and turned toward Fanny. "But my clever little pretty, here, looks wide-awake! Come and sit beside me, Lady Fanny, and I shall butter you a scone."

Fanny darted a cool, assessing glance at her sister, then complied. As Angela fussed over her, the six-year-old examined the beautifully gowned woman. She'd been told Lady Tamarand was not only Lady Helene's stepmother, but her dearest friend.

But she didn't believe it, and she knew Lottie didn't believe it either. The lady was very pretty, but she knew her stepdaughter was a lot prettier—and she didn't like it. Fanny could tell from the way she looked at Princess Holly. The way she said "Lady Helene" . . .

But she'll always be Princess Holly to me! She's much more a princess than this old marchyness could ever be!

Right then and there, Fanny made up her mind to something: She didn't like Lady Tamarand one bit! No, nor her stuffy husband. What's more, she'd spied that *fee-awn-say* striding from the house yesterday, and she didn't like him either. She didn't like the lot of them!

❧ Twenty-One ❧

Four pairs of china blue eyes watched in silence from the top of the stairs. They never left the adults in the foyer below. Not until Holly, Nicholas, and Maud left for the waiting carriage. When the door shut behind the grown-ups, a quartet of voices erupted.

"He's not taking the new phaeton, dash it!" said Michael. "That's a bang-up gig, if I ever saw one!"

"He can't, with the ladies all in trim," his twin pointed out reasonably. "A high-perch phaeton's no gig for silks and fallals."

"Wasn't our princess bee-yoo-tiful?" Charlotte asked dreamily.

"Complete to a shade," said Fanny, "especially with Uncle all rigged out beside her. They'd make an absolutely famous fairy-tale prince and princess!"

"But for Uncle to be the prince, he'd need to be married to Princess Holly, wouldn't he?" Charlotte asked.

Fanny nodded sagely, a squint beginning to form.

"Well, that can't happen," Martin stated. "She's engaged to wed that Lord Regis."

"Yuck!" his twin exclaimed. "Lord Regis is a disaster at the ribbons! He'd never do for a prince. Can't have a prince who's cow-handed with his high-steppers!"

"We can't have Regis at all," said Fanny abruptly. "Princess Holly doesn't have a *tendre* for him. And everyone knows a fairy-tale prince and princess must have a *tendre* for each other!"

"She doesn't?" Michael asked, quite at sea.

"Honestly, Michael Sharpe, don't you know *anything*?" Fanny's voice assumed that superior air the twins had begun to relate to her femaleness lately; they looked at each other and nodded knowingly as she went on. "She loves Uncle Nicholas, you sapskull!"

They'd all seen the pair kissing that day, of course. But Martin and Michael had been reluctant to discuss the incident, even between themselves. Their concept of war heroes in no way included the yucky business of kissing ladies!

"And *he* must love *her*!" Charlotte piped with sudden inspiration. "Else, why'd he kiss her that way in the drawing room?"

"Just." Fanny ignored the faces her brothers pulled at Lottie's reminder. "And that means we've a problem on our hands."

"We?" The twins spoke in unison.

"What problem?" Lottie asked.

Fanny gave them an impatient look. "If Princess Holly loves Uncle . . ."

"And Uncle loves her . . ." Lottie reminded.

Fanny gave a decisive nod. "Then she mustn't marry that *fee-awn-say!* It's all wrong!"

"Capital!" exclaimed Michael, thinking of the bungled ribbons. "How do we stop her?"

"Well . . ." murmured Fanny, getting the squints again, "I was just thinking . . ."

Holly stood between Nicholas and Maud at Almack's, trying to gauge her own mood. She was feeling off balance again. Not that this was anything new where she and Nicholas were concerned. But ever since he'd come roaring back into her life a few days ago, the feeling had intensified.

After that drugging kiss in the drawing room, he'd been acting the complete gentleman in her company. No sardonic smiles. No dire warnings. No putting her in her place with looks. And definitely not with sudden kisses!

She knew it all had to do with the arrangement he and her father had ironed out between them. Nicholas had taken it upon himself not only to guard her safety, but to facilitate her reentry into society. To do this, it made sense that his own behavior be exemplary. She ought to be glad of it.

So why was she feeling such a niggling sense of loss?

She gazed around the main assembly room, trying to familiarize herself with it. She'd been here many times, Angela had informed her. But this was the first Wednesday evening she'd seen it since her return.

Her father had thought it unwise to risk her being shunned by one of the high-stickler patronesses while they were trying to face down all the rumors. He'd retained their vouchers, but there were all sorts of ways the *haut ton* could make its disapproval known. The Cut-direct was said to be the most devastating.

She'd been amazed to learn Nicholas had come by his own vouchers. More amazed that he'd insisted on bringing Maud and her here tonight. She remembered all too well his snarling disdain for the *haut ton*.

But most impressive was the number of people here who knew him, greeted him warmly by name. He might disdain them, but they, apparently, didn't know it. Even the arch *grand dame* Lady Castlereagh—Angela had named her the worst high-stickler of all—had welcomed them. With smiles!

"So good to see you again, m'lady," the patroness had said to Holly. "But do tell me, how is Major Sharpe's little ward getting on? So like you, if I may say so, to be keeping a bedside vigil for an ailing child!"

As they'd rehearsed, Holly explained the child was improving. That she no longer needed her constant vigil— Good Lord! Where had that tidbit come from?—but still begged for her company when she was awake.

Still smiling, the patroness had patted her hand, told her

to keep up the good work. "Such selflessness is a treasure to see in one so young," she'd said.

Holly had begun to relax after that. True, there were a few subtle looks, a covert glance or two in her direction; but by and large, it was clear none would dare the cut—direct, or otherwise. And she suspected it was largely because of Nicholas.

They couldn't dance, of course. Nicholas and Maud were still in mourning. Holly wasn't in black gloves, but as a guest in their home, showing similar respect would garner approval. And the *ton*'s approval, her parents and Trevor had repeatedly told her, was her singular goal. Her duty.

As it was her duty to wed the man she was pledged to. That had been implied, if not stated outright. Her father and stepmother were making plans to set the wedding date, announce it in the papers shortly.

And she would let them.

She would wed Trevor Regis, even though it was Nicholas she loved. Loved so deeply, she felt it in the marrow of her bones. With a passion that frightened her.

And she was terrified of letting him know it. *On-dits* were already flying over Lady Harlowe's ignominious downfall from the Olympus of Nicholas Sharpe's regard. "Poor Lydia!" she'd overheard a matron whisper cattily in another's ear at an "at home" yesterday. "How the haughty have fallen!"

I'll die before I let them say that about me! Before I become another pitied female on Sharpe the Bastard's discard pile!

"Why the frown, sweet?" Nicholas questioned as they circled the dancers in the stuffy room. Beside them, Maud looked dignified and properly somber in a new black gown she'd ordered from a fashionable *modiste*.

"Oh, um—the dancing!" Holly quickly improvised. "I'd heard about the waltz, of course, but now I see it performed, I wonder the patronesses allow it."

Nicholas chuckled. "This is a rather tame form of the dance, actually. If any attempted the style I witnessed abroad, Mr. Willis would toss them out on their pampered ears."

He grinned at her when she looked confused. "On the Continent, sweet, men and women don't just clasp each other lightly with their hands when they waltz. They, ah, align their bodies somewhat closely!"

Holly tried to picture it, and gave up, blushing. It was enough to provoke another chuckle from Nicholas, and she was glad when a familiar voice distracted them.

"Nick! We were wondering when you'd turn up!" Diana Wickham used her fan to wave them over to a corner where she and Rex appeared to be avoiding the crush.

The earl and countess exhanged greetings with the women while Nicholas marshalled excuses for not visiting with the pair. He'd turned down several recent invitations. Whitehall had ordered him to abandon Braithwaite temporarily. They'd had an opportunity to plant some false information in Rex's way, and were waiting to see if he took the bait. They'd no wish to scare him off with Nicholas's spying, no matter how subtle. If Rex was the traitor, he could be caught this easier way.

As it turned out, excuses weren't necessary. "We've heard all about Nick's poor little niece," Diana told Holly. "It explains why we've not heard from him. He must have been worried sick, if he took to collecting you straight from Rotten Row!"

Diana leaned over, whispering to Holly behind her fan. "Not that it wasn't the most romantic thing I've ever heard! But is the child feeling better now?"

Holly gave her the rehearsed response, and the countess nodded. Then she covered an aside with her fan again. "And what about the amnesia, Helene? Is it—that is, are you . . . recovered?"

She seemed uncomfortable with her question, and Holly wondered about it. Perhaps Diana wasn't sure how to deal with being privy to more than others knew. As far as the *ton* was concerned, Lady Helene had suffered some vagueness of memory with regard to her ordeal, but nothing had been

given out about actual amnesia. They'd felt the less said of it
—or any of the details—the better.

Holly informed her there were still gaps in her memory,
but not to fret about it; most of what she required to be
back within society had been filled in for her by her family,
and she was dealing well with the situation.

"Well, that's a relief," said Diana. "But please, my dear,
rely on us if the need arises. You must know we'd be only
too happy to help!"

She proceeded to demonstrate by ushering their party
through the assembly rooms like a doting mother hen. Hail-
ing friends and acquaintances left and right, she made it
clear Lady Helene was still her friend, and up to snuff in
every respectable respect.

At one point during it all, Rex Wickham caught Holly's
eye, and winked at her. *See,* he seemed to be saying, *we said
you could rely on us. Trust us. We're your friends.*

Nicholas caught the byplay, and felt suddenly uneasy
about Holly's having any contact with Rex. Quite inadver-
tently, he'd just overheard some gossip as they'd circled the
rooms. A piece of information about Braithwaite that was
deeply disturbing, especially as he'd not heard it before. Rex
had apparently been gambling recklessly at cards lately, and
was courting ruin.

Had the threat of being dished up been dire enough to
make him sell expensive information? Nicholas glanced impatiently at the clock, wondering if he could locate a certain
"fishmonger" without waiting for the stalls to open in the
morning.

Holly smiled as Maud invited her to make herself comfortable. They were in the small sitting room adjacent to the
older woman's bedchamber. Holly wasn't certain what had
prompted Maud to ask her to join her here for breakfast,
but she suspected an intimate chat.

She was hardly prepared for *how* intimate when Maud
fired a question at her seconds after they'd buttered their
toast.

"Forgive my bluntness, gel, but what are your feelings toward Nick? Are you in love with him?"

A piece of toast held midway toward her mouth, Holly said nothing. Couldn't, as her eyes flew to Maud's. She felt her face grow hot, looked quickly away.

"Thought so," Maud said kindly. "A woman doesn't kiss a man that way without feeling a *tendre* for him. Not an innocent like you, at any rate."

Hearing herself called an innocent deepened the blush. Holly wasn't at all comfortable with the description. Despite Nicholas's attempts to disabuse her of believing otherwise. Awareness of her violation ran deep, especially now she was back among the *haut ton*.

"Then, if I may ask," Maud went on, "why on earth haven't you broken with Regis? You must know by now, the man's interested primarily in your fortune!"

She did know it, of course. She'd simply chosen not to think about it. Easier that way . . .

"Not that I'm impugning the system that encourages that, mind you," Maud told her. "Families of heiresses have compounded with out-at-heels noblemen for generations. Alliances among our class need to be practical. No doubt Regis has something your father values in return . . . useful lands on his Irish estates, most likely."

She clasped Holly's hand, urging eye contact. "But that is not to say the heiresses always go along. Some have been known to follow their hearts, my dear. And given the tenderness I've witnessed in yours, I'm surprised you haven't put yourself among them."

Holly still didn't look at her, and when she answered, it was slowly. As if feeling her way carefully through the jumble of emotions beating about inside her.

"Aunt Maud . . ." She glanced briefly at the old woman's face, saw the kindness there, went on. "You mentioned, just a few moments ago, my . . . innocence. But surely you recall the . . . the circumstances under which I arrived at Caerdruth! The physician—"

"I know what you're thinking, gel, and it's nonsense! It doesn't matter that—"

"Oh, but it does! And I'm not just speaking of the *ton*'s reaction, if it were definitely known. I'm speaking of my own!"

"Your own? But I don't understand. It's your love for Nick we're considering here, gel, and I know him. He'd never let what happened—"

"But you'll agree, won't you, that Nick is a man of . . . of appetites? Passion?"

Maud smiled ruefully. "You'll get no argument from me on that, child."

"Then perhaps you'll understand when I tell you I . . . I'm not certain of myself where passion is concerned. Aunt Maud, I still don't know if I can surmount knowing what happened to me! I . . . I have all these doubts, you see. About myself as . . . as a woman."

Maud studied her a moment, then nodded tentatively. "You're not certain you could be . . . fully intimate with Nick? But you forget, I saw the way you were kissing him, my dear, and if he loves you—"

"But I've no assurance of that at all! On the contrary, I've all sorts of evidence I'd simply be one more female in a long line of Sharpe conquests! I may be in love with *him*, but I'm quite afraid he doesn't—doesn't . . ."

She bit her bottom lip, unable to finish, and Maud thought about arguing with her. She more than suspected Nick loved her, even if he didn't acknowledge it. Not even to himself.

Nick played a deep game with his emotions. Had, ever since he was a green boy. And the business with Judith had left him doubly certain he mustn't trust them.

But Maud could see all the arguments in the world wouldn't persuade the child. She was riddled with insecurities about herself, and Nick's deep game wasn't helping!

"Perhaps you can tell me this," she ventured. "If you're worried about Nick's not loving you, as well as your doubts about being, ah, a wife to him, how does that justify a marriage to Regis? *He* doesn't love you, and you'd still have to—"

"But don't you see?" Holly cried. "It wouldn't matter with Regis! Since he's made no secret of why he offered for me, he couldn't feel cheated by my lack of . . . of total passion in the marriage bed! He'd have his fortune, and that would be enough.

"But I've no right even to consider Nicholas," she went on. "No right at all. Even if he did come to love me, which isn't likely. Oh, I've no doubt he feels a physical attraction for me. And I, God help me, feel desire for him too!

"But that makes it all the more impossible to set my sights on him as a husband! Nick would never settle for doubts in the marriage bed. And he deserves more than *half* a woman in it!"

Maud sighed, and when she murmured something about this being worse than gypsies, Holly was reminded of the fey creature she'd met initially. Which was odd, because she hadn't thought of Maud that way in weeks.

"Drink your breakfast tea before it goes cold, my dear," Maud told her. "It's time I revealed a piece of family history I've been carrying about for more years than I ought. But once you've heard it, perhaps you'll understand why I chose to put it out of mind. Until now.

"Do you recall our previous discussion about the Sharpes?" she asked Holly.

"About Nicholas's father and—and his mother, you mean." The tale of the old earl's unrequited commitment to Nicholas's mother, of her desertion of him and their child, haunted Holly sometimes. Especially when observing Nicholas in one of his darker moods.

"I do," said Maud, "and the business about Aubrey and Judith as well. But it's the older pair I mean to enlighten you on this morning. Especially since I'm the only one who can."

Holly threw her a puzzled glance, and Maud smiled ruefully. "You see, my dear, after the old earl's death, I was the only one left who remembered."

Holly set aside her teacup, intrigued. "Remembered?"

"Catherine—that wild child who bore him a son, and then left them both to run off with gypsies—was my *daughter*. Nick, dear Holly—although I've never had the courage to tell him—is my grandson."

❧ Twenty-Two ❧

She crouched in the corner of the moving carriage, trying not to panic. Outside, lightning flashed, and rain beat down on the roof with a thrumming sound. Thunder rolled in the distance. She barely heard it. She focused on the dark-cloaked figure who held the riding crop . . . on the feral smile she could see when the lightning flashed.

She had to get away! But how? How? They were moving very fast. Still, had to—

The figure was upon her before she got her hand near the door. A gypsy! What were gypsies doing here? No, not a gypsy. It was—

She struggled like a wild thing, fear rising in her gorge. The choking sense of panic made it hard to breathe. Merciful God, she had to—

No use! So much stronger than I am! Can't even move! "Dear God, have pity! I've done you no wro—

"No! No, don't, please!"

Pain tore through her center like a knife. She opened her mouth, screamed . . .

"Holly, for God's sake, wake up!" Nicholas threw himself on the bed, reached for her, pulled her roughly into his arms. He'd made up his mind when the screams woke him; he'd be less gentle this time. Maybe the shock would pull the nightmare back with her, where they could face it—

"Depraved . . . *monster!* Let me *go!*" Holly clawed at him, bucking under his weight like a crazed animal, and thrashing her head from side to side. It was all he could do to hold her. Yet he did, calling her name. Then again, louder.

She came awake with a start. He felt the change at once. She stilled instantly, and he saw the shock of recognition on her face. Wide eyes glistening with tears in the moon washed room.

"Nicholas . . . ? Oh, God, Nicholas!" She began to sob, soft, broken sounds, and notions of being rough with her fled his mind.

He cradled her against his chest, running his hand over her hair. He stroked her shoulders, her back, wanting to absorb her pain. Murmuring her name again and again, he began to feel something unfamiliar . . . strange. There was a sense of aching tenderness, and the embryonic beginnings of a new emotion he didn't want to name.

He pushed the feeling back, unable—unwilling, if he were honest with himself—to examine it. She was quieting now, and he concentrated on his earlier purpose. "Tell me about it, Holly. Can you recall something?"

She hesitated, then nodded, pulled away to look at him. "The—the storm again . . . and a c-carriage. S-someone was in the carriage with me . . . someone . . . I couldn't see his face, b-but he w-wanted to—Oh, God, Nicholas—I can't *remember!* Why can't I re—"

"Shh . . . it's all right." She'd begun to tremble, and Nicholas pulled her back into his arms, her head tucked beneath his chin. "You needn't, if it's too pain—"

"A riding crop!" She gripped the front of his shirt, her hands balled into white-knuckled fists. "I remember a riding crop, and—"

"Holly, don't." The trembling had grown severe, and he realized he couldn't press her. Cartwright had warned him about trying to force things; the human mind had a powerful control over us, he believed, and would not be coerced into giving away what it regarded as essential to the preservation of self.

"No more, sweetheart," Nicholas went on. "I shouldn't have asked. Hush, now."

Her arms slid around his waist, and she pressed tightly against him. He was her anchor. In a treacherous maelstrom, her only safety. She wanted nothing beyond the shelter of his arms. Nicholas . . . only Nicholas . . .

Seconds passed, and the room grew still, but for the ticking of the mantel clock. Holly felt her heart beating in tandem, much slower now that the panic had passed. But a new awareness crept in, winding around her senses like smoke. Desire, heavy with need, stole in on cat's paws . . . *Nicholas.*

"Are you cold?" he asked, deliberately misinterpreting her shudder. He felt it too, of course . . . desire rushing in, in the wake of what they'd shared. Recalling the other times this had happened, he'd been prepared for it.

Prepared, as well, to thwart it.

Maud had come to see him in the morning, telling him of Holly's decision to go through with the marriage to Regis, despite having no feelings for the man. Despite knowing why he'd offered for her. When Nicholas asked for reasons, the old woman had declined to explain. She abruptly changed the subject, and he'd soon been too caught up in what she was saying to think of anything else. Aunt Maud . . . his grandmother! It was almost too much to absorb!

He focused on her other message: Holly . . . set on Regis. If it was true, he had no right to be with her this way. No right to act on the desire rolling over him like an avalanche.

He ground his teeth against it as she eased away to look at him. *Ah, Christ, Holly! Don't look at me that way! I'm only a man!*

She said nothing, only reached out to touch his face with her fingers. He felt them tremble as they traced the contour of his cheekbone, lowered to seek the shape of his mouth . . .

"Holly . . ." His voice sounded rough in the quiet room. Raw, and thick with need. Despite the warnings clanging in his brain, he covered her hand with his own, pressing it against his lips.

She shuddered again as she felt the kiss on the sensitive skin of her palm. He was beyond pretending it meant something other than a longing that matched his own. The dam broke. Desire thundered through him, and he caught her to him with a ragged groan.

Holly felt his resistance melt, had a moment to savor a fierce, impending joy before his mouth closed hungrily over hers. She'd sensed the tension in his body, the readiness to withdraw. To leave her alone again, perhaps with some platitude about sleep.

But now he was hers. Hers! Tomorrow would come, and with it, duty, and time for regret. But for this moment in time, Nicholas was hers. She would love him, and take the memory to her grave.

The kiss was fierce, devouring. She reveled in it, meeting his darting tongue, thrusting her arms about his neck in a frenzy of need. They clung together, rolling as one amid the tangled sheets. Now she was beneath, savoring the weight of him, the strength; he shifted, and she was above, stretched along his length and giddy with the feel of him. Of hands that found the softness of her buttocks and pressed her against his turgid heat.

Nicholas sensed the urgency in her. It equaled his own, and for a moment he let it rage. But then his hands met the row of tiny buttons on her sleeping gown. A prim reminder. She was still an innocent in need of tender care and slow hands. He could never chance triggering the fear again. She'd come so far, and he'd die before he let his own lust spoil it.

Ruthlessly biting back his passion, he eased her beneath him, and gentled the kiss. He threaded his fingers through her hair, held her head between his hands, and began to nibble and tease at her lips with teeth and tongue. She moaned softly at the subtle onslaught, stilled willingly to meet the slower pace.

He became absorbed by the taste of her, the textures . . . teeth and tongue, and silken lips that parted beneath his gentle probing. So absorbed, that when he felt the rake of her nails along his bare chest, he pulled away in surprise. She'd undone the buttons on his shirt, and he hadn't even realized!

"Minx!" he accused with a shaky laugh, then gasped as her nails found the flat discs of his male nipples, made them contract. He caught her wrists, pinning them firmly to the bed on either side of her head as he strove to gather his wits. "How the devil did you manage—"

"I had a splendid teacher," she whispered throatily.

Heat shimmered between them. Their eyes locked as each recalled that earlier lesson with buttons. Remembrance created the moment anew, and Nicholas clenched his jaws against the rush of heat to his loins.

He fought the battle, barely keeping himself in check. He wanted nothing more than to raise her gown, release the swollen shaft that strained against his breeches, and take her then and there.

But he made himself wait, his smile slow and lazy as he cocked a brow at her. "So it's lessons m'lady recalls, is it?"

The smile became a teasing grin, and Holly felt her mouth go dry. "Perhaps," he drawled musingly, never releasing her gaze, "she wishes another?"

Pleasure rippled along her spine. A thrill of anticipation as she caught his intent. Liquid heat gathered at the juncture of her thighs, and her woman's place throbbed. She squirmed against him, provoking a knowing chuckle.

Then suddenly he shifted, and strong hands laid her gently on her belly. "Shh," he whispered when she turned her head, and a question formed on her lips. He swept the long tangle of hair from her back, bent to place a kiss on her shoulder, another at her ear. "Relax, darling," he murmured. "This is for you . . . for pleasure."

He began to run his hands over her . . . shoulders

. . . length of back . . . waist and hips . . . thighs. Light, caressing strokes that had her sighing his name.

"Like this, do you?" he murmured lazily.

"Mmm," was all she could manage, and she heard him chuckle softly.

"Thought so," he told her in that same indolent tone. Then, suddenly, his touch became more localized . . . intimate. She felt a hand curl beneath her, cup and fondle a breast. He squeezed the nipple, then again, harder. A shaft of pleasure lanced to the place between her thighs, and she moaned.

The moan became ragged when his other hand stroked upward from the backs of her knees, over her derriere, then higher, sweeping the hem of her gown with it. Cool air caressed the skin of her buttocks, but she was burning, burning.

She felt him shift again, and then his mouth was on her, feasting on what he'd bared. His lips brushed and nibbled lightly along her spine . . . then lower, lower, until he pressed a kiss at its base. At the same moment his fingers stroked the cleft of her buttocks, and she thought she heard herself whimper. When they delved between her thighs, finding the slippery heat of her woman's flesh, she knew she sobbed his name.

She never learned how he managed the buttons himself. But her gown was a twist about her waist when he turned her toward him again. She gasped as she found herself seated astride his hips. He leaned indolently against the headboard, his hands skimming her waist. And he gave her that knowing, lazy grin again, but his eyes were heavy-lidded, his voice husky as their gazes met.

"My shirt, darling . . ." he said. "Remove it."

She swallowed, keenly aware of the bulge beneath his breeches as it pressed against the apex of her thighs. Her fingers shook as she pushed the cotton off his shoulders, slid it down.

Moonlight limned the contours of his arms and shoulders . . . corded strength that rippled and flexed as he shrugged the garment away. She ran her eyes greedily over a muscled chest that tapered to a lean, hard waist. Moonlight streaming in from the windows silvered the mat of hair she'd felt with her fingers. She reached out, eager to touch it again, but he stayed her hands with his.

"Not yet," he murmured huskily, then placed her hands at the top of his breeches. "First these, m'lady. Undo them, if you would."

She released a wavering breath she hadn't realized she was holding, set to work with clumsy, unsure fingers. Her attention kept straying from the closures to the turgid mound beneath, and she could hardly keep a thought in her head.

The task seemed to take forever. At one point it seemed utterly hopeless, and she heaved a sigh, raised imploring eyes to his. He flashed that reckless grin, but she thought it seemed strained as he shook his head no.

She called him wretch, and other things under her breath, but he laughed softly and urged her on. Then, without warning, his hands slid to her breasts. He cupped them, as if to test their weight, and she squirmed helplessly when his thumbs teased and worried her nipples into hard, thrusting buds.

It was too much. She sucked in her breath as a shudder claimed her. "N-Nicholas . . ." she managed, then had to stop. Below, the hard, velvety length of him sprang free, and she felt its heat against her naked thigh. She uttered a soft cry, and gripped his shoulders to steady herself.

"Lesson completed," he rasped before his mouth captured hers in a drugging kiss.

Holly lost all sense of time and place as her body melted into his. She perceived his hands on her hips as he positioned her, but dimly, as if in a dream. The night, the room, the moonlight faded away. The center of her world became his voice, urging, encouraging, and the hot swollen shaft that pushed slowly into the slick heat of her.

Nicholas felt sweat bead his brow as he pressed slowly home. She was tight and hot, yet open to him as the slippery moisture of her eased his entry. But it was hell, pacing himself this way. He'd brought them both to a fever pitch. He wanted to thrust, and plunge, and lose himself in a storm of mindless rapture.

But he couldn't. Not yet. Everything that passed between them had been carefully orchestrated. Designed by him to keep her fear at bay while he made this perfect for her. Even her position astride. She had to feel less vulnerable this way, less—

"Nicholas!" Her sharp cry echoed in the room, and she fell against him, taking him to the hilt. He groaned her name as he felt the first spasm claim her, and he knew his wait was over.

"Yes, sweetheart—yes!" he urged as he rolled and took her with him. She bucked to meet his thrust, then again.

A roaring filled his ears, and he picked up the rhythm, moved with her in the cadence of the age-old dance. Soon they were riding the crest, and he felt her climax a second time.

Joy and triumph surged through him. She was sweet, and whole, and a miracle in his arms. He felt her come yet again, and he cried her name.

"Nicholas!" she sobbed, and he thought the ecstasy would kill him when he spent himself in a shuddering release. It took him out of himself, and he was soaring, soaring . . . at one with the woman in his arms, and mindless among the stars.

Nicholas lay awake in the moonlit chamber. Beside him, nestled against his side, Holly stirred dreamily in her sleep. He pressed a kiss to her brow, smiled as she snuggled closer.

His body was replete, but his mind chased itself in circles, never more awake. She'd just given him the most satisfying bedding of his life, yet even as he savored it, he wondered why he'd let it occur. What had happened to all his lofty thoughts of that other time? He'd given her his seed, and right now, she could be carrying his child.

A sardonic smile shaped his mouth. So much for Sharpe the Bastard and his lofty intentions!

A frown replaced the smile. She was set on wedding Regis. Christ, the very notion made him sick!

Yet what did he have to do with it? Say about it? He was only her first bed partner, and a guilt-ridden one at that.

A vague restlessness stirred behind his thoughts. He closed his eyes, and images beckoned . . . the color of her eyes the first time he'd seen them . . . the way they caught the light when an idea took hold . . . the sound of her laughter. And finally, that sense of aching tenderness he'd felt when he comforted her tonight.

Christ, what was wrong with him? He'd never let a woman invade his thoughts like this before! Not even Judith, and he'd been an infatuated boy at the time.

The mere thought of Judith had him scowling, and he eased himself away from Holly and left the bed. He glanced down at her as he gathered his clothes, and the scowl deepened.

She'd murmured something about him not leaving her as she drifted off, but that was ridiculous. Her abigail, or God knew who else, would be coming here in a few hours. He could well imagine what would happen to all their efforts to free her name from scandal then!

But damn it, Holly—what's it all for? So that you may go trailing off to the parson's mousetrap with that fortune hunter? Be a dutiful little, scandal-free wife for Regis?

Muttering a vicious oath under his breath, Nicholas strode toward the door. But as he passed her dressing table, he saw something that suddenly made his blood run cold. In a dusting of talcum powder on the moonlit floor, he saw a man's booted footprint—and it wasn't his.

❧ Twenty-Three ❧

Holly awakened slowly, basking in the afterglow of dreams too delicious to relinquish all at once. Her limbs felt oddly heavy, weighted by a pleasant lethargy. Other parts of her body felt strange as well . . . the tips of her breasts . . . the place between her thighs . . .

She moaned softly, beginning to recall . . . Dear God, had they really . . .

A subtle ache between her thighs told her they had. Remembrance teased her further from the haze of sleep, and a dreamy smile tugged at her lips.

Ah, God, Nicholas . . . She stretched languidly, reaching for—

Gone! A piercing sense of loss brought her fully awake. She felt the hot sting of tears, and her vision blurred as she stared at the empty place beside her on the bed. Her sob echoed in the quiet room.

"What the devil are you crying for, you impossible baggage?"

She gasped, eyes flying to the chair by the window. "N-Nicholas!"

"Damned right it's me! And now perhaps you'll tell me what's prompted these waterworks! When a man sits up half the night at a woman's request, one might think he could expect a pleasant greeting from her. A 'good morning, Nicholas' would have answered nicely, I should think."

He was scowling as he rose and walked toward her.

"You did stay!" With a watery laugh, Holly scrambled off the bed. Caught in the surprise of finding him there, she forgot her deshabille, and flung herself at him with a small, glad cry.

Nicholas laughed as he caught her to him. "Silly chit! Of course, I stayed!" He ignored an inner voice that reminded him he'd not intended staying; that he'd only changed his mind when he saw a chilling footprint on the floor.

Holly closed her eyes, savoring the feel of his arms around her. Dear God, but she loved this man! She knew she could never wed Regis now. But she wouldn't think of that. Nicholas was here, and at this moment nothing else mattered.

As he held her, Nicholas tried to make sense out of what he was feeling. His annoyance had vanished. Whether it had gone at her unexpected tears, or for reasons he'd no wish to examine, he didn't know. But it was gone.

In its place was an odd feeling of how right she felt in his arms. He'd never felt this before. But he knew instinctively this woman had become important to him in ways he wasn't prepared to deal with.

He disengaged at once, setting her away from him . . .

And groaned. The twist of sleeping gown, which he'd never entirely removed last night, had puddled around her feet, and she stood there totally unclothed. Perfection. He knew as he ran his eyes over her, that if he lived to be an old, old man, he'd never see anything lovelier.

His eyes went to hers. They were huge in her face. Two deep pools of liquid green. Their pupils were dilated. "Ah, Christ!"

She moaned as he caught her to him. Mouths joined as they came together in a tangle of limbs and unleashed hunger.

This time there were no preliminaries. Holly hadn't time or will to think as he deftly undid the closures she'd fought with the night before. Her feet left the floor, and she felt his hand beneath her buttocks before she realized enough to wrap her legs about him. She had a fleet second to wonder if such things were possible before he thrust inside her, and all thought ceased.

It was instant, full-blown passion, and as new to Nicholas as it was to her. But she was sleek and wet, and more than ready. She climaxed with the first hot spewing of his seed. It was over in a matter of minutes.

"Are you all right?" They stood there, weak with repletion, in the middle of the floor, and Nicholas could barely speak. He'd released his hold enough to lower her to the carpet, and she sagged against him. He could feel the wild crescendo of her heartbeat. Like his, it was only beginning to slow.

"I love you." She murmured this weakly against his chest, then seemed to freeze. With a gasp, she pulled sharply away, her hand over her mouth.

Nicholas too, seemed frozen as they stared at each other. Dozens of women had told him they loved him after having sex. Judith had been the first. It meant nothing. But as he took in Holly's look of chagrin, he had a suspicion that her declaration was different.

Caught utterly off guard, he said the first thing that sprang to his mind. "Then why the devil are you wedding Regis?"

Relief washed over Holly. At least he wasn't laughing. Or pitying her.

The relief vanished, replaced by the bitter realization that he'd made no declarations himself. It only confirmed what she'd told Maud: Nicholas didn't love her.

Covering her hurt with anger, she lashed back at him. "That's no business of yours!"

The gray eyes flashed a warning as he seized her roughly by the shoulders. "Isn't it? What if you're with child? Is that what you'll tell the babe that at this moment could be growing in your belly? Or will you tell it anything at all?"

A child? His child . . . The blood drained from her face. She hadn't even thought—"Nicholas, I—"

"Nicholas—what?" He sneered at her. "But perhaps you

won't tell it anything. Simply pass it off as that jackal's. Or will you take an easier route? Will you give it to the jackal to raise—as his bastard?"

She sucked in her breath with a sharp, audible hiss. Her arm came up, and she struck him hard across the face.

He never even winced. He merely looked at her, and his eyes were ice. Then he strode silently to the door.

Holly watched it shut behind him, then sank to the floor in sobs.

Maud paced the length of the carpet in her chamber, well aware it had been years since she'd displayed such agitation. Since Catherine . . . wild child of her womb. Nick's mother.

As she paced, she talked to herself. "You owe that boy something, Maudie, my gel. For your years of silence. For your cowardice! Who knows how he might have fared if he'd had a true grandmother to turn to!

"His sire was a brute, and perhaps no one could have stood up to him, but you might have tried! Or at least been there for the lad when he hungered for a loving touch . . . when he needed a woman's soft, maternal hand.

"But where were you? Hiding away inside yourself, that's where! Nursing your own wounds, with poor Nick left to find his own way. Left to bury his finer instincts inside all that hard, unfeeling armor!

"Well, you're done hiding, Maudie. It won't answer! This may be the lad's last chance for happiness, and it's up to you to—"

A knock on her door ended the monologue, and she called for Holly to enter. She'd found the poor child in tears that morning, having gone to Holly's room when she failed to turn up at breakfast. In tears, and not wearing a stitch as she'd huddled amid the bedclothes.

It had all come tumbling out, then. The reasons for her despair: Holly's giving herself to Nick . . . unwittingly letting him know she loved him . . . then their bitter, angry words.

And that was when Maud had decided she must do something. She'd come to love this girl like a daughter. It was almost as if God had taken pity on her for all her years of bottled-up love for a child who'd neither wanted nor needed it; as if He'd sent her this motherless girl in Catherine's place. To love. To help! Just as she must help Nick.

It simply couldn't be a coincidence that in helping the one, she'd also be helping the other!

"Thank you for coming, my dear," she told Holly. The child looked a sight, with dark shadows under her eyes, and their rims red from weeping. But Maud said nothing of this, assuming a brisk, no-nonsense air as she led her to some chairs by the windows.

"No doubt you're wondering why I asked you here," said Maud, "so I shan't beat about the bush. The facts are that you love my grandson, and Nick, I'm certain, loves you, although—"

"Oh, Aunt Maud—"

"Now, hear me out, gel! I've been alive a deal longer than you, and it's entirely possible I've acquired more wisdom in the process!"

Holly sighed tiredly, but gave an acquiescing nod.

"As I was saying," Maud went on, "I believe Nick returns your feelings, although he's too blind and stubborn to realize it. In fact, it's worse than stubborn blindness, now I think on it. I think he's afraid to—"

"Afraid?" Holly couldn't even associate the word with Nicholas. "Why should Nicholas be—"

"Because he was brutally taught, at a very early age, that to allow himself to feel any sort of tender emotion was to expose himself to the worst sort of abuse. Love, in young Nick's world, brought pain."

Maud looked at her sharply. "Can you blame him, then, for trying to make himself immune to it? For building a hard protective shell about his heart, and pretending that, for him at least, love doesn't exist?"

Holly looked doubtful. "Even if it's true, what difference

in the end? All well and good to say he loves me, but if he won't acknowledge it—"

"Then we must force him to acknowledge it! For his own good—and yours, gel."

Holly closed her eyes and shook her head. She couldn't imagine forcing Nicholas to do something he'd no wish to do. Easier to imagine him afraid! "How?" she asked. "We're only two powerless women who—"

"Who love him enough to try? And never say powerless. I shan't, in any case!"

Holly looked at her. How had she ever imagined Maud was cakey and bird-witted? Fey and inconsequential, and therefore weak? The woman across from her had a look in her eye to give anyone pause. Fey, or not, Maud already had her love; now she would have her attention as well.

"What did you have in mind, Aunt Maud?"

The old woman grinned at her. "We're going to convince Nick to give a party to celebrate your forthcoming nuptials to Regis."

Holly considered taking back all she'd concluded about bird-wittedness. "Never say you're serious!"

"As a vicar with a sermon! Now, listen carefully, gel . . ."

Maud outlined the scheme she'd hatched. She was already convinced Nicholas found Holly's commitment to Regis intolerable. His words to Holly in the heat of argument said as much. By having him host a party that feted the couple's engagement (to coincide with the imminent announcement of the wedding date in the papers) they might just push him into realizing he loved her. Into realizing he ought to replace "the jackal."

Holly pointed out the Sharpe household was in black gloves. That people in mourning couldn't be having parties.

Maud was undaunted. "It needn't be an elaborate affair. A quiet 'at home' with no dancing. Not even the high-sticklers can object to that!"

How to convince Nicholas to give such a party posed a greater problem in Holly's mind, but Maud had thought that through as well. "Nick may be stubborn, but he's not without honor," she told her. "He promised your father he'd do the right thing by you, you'll collect. Said he'd do all he could to help reestablish you among the *ton*, didn't he?"

"I own, he did, but if Nicholas can't abide my wedding Regis—"

"Trust me, gel. By the time I've done with the lad, he'll be convinced he *must* give this party. I'll have him believing you need it to cement your credibility within the Polite World. For fear of appearing peevish, he wouldn't dare refuse! Trust me."

Doubts and what-ifs assailed Holly. But as she met the old woman's eyes, she found her heart suddenly beating faster, hope fluttering crazily in her breast. "I love you, Aunt Maud," she told her. "And I shall!"

The day of the party dawned bright and sunny. They were heading into the warn season now, and Maud knew they'd barely scheduled the fete in time; in less than a fortnight the entire *ton* would be off to their country houses, or at Bath, or Brighton with Prinny.

As it turned out, the *crème de la crème* had accepted. Nick cynically ascribed his own reasons to this. "Those rabidly nosey twits," he'd told Maud, "wouldn't miss their chance at a potential tidbit for the gossip mills! Decline? They wouldn't dare. Might miss something juicy!"

Lord and Lady Tamarand had been particularly pleased with Maud's idea, and Regis had been greatly mollified. To Nicholas's disgust, he'd even sent a letter saying he'd been rash in his earlier judgments, and that he hoped he and Major Sharpe might become friends.

As with most fetes, the guests weren't scheduled to arrive before nine, and even that was early by *tonnish* standards. The only difficulty this presented had to do with the children. Fanny had come to Holly and begged that they might be allowed to attend.

"We've never, *ever* attended a party before," she'd said

plaintively. "Not even Harry! And Lottie and I want ever so much to see all the ladies in their splendid gowns! And especially to see you there!"

"But you've seen me in my new gown," Holly had hedged. Angela had sent her personal *modiste* to Sharpe House, and Lord Tamarand had paid an enormous sum for the tissue-fine creation hanging in Holly's wardrobe. It was tinted a new color the *modiste* called "apricot," with deep green accents, and with it she'd wear the Lansdowne emeralds.

"Oh but, Princess!" Fanny had pleaded. "It won't be the same! We just know you'll be the most beautiful lady at the party. But how are we to appreciate how beautiful, if we don't see you outshining the others?"

Suspecting the child would have made a fine barrister if she'd been born male, Holly had agreed to speak to Maud about it, although the decision would have to be made by Nicholas.

The night of the party arrived. With the exception of Harry, the youngsters were allowed to make a brief appearance before retiring to their beds . . . "to be seen, but not heard," as their uncle had put it. Young Lord Sharpe, of course, was counted an adult, and allowed to remain as long as he wished.

"Don't see why Harry wants to stay anyway," Michael mumbled when the time came for them to go upstairs. "Grown-ups' parties are devilish boring!"

Martin nodded vigorously as they trudged upstairs with Charlotte, who was yawning and rubbing her eyes. All four younger children had again been the recipients of Lady Tamarand's effusive attentions. She'd cooed and fussed over them until the twins began to squirm. Finch's quiet reminder that it was their bedtime hadn't come a moment too soon!

"Fanny was right about that stepmother," Martin said. "I don't like her either, and—Michael . . . where *is* Fanny, anyway?"

His twin looked behind them and saw only Charlotte

trailing sleepily in their wake. He shrugged. "Perhaps she went to the refreshment table to pinch a strawberry tart. Hope she pinches one for us! Awfully tasty. Best thing about the whole silly party!"

Fanny was nowhere near the refreshment table. Yet it had been her unseen presence beneath that cloth draped piece of furniture which was responsible for where she presently was: secluded in the twins' bedchamber, and near bursting with important news!

Michael would have been right about her original hiding place; she'd stashed herself under the refreshment table in hopes of making off with a few of the strawberry tarts when no one was looking.

But what she'd come by instead was an earful. Having already purloined the pastries, she'd been about to make her escape when she heard a female voice just above where she sat.

"I'll meet you in the side garden, darling, in half an hour," the woman had murmured. "It's just outside the French windows in the smaller drawing room. But be careful, my dear. If he sees either of us leaving, he'll no longer believe my promise that our affair's over."

Fanny would have recognized that voice anywhere. It was Lady Tamarand!

The male voice that answered was more difficult. So when the man had whispered that he was already savoring the stepmother's kisses, Fanny had dared a peek from beneath the tablecloth. The *fee-awn-say!*

Fanny was righteously indignant. And furious. She hadn't known exactly what Lady Tamarand meant when she spoke of their "affair"; but she certainly knew Princess Holly's *fee-awn-say* had no business giving kisses to that stepmother!

So Fanny had waited until the coast was clear, and then managed to make her escape. She'd been so excited, she hadn't even remembered the tarts.

But tarts were unimportant now. She'd seen Finch speaking to the twins, and known he was sending them to bed.

And since what she had in mind would be best if she and her brothers did it together, she'd decided to take the servants' stairway to reach their chamber ahead of them before an adult could stop her.

Any moment now, those two sneaks would be going to the side garden for their kisses. Kisses that were wrong.

But they were good for one thing: proving to the princess that she must never wed that awful Regis! Before the pair sneaked into the garden, Fanny planned to collect the twins. The three of them would spy on that odious couple. Then they'd all go straight to Princess Holly and—

The door swung open, barely missing Fanny in the process.

"Dash it all, Fanny! How'd you get here ahead of us?" Martin demanded.

"Never mind that," said Michael. "Did you get us some tarts?"

"No, but I've brought you something even better!" Ignoring their scowls, she hurriedly imparted what she'd learned. The twins were resistant at first. Who cared about disgusting kisses anyway? But when she explained the import of *these* kisses, and then went on to explain how she needed their help, they quickly fell in with her plans. The temptation to play spy was just too great to resist!

"Now we've got to hurry!" Fanny finished breathlessly. "Any minute now, those two sneaks—"

"Lady Fanny! I thought I heard your voice in there!" Finch's admonishing tone had the three of them looking at one another with chagrin.

The majordomo chastised Fanny, and sent her off to her bedchamber to join her "*obedient* little sister." She barely had time to hear Michael whisper that it would have to wait till morning, but that he and Martin would back her up.

But Fanny had no intention of waiting till morning. Even if the twins told a clanker, pretending they'd been with her when she overhead the nasty business, she doubted anyone would take them seriously.

She'd tried to tell both the princess and Aunt Maud

about her dislike of that stepmother and the other two, but neither had taken that seriously. "It's not the Way of Things to be disliking people because they give you 'bad feelings,' gel," Aunt Maud had told her. And Princess Holly had simply smiled and told Fanny that perhaps she just wanted time to come to know these people better.

No, thought Fanny as she walked thoughtfully in the direction of her chamber. It simply wouldn't wait till morning. Not when they'd be armed with no more than an overheard conversation. A conversation she couldn't prove had happened!

Fanny knew exactly what she'd do. It only wanted waiting until Finch returned downstairs, and then making for the servants' stairwell herself. She'd need to be very brave, but she could do this without the twins. And wouldn't they be surprised when she told them in the morning! And Harry and Lottie too. The whole lot of them would!

But as it turned out, Fanny never saw her siblings in the morning. She never made it to her bed.

ᔰᔥ Twenty-Four ᔥᔰ

"**M**artin, are you awake?" Michael plunked himself down on his brother's bed, well aware it was an hour earlier than they usually arose. But he'd already been awake for half an hour, and he couldn't wait any longer. Fanny's news, and the bumble bath Finch had made of their spy mission was burning a hole in his brain. "Martin," he repeated, "are you—"

"Dash it, Michael!" Martin groused. "If I wasn't, I am now!" Of the two, he'd always required more sleep, and it didn't help that they'd lain awake past their normal bedtime last night, discussing the business with Fanny.

"Splendid!" Michael exclaimed, unfazed by his twin's grumbling. "Come on out of the clothmarket, you slugabed! We've got to fetch Fanny, and see what's to be done!"

Martin yawned and sat up groggily. "What time is it?"

"Time to do something, you paperskull! What if Fanny's already up and doing it herself? D'you want her getting the jump on us? A girl?"

This had the effect he'd known it would. His twin blinked, then hastily rubbed the sleep out of his eyes as his brother handed him his shirt and breeches.

As Martin dressed, Michael peppered him with questions. "What d'you suppose we might do? Should we go to Miss Holly? Would she even believe us without proof? We can't let Fanny go it alone, can we?"

"We told Fanny we'd back her up," said Martin as he fumbled for his shoes. "Means we'll have to tell a clanker. Pretend *we* overheard it too. Miss Holly would be more inclined to believe the three of us, instead of one silly girl who's given to squints!"

"Right!" Michael nodded decisively, handing him the second shoe. "And what's bad about a clanker if it's for a good cause? Ol' Fanny needs us, and if she's clever, she'll know it. But we'd best hurry. Can't always trust a girl to be clever about these things."

They hurried out to the hallway and made a beeline for their sister's room. Michael had just raised a fist to knock on the door when a familiar voice stopped him cold.

"Master Michael!" exclaimed Finch, who'd already learned to tell the difference between the twins. "What are you about, sir? And you, Master Martin!"

Michael dropped his hand with alacrity, and both boys turned toward the majordomo. "Um, we thought we'd, ah, collect Fanny for, um . . ." Michael glanced helplessly at his twin.

"For a jaunt in the garden!" Martin supplied. "There's this queer sort of rock we spied there yesterday, and Fanny's awfully clever about rocks. She'll be able to tell us—"

"Not at seven in the morning, she won't, lads. Now, come away from there, and we'll see about some breakfast for you. Cook's got her hands full, what with the aftermath of the party, but I'm sure she'll be able to find something for a pair of early risers."

The twins exchanged frustrated glances as he led them briskly away from the girls' sleeping quarters. Beset by visions of Fanny getting the jump on them, each privately cursed their ill fortune, not to mention wide-awake servants.

But suddenly their luck took a turn for the better. As they reached the bottom of the stairs, a knock on the front door drew Finch's attention. He sent them toward the breakfast room on their own, and as the servant went to answer the door, they spied Nicholas coming down the stairs.

The twins exchanged glances, nodding archly at each other. Uncle Nicholas was a man of the world. They could tell him the news. Man to man, and leave the females out of it!

Nicholas waited as patiently as he could while the twins began their tale. He needed to reach Whitehall with some disturbing news he'd come by last night, and the sooner the better. Intent on his mission, he was listening with only half an ear until the import of what they were saying began to penetrate.

"Hold a moment, Martin," he said, "and repeat what you just said."

"Lady Tamarand and that Lord Regis, sir . . . they were meeting in the garden last night. In secret."

"For kisses!" Michael supplied, the look on his face making it clear what he thought of such business.

"You're certain of this? You heard them?"

The twins shot uncomfortable glances at each other, but their uncle missed the exchange as Finch rushed up to him with an official looking envelope in hand.

"Message for you, sir," said the majordomo. "The man who delivered it said it was urgent."

The twins exchanged groans as Finch ushered them toward the breakfast room with admonitions about foot-dragging.

Michael glanced helplessly over his shoulder, but his uncle was absorbed in the letter he'd been handed. He could only hope Uncle would carry on with what they'd related. At least they'd been spared having to boldly face things out with him. Michael had a good suspicion Uncle Nicholas would know a clanker when he heard one!

Nicholas's jaw dropped as he read the message. From Whitehall, it consisted of two sentences: "Come at once,

using prescribed arrangements for secrecy. Regis was found
dead early this morning."

It took him little time to reach the government offices at
that hour of the morning. The *ton* slept late, and the West
End held almost no traffic. This also made it easier than
usual to slip in through a service entrance unobserved.
Nicholas was admitted to the office of Castlereagh's man by
a uniformed guard exactly half an hour after reading the
message.

Sir Anthony Smythe greeted him grimly as he entered.
Nicholas nodded, but his eyes were already on the silent
figure sitting across from Smythe's desk. Lord Basil
Tamarand glanced at him, but said nothing as Smythe gestured Nicholas to the empty chair that remained.

Sir Anthony quickly filled him in. Lord Regis's body had
been found floating in the Thames shortly before dawn by
an alert member of the watch. The corpse had a knife in its
back.

Nicholas digested this information, and his eyes went to
Holly's father as Smythe explained the marquis's presence.

"Lord Tamarand is here for questioning because he was
overheard quarreling with his future son-in-law last night
. . . at *your* party, Major Sharpe."

Tamarand and Regis at odds? This was the first Nicholas
knew of it. But then, he'd been busy pursuing different
game last night. "Overheard by whom, Sir Anthony?"

"Several of the guests, actually," said Smythe after a subtle clearing of his throat. "Their names are unimportant at
the moment."

So Whitehall had other spies out. Nicholas had supposed
as much, wondering mildly who they might be as Smythe
went on.

"Fact is, it doesn't matter because his lordship admits to
the quarrel. Isn't that so, m'lord?"

"Yes, but I didn't kill him."

Nicholas saw the first sign of emotion on Tamarand's face
since he'd entered the room. The man was furious.

"So you've said, m'lord," Smythe told him. "Would you please tell the major what else you said of the matter?"

Tamarand eyed him coldly. "I don't see why I should. What's Sharpe to do with the business, anyway? He was merely the host at—"

"At the last place Lord Regis was seen alive," Smythe finished smoothly. "Now if you would be so kind, m'lord . . . ?"

Tamarand heaved a disgusted sigh. "I said I didn't kill him, but that I wished I had!"

Nicholas eyed him sharply, a suspicion beginning to niggle at the back of his mind. "Why?"

"Because the bleeding scoundrel was cuckolding me, damn it! I caught him at it! Trysting with my wife! God, what a fool I've been!"

Tamarand bent his head in anguish, and under the guise of allowing him some privacy to recover, Smythe led Nicholas from the room.

"What else?" Nicholas asked when they'd retreated a distance down the hall. His head was spinning with recollections of those earlier rumors about Tamarand being out for blood. And with the rattlings of his young nephews who, it seemed, knew what they'd been talking about.

Sir Anthony went on to say Tamarand had been found shortly after the discovery of the body. He was returning from a royal park where he'd been preparing for a duel. He had his seconds along, and they'd sworn to being with him since he'd left the party at Sharpe House.

"Unless they're both lying to protect him," Smythe finished, "the man has an air-tight alibi."

Nicholas nodded. "They could be, of course. But I'm inclined to believe them—and him. I've been observing the man, as you well know. Tamarand's not the sort to be stabbing an enemy in the back. He'd be far more likely to shoot the bastard in a duel."

"How is it you'd no knowledge of the quarrel, Major?" Smythe asked. "As I can only assume, that is. You left it

to us to come to *you* with the news—and not the reverse."

Nicholas looked at him gravely. "I assume it took place
while I was pursuing another avenue last night . . . learning something, I think, which should be of considerable
interest to you, sir."

"And that is . . . ?"

"While keeping my ear to the ground," Nicholas said
tightly, "I learned that Regis recently won an enormous sum
from the earl of Braithwaite at cards. A sum Lord Wickham
could in no ways pay without being completely dished up."
Nicholas's eyes were grim. "Ruined, that is, Sir Anthony.
Ruined beyond remedy."

Nicholas urged Lucifer to pick up the pace as he made his
way back to Queen Street. A vague uneasiness which had
begun with the news of Regis's murder was growing steadily inside him.

Holly . . . Her name seemed to echo through the ring-
ing of the stallion's hooves on the cobbles. *You've got to get
to Holly!*

He made Sharpe House in half the time it had taken him
to reach Whitehall. Flinging the stallion's reins at the groom
Finch had hired, he charged up the front steps and through
the door.

"What the devil . . . ?"

All bedlam appeared to have broken loose. Noise and
movement wherever he looked. Servants shouted and
rushed about for no apparent reason, including a pair of
chambermaids in tears. Harry hovered anxiously over the
twins and little Charlotte at the base of the stairs. The boys
gestured wildly toward the top of the staircase, and Lottie
was sobbing. He saw Finch conferring anxiously with Maud
near the drawing room doors; she wrung her hands and
seemed near tears as well.

With a deliberate motion, Nicholas slammed the front
door behind him. The noise ceased. All heads turned his
way.

"Excellent," he said into the silence. "Now, what the deuce is going on?"

His hand came up as everyone started to speak at once. It stopped them. Nicholas sought out a calm face. "Mr. Finch . . . if you please?"

The majordomo may have looked calm, but Nicholas saw his lower lip tremble ever so slightly before he answered. "Thank God you've come, sir. It's the little lass . . . Lady Fanny. She's gone, sir."

"Gone?"

"Gone missing, sir."

"When? When did—"

"We discovered it just a short while ago, sir . . . perhaps twenty minutes. Her bed's not been slept in, you see."

Nicholas started to reply with a remark about the chit's penchant for hoydenish mischief when he saw a look of alarm pass between the twins. He bit back an oath, and fixed them with a piercing gaze. "Martin, what do you and Michael know about this?"

Nicholas had to admire the lad. Without tears or hesitation, Martin quickly described Fanny's role in the news he and Michael had imparted earlier. But a feeling of dread began to settle in as the child went on to describe their aborted plan to spy on Regis and the stepmother.

Aborted for the twins, Nicholas realized as the dread crept steadily through his gut. *But not necessarily for Fanny.* The dread began to gnaw and tear, and it was all he could do to beat it back.

Yet it was nothing compared to what he felt when Maud rushed forward.

"Oh, Nicholas, I fear that's not the end of it!" she cried. "Holly's gone missing too!"

"Christ! When? How?"

His grandmother looked as ancient as he'd ever seen her as she stammered out her reply. Upon learning the news of Fanny's disappearance, and then the twins' tale of what they knew, Holly had fainted. She'd been carried to her room by Finch, who then left to fetch some hartshorn, and send a footman for a physician.

"Wh-when I went up to ch-check on her a short—a short while ago," Maud finished, "sh-she was gone! Oh, merciful heaven, *both* of them! Whatever can it mean?"

The dread became an icy lump of fear in the pit of Nicholas's stomach. He had a chilling idea of what it could mean, and his mind raced with all the implications: Regis dead, and the murderer still at large . . . Fanny bent on spying on Regis, perhaps just at the critical moment when the killer made his move . . . Holly—

His mind drew a blank at her connection with the matter. Yet he knew as surely as he stood there, that Holly's disappearance was somehow—

A banging on the front door intruded, and Nicholas spun toward it. A footman dashed across the foyer to open the door, admitting the groom Nicholas had just left in charge of Lucifer.

"Oh, sir!" the man blurted as he wrung his cap in his hands. "It's your new 'igh perch phaeton! It's been taken, and them fine bloods with it!"

Nicholas felt the fine hairs on the back of his neck rise. "Who, man? Who took it?"

" 'Twas 'er ladyship, sir. The stable lad told me. Said 'e couldn't stop 'er!"

Nicholas forced a calm he didn't feel. "Lady Helene, do you mean?"

"Aye, that be 'er. But please don't be blamin' the lad, sir! When she told 'im where she was goin', 'e figgered 'er ladyship knew—"

"What was that?" Hope flared like a rocket as Nicholas seized the man by the shoulders. "What did you say?"

"I—I asked ye n-not t' blame the—"

"No, the rest! Did you say she told the lad where she was going?"

The groom managed a shaky grin despite the flint-hard eyes that pinned him where he stood. He'd no sooner given the fashionable address in Grosvenor Square than Nicholas was bounding out the door.

Grosvenor Square! Nicholas's pulse thundered in his ears as he leapt on Lucifer's back. Tamarand lived in Grosvenor Square!

ཉ Twenty-Five ཉ

Nicholas's high-perch phaeton raced along South Audley Street as if its driver had been born to the ribbons. The fine pair of matched grays were spirited, but they posed no problem for the skilled hands of Helene Tamarand.

And it *was* Helene who tooled rapidly along the elegant thoroughfare. Not Holly. Her entire past had come tumbling down on her with Fanny's disappearance . . . and with the news of Regis and Angela. She remembered everything.

And she almost wished to God she didn't.

But she couldn't afford to hide any longer. Even though terror stalked with every recollection, lodged in her throat till she thought she might vomit. She'd never known such fear! What she'd felt on those rain-swept moors paled in comparison.

Because that terror had been for herself, for her own safety. This was for Fanny.

Dear merciful God, let me find her! Let me be in time! She's only a child! An innocent!

But she collected how her own innocence hadn't been enough to protect her. Those monsters had—

Her thoughts careened wildly back to the beginning. To that terrifying moment when the nightmare began . . .

* * *

Helene was sitting in Regis's carriage as it stood in the courtyard of an inn. She was on her way to the coast with her fiancé and stepmother, where they would all board a packet for Ireland; she was to meet Regis's family, now the engagement had become official.

The pair had left her alone when she pleaded a headache, saying they'd try to procure them all something hot to drink. The headache was growing severe, no doubt worsened by the rumblings of thunder overhead, and the merciless pounding of rain on the carriage roof.

Her gaze fell on Angela's portmanteau lying on the floor. She collected her stepmother saying she never travelled anywhere without her vinaigrette and headache powders. Surely Angela wouldn't mind if she rummaged through the bag; she'd be able to take the powder the moment they returned with the beverages.

The bag was stuffed to capacity with all manner of things, from an elegant gilt-edged fan, to toiletries, to—

Her hand stilled on a likely looking vial she'd just located as something else caught her eye. A small notebook near the bottom. It was so well thumbed, it appeared battered. Odd . . . it wasn't like Angela to own anything that looked so shabby.

But what gave her further pause was the piece of parchment she spied sticking out of the notebook. It bore her father's handwriting.

She was a well-bred young woman, and knew she shouldn't snoop. Yet the temptation tugged at her. Angela was family, she reasoned; surely she wouldn't take it amiss if her stepdaughter were to take a peek—just a tiny glimpse.

She withdrew the parchment, began to peruse it. . . .

In short order, she was puzzled, then incredulous, and finally shocked. She was reading a top-secret memo to her father from the war office! In it were details of battle strategies, dates of planned attacks on enemy fortifications, exact numbers denoting the strength of British troops to be used against Napoleon's forces.

Her heart beating wildly in her chest, she hastily thumbed through the ragged notebook. It contained a deal of similar information. Written by someone who was obviously spying for the French.

And the handwriting was Angela's.

Noises outside drew her attention. Trying desperately not to panic, she hurriedly stuffed the damaging information back inside the portmanteau. *Must find a way to tell Trevor,* she thought. *Trevor will know what's to be done.* She hoped the smile she pasted on her face was believable as Angela and Trevor climbed inside the carriage.

But perhaps it wasn't, or perhaps the trembling of her hands on the mug of grog Angela handed her gave it away. She only knew that before the driver had even whipped up the horses, Angela was remarking on Helene's apprehensiveness to Trevor.

There was a sly smile on her stepmother's face as Angela eyed her appraisingly. Helene tried to pretend nonchalance, but icy fingers of dread crept along her spine as Angela continued to hold her gaze—and reached for the portmanteau.

Things happened fast after that. The first jolt of terror hit when Angela announced to Trevor that "it seems our little secret is out." Trevor—whom Helene had thought to go to for help! He was part of it!

Worse, she quickly learned he was not only Angela's accomplice, but her lover! They'd been intimate for years, and spying for the French all that time! Angela's real name was Angelique, and while her father had been English, her mother was French. The English father had deserted them when Angela was a child, and she'd hated the English ever since.

Yes, Regis was a part of it, but it soon became apparent that Angela was in charge. Fear became a living thing that clawed at Helene's belly as Angela coolly informed Regis they must do away with her. They would need to make it appear an accident, she told him.

A faint thread of hope arose when Regis balked at this.

He angrily reminded Angela that he was desperate for Helene's fortune. She'd promised it to him when she wed Tamarand!

But Angela was adamant. Helene could have them hanged with what she knew, she reminded him fiercely. The pair continued to argue while Helene hunched in the corner of the carriage, choking with fear.

Regis insisted he was quite capable of keeping a wife quiet, even if it meant maintaining her under lock and key on his Irish estate. And once they succeeded in bringing Napoleon back from exile—once they won the war for good—it wouldn't matter what the chit knew.

Then he added something that made Helene's stomach clench. Snidely, he informed Angela he was tired of her worn-out predictability in bed; he was looking forward to tasting Helene's untried charms, and he wouldn't be cheated out of them. He'd always been partial to virginal flesh, and he'd see Angela in hell before he relinquished his prize!

Angela looked as if she might kill him. Helene had never seen her this way. The beautiful features were distorted with rage. But there was something else.

Angela's eyes glittered strangely. They had an odd, undecipherable look in them. No, it was worse than odd. It was . . . unnatural. Helene had to turn away when she saw it.

But a moment later she was gazing back at her stepmother in horror. With Regis's remarks about virgins, Angela's rage had mushroomed. She was spitting obscenities at him with a vengeance. She told him she knew all about his penchant for "little girls." About a certain house he frequented . . . an "abbey" near the East End where ten-year-old virgins might be had if the price was right.

Helene fought nausea as she began to comprehend. *Little girls . . . Sweet God in heaven!*

Angela and Regis continued to taunt and rage at each other as the carriage made its way steadily westward in the storm. Holly seized onto a thin hope that perhaps the carriage driver might help her; it was dashed when she learned he was a loyal Frenchman, and one of Napoleon's spies himself.

The storm was climbing toward its peak when the pair at last reached a compromise that boded ill for Helene. It was decided Trevor would be allowed to bed his "precious virgin" aboard the ship that carried them from the coast. But then a "tragic accident" would occur: Helene would be washed conveniently overboard. For a rich marriage, Angela told him smugly, he would be forced to look elsewhere.

Helene never learned how they came to be near the Cornish coast. Perhaps the storm diverted them from Wales, where she'd supposed they were headed. None of it mattered. She only knew the choking fear that grew with every mile made it nearly impossible to think. And she desperately needed to find a way out. The word *escape* became a pounding refrain in her mind.

She realized that perhaps her only chance may have come when they made a final stop to change horses. Regis left the carriage to see about this while Angela remained inside to guard Helene.

Then the real nightmare began.

Angela had been fuming ever since her lover's biting setdown over her diminished sexual attraction for him. She'd been especially enraged by Regis's taunts about his preference for virgins, and for Helene in particular.

That unnerving look had returned to her stepmother's eyes. It had grown when Regis went even further, sniping at Angela by saying her beauty couldn't hold a candle to Helene's.

Helene was beside herself with terror when she finally realized what she was seeing; she recalled glimpsing something similar once, in the eyes of a tenant on her father's country estate . . . a man she'd later learned was sent to Bedlam.

Angela wasn't right in the head. In fact, she was quite likely stark raving mad.

Panicking with this realization, Helene made a wild bolt for the door. A mistake. Angela was on her before she got her hand near the handle. She was a deal larger than Helene to begin with, but Helene couldn't believe how strong Angela was! She struggled wildly, but that combined size and strength made it almost impossible to move.

Helene's hands clenched on the reins, sending Nicholas's sensitive grays lurching to the side of the road. She barely managed to resume control as what had happened next passed before her in a blur of indistinct images.

She heard herself pleading, asking what she'd ever done to deserve this. Angela's mocking laughter rang in her ears. The images whirled and spun in her brain, coming faster now . . .

Angela's feral smile . . . vile accusations shrieked at the top of her lungs . . . *You stinking virgins who simper and strut your innocence while a real woman must take a hind seat!*

Angela's hands on her throat . . . herself thrashing in terror . . . a riding crop in Angela's fist . . . the weight of that madwoman upon her . . . a strong, rough hand shoving her skirts upward . . . a stockinged knee between her thighs . . . the cool leather handle of the riding crop against sensitive flesh, and—

"*Noooo!*"

Her scream cut across the rumble of the phaeton's wheels. The grays flattened their ears and would have bolted, but years of experience came instinctively to her aid; she held them in check. After a precarious swerve to the left, the vehicle straightened, and they raced on toward Grosvenor Square.

While her mind reeled with the hellish truth. With that first realization of the vicious thing that had been done to her. *Regis* hadn't raped her! It had been that monster in woman's guise—*Angela*—tearing through virgin flesh with the handle of a riding crop!

Dear God, no wonder the memory was dim! Even now she shrank from recalling the thing. But she pushed on, though what had happened after was also blurred and fuzzy.

She vaguely recalled Regis returning to the carriage . . . his rage at what Angela had done . . . the pair of them at each other's throats . . . her own mindless fear as she managed somehow to bolt from the carriage while they concentrated on each other . . .

Helene shook her head, trying to clear it as Grosvenor Square came into view. What else? She wanted as much detail as she could recall before she reached her father . . . before she accused Angela.

She vaguely recalled outdistancing her pursuers somewhat . . . and there was something about how she must try to leave a false trail, wasn't there? She wasn't certain. It all paled beneath memories of panic and fear . . . of the merciless, unending rain . . . and finally the miracle—lights in the distance. Caerdruth—and Nicholas.

A groom came up to take the horses while a footman helped her descend from the phaeton.

"Cool them down, please," she told the groom as he admired the handsome gig and blooded cattle. "But have them ready to travel. I may require them shortly."

The man nodded deferentially, but Helene was already racing toward the front door. The footman leapt ahead to open it for her, and she strode into the spacious entry hall. Manning, their longtime majordomo, appeared, and she asked for the marquis.

"I'm afraid he's not here, m'lady. He was called away on some business, and—"

"Business? Where?" She tried not to panic. *Dear God, if Father isn't here* . . . She realized she really hadn't planned on such a likelihood.

"Ahem, I regret I can't tell you, m'lady. His lordship never said. He returned from your party last night only to leave again a few hours later. Lord Haverill and Sir Henry Marsden were with him, and . . . well, truth to tell, m'lady, we've not seen him since."

Haverill and Marsden? Old friends of her father's . . . but what were they doing here at that late hour? And where could they all have gone?

"Ah, her ladyship is at home, m'lady," Manning offered.

"Is she?" Helene tried to contain the fear and disgust that boiled through her. But Fanny was missing. And there was every reason to suspect the child's disappearance was connected to Angela. *Angela and Regis,* she thought with a wild surge of panic. "Where?"

The servant directed her to her stepmother's chambers, and she forced herself to ascend the stairs. As she made for the suite of rooms at the end of the hall, she tried to think what she must do.

Angela had no idea she remembered anything. No one did. If she behaved as she had been, pretended she was still in the grip of amnesia, perhaps she could inveigle her into revealing something about where the child was. *Fanny. Dear God, please* . . .

She almost ran into Betty, Angela's abigail, coming out of the door to the sitting room. The girl was breathless, looking quite harried as she bobbed a curtsy to Helene. The maid quickly excused herself, saying her ladyship wanted the carriage brought round, and she'd best hurry.

Helene pondered this information as she let herself into the sitting room and made for the bedchamber beyond. The carriage? Perhaps she'd not come a moment too soon. Angela almost never rose at this early hour. Where was she off to in such a rush?

The inner door was ajar. Helene hesitated briefly, took a steadying breath, and entered. Angela didn't notice her. She was busy throwing objects into a portmanteau. The same portmanteau that—

"Betty, I thought I told you—" Angela's brows rose as she spied Helene. "Well, well, well . . . what brings you here so early, Helene? The party can't have ended until—"

"I wished to speak with Father." Helene clutched the sides of her pelisse to keep her hands out of sight. They were shaking. "Do you know where he might have gone?"

"No . . ." Angela hesitated as if debating what to say. Her eyes scrutinized her stepdaughter's face, and Helene resisted the urge to squirm under the penetrating gaze.

"But perhaps you ought to tell me what it is you wished to see him about," Angela went on as she turned back toward the open portmanteau. "I might be able to help."

"Oh, I hardly think so, Angela. But don't let me keep you from your packing. Um, might I ask where you're off to? I wasn't aware—"

Suddenly Angela whirled about, and Helene's stomach lurched as she recognized the feral smile.

"The amnesia's gone, isn't it?" said Angela with a note of triumph. "I always wondered if I'd be able to spot it when your memory returned, and I have! You see, I know you very well, Helene."

Helene wasn't about to argue. The pistol Angela had withdrawn from the portmanteau was pointed straight at her.

Nicholas had Lucifer at an all-out gallop. His mind raced with the implications of Holly's destination as he tried to piece out what it might signify. Had something about Fanny's disappearance alerted her? Told her that was where the child might be?

Or was she trying to head off a confrontation between her father and Regis? And if Tamarand had murdered Regis after all, what would that bode for her if she came across him?

The possibilities came and went in his mind. Why had she run off without a word? Had she suffered more of the nightmarish visions when she fainted?

Fainted . . . She'd fainted at the distressing news . . . and regained consciousness shortly thereafter. With her memory restored?

It was a possibility. And if she recalled the past, something about it had taken her to her father's house. Christ! Where was Tamarand now? Had Whitehall released him? Was she going to the one place she should be avoiding? By

God, he'd kill the bastard if he laid a hand on her! And the child! What about Fanny?

He cut a corner hard, and the stallion stumbled, nearly losing its footing. Nicholas brought the animal through the stumble, urged it on. There was a sick feeling inside his gut that he recognized as fear. Fear such as he'd never known on the battlefield, when the danger had been to himself.

Holly! his mind kept screaming. *Holly, please be safe!* And at that moment Nicholas knew the truth. He loved her. Loved her as he'd never begun to love Judith, or any other woman. Although that other fear nagging at his gut told him he'd begun to love those worrisome children as well.

But Holly . . . maddening, impossible creature that she was, Holly was *everything*. She meant more to him than his own life! He'd *kill* before he ever let anyone hurt her again!

❧ Twenty-Six ❧

"You'd be a fool to kill me with that pistol." Helene addressed her stepmother with a bravery she didn't feel. "The noise would bring the entire household down on you. And whatever else you may be, Angela, I don't believe you're a fool."

Angela's smile was wolfish. "But who says I plan to kill you with it, darling? All I need do is . . . maim you. A ball in the knee, perhaps . . . enough to cripple you for life—yet leave you able to limp out of here as my hostage.

"But it may not even come to that," she added enigmatically, "although a little maiming would suffice, I think. Don't you?"

"You won't get away with it. Father will hunt you down—"

Angela's laughter echoed her condescending look. "Basil? Now there *is* a fool! He's mad for me. How else do you think I was able to come by all that information over the years?"

"You used him as much as you used me."

"Oh, at least, dear girl—at least!"

Helene kept her eyes on Angela's face, concentrated on keeping her talking. She was shocked to realize she had a morbid curiosity about what motivated the woman; more importantly, however, the longer she kept Angela talking, the more time she bought. And she needed to learn where Fanny was!

"I suppose I understand about Father," she said carefully, "but why me? I never did you any—"

"Didn't you?" Angela's face twisted, and Helene had to force herself not to back away from the menace in her eyes. "Well, let me disabuse you of your naiveté right now, you little bitch!"

Angela took a step toward her, and the pistol never wavered. "Have you forgotten what happened when we came out together? You dewy-eyed little virgins are all alike! You lower your eyes and smile, and every man in the room falls all over you! 'Lady Helene Tamarand, the Belle of the Season,' they called you! I'd have killed you then and there if I'd been able to find a way!"

"Angela, I never—"

"*I* was the one they ought to have celebrated. Me! It was all arranged. *Merde,* when I think on it! All those years of Maman scrimping and hoarding away the favors her protectors bestowed on her . . . the jewels, the precious trinkets —it was all supposed to be for *me!* For *my* triumph!"

Angela's eyes began to take on that eerie glitter Helene recalled only too well. "My English sire, Lord Phipps, left us penniless, you see. He wouldn't even have married Maman, but in that, she was too clever for him. She refused to accompany him from France without the banns being read, and a visit to the priest. And m'lord was at that time too head-over-heels to refuse.

"He married her all right," Angela spat, "but a deal of good that did us! A few years later, he left us both—to go haring off to America after some milquetoast virgin! We'd word he secured a divorce to wed the bitch, and Maman and I were left to rot!

"But Maman was more careful after that. She still had her beauty, and continued to use her title. Together, they bought her the favors of a number of well-heeled gentlemen over the years. I was placed with some genteel, impoverished English cousins in the country, and Maman sent them everything she could for tutors, and dancing masters, and the like. I was being raised as a proper lady, you see.

" 'You'll be the belle of your Season, Angelique,' she used to tell me when she came for her visits. 'We'll show those English dogs . . . we'll show them all!' "

Angela took another step forward, and her eyes narrowed. "But do you know what happened in the end, my sweet innocent? Maman died two years before I was ready —of the pox! I was beside myself with grief—with anger! But still, I managed to pull myself together.

"I'd already met Regis, and he helped me secure the patronage of Lady Jersey. And that, along with the last of Maman's jewels, was enough to see me launched. Maman would have her victory even from the grave, I told myself. And she would have"—Angela drilled Helene with her eyes —"if it hadn't been for you!"

Helene sought desperately for something to say. She had to keep her talking! "You managed well enough for yourself nonetheless. Father wasn't exactly a poor catch. If you'd given up the notion of spying, not to mention Reg—"

"Regis! That fool! He was besotted with you like all the rest! Him, and his taste for little innocents!"

Angela snickered, and suddenly Helene's blood ran to ice. She remembered all the fuss Angela had made over the children, calling them her little innocents . . . yet she hated innocents! *Dear God—Fanny!*

"Where"—she had to clear her throat of the lump that had formed—"where is Lord Regis now? Waiting somewhere for you, I suppose?"

The blue eyes went cold. "Dead."

"D-dead?" Helene didn't know what to think. If Regis was dead, at least he couldn't be holding Fanny somewhere, doing—she couldn't even think it.

"I killed him." Angela said it blandly, as if she were announcing a shopping purchase. "He refused to abandon the marriage to you, you see. Insisted on having your dowry, even though I told him he was playing with fire, that you could regain your memory at any time.

"Which, of course, you've done, haven't you?" Angela's smile became sly. "I ordered him to kill you in your sleep several nights ago. Did you know?"

"I—in my sleep?"

"Why, yes. But he bungled it, the stupid toad! Came back ranting about a screaming nightmare you had—loud enough to wake the dead, he said, and . . ."

Angela cocked her head to one side, eyeing Helene almost coyly. "Just how much of a virgin are you these days, Helene? Regis seemed concerned about it, you know. Said that handsome stud Nicholas Sharpe seemed to have no trouble finding your chamber, and . . ." Her words trailed off insinuatingly.

Helene felt nausea rising. Had Regis seen her and Nicholas together? Had he—*Dear God, don't think about it! Concentrate on Fanny. You've got to find out where they took her!*

But time was running out. She saw Angela glance at the clock, then toward the windows facing the drive. She could hear a carriage approaching from the stables at the rear of the house. There was no help for it but to ask outright, and perhaps a miracle would happen. *God please, we need a miracle right now!*

"What have you done with Nicholas's niece?" she asked, then held her breath.

"Ah. The bold little innocent who dared to spy on us, do you mean?"

Helene waited, saying nothing. Angela's words had just confirmed that they'd caught Fanny eavesdropping on their tryst. Now if she'd only say what they'd done with her after that . . .

"Such a little angel." Angela crooned the words. "So innocent. Almost like . . . a nun, wouldn't you say? And do you know what else, dear Helene? She's the reason you're going to help me get away. The reason I'll reach the sloop that's waiting to take me to France. In fact, if you ever want to see that little angel again, you're going to do exactly as I say!"

* * *

Nicholas galloped headlong onto the drive fronting the Tamarand mansion. He recognized his high-perch phaeton, as well as the Lansdowne carriage as he reined Lucifer in. At least Holly was there, he thought with a measure of relief as he slid off the stallion's back. But if Tamarand had just arrived in that carriage . . .

Flinging the black's reins to a groom who came rushing forward, he was already at the door when a pistol shot rang out, and then another.

"Christ, no!" He shoved past the servant who opened the door, withdrawing from his waistcoat the pistol Sir Anthony had insisted he carry. The servant backed away, and Nicholas raced toward the staircase. The shots had come from the second floor, and he took the stairs two at a time, praying he wouldn't find what he feared.

Servants were shouting and running toward the far end of the upper hall. He lunged past them. *Holly!* his mind screamed. *Oh, sweet Christ, not Holly!*

A door near the end had been left ajar. Pistol raised, Nicholas stumbled through it. He caught his breath, and halted.

Poised before an open inner door of what was obviously a woman's sitting room was Basil Tamarand. He stood absolutely still, and in his hand was a smoking pistol.

"Hold it right there, m'lord." Nicholas trained his own weapon on the marquis as he advanced toward him.

Tamarand didn't move, didn't say a word. He simply stared into the adjacent room.

Then Nicholas reached the doorway and stopped in his tracks. Angela Tamarand lay on the carpet in front of an opulent tester bed. There was a smoking pistol in her outstretched hand. And a bloody, gaping hole in her chest.

But Nicholas's gaze had already gone to the slender figure who stood a few yards away from the body. Holly hadn't moved, and he noticed her eyes were unfocused.

"Holly?" He said it softly, unsure of her mood.

There was no response, and her face looked bloodless. It reminded Nicholas of the time he'd first seen her, on a stormy night in April. He felt something inside him threaten to crumble as a terrible possibility occurred to him: Had the amnesia deepened into something worse? Had she lost her mind completely this time?

"Holly," he repeated gently, and held his breath as he opened his arms to her. "It's Nicholas, love. Talk to me, sweetheart . . . please?"

"Blood . . ." she murmured, "so much blood . . ."

"Holly?" He whispered the name, like a prayer.

She turned slowly . . . looked at him, then seemed to crumple, sinking toward the floor with a sob.

Nicholas caught her, her name breaking from his throat in a hoarse cry this time as he wrapped his arms about her. He thought he might never let her go.

Holly felt his arms close about her like a benediction. Nicholas . . . it was truly Nicholas, and nothing in the world mattered but the safety of his arms.

She started to cry then, deep, wrenching sobs that were his name, and he sagged with relief. She knew him. She was going to be all right.

How long they stood there like that, neither knew. It was enough to hold each other and let the nightmare pass. But reality crept in soon enough . . . a nagging awareness in the back of Holly's mind that finally had her pulling away to look at him.

"Oh, God, Nicholas—Fanny! What about Fanny?"

"I know," he said grimly. He glanced at Angela's body. "Did she say anything that—"

"What *about* the child?" It was their first reminder they weren't alone, and as one, they turned toward Lansdowne.

Basil Tamarand looked older than his years as he told of his release from Whitehall, and then coming home to discover his wife holding his daughter at pistol point. Angela had spotted his reflection in the sitting room mirror. She fired at him, but wildly, and missed. And then he killed her. That explained the two shots Nicholas had heard.

Holly realized neither of them knew what she'd recalled with the return of her memory. Servants were gathering at the door to the hallway as she began haltingly to fill them in. The marquis spoke briefly to them, and hurriedly shut the door. Both men listened as Holly stumbled through the details of her nightmarish trip in the storm with Regis and Angela.

Her voice began to shake when she related what Angela had done to her. Her father wept openly, and Nicholas's jaw tightened, though he said nothing. But there was pain in his eyes as he drew her back into his arms.

Holly felt calmer when she'd finished, and she immediately thought of Fanny. "Nicholas, they took her . . . did s-something with her." She hurriedly explained about the ugly suspicions she'd gleaned from what Regis and Angela had said.

Nicholas grated out an obscenity, but Holly never heard him. Her mind was racing over the more recent of Angela's rantings. She seized on something she'd thought odd at the time, then made a connection with another detail from the night in the carriage.

"Does the word *abbey* mean something to either of you?" she asked. "I mean, isn't it East End cant for—"

"Brothel," Nicholas supplied.

Holly nodded and told them how Angela had used the word that time to describe such places in the East End, with particular reference to Regis's perverted sexual appetites. "And just now Angela talked about Fanny being like a nun," she added hurriedly. "God in heaven, do you think he took Fanny to—"

"I know of only two such places that would be fastidious enough for the likes of Regis," Nicholas said tightly. He leveled a look at Tamarand. "To save time, m'lord, I suggest we each search one of them."

Tamarand nodded as Nicholas checked the pistol he'd returned to his waistcoat.

"I'm coming with you," Holly told them. She saw the immediate refusal in their eyes and shook her head. "Don't even try to talk me out of it. I love that child like a daughter, and if she's been taken to such a place, she'll need the comfort only a woman can offer. A woman, I might add, who's familiar with the terrors such things can hold."

The two men eyed her silently for a moment. Neither could miss the chin held at a stubborn angle, the adamant look in the green eyes. Both had seen that fierce determination more times than he liked to recall.

Nicholas heaved a sigh and nodded. "If it's all right with you, m'lord, I'll take her with me in my phaeton."

Tamarand hesitated, then reluctantly agreed, and Nicholas quickly gave him directions to a place in Cheapside called The Cat and Kittens. He and Holly would be searching somewhat farther afield, he told him—an exclusive little "abbey" in Whitechapel called The Sparrow's Nest.

"I pray to God one of us finds the child!" the marquis said fiercely as they headed for the door.

More to the point, Nicholas thought grimly, *that we find her in time!*

Holly kept her mind carefully blank as Nicholas raced his team eastward. If she let herself envision what might be happening to Fanny, she knew she'd go mad. She'd no idea how long it took to reach the narrow alley barely wide enough for the phaeton; she'd shut out time along with uglier realities. She only knew, when they pulled up before a nondescript building at the end, it seemed a lifetime since they'd left Grosvenor Square.

Nicholas turned to her after he brought the team to a stop. His face was grave. "What we see inside might not be pretty. Are you certain you want to—"

"I'm certain, Nicholas. It can't be any worse than what I'd be imagining if I waited out here."

He nodded, realizing he couldn't leave her alone in such a neighborhood in any case. She had more courage than any man he'd fought with in battle, but he wished to God he'd been able to convince her to remain behind. "Let's go, then," he said grimly.

Gaining entry posed no problem. The footman who answered the door ran assessing eyes over the quality of their clothing, and admitted them at once.

"Stay close by me," Nicholas murmured to Holly before asking the servant to fetch his employer. Holly needed no such reminder as she took in the surprisingly opulent interior. Though far more richly decorated than the building's facade had led her to expect, the large room she found herself in had a vaguely sinister quality about it.

The furnishings were lavish, with fine, polished woods, and silks and velvets predominating. Frescoed ceilings were surrounded by gilded moldings, and hand-painted fabrics lined the walls. But as her eyes grew accustomed to the dim light, she began to notice the details of those frescoes, the nature of the scenes displayed on the walls.

They were pagan in nature, all depicting some sort of bacchanalian . . . rites, she supposed. Naked wood nymphs gamboled in classical forests, with satyrs in hot pursuit. But not just in pursuit—in various positions that, even to her untutored eyes, could only signify copulation!

Averting her gaze from a particularly lascivious scene involving a nymph with two of the half-human beasts, she found herself staring at a design on the carpet that was even more graphic. Dear heaven, she didn't know where to look!

Alerted to her discomfort, Nicholas grasped her hand and gave it a reassuring squeeze; he kept ahold of it as a large, corpulent woman with improbable red hair descended the carpeted staircase ahead of them.

She was dressed in an elaborate morning gown of carmine velvet, and her ample bosom nearly spilled out of a neckline that was indecently décolleté. Jewels glittered from rings adorning every sausagelike finger, and as she drew closer, Holly could see she was no longer young: Her heavy application of maquillage had gathered in the creases of the crow's feet fanning her eyes; it emphasized the deep lines running from nose to mouth. She was fifty, if she was a day, although the hard black eyes she trained on them looked as if they'd seen centuries.

But they brightened appreciably, and she smiled when

she neared the wall sconce at the base of the stairs—and got a better look at Nicholas. "Good day, yer lordship," she purred, ignoring Holly entirely. "I am Mother Sparrow. It's a mite early in the day, but The Sparrow's Nest is always ready to accommodate the, er, tastes of the gentry. 'Ow may I be of service?"

Not deigning to disabuse her of his social status, Nicholas went straight to the heart of the matter. "We have reason to believe you've a child on these premises who was brought to you under false pretenses. We've come to fetch her."

Mother Sparrow's smile disappeared, and the black eyes became slits of suspicion. "False pretenses! What false pretenses?"

"The girl is an earl's daughter and was plucked from her home by a man named Lord Trevor Regis. I've no idea what you paid him for the child, but it would behoove you to know, madam, that Regis was found murdered this morning."

He watched her brows climb nearly to her hairline. "For reasons having to do with his involvement in the kidnapping," Nicholas added insinuatingly.

This last had the effect he'd known it would. The abbess ran her tongue nervously over rouged lips, and she glanced anxiously at Holly before returning her gaze to Nicholas. "Ye're not from the magistrate's? I'm an honest, law-abiding subject of—"

"Rest assured, we are not. The child is my niece, and if you don't surrender her at once"—Nicholas's voice grew ominously soft—"I shall be happy to demonstrate a deal I know about making sparrow pie."

Mother Sparrow swallowed audibly. "F-flaxen 'air . . . ch-china blue eyes?"

Nicholas felt Holly's hand tighten in his, and he gave it another reassuring squeeze. "Where is she?" he asked the abbess. "And I warn you, madam, if one tiny hair on the child's head has been ill-used, you'll be wishing you'd never set eyes on her—on either of us."

The abbess began to talk so fast, she nearly babbled. "Ill-used, yer lordship? Oh, never say so! She's a rum un, she is, yer little lady! Why, we all love 'er like a daughter! And so well travelled! Why, the places she's been! The things 'er big blue eyes 'ave seen! She's 'ad us all in transports!"

Nicholas and Holly exchanged troubled glances. Well-travelled? Perhaps this wasn't Fanny after all. Fanny had never been out of Cornwall before the recent trip to London!

But Mother Sparrow was already showing them up the stairs. There was nothing for it but to follow, and pray the woman had misunderstood the child somehow.

She led them to a large sitting room with a decor similar to that of the downstairs. It was dotted with lavishly uphol-stered settees and divans, and on these lounged about a dozen women in various states of deshabille. That each was a painted whore was obvious, from the display of legs and half-naked breasts, to the diaphanous nature of their gar-ments.

But what drew their eyes—indeed, drew the eyes of all the women as well—was the small towheaded creature sit-ting cross-legged on the carpet, in the middle of the room.

Fanny. She had her back to the door and didn't see them; but they recognized her instantly from the jaunty way she held her head, the familiar gestures she made with her hands. As for Holly and Nicholas, they were momentarily too flabbergasted to make a sound that would let her know they were there.

She was dressed in an outlandish concoction that made Maud's wilder ensembles look tame by comparison. Brightly colored scarves were wound about, or hanging from, every part of her. A citron yellow one about one arm . . . an orange, about the other. A pair in pink and laven-der draped her narrow shoulders . . . and yet another patterned in a green and purple paisley was wrapped about her neck. This was left to hang down her back, while sev-eral in shades ranging from vermillion to pea green, to a blue that hurt the eyes trailed, fanlike, from her waist to the carpet. She resembled nothing so much as one of those court jesters of old, with their coats of motley—or perhaps an exotic genie from the *Arabian Nights*.

". . . and then I looked that Sultan of Cathay straight in the eye," she was saying, "and told him he'd never met a clever elephant until he met my Methuselah! Two stories high if he was an inch, Methuselah was, and clever as the devil! Why, that elephant knew . . ."

While Holly and Nicholas gaped, Mother Sparrow murmured to them in low tones, obviously not wishing to intrude upon the storyteller's hold on her audience. "She's been tellin' them tales of 'er travels all night, yer worships. Never onct stoppin' t' take even a bite of the good food we fetched 'er. I do wish ye'd tell me one thing, though . . ."

"What . . . what would that be?" Holly dragged her eyes from Fanny, managing to respond despite her astonishment.

"I wish ye'd tell me," said the abbess, "why it is the poor child *squints* so!"

❧ Twenty-Seven ❧

In the drawing room at Sharpe House, Fanny was the center of attention, much as she'd been at the brothel. Each of her siblings had one of the scarves the whores had given her tied about one arm. Holly was reminded of the favors medieval ladies bestowed on their champions, but done in reverse; Fanny was the champion today.

She had everyone's rapt interest. Even the adults were fascinated. And among the younger set, there wasn't a single remark about squints as Fanny explained how she'd held "all those silly sparrows" enthralled in their nest until rescue came.

"It was all terribly exciting," she told them. "I began my stories as soon as I got there, but at first I'd only that fat Mother Sparrow to tell them to. The sparrows were busy with their gentlemen callers, you see."

One of the adults—Holly wasn't sure who—made a choked, clearing-of-the-throat sound at this, but Fanny was oblivious to it. "But by the time word got round," she continued, "they began to gather, one by one. Pretty soon that odd chamber was fair to bursting with sparrows! And let me tell you . . ."

As the child went on, Holly's eyes drifted to the others in the room: her father, looking tired and perhaps relieved, yet indulgently amused by what he was hearing . . . Aunt Maud, holding Lottie on her lap, and smiling . . . Diana and Rex Wickham, who'd come to offer their help when the servants' grapevine told them of Fanny's disappearance, and had stayed to hear of her miraculous recovery . . .

And Nicholas.

What was he thinking? She'd felt his eyes on her countless times since they returned home with the child, but they'd not talked privately. First, there'd been the need to inform the marquis of their success. And then Nicholas had gone with him to the authorities to give an official report on all that had happened.

But there'd been moments since then when he might have drawn her aside, had a word with her; she knew he'd something on his mind by the way she caught him looking at her from time to time. Yet he hadn't.

Holly felt anger rising. *Damn him! He's withdrawn into that shell! Become Nicholas Sharpe, the brooding enigma, all over again! Well, I shan't put up with it this time! I know who I am now, and it's no hen-hearted ninny he's dealing with!*

Her chin set at that stubborn angle Nicholas would have recognized as boding him no good at all, Holly quietly stole from her chair. She began to make her way unobtrusively toward where he was standing, beside the French windows. Had Nicholas noticed, he wouldn't have liked the look in her eyes, either.

But Nicholas was preoccupied, for once unaware of Holly's movements. She did consume his thoughts, however. Entirely.

While he'd been in the throes of apprehension and fear for her and the child, the startling discovery that he was in love with her hadn't had a chance to settle. There'd been no time, no peace of mind, to reflect on it.

But now there was. Time, at least. Peace of mind was another matter. He'd had none, from the minute he'd begun to examine what his feelings meant, where they might lead.

In one instant, he longed to tell her, and in the next, called himself a fool for even thinking it. She was a titled heiress, damn it! The daughter of a wealthy and powerful lord!

And he was Sharpe the Bastard.

Ever Sharpe the Bastard, and penniless and landless, to boot. He smiled sardonically, recalling his recent willingness to consider Witherspoon's suggestion after all. Recalling how he'd paid court to Lydia—and her fortune. So why did it stick in his craw to contemplate doing the same for a woman he loved?

Loved. Christ Almighty—the very word scares the hell out of me!

She's not Judith, a silent voice reminded.

No, and if she were, I'd have no problem offering for her. I was never really more than infatuated with Judith. But I love this woman, damn me, and she's been used by scoundrels enough! I cannot—will not—use her myself. I may be a bastard in fact, but I'll be damned if I let myself act the bastard with her!

The inner argument had him scowling by the time Holly stole up to him and plucked gently at his sleeve.

"What the devil do you want?" he ground out under his breath. But the stricken look in her eyes had him murmuring an immediate apology. "Sorry. Must be tired."

Holly swallowed with apprehension at the bleak look in the gray eyes. They looked like winter itself. *Oh, my love! I want to erase that look forever! I want to make you smile . . . laugh! If only you'll let me. I don't even care if you can't love me. Just let me love you!*

"I . . . I wonder if I might speak with you, Nicholas," she managed quietly.

The scowl was back. *Damn it, Holly! Don't you know how it hurts? To be near you, and know I can't have you? To ache with wanting you, and know I'll never have you in my arms again? Or—oh, Christ!—in my bed?*

He heaved a sigh, looked at her. "Where?"

"We could slip out to the garden," she said. "Right now, I mean. No one will miss us." And when he didn't answer, "Please . . . ?"

*   *   *

The garden was wrapped in the balmy air of an early summer evening. Birds chirped among hidden branches as they settled in to roost for the night. Long shadows cast by the lingering dusk stretched across clipped hedges and graveled pathways. Holly thought about how peaceful it seemed as she and Nicholas found seats on a stone bench near the central fountain.

Yet she was feeling anything but peaceful. Her love for this man had her insides tossing about like leaves in a storm. The look on his face was so off-putting, it made her want to run back inside and hide.

But the time of hiding was past. She was entirely herself now. She was no longer the scared rabbit who'd been prepared to doom herself to a loveless marriage simply because the one she loved was incapable of loving her back. Half a loaf was better than none, her old nurse used to say. She meant to fight for her love. Even if the one she had to fight was Nicholas himself!

She glanced at him, and felt her breath catch. Dear God, but he was beautiful! He was looking straight ahead, not at her, and his profile reminded her of some ancient pagan god out of myth.

She ran her eyes over the high, angular cheekbones. Softened by the fading light, they still retained an ineluctable impression of nobility and power. There was the straight, perfectly proportioned nose . . . the strong, square chin . . . the sculpted mouth that had always made her weak with longing, even before she'd known the mindless havoc it could wreak on her body.

She shivered with remembered pleasure and had to grip the edge of the bench to quell the curling sensation that wound its way up from below her belly. "Nicholas . . ." she began, then had to stop and swallow, begin again. "Nicholas, do you collect asking—asking me why I intended wedding Regis?"

He glanced sharply at her. "Yes," he said tightly.

She forced herself to hold his gaze. "And—and do you

collect what I said—blurted out quite unintentionally, actu-ally—that prompted that—that question?"

There was a brief hesitation, then a curt nod.

Holly took a deep breath, released it in a rush. "Well, suppose I were to tell you I'd no intention of going through with it. That I'd made up my mind not to marry him, no matter what."

There was a long silence in which he studied her face. "No matter what?" he questioned at length. "Not even if you were with chil—" He gave her a sudden, penetrating look. "Christ! Are you telling me you're—"

"No—no, of course not! That is, even from what little I know, I'm certain it's much too soon to tell."

She nearly shrank from the look he gave her. "But that means it's too soon to be sure either way, doesn't it?" He put the question to her much too softly; his voice didn't match the bleak, glacial eyes. "You *could* be carrying my child, couldn't you?"

She raised her chin a notch, boldly met his look. "I could. And I want you to know, Nicholas, I'm praying that I *am*!"

"What? What the devil are you telling me? Why in hell would you *want* to be carrying my bastard?"

"Not your bastard, Nicholas—your *child*! *Our* child! A child I long to carry because it would be a child I conceived in love! And I would love that child, and cherish it! Just—just as I love and long to cherish its father!"

Nicholas swore softly, ran a hand haphazardly through his hair. "You don't know what you're saying!" he told her, and there was anger in his voice, but something else as well. "Nobody loves a bastard, Holly. Take it from one who knows!"

"You're wrong, Nicholas! *I* love a bastard. With all my heart, and if the stubborn fool w-would consider offering for me, our child wouldn't *be* a bastard!"

She looked straight at him, her heart in her eyes, and Nicholas wanted to scream at her, yell his rage and pain to the heavens. "Holly, it's no good, don't you see? I've noth-

ing to offer with! I'm not just an untitled bastard. I'm penniless, landless!"

"But *I'm* not!" she cried. "For God's sake, Nicholas, do
you think, if I were willing to marry someone like Regis,
who was also in need of a fortune, I'd be less willing for a
man I love?"

"Regis was willing to use you," he said stiffly. "I'm not!"

"But that's silly! It's done all the time among honorable
people of our class." A memory flashed in her mind, and
she narrowed her eyes. "And if you're so set on being noble," she added, "perhaps you'll tell me how that fits in with
a certain wealthy widow you were being seen with not too
long ago! W-word was out, you were courting her!"

"That was different!" he said hotly. "I wasn't in love
with—"

As he clamped his jaw shut, looked sharply away from
her, Holly's heart took a soaring leap. "N-Nicholas . . . ?
A-are you saying . . . ?" She couldn't finish. The hope
thudding in her breast was too fresh . . . too achingly
new to trust.

He muttered something under his breath, turned to face
her. "That I love you? Yes! Yes, dammit, and a lot of good
that will—"

He got no further as she threw herself at him with a glad
cry. Utterly helpless to stop himself, he caught her close,
murmured her name brokenly against her hair.

The night, and the garden, and the sweet, piercing joy
rocketing through her were too much for Holly. She began
to sob softly, brimful of emotions too great to contain.

"Holly . . . oh, Holly, love, please don't cry!" Nicholas's
voice quavered as he pressed consoling kisses against her
hair, her brow . . . tasted the salt of tears on her cheeks.
"I know it's all so damned hopeless, but we've got to—"

"Hopeless!" She pulled away sharply, looked at him.
"Don't you dare say so, Nicholas! Now that I know—God
as my witness, you impossible man, I'll *never* let you go!
Never!"

He wanted to smile, despite the pain tearing at his heart.

She looked so damned resolute sitting there! An angry, adorable kitten, spitting at him with fire in her eyes. He'd never meant to love her. Yet it had happened, and the thought of living his life without her was killing him!

Holly saw the shifting emotions cross his face, and began to panic. Nicholas could be stubborn. And proud to a fault. He'd cling to his pride, even if it doomed their one hope of happiness. If she let him, that was, and she'd no intention of doing that!

"Do you really love me, Nicholas?"

"More than my life," he answered softly . . . bleakly.

Holly felt tears threaten anew, but managed to nod, as if she'd made up her mind to something. "Then, if you won't offer for me, you leave me no choice. I shall have to *make* you wed me, you stubborn man."

"What the devil do you mean by that?"

She gave him as sardonic a smile as any he'd ever given her. "I shall go to my father and tell him you had your way with me not a fortnight ago! He'll force you to—"

"The devil, you will! Christ, woman, are you mad?"

"Mad for *you*, yes!"

"I won't let you—"

"Can you deny it?" she asked. "That you were the one who had my true virginity? That we made love all night long in my bed? And that, right this very moment, I could be carrying your child—and perhaps the *male heir my father's always wanted*?"

Nicholas gaped at her. "Jesus, woman, but you play a hard game!" he muttered as he considered this new aspect of her. So unsuspected under that innocent mien! She had more balls than any man he could think of—except perhaps himself! If she *was* carrying their child . . . Christ, what sons they'd make!

"I play for keeps, Nicholas," she said softly. "It's what this is all about."

Nicholas swore under his breath, admiring her courage even as he cursed her foolishness. He was about to try a final argument that appealed to the good sense he'd always known she had, but at that moment a quiet voice intruded.

"I beg your pardon, sir, but this arrived for you earlier in the day." Finch stood before them, and held a heavy-looking envelope in his hand. "With all the excitement," the majordomo added, "I regret to say I quite forgot about it. So sorry, sir."

It had grown quite dark in the garden, and the servant held out a lighted candelabra. "In case you wished to read it straightaway, sir," he added.

Nicholas took the device from him, thanked him. They watched the servant retreat to the house, the silence between them pregnant with all that had gone before.

"Well . . . ? Aren't you going to open it?" Holly asked. Perhaps this would provide an interlude which would allow their emotions to settle. She'd meant every word she said, and she wanted to give Nicholas time to realize it.

Nicholas nodded absently, noting the seal on the envelope; it belonged to James Witherspoon.

Holly calmly took the candelabra from him, held it high for Nicholas to read.

It was, as he'd suspected, the promised copy of Aubrey's will. It held surprisingly little interest for him at the moment; what lay between him and Holly was uppermost in his thoughts. With a sigh, he began to read it anyway.

And several minutes later found himself growing astonished . . . then amazed . . . then—

"By God . . . by *God!*" he cried, hardly able to credit what his eyes were seeing, even as a wave of happiness beckoned.

Holly grew alarmed. "What? What is it?"

Nicholas gave a whoop of elation and turned to her, the sheaf of papers dropping to the ground. His face was a study in pure joy as he carefully took the candelabra from her, set it down on the bench, and drew her to her feet.

Holly was uncertain of his mood, despite the delight she thought she detected; she'd never seen him this way. "Nicholas . . . ?" she questioned as she searched his face.

"Holly/Helene Tamarand . . ." he said as he drew her into an embrace that pressed her intimately against him. Holly shivered with a surge of desire so great, she couldn't breathe. She found herself gazing up into eyes more silver than gray; they were studded with a joy she'd remember to the end of her life.

"Woman of my heart . . . my life," Nicholas continued as absolute love blazed in his eyes, "will you do me the honor of spending your life with me? Of bearing my children? Of becoming the wife I shall love and cherish to the end of my days?"

❧ Epilogue ❧

"Mmm . . ." Holly stretched lazily as Nicholas nuzzled her ear. She was all muzzy from sleep, although she'd meant to take only a short nap. It had been three months since the twins were born, but her husband still insisted she get plenty of rest. She rarely argued—not when it meant she could expect to be awakened in such a delightful manner.

She made another appreciative sound, deep in her throat, while Nicholas continued his delicious assault on her ear. But a second later she felt her breath catch as he sank his teeth into the lobe.

They were making love in their bed at Trevellan, which now belonged to Nicholas. Judith—with Aubrey's full consent, and help—had placed the estate in trust for Nicholas under the English system of equity for married women.

The trust had been set up and executed through their wills. Each had stated that Trevellan should pass in its entirety to Nicholas in the event of both their deaths, providing he survived them.

Holly would remember to her dying day, the look on Nicholas's face when he'd explained the contents of his brother's will. That had been a little over a year ago, and he'd just proposed to her. There'd been nothing of the reserve she'd expected with his offer of marriage; but then, she'd been prepared to wrest it from him.

Instead, he'd asked her with a free and joyous heart . . . and with his pride intact. She'd never known Aubrey or Judith, but she thanked them in her heart every day for the wonderful gift they'd given her husband. Not just for Trevellan, but for helping to restore his faith in people. Coming as it had, from two who'd betrayed him, it went a long way toward erasing the bitterness that betrayal had caused long ago.

No, she'd never known those two unfortunate souls. But she hoped they were somehow aware of her gratitude for what they'd done . . . perhaps by knowing how their children were well and truly loved by her and Nicholas.

"You're not concentrating, love," Nicholas murmured against that same ear, and she shivered when warm breath caressed sensitive nerve endings.

They were engaged in Nicholas's devilish, arousing game that required the unbuttoning of her sleeping gown. Normally she didn't change into sleepwear for a mere nap; but this afternoon Nicholas had handed her a package as she went to lie down. She recalled the look in his eyes as he'd told her to open it; and when she had, how they'd met hers . . . and how his grin had been slow and lazy as he told her to wear it for her nap. The result was that she'd hardly been able to get to sleep at all!

He'd bought her several sleeping gowns since they were wed. This one was a satin creation he'd ordered made for her by a French *modiste* on their recent trip to Paris. The deceptively innocent garment had two dozen tiny buttons, if it had a one!

"Surely you can manage to concentrate better than that, pet," he teased. He used his thighs to give hers a caress, and then a suggestive squeeze.

"H-how can I, when you're—"

"Does this help?" he questioned as his fingers did something wicked to the tips of her breasts. These were already peaking against the satin, but with his skillful manipulation, they became hard, outthrust buds.

"Hmm," he murmured when she sucked in her breath. "I

can see it's helping . . . *some*thing . . ." He was behind her, but she could picture his indolent grin from the lazy timbre of his voice.

But his fingers had stilled, as she'd known they would when she failed to undo another button. Her own were trembling with the desire coursing through her body, and she could barely think.

"Devil!" she accused, and shuddered when his low laughter vibrated through the lips and teeth he used to nibble at her neck.

But she managed another of the tiny, satin-clad closures, and he rewarded her in a deft maneuver that had her moaning. "Oh, God, Nicholas, I can't—"

A sharp cry of pleasure broke from her lips. One of his hands had strayed to her mons, and he cupped it possessively. The fingers and thumb of the other hand squeezed a nipple, began to twist it gently back and forth.

"Can't what, love?" he murmured thickly as Holly felt his finger press into the cleft below. Felt, as he did, her wet response dampen the satin as desire swelled and built inside her.

"Can't—*wait,* damn you!" She gasped as he suddenly withdrew his hands. Then she clenched her teeth; Nicholas seemed content merely to wrap his arms about her waist from behind. He was driving her mad!

"Oh, but you will . . ." he taunted devilishly as his mouth began a devastating assault along the column of her neck. "Unless . . ."—he nibbled just below her ear—"you manage . . ."—he ran his tongue along the sensitive flesh beneath that ear—"to undo . . ."—he pressed his lips to the pulse at her neck, where it met the shoulder—"another button . . . ?"

She hissed something naughty in the French she'd picked up in Paris, and he chuckled wickedly. He followed swiftly with a quick, playful nip that had her moaning his name aloud. But still, he didn't relent.

Yet she knew he wanted her too. His voice had begun to take on a husky quality she recognized. And she could feel his arousal jutting against the sensitized skin above her buttocks, which were nestled between his thighs.

Then all at once, he pulled her hips hard against him with a sudden movement that caught her completely unaware. A jolt of desire sluiced through her, and she gave a sharp, breathless cry.

"N-Nicholas, you beast . . ." was all she was able to manage before his hands grasped ahold of hers and returned them to the half-undone row of buttons.

"One more, love . . ." he whispered enticingly. "Surely you can manage . . . one . . . more . . . tiny . . . button . . . hmm?"

With each word, he drew the palms of her hands over her nipples. Her breasts felt oddly heavy, and she could feel how hard and tight their peaks had grown. They began to throb and tingle with each pass of her hands as he guided them, had them skillfully doing his bidding.

Soon he had her hands at the final button. She fumbled at it with clumsy fingers as Nicholas murmured encouragement. He urged her on with whispered phrases that painted delicious images in her mind, and drove her insane. But in the end, he stilled her hands with a quiet word, and performed the task himself.

The gown landed on the floor with a silken whisper as he turned her in his arms. Nicholas smiled as he ran his eyes over her.

"You're exquisite, darling . . . so beautiful, I sometimes need to touch you, just to convince myself you're real . . ." He ran a hand lovingly over her shoulder, across to her breast. He cupped it wonderingly, as if in awe at its perfect shape.

The smile widened, became a grin. "I even admit to being a bit jealous in the days when Nathaniel seemed to claim the attention of these more than I."

Holly laughed shakily, for her desire hadn't ebbed. Nathaniel was their son. He'd followed his twin, Alexandra, into the world by two minutes, and spent the first few weeks of his life howling as if in protest at having been born second. Holly had defied convention by nursing them herself whenever she could. But Nathaniel's voracious demands had often left her surrendering his placid sister to the wet nurse they'd hired.

"I do believe your body's even more beautiful now," Nicholas was saying. "Motherhood becomes you in every way, love," he added as their eyes met . . . held.

And then he was kissing her . . . lingeringly, thoroughly, while she clung to him with unsteady hands. He'd somehow managed to remove his own clothes, and this was the first touch of flesh against unclothed flesh. Holly could feel her sensitized breasts pressing against the crisply curling hair of his chest. She felt as well, the rapid acceleration of her heart as their bodies meshed.

Nicholas's lovemaking had been deliciously controlled until this point. But now it was as if he couldn't wait any longer. She felt desire thundering through him as he readied her for possession.

His hands, his mouth, were everywhere, provoking sharp little cries from her as he used his knowledge of her body to bring her to a fever-pitch. She began to twist and arc beneath him, begging for completion, and at last he gave her what she craved.

They came together with a fierce mutual hunger. Bodies joined, each cried the other's name aloud as they rode the crest of the wave, and found repletion on the wide, mindless shores beyond.

It was always this way between them now. As if they were making love for the first time. Despite their growing knowledge of each other's bodies, each time seemed somehow fresh and new. And when it was done, as they held each other close and their pulses slowed, each marvelled at the perfect peace that filled their hearts and minds.

"Penny for your thoughts, love," Nicholas murmured against her hair when at last he could think clearly.

His finger traced lazy circles around the tip of one breast as he held her close, and Holly sighed with pleasure before summoning the energy to reply.

"I was thinking of how peaceful I feel . . . and how wonderful life is for us now. It's sometimes hard to believe how this all began."

She shifted until she was leaning on his chest, looking down at him. "Do you ever think about it?"

Nicholas folded his arms about her waist and hips, drawing her lower body snugly against his. They were both slippery from the seeds of his lovemaking, and Holly succumbed to a tiny aftershock of pleasure with the contact.

Nicholas grinned, recognizing the tiny tremor that ran through her. It wouldn't take much to make him hard again. He'd never wanted a woman as much as he wanted Holly, knew he never would. There'd be a repeat of pleasure before the afternoon was done. But for the moment, all he wanted was to converse desultorily with his wife. A pleasant interlude between lovemaking. He wished she'd chosen something else to talk about.

"I think about it," he said. "Most often when there's a storm coming on. It's odd . . . I used to love those storms as a lad. Now I know I'll never witness a coastal storm again without recalling that night."

Holly felt him tense and bent to place a soft, reassuring kiss on his lips. "But never say they trouble you, Nicholas. After all, it was that storm that brought us together. And I —Oh, love, I'd endure a hundred of them if I knew they'd bring you into my life!"

Nicholas met her eyes, and the look of love in his was so intense, it took her breath away. "I love you, Holly," he whispered before he claimed her lips in a kiss so tender, it brought tears to her eyes.

"What's this?" he asked as he touched the moisture gathering on her lashes with the tip of his finger.

"Just a little joy . . . leaking over at the edges," she murmured with a tremulous laugh.

He kissed each eyelid, then pulled her head gently against his chest. They remained quietly in this embrace for a time. But all at once, after a few minutes had passed, Holly gave a gasp. She sat up, looked at him.

"Nicholas! I've just recalled something else from that night!"

"Have you?" He sounded dubious. "I wasn't aware there was anything you hadn't—"

"Oh, but there was!" she said excitedly. "Don't you collect wondering why Angela and Regis would have thought it safe to declare me dead when they hadn't succeeded in killing me? Hadn't even been able to find me in the storm?"

"And thank God for it," Nicholas said with a grimace.

"Yes, darling, but listen! I've just recalled *why* they thought themselves safe!"

"Go on." It was clear he was less than thrilled with the turn the conversation had taken.

"It was because I led them to *believe* I'd died. I laid a false trail!"

"What sort of false trail?" He was intrigued in spite of himself.

"Well," said Holly, excitement lacing her words, "I was wearing this cloak, you see. It was velvet . . . a dark green velvet. Yes, I remember it clearly now. Nicholas, I made them believe I'd tumbled off that cliff—you know the place. It was where I rode that day when—"

"When you were mad enough to think you could ride Lucifer without consequence," he said irritably. Since their marriage he'd spent long hours training the stallion to obey his wife's commands; Lucifer now accepted Holly on his back as easily as he did Nicholas. But those lessons had been accompanied by many a husbandly lecture about her headstrong ways, how she must never again jeopardize her safety as she had that day. "Yes, I remember" he added grumpily. "Go on."

Holly grinned at him, too caught up in what she was saying to be fazed by a little husbandly irritation. "I deliberately removed that cloak, Nicholas—and hung it on the branches of a tree that grew at the edge of the cliff! When they saw it, they had to think I'd plunged to my death at that very spot!"

"Excellent!" he said with some of the old sarcasm. "A lovely image to warm me each time one of those damned storms arises!"

Holly just laughed, giving him a resounding kiss on the mouth. "But you must hear what else I now collect, darling!"

He couldn't believe it. She sounded triumphant!

"Guess, Nicholas! Guess what kind of a tree it was!"

He looked at her as if she'd sprouted wings, or something equally fantastical. "I know you're going to tell me anyway, you impossible wench, so get on with it!"

Holly's grin was ear to ear. "Nicholas—it was a *holly* tree!"

There was a moment of stunned silence. And then a low rumble issued from his chest as her words sank in. Nicholas met her eyes, and mirth spilled from him. Holly grinned, and then began to giggle helplessly. In seconds the room rang with shared, uncomplicated laughter.

It was a sound that would follow them all their lives.

HERE IS AN EXCERPT FROM *GABRIELLE*—THE
NEXT HISTORICAL ROMANCE FROM VERONICA
SATTLER AND ST. MARTIN'S PAPERBACKS:

❧ Chapter One ❦

Paris, France: 1793

Evening shadows stretched across shrubs and graveled walks as
a slender figure slipped through a side door to the garden. Brielle
Lafleur went very still and looked around. Not yet full dark. They
must arrange to meet later from now on, she realized; it was only
early April, but already the days were noticeably longer. And everything depended on not being seen.

She caught a furtive movement amid the deeper shadows at the
far end of the walled enclosure. *Bien.* He knew how to hide, that
one. Glancing up at the windows of the mansion that loomed at
her back, she could perceive no movement. Still, one could never
be certain someone wasn't watching. Especially these days, since
the *Comité de salut public* had been given virtually dictatorial pow-
ers.

The mere thought of the Committee of Public Safety made her
shiver. Brielle paused a moment longer, gathering her courage.
Then, her breathing shallow, she edged her way carefully along
the periphery of the house.

It seemed like eons before she reached the pocket of midnight
shadow where the man waited. She let out her pent-up breath in
relief as she made out his pockmarked face. With mild surprise,
she realized his appearance no longer frightened her. She'd come
to know things far uglier than a man's face.

"It took you long enough, sister!" hissed the man known to her
only as Le Feu.

Brielle merely shrugged. She'd learned by now that Le Feu was
always irritable; his manner, too, had lost its power to intimidate

her. What mattered was the power he and their small band of conspirators could summon over weightier things. *Things like— please, God—Maman's life*! she reminded herself with desperation.

Le Feu scratched the bearded stubble on his chin and grinned. The show of yellowed teeth seemed to her less amused than leering. "Full of the sangfroid these days, eh?" he asked in the rapid guttural French of the Parisian streets.

Unlike the man who'd sent him, Le Feu had humble origins, and in the beginning she'd wondered why d'Albret had trusted him. Why would this peasant attach himself to a group with Royalist loyalties? But she no longer wondered; money, she knew, could buy almost anything.

When his gibe provoked no reaction, the grin faded and suddenly Le Feu was all business. "You've not found it, I take it."

Mutely, Brielle shook her head, willing away the sting of tears. It was the same response she'd given for weeks now, and its very repetition had begun to feel like a personal admission of failure. "But there are easily a dozen chambers I've not yet been able to search," she told him. "I said it would take time. A menial doesn't have free access to every part of the house, don't forget. If only we knew which chamber Maman occupied!"

"If only, if only!" Le Feu sneered. "If wishes were horses, then beggars would ride, Citoyen Lafleur!" The term of address was sneered, too; unlike the reverse, he knew who she really was.

Born Gabrielle Marie de Saint-Germain, she was the only child of Louise de Saint-Germain, Comtesse d'Auxerre—one of Queen Marie Antoinette's favorites. But her very life depended on concealing it. To all and sundry in the household of Minister Jean Roland and his wife, she was pretty Brielle Lafleur, a humble serving maid.

And Gabrielle's wasn't the only life at stake. Her mother was imprisoned in the Temple along with the queen and the royal children. The comtesse had been arrested in Varennes the same day as the king and his family. The good citizens of the Republic had executed that king in January, and Gabrielle had no reason to doubt her mother and the others would suffer the same fate— unless there was an escape.

An escape that had become Gabrielle's chief reason for living. To save her mother, Gabrielle knew she would do anything, pay any price. Maman was all she had left in the world. They had lost everything—their lands, their titles, their way of life—yet all of that could be borne as long as there remained the hope of saving Louise from the hungry maw of the guillotine.

As if he'd read her thoughts, Le Feu chose to remind her of that infamous instrument of death. "La Guillotine will not be pacified with excuses, mademoiselle! She craves *heads*! Pampered, aristocratic heads! And those who would thwart her hunger require *money*. Without the Queen, nothing can be accomplished—and it is *your* duty to find her!"

Brielle nodded grimly. The Queen he spoke of wasn't the one they'd imprisoned, wasn't even a person. The object of her search was a fabulous sapphire surrounded by diamonds and set into a pendant. Called the Queen of the Sea because of both the jewel's color and the long sea voyage taken by the Eastern potentate who'd traveled to present it personally to the old king, it was as beautiful as it was priceless.

Except that now it did have a price: Maman's life. The plans for extricating her mother and the royals were all but in place. They awaited just one thing: the huge funds necessary to bribe guards and others whose silence was essential. And nothing less than the famous gem given as a gift to the Comtesse d'Auxerre by Louis XV could provide such staggering funds.

But no one except Maman knew where the pendant was. It wasn't found on her when she was arrested, nor by those who'd confiscated the comtesse's property. But it had last been seen on her mother's person when Louise was a guest here, at the minister's home. That was shortly before she traveled to Varennes, where she'd joined the royal family in their abortive attempt to flee the country.

Gabrielle shivered, recalling how close she'd come to being captured too. Only luck and Maman's quick thinking had saved her. Her mother had sent her on ahead to Varennes before Louise herself left Paris. And she'd never let on to Gabrielle that they were to accompany the royals in their flight from France. In retrospect, Gabrielle realized Louise had been thinking of her daughter's safety: If Gabrielle knew nothing, she couldn't betray herself through nervousness. And the same reason had to account for Maman's sending her on ahead; too much might have been made of an aristocratic mother and daughter leaving Paris together in these dangerous times. Her mother had done everything possible to avoid drawing attention to their flight.

Would that the king had been as careful! Poorly disguised, Louis was detected by a peasant who'd never even seen the monarch in person. But the man had recognized Louis XVI's profile—which was stamped on coin of the realm scattered across France!

Thinking of coin reminded Gabrielle of something still in question the last time she'd seen Le Feu. "Has he secured a buyer for the sapphire?"

There was no need to name the *he* in question. They both knew their plot was the brainchild of Antoine d'Albret, that no one but d'Albret had the connections to bring everything about. Antoine d'Albret . . . former court gallant often called the handsomest man in France—and Louise de Saint-Germain's lover for the past ten years.

Nicknamed "Le Chat" for his ability to shift with the political winds at Court and always land on his feet, d'Albret had once again lived up to his sobriquet. When he perceived early-on how the tide was turning against the forces of the *Ancien Regime,* Antoine quickly took steps to align himself with the revolutionaries. He now moved among them with ease.

To give him his due, he'd urged Louise to do the same, but Maman had refused; she could never desert her friends, her heritage, she'd told him. No, nor even the Austrian who'd been so kind to her and Gabrielle in the years since Gabrielle's father died; silly and vain though she was, Marie Antoinette deserved her loyalty.

But Antoine d'Albret had no loyalties. Unless they were to himself. It was one of the reasons Gabrielle had never liked him very much. How could one trust such a man? And yet here she was, placing all of her trust, her every hope, in this handsome shape-changer.

Maman had loved him passionately for years. That, and that alone, stood behind Gabrielle's alliance with d'Albret. If Maman loved him, there had to be a reason. She'd deliberated long and hard on it, but finally Gabrielle convinced herself he loved her mother too, and meant to get Louise out. Why else would he risk so much to involve himself in this plot? Besides, she had no one else to turn to.

"Finding someone desirous of buying the Queen was never in

question," said Le Feu, bringing her back to the moment. "Making sure there were funds to *back* the desire—now, *that* was a problem!" he added with a sly smirk.

"You know what I meant!" Brielle snapped, then instantly regretted her loss of composure. It wouldn't do to antagonize him. *Le bon Dieu* only knew what the man was capable of! "Sorry," she murmured. "I find myself impatient to see this business completed."

Le Feu grunted unsympathetically. But he informed her that a wealthy merchant who happened to be from the sapphire's country of origin had the funds to acquire it.

"But for him to acquire it, mademoiselle," he told her accusingly as he turned to leave, "it must be *found!*"

Gabrielle watched him melt into the night as stealthily as a wraith. It was completely dark now; she noted that lights had appeared at many of the windows of the Hotel Liberte, as the mansion was now called. Soon they would be wondering where she was. Madame Roland was fond of entertaining—usually with an aim to furthering some Girondist cause—and Gabrielle was expected to serve at her dinner party tonight.

Still, she remained for the moment where she was, silently contemplating the things she'd discussed with Le Feu. And then the things she had not.

Because she'd learned to be wary, there was one very significant piece of information Gabrielle hadn't shared with her conspirators. Only she knew the true reason the Queen of the Sea was missing: It had been hidden by Louise for her daughter to use in the event their flight failed. Of course, this presupposed that Gabrielle would remain at large, but she now knew Maman had taken very specific precautions to prevent her daughter's capture.

A bittersweet smile etched Gabrielle's lips as she recalled the argument they'd had the morning of the arrest. Maman had forced her to dress in rags bribed from a scullery maid at the inn where they'd met, allowing her only that plain black mourning cloak of Maman's to conceal her humiliation.

Humiliation! She wanted to laugh and weep at the same time. That "humiliation" had saved her life. That, and Maman's quickness. Louise had chanced to look out the window of their carriage and seen the king's coach being halted up ahead. She'd suddenly thrust her daughter from their vehicle, telling her to pull up the hood of the cloak and walk slowly away with head bent. "Make for the nearest church, Gabrielle," she'd said. "I'll do what I can to distract them. But if anyone stops you, you are a simple scullery maid in mourning, on your way to pray for your dead! Now go, and don't look back! If you love me, go!"

Those were the last words her mother had said to her. But not her last message to her daughter. Later, after they'd questioned her and let her go, Gabrielle had sat, shaking, in the deserted church in the village, wondering what to do. News of the arrest had spread like wildfire throughout the area even before she reached the sanctuary.

It was when she'd knelt to pray that she heard the odd rustle of paper against her skirts. And found the message. Pinned to the ragged petticoat was a piece of paper written in Maman's hand. That it had been intended solely for her daughter was beyond doubt. Besides the manner in which it had been passed, it was written in English, which both of them spoke fluently; Papa had had a scholarly interest in English literature, had insisted they learn it, even speak it at home.

Standing in the darkened Parisian garden, Gabrielle silently recited the verse she'd committed to memory:

> Blue as the sea, and queen I am,
>   Beauty as rich as the ages.
> Gift of a king, and rare to behold,
>   I am thy passage when infamy rages.
> Hasten to mantel, search out the coat;
>   Find me concealed beneath turret and moat.
> Then fly away—flee! And never return!
>   Thou art the future—the past, thou must spurn!

Gabrielle sighed. There was no doubt about the pendant's purpose, as Maman intended it. Her mother had wanted her to use it to get away, begin a new life—alone. She never meant for Gabrielle to use it to free her . . . Thou art the future—the past, thou must spurn!

But how could she spurn her own mother? The mother who'd given her life, nurtured her, been both mother and father to her after Papa died of the fever? The mother who'd loved her enough to sacrifice her own safety for her daughter's?

"Forgive me, Maman," she whispered into the darkness. "But I could no more desert you than desert myself! And if all goes well, we'll both be free to laugh together, love each other again!"

But first, she had to find the sapphire. And to do that, she needed to know what the rest of the verse implied. But it wasn't proving easy. She'd been trying to piece it out for weeks . . .

She kept coming back to the word, *mantel—what* mantel? Nearly every blessed fireplace in France had a mantel! But d'Albret was certain the pendant was hidden in the Roland mansion; it was the reason he'd gotten her the position here.

So she ought to search the mantel in the chamber Maman had used when she'd been Madame Roland's guest at the *hotel* all those months ago. Secret caches were common enough in such structures among the grand houses of the French aristocracy— architectural testaments to the intrigues of court life in an earlier age. But the damnable mansion had over forty chambers, and she hadn't even been *in* many of them!

Well, there was nothing for it but to search the place at random until—

Gabrielle froze, feeling the tiny hairs on her arms rise. In the distance, somewhere along Paris's dark streets, she heard the ominous rumble that could only mean one thing.

Mon Dieu! They were even rolling at night now!

She could still recall the first time she'd heard that sound. And seen what caused it. Tumbrels, lumbering along the cobbled streets. Tumbrels . . . carrying the condemned to their deaths. To the Place de La Revolution where La Guillotine waited.

The sound had sent a forbidding chill down her spine then, and it still had the power to make her weak with dread. Any day now, Maman could be in one of those death carts, and—*No!* She wouldn't think of it! That way, surely, lay madness, and then they'd both be lost.

She would concentrate purely on her task. *Find that damnable pendant, Gabrielle!* she told herself as she slipped silently toward the house. *Find it—or be forever damned yourself!*

❧ Chapter Two ❦

Jason Trace's face revealed nothing as he joined his aide outside the chamber where the Committee of Public Safety met. But Conor O'Shea had been his friend for years, knew him too well to miss the ominous look in Jason's eyes. They glittered like chips of obsidian.

"Problems?" Conor murmured as he shuffled a sheaf of official-looking papers and tucked them under his arm.

"Not here." Jason dipped his head toward the exit, indicating they'd discuss the matter outside. They spoke in English, but any of the men milling about the antechamber might comprehend; Jason had no doubt the Committee would spy on them if it could.

The Rue Madeleine was nearly deserted as they made their way toward the American ministry on foot. The minister had offered them his carriage, but both Trace and O'Shea were athletic; after the inactivity of their sea voyage, they'd welcomed an opportunity to stretch their legs.

"*Now* would ye be after tellin' me what's fashin' ye, man?" Conor's speech still carried the lilting accents of Ireland, where he'd been born. They were softened somewhat by the easy drawl of his adopted land, but not even twenty years in Virginia had been able to erase them entirely. "Didn't they take it well?" he added with a frown.

"Oh, they took it well enough." Jason's eyes scanned the street on either side as they walked. They'd been in Paris less than forty-eight hours, yet had already witnessed some ugly things: a blood-thirsty rabble, screaming for vengeance as those accursed tumbrels passed . . . bands of brigands roaming the streets, looking for trouble. Both he and Conor were armed with pistols beneath their coats.

"It wasn't as if they had any choice," he went on. "If nothing else, the majority of the men on the Committee are realists, and they know a neutral stance won't harm them. But there are definitely some who resented Washington's decision, who felt we ought to align with them in their bloody damned war."

The war he spoke of had its first rumblings in July of '89, following the storming of the Bastille. But it broke out in earnest after the execution of Louis XVI; monarchical Europe, particularly Austria and Prussia—and now England—had not taken kindly to the regicide of an anointed king.

"Hah!" Conor snorted. "As if there were any chance o' that after their latest outrage! Lafayette, a traitor? Next, they'll be after declarin' the Virgin Mary and Our Lord guilty o' treason. No wonder Washington's proclaimin' us neutral. They're lucky we didn't join the other side!"

"There was never a chance of that, Conor, and you know it. The chief tenet of Washington's foreign policy is to keep the United States out of foreign wars. He'll see we stay neutral as long as he's in office."

Conor gave him a sidelong glance. "Unlike one or two others we know, if they got the chance, eh?"

Jason threw him a grin. "Let's just say the Secretary of State's a francophile and can't help himself, shall we?"

"A what?"

"Tom Jefferson's been in love with France since his years here as minister. Lump that together with the republican leanings of the man—he penned our own Declaration of Independence, don't forget—and you can begin to understand why he urged Washington to support the French."

"Aye, while Hamilton prodded him to align with England and the Coalition—but that would have been over auld Tom's bloody body! Is that what ye'll be tellin' Roland and his Girondist friends this evenin'?"

Jason nodded, giving him a wry smile. "But in more . . . diplomatic terms, shall we say?"

Jason was a planter, not a trained diplomat; still, he'd picked up a great deal from his father, who was to have carried out this assignment originally. But Alexander Trace had broken his leg in a hunting accident at the last minute. On the elder Trace's recommendation, Washington had asked Jason to step in as his special envoy.

"And ye'll be tellin' them all quite *off the record,* o' course!" Conor exclaimed with a chuckle.

Jason chuckled too. His official mission was to inform the French of the Proclamation of Neutrality, which would be issued later in the month; in this way Washington hoped to head off problems or confusion over the United States position before it became official.

But what had them chuckling was their second, *un*official mission. The one the President knew nothing about—and which would likely have him swearing like the old soldier he was, if he ever found out. Washington's Secretary of State had not accepted neutrality lying down; Jefferson had secretly asked Jason to meet with the moderate Girondists who were in power and assure them the French still had "friends in high places" in the U.S. And because Jefferson was *his* friend, Jason had agreed to do it.

When a frown suddenly replaced the amusement on Jason's face, Conor eyed him archly. "Havin' second thoughts on the matter?"

Jason shook his head. "Just wondering if ol' Tom would have been so enthusiastic if they *had* guillotined Lafayette."

Conor nodded. Lafayette had escaped capture and execution only narrowly; he'd defected to the Prussian army after learning the National Assembly had declared him a traitor the previous August. "Is that what had ye lookin' so fierce, then?"

"Indirectly. Conor, there's—"

Jason broke off abruptly as a sound in the distance drew their attention. It traveled from the Place de la Revolution across the streets and avenues of Paris on the balmy spring air: a muted roll of drums, followed by a jubilant shout of many voices, all raised in unison.

The two men exchanged grim looks in the silence that followed. Another "enemy of the Republic" had lost his head.

"Dammit, Jason," Conor muttered, "it's not civilized! Those *sans-culottes* stand in that square and cheer as if they've witnessed a bloody weddin'! The bloodthirsty bastards are *runnin'* this damned revolution!"

"Not quite," said Jason as they resumed walking. "But there are those who know how to play to their sympathies, manipulate them to their own ends."

"The men in that chamber?" Conor hadn't joined Jason inside the chamber because it would have been pointless; unlike Trace, he didn't speak French.

Jason nodded. "The upper bourgeoisie, those extremists that call themselves Montagnards and Jacobins. Although, of the two, I fear the Jacobins are the most dangerous. Georges Danton heads the other group, and he strikes me as at least rational. But I'm not sure he has the power to withstand the radical bent of the Jacobin leaders—Marat and Robespierre, in particular."

Conor noted that the dangerous look was back in Jason's eyes. "What in hell did they *say* t' ye, man?"

"They asked how men who'd recently fought their own revolution against tyranny—and won, but only with French help—could stand dishonorably by and not return the favor."

Conor nodded. "We were expectin' that, o' course. What did ye tell them?"

"That we'd neither killed a king, nor indulged in a national bloodbath. I told them there were any number of Tory Loyalists who, now that our war was behind us, enjoyed a peaceful co-existence with their Patriot neighbors. Ours, I said, was a triumph of reason and enlightenment over the forces which had attempted to suppress those nobler aspects of the human spirit."

Conor grinned at him. "Holy Mother o' God, I do believe ye've missed your callin'! With a gift for blarney like that, ye ought t' be runnin' for Congress!"

Jason flashed a grin, but shook his head. "No, thanks." He'd seen what holding office had done to men like Washington and Jefferson. Each had to drag himself up North for most of the year when he hated doing it. He knew they were dedicated, admired them for it. But he also knew nothing would please them more than to retire peacefully to the Virginia homes they loved better than anything. The way he loved Fairhills.

"But we were speaking of the Committee," Jason went on. "When I mentioned the horror felt by men of reason at the blood-letting, do you know what Robespierre said?"

He placed an arm on Conor's, halting their progress as he met the other man's gaze with grim eyes. "He said it was necessary, and that there was *far more* to come. He spoke of a 'reign of terror' which would bathe France in blood until every last enemy of the Republic was silenced. A *reign of terror*, Conor—'without recourse, or pity, or remorse.' "

Conor suppressed a shudder, recalling the frenzied cheers of the mob. "They've already begun t' slaughter innocents, the minister's wife told me. She saw a humble seamstress's assistant in one o' the tumbrels not a week ago. A child barely into her teens. What harm would they see in a poor creature like that, can ye tell me? What threat could there possibly be in a wee lass?"

Jason shook his head, and Conor glanced sharply at him as they walked on. The Irishman thought for a moment he'd detected a sardonic smile on his friend's lips, but perhaps it was a trick of the light. The unfortunate lass *had* to have been an innocent. Even Jason must see *that*.

But his friend's feelings about females were never to be taken lightly. Jason Trace deeply distrusted women—and Frenchwomen in particular.

Not that he didn't have his reasons. The French woman who'd given birth to Jason had abandoned her husband and young son years before—to return to France with an old lover. Jason last saw Juliette Trace when he was a boy of six, and her heartless departure had left him bitter. He was now thirty-six years old, and still single. Deliberately single. Conor doubted he'd ever wed, although he knew Alexander still had hopes that he might.

But Alexander Trace was a different kettle of fish entirely. Strange, Conor thought, that the Frenchwoman's desertion should have affected her husband and son so differently. But gentle, optimistic Alexander was an idealist who never really saw bad in anyone. He'd told Conor once that he'd forgiven Juliette long ago, and hoped she was happy.

Not so, Jason. And perhaps their differences weren't so strange when one remembered that Jason wasn't Trace's natural offspring. Not that the elder Trace hadn't raised and loved him like his own. But Jason's biological sire was that same former lover—the one Juliette ran off with. She'd been pregnant when Alexander met and married her in France, never letting on about it till they were crossing the sea to his home in Virginia!

What made it all so ironic was that it was the natural father who'd not wanted his own son; according to Alexander, it was he

who convinced Juliette to leave Jason behind when the pair went
back to France.

Conor sighed. Small wonder Jason sometimes acted as if he had
devils charging around inside him! Hard and cynical, that's what
he was. As different from Alexander as night from day.

Still, a man couldn't fault him for the son he'd turned out to be.
How he loved Alexander! And he was fiercely protective of him,
too. As Jason saw it, Alexander was a softhearted romantic who'd
be easy prey for the unscrupulous if Jason weren't there to look
out for him. Because Jason might be many things, but softhearted
and romantic weren't among them!

They arrived at the ministry without incident and made their
report to Gouverneur Morris; the U.S. envoy had elected to stay
out of the matter until the Proclamation became official. It was
dusk by the time they'd changed clothes and departed for the
Roland home on Jefferson's errand.

Informed only that they were dining with friends, Morris had
again offered the use of his carriage. This time they'd accepted;
Paris had become too dangerous to negotiate on foot after dark.

Jason gave the driver their destination, and the carriage lumbered slowly up the Champs-Elysees toward the Hotel Liberte.

"They live in a hotel?" Conor asked as he settled his large frame
against the plush squabs of the seat.

Jason smiled, shook his head. "*Hotel* is the French word for
mansion. Roland and his wife are from the well-to-do upper bourgeoisie. Some of them live as well as did those aristocrats they
helped oust. I doubt their home was always called the Hotel
Liberte, though. The revolution has seen to the renaming of a lot
of things, apparently."

Conor nodded. The damned frogs had even renamed the
months of the year! Well, it was an odd, uncomfortable place—no
doubt about it. For his money, the day they left for home couldn't
come too soon!

He'd come along on this blasted business because Jason had
asked him, and Jason was his closest friend. But if he had it to do
over again, he wondered if he would. Like Trace, he was a planter;
their plantations neighbored each other on the western bank of
the Rivanna River, just south of Charlottesville. It was land he
cherished.

He'd come to the Colonies as a lad with nothing save the

clothes on his back and a willingness to work hard. But he'd made the most of the opportunities offered by the brash new land; today he was a man of considerable property, and proud of all he'd achieved. What did he know of diplomacy and foreigners? Why wasn't he home where he belonged?

But as his gaze fixed on the profile of the man sitting beside him, Conor knew the answer to that. Jason Trace was more than a friend; he was the sort of man who commanded loyalties. The sort you'd follow unquestioningly, as Conor had . . . many times.

Jason had been his commanding officer in the War for Independence. One of Washington's youngest junior officers at the outset, Trace had risen swiftly during the course of the war, and with good reason. He'd been a brilliant tactitian, leading his company of dragoons out of a number of situations others would have given up as lost.

And Jason never asked of his men anything he wasn't willing to ask of himself. Moreover, he'd saved Conor's life during Greene's hellish retreat from North Carolina in '81. By the time the war was over, Conor knew he'd follow Jason Trace into hell itself if he asked it.

And perhaps I already have, Conor mused as he surveyed Paris's darkened streets. It wasn't the first time he wondered if even their diplomatic immunity protected them from the savagery they'd witnessed. He was the last man to question a people's quest for freedom; but in his judgement, in the France of 1793, the quest had become a plunge into madness.

And they were mad to be in the thick of it. Worse, Jason had decided to prolong their stay, which ought to have ended with tonight's errand. And for what? A bit of morbid curiosity, that's what!

After their missions were completed, Jason planned to travel to the interior wine country! And what did he hope to accomplish with it? What sense did it make? Had the French infected him with their insanity?

Reminding himself it was just one more example of the devils besetting his friend, Conor heaved a sigh.

"Something troubling you, Conor?" Jason's voice seemed startlingly loud in the close confines of the carriage.

"Ach! I was just wishin' ye'd reconsider this mad idea ye have t' travel t' the . . . er, Bourgogne, is it?"

Conor's accent made hash of the French place name, and Jason grinned at him. "It's bad enough you mangle our former king's English, man—must you murder the French as well?"

"Better than *riskin'* murder, I'm thinkin'! They say the provinces have seen more beheadin's than that bloody square!"

"I've not asked you to come with me, Conor." All traces of humor had left Jason's voice. "In fact, I'd rather you didn't. This is something I . . . need to do, and I won't burden anyone else with it. But I *will* do it." '

Conor nodded, suppressing another sigh. Insanity, that's what it was. Jason despised his mother for what she'd done. Why elect to travel to the place where she'd lived? Why deepen the bitterness by going out of the way to visit the place where she'd conceived the son she deserted? *Ach, Jason! You're my dearest friend, but sometimes I wonder just what it is that makes you tick!*

Conor's frustrating thoughts were curtailed by their arrival. He gave himself over to marveling at the vast richness of the place. The size of it!

Lit by the blaze of dozens of torches, the building's creamy stone expanse and sculptured friezes shone grandly in the night. They entered through a main gate that led into a spacious courtyard, and he had to crane his neck to take in the gambrel roof towering overhead.

"Holy Mother o' God, Jason! And I thought *we'd* built grand houses!" The Trace big house at Fairhills and his own at Ballyshea could both fit inside this edifice—aye, and Jefferson's precious Monticello, too!

Jason nodded. "Now, perhaps you can understand why the Girondists wield some power. They're not tainted with the oppressive reputation of the *Ancien Regime,* but there's no shortage of wealth."

A swarm of servants hastened to accommodate them. Grooms led their vehicle toward the stables in the rear; footmen rushed out to assist them up the stairs; still others ushered them deferentially into the reception hall.

Here again, Conor had to stop and marvel. The hall was huge and richly appointed, with a painted ceiling vaulting high overhead, its gilded friezes framing the work of what had to be a major artist.

He noted Jason, too, had halted in his tracks. His gaze was on the pink marble staircase that dominated the hall and led to the upper stories. Or rather, what was *on* the staircase.

A petite, slender serving lass, judging by her dress . . . a simple frock in the tricolors of the revolution—red and blue striped skirt, accented with crisply starched apron and mobcap in white. But she didn't move like any servant *he'd* ever seen.

And her face! Framed by a jumble of reddish-gold curls that ran riot beneath the confines of her cap, it was a face, Conor thought, to make young men dream, and old men yearn to be young again. As she drew near, all he could think was that this was the way angels were supposed to look.

Jason noted his friend's rapt gaze and arched an eyebrow at him. "A fetching piece, hmm? But she's lucky to be here in this place and time. She wouldn't have lasted a day under the *Ancien Regime!*"

"Why not?"

"It's the way she carries herself. As if she were a goddess . . . or a queen. I'd heard French servants were haughtier than their English or American counterparts, but I can't imagine one of the old aristocracy putting up with this! And her beauty would have doomed her for sure! Can't say I'd mind tasting it, though . . . on a big, wide French bed," he added with a grin.

Conor had begun to shush him, the girl being almost upon them; but then he realized they spoke in English, so he didn't bother, even though he saw the lass dart a look at them.

But a moment later, he found himself wishing he had.

"You are Monsieur Trace and Monsieur O'Shea from the American ministry?" The girl spoke in only slightly accented English! Conor noted Jason had the grace to flush as he nodded.

"Welcome, and good evening, gentlemen," she went on, but Conor noted she didn't meet their eyes. "I am Citoyen Lafleur, and because I speak English, I've been chosen to show you into the salon. Won't you follow me?"

GABRIELLE BY VERONICA SATTLER—AVAILABLE NEXT YEAR FROM ST. MARTIN'S PAPERBACKS!